William Dunn Macray, Selborne Priory

Calendar of Charters and Documents

relating to Selborne and its priory, preserved in the muniment room of Magdalen college, Oxford - Vol. 1

William Dunn Macray, Selborne Priory

Calendar of Charters and Documents
relating to Selborne and its priory, preserved in the muniment room of Magdalen college, Oxford - Vol. 1

ISBN/EAN: 9783337423827

Printed in Europe, USA, Canada, Australia, Japan

Cover: Foto ©Andreas Hilbeck / pixelio.de

More available books at **www.hansebooks.com**

CALENDAR

OF

CHARTERS AND DOCUMENTS

RELATING TO

SELBORNE AND ITS PRIORY

Preserved in the Muniment Room of

MAGDALEN COLLEGE, OXFORD.

EDITED BY

W. DUNN MACRAY, M.A., F.S.A.

Fellow of Magdalen College, and Rector of Ducklington, Oxon.

London:

SIMPKIN & CO. LIMITED, STATIONERS' HALL COURT.

Winchester:

WARREN & SON, HIGH STREET.

1891.

WINCHESTER:
PRINTED BY WARREN AND SON, HIGH STREET.

ERRATA.

p. 46, l. 26, for "capellenum," read "capellanum."

p. 52, l. 5.—The date should probably be "*c.* 1305." Compare the third article at p. 81, of which the date must be "*c.* 1305."

p. 64, l. 10, *dele* 1270 in the date. Compare the third article on p. 68, which should be dated "*c.* 1270–80."

p. 68, l. 3 from bottom, for "*c.* 1280," read "after 1291."

p. 70, l. 19, for "Urbemvetenem," read "Urbemveterem."

p. 74, the two charters dated "[*c.* 1290]" and "[*c.* 1290–1300]" should be dated "[*c.* 1270–80]."

p. 79, l. 16, for "for," read "from."

p. 111, l. 32, for "quyshonya," read "quyshonys."

p. 119, l. 26, for "Sept. 6–10," read "Sept. 6–11."

PREFACE.

THERE are not many instances of the existence of original monastic muniments preserved together in their entirety from the foundation of the house to which they relate up to the time of its extinction. But such an instance occurs in the case of the Priory of Selborne. And the preservation of its records is due to the one cause which in every such instance has alone been the means of preserving them from dispersion and destruction, namely, the transfer of the monastic property, *en bloc*, to some collegiate foundation, which then laid up safely in its muniment room the documents which came with that property. But even in these instances the term "muniments" has to be taken in its strictly limited sense of "title-deeds." It was as title-deeds to property, not as historical documents of value in themselves, that the charters were preserved; and consequently such rich sources of information for later ages as sacrist-rolls, rent-rolls, farm-accounts, obit-rolls, and the like, and even, sometimes, for all that appears to the contrary, the contents of libraries,[1] were disregarded.

In the Founder's Tower at Magdalen College, Oxford, the whole series of deeds relating to the foundation, enrichment, and dissolution of the Augustinian Priory at Selborne is preserved. They were calendared for the College by the Editor of this volume many years ago, together with the rest of the vast collection of charters preserved in the same place. And here, by the ready permission of the College, the members of the Hants Record Society are presented with that portion of the calendar which describes the deeds directly relating to the Priory

[1] None of the few books mentioned at p. 145 appear to be now in the library of Magdalen College.

itself, the place in which it was situated, and the immediate neighbourhood; a portion which for the purpose of this publication has been carefully compared with the original documents. The number of documents here described, or (as in the case of those of special importance) printed at full length, is 388; others, chiefly relating to property at Alton and Bramdean, number about 125, at Petersfield 167, and for Basing and Basingstoke 72. The calendar of many in the latter portion is printed at pp. 651—659 of the exhaustive *History of Basingstoke*, by F. J. Baigent and J. E. Millard, D.D., published in 1889.

Besides these, there are upwards of 1200 deeds in the same muniment-room relating to Enham, King's Somborne, Otterbourne, and other places in Hampshire (see *Eighth Report of the Historical MSS. Commission*, pp. 263-4); and of what value the calendars of these must be for the history of the county and of families connected with it, the readers of the present volume will be able to judge.

It is hardly necessary to dwell in this place upon the history of a Priory which has been narrated, largely from the documents here described and with general accuracy, in so universally known a book as Gilbert White's *Natural History of Selborne.* But those who examine its history will not wonder that its existence was comprised within the narrow limits of two centuries and a half. There seemed to be no actual reason for its existence in the district where it was placed. It was founded in an age when such founding was a fashion, and when already the number of like houses was becoming excessive; and founded where it was not needed, like the early homes of piety and progress, for the spread of religion, or for the relief of the sick and needy,[1] or for the promotion of agriculture and reclamation of

[1] It is noteworthy that the only instance of a distinctly charitable benefaction (although the house was said to be partly founded for "pauperum susceptionem,") occurs in the year 1235, at the very outset of the Priory's life, in the gift of land charged with an annual dole of six pairs of shoes to poor parishioners of Selborne; while the strict injunction in 1387 by William of Wykeham that in future the old clothes of the Canons should be given to the poor shows that the rule of the Order in this respect had been disregarded.

waste lands, or for the advancement amidst a growing population of arts and learning. And its founder, although an able statesman and ruler, over whose death the historian Matthew Paris mourned as an irreparable loss to the nation, was not a man of God to inspire holy work and workers. His gifts to "religion" in the technical sense of the time were great, but were not necessarily therefore in a later sense "religious." By grant of a manor from King John he founded the Abbey of Hales Owen in Shropshire; by a similar grant from Henry III the Abbey of Titchfield in Hampshire; a Dominican Friary at Winchester, and, best of all, a Hospital at Portsmouth, while he largely aided the Church of St. Thomas the Martyr at Acre; and so he seems to have given ungrudgingly of his wealth for objects which promised to perpetuate his name and keep it in remembrance to his personal honour. But Selborne evidently had no sufficient *raison d'être*; no special good work to do to keep it alive. And so we need not wonder at its early corruption and its sure decay. The injunctions given by William of Wykeham after a personal visitation, in the course of which he declares he found not merely disregard of rules and of the vow of profession but also of due and decent behaviour, show how great the laxity had become; the Prior and Canons, without being guilty of any gross and crying scandal (although there is even some small intimation of this), had become a society of worldly gentlemen living carelessly and very much at their ease. And upon careless spendthrift living followed indebtedness, dilapidation of buildings, and inability to maintain the statutable number of members; evils which Bishop Waynflete subsequently endeavoured in vain to remedy by the appointment and removal of several Priors in rapid succession. In 1478 we find that a visitation under the authority of the General Chapter of the Augustinian Order was held at Selborne, which very probably may have been in consequence of representations from the Bishop; and it is to be wished that the report of the official examination then made were forthcoming. In that year, however, Peter Bernes, who was then Prior for a second time, resigned his office, very possibly as a result of the enquiry. At last, when in 1484 there was no one left but the Prior, an old man of seventy-two, Wayneflete took the final step of procuring the suppression of the useless house, and of transferring its endowments to a better object. But all was done with a care which justified to the world the course that was taken; a duplicated process of enquiry showed by sworn witnesses the actual state of things; the Prior, the next succeeding Bishop of Winchester and the Prior and Convent of St. Swithun gave their several consents; and the transfer was confirmed by the Pope. And for five years afterwards, at least, the Prior lived to receive from the College an annual pension of £6. 13*s*. 4*d*., two-thirds of the income which his predecessor had received; while the founder of the Priory was, by Wayneflete's order, commemorated at one of the quarterly obits observed at Magdalen College.

The entries relative to the family of Gurdon or Gurdun enable us to correct the account given by Gilbert White. He supposed that there was but one Adam Gurdun, the outlawed adherent of Simon de Montfort, who in 1266 fought his famous duel with Prince Edward, and that he married three wives, confusing in this way homonymous father and son. The pedigree really runs in this form:—

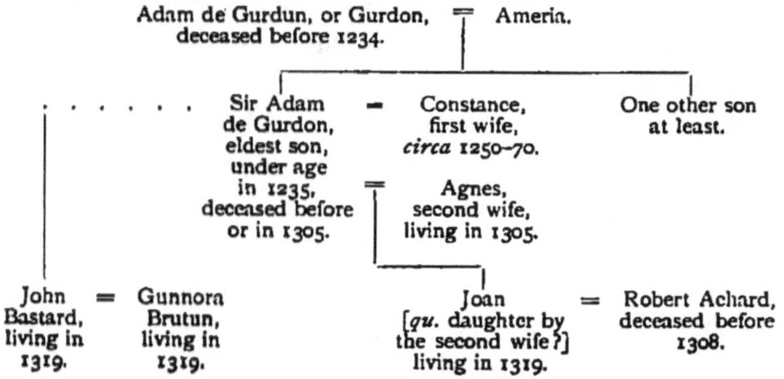

Of the prevailing pestilence and scarcity, involving a great rise in the price of all articles in common use, which are mentioned under the year 1352 as reasons for increasing the income of the then vicar of Selborne, there are notices in the Chronicles of Higden, Geoffrey Baker, a continuator of Murimuth, and Walsingham. The latter records that England, always so fertile, was in the following year driven to seek corn from other countries, no rain falling from March to July, and that the Duke of Zealand sent many ship-loads; while Baker mentions that corn was also imported from Ireland.

In the Church of the Priory there were, besides the high altar, altars of the Blessed Virgin, of St. Peter, St. Stephen, and St. Katherine. The inventories of church goods in the years 1442 and (probably) 1445, as well as that of goods and books remaining in 1490, are interesting, particularly in the enumeration of the few relics which the Priory (as a necessary part of its furnishing) possessed. The ear of St. John, as entered in the table of 1442, becomes three years after the bone of the ear-finger (*i.e.* of the little finger) of St. John Baptist, which seems to show some doubt alike as to its ownership and its anatomy. The ring of St. Hippolytus, bishop of Ostia in the first half of the third century, would scarcely have been looked for in an obscure priory in Hampshire in the fifteenth. But for the authenticity of the remainder of the relics the Sacrist could no doubt speak with a little more certainty; the ring of St. Edmund Rich of Canterbury, who was primate when the Priory was founded, and the chafing-dish and comb and a finger-joint of St. Richard of Chichester, who died twenty years after the foundation, were no doubt veritable relics of the persons whose names they bore. It is curious that the joint-bone (if that is the meaning of the unregistered word "junctorium") of the latter would seem to have been acquired during the short interval between the two inventories of 1442 and 1445, since it is not mentioned in the first of these. There were also five relics undescribed, enclosed in a small cross. Nothing has been left on record to show what became of these relics after the suppression of the Priory. Probably they were removed to the College, but no notice of them has been met with in registers or inventories there.[1]

In 1251 we find an agreement made beforehand with Sir James de Norton, with regard to possible future disputes as to trespass by cattle, for the referring of such cases to the arbitration of good men meeting in the churchyard of Selborne, instead of having recourse to suits at law. In 1253 Aylmer de Lusignan, de Valence, half-brother of King Henry III, for ten long years, from 1250 to 1260, the justly unpopular bishop elect, but not consecrated, of Winchester, and who died very shortly after consecration, is found borrowing "for his necessity" the large sum of 200 marks from the Priory, to be repaid in two years and a half. In that year, as we learn from Matthew Paris, an aid of forty shillings from each knight's fee was granted to the King for the knighting of his son Edward, and a writ was issued for compelling Aylmer's tenants to pay their quota;[2] possibly the "necessity" which demanded the loan may have arisen from difficulties in connection with this taxation.

The succession of Priors of Selborne is as follows. The names and dates placed within brackets are supplied by Gilbert White, and in the last edition of Dugdale, but do not occur in these charters or in the others preserved in Magdalen College. The dates are the earliest and latest for which authority can be found.

[1] It may be worth while to note here the meaning of some words in these Selborne inventories which are not of frequent occurrence. *Offertoria* = chalice-veils; *ridelli* = curtains; *costrellum* = a large wooden jug; *tunicæ de ray* = tunicles of striped cloth; *par vestimentorum de borde Elesaunder* = a pair of chasubles with border of Alexandrian work, *i.e.* of striped silk. In a very long sacrist's inventory of vestments, books, ornaments, etc., for use in Magdalen College Chapel in 1481, we have for the seven altars, for week-day use, "xii paria vestimentorum sacerdotalium de Bordalysaundere cum scutis de aliis in dorso"; and again, "duos pannos de Bordalysaunder chekere pro ambonibus."

[2] M. Paris, edit. Luard, vol. vi, p. 250.

1234—1258, *dom.* John.
1261, R[ichard] of Kent. The editors of Dugdale give "Nich. de Cantia," a misprint for "Rich. de Cantia," to whom the temporalities were restored 24th Dec. 46 Hen. III, 1261.[1]
1267—1271, *dom.* Peter de Disenhurst, *or* d'Isenhurst.
1277—1291, Richard.
[1299, March—1324] William [de Basing]. Died 17 Edw. II, 1324. The royal licence to elect his successor is dated 25 Aug.[2]
[1324]—1339, *dom.* Walter [de Insula *or* de L'Isle.]
[1339, John de Winton.]
1352—1357, Edmund (not in White or Dugdale).
1364—1366, Nicholas (not in White or Dugdale).
[1377]—1392, Thomas [Weston].[3]
[1410]—1413, John Wynchestre.
1415—1453, John Stepe.
[1454—1468], Peter Bernes.
1468—1471, John Morton.
[1471, William Wyndesor; prior for a few days, but removed because irregularly elected.]
[1471, Thomas Farwill, *or* Fairwise].
[1472—1478], Peter Bernes, re-elected.
1479, John Scherpe, *or* Sharp.
1484, Thomas Assheford.

One name of which casual mention occurs must not be passed over without notice. In the writ directed in 1425 to Thomas Chaucers (*sic*) as keeper of Wolmer Forest, we meet with the eldest son of the poet as holding an office which does not appear to be named in connection with him in printed accounts elsewhere.

With regard to place-names in the Index the Editor has endeavoured (with the kind assistance in several instances of the Dean of Winchester) to group the names of hamlets, manors, lands, etc., under the parishes to which they belong. But ignorance on his part of the archaic or extinct forms of local nomenclature in Hampshire may possibly have involved mistakes

[1] MS. note by White Kennett in his copy of the original edition of the *Monasticon* in Gough's collection, Bodl. Lib.

[2] MS. note by the same, *ibid.*

[3] A deed with the date of 1392, in which Prior Thomas occurs, is among the charters in Magdalen College relating to Bramdean.

here and there which those who know the difficulty of verification in such cases will, he is assured, forgive. A few names of hamlets which occur often, *e.g.* Oakhanger in its different forms, he has indexed separately, on account of their greater prominence. With regard to this name a happy conjecture was made by J. M. Kemble in his index of places in the *Codex Dipl. Anglo-Sax.*; he there affixes to the name *Achangra* the guess, that its present form might be expected to be *Oakhanger* if such a place should be found in Hampshire.

No formal Register of the Priory exists in Magdalen College, nor is one to be found in the Public Record Office, the British Museum, or the Bodleian Library.

CHARTERS AND DOCUMENTS RELATING TO SELBORNE PRIORY.

[*c.* 1190—1200.] Grant from Ralph de Herpendena to William de Venuiz to make a ditch through the middle of his land, so that the water may come to the mill of the said William, as great and as long as he pleases, and this ditch the said William owes (*debet*) to hold of the grantor and his heirs by an annual rent of 16*d.* This is done with the consent of the grantor's lord, Gillebert Oin, of whom he holds his land; with whose seal he has sealed this deed because he has no seal of his own. Witn.: Roger de Newburgh (*Nouo Burgo*) Rich. de Herierd, Philip de Stane, Peter de Stane, Rich. de Burhunt, Rich. de Nortune, Peter de Venuiz, Hugh de Craucumb, Osm[er], Roger the Forester, Rob. Oiselur (*i.e.*, the Fowler), Peter de Heges, Will. Foxele, Henry Wiard, John de Chaltun, Robert son of Elur[ed], John de Westcote, Hugh the chaplain of Aweltun, who wrote the deed.—[388.]

Seal lost, but its silken strings remain.

[*c.* 1200.] Grant from Ralph de Harpendene to William de Venuz of the water-course of Beme, through the middle of the land of the grantor, to make a pool for his mill of Sidenemed as large and as deep as he pleases, by the grant of the lord of the said Ralph, Gillebert Oin, of whom he holds that fee; paying annually to the grantor a quit-rent of sixteenpence. Witn.: Will. Peche, Reginald de Halesete, Peter de Heyes, Will. Swele, Robert son of Elured, John de Westcote, Henry Wiard, Henry Waleis, Geoffrey de Staiford, Alan son of Peter de Heyes, Nicholas son of Robert son of Elured, Hugh de Craucumb, John son of Richard the clerk, Gillebert de Dene, Alan de Holt, Robert Oiselur, Osm[er] the forester, Roger the forester, Geoffrey de Venuiz, Hugh the chaplain of Aweltun.—[307.]

Round brown seal; a kind of fleur-de-lis: "Sigill' Rad. de Harpedene."
A copy on paper, made towards the end of the fourteenth century.—[308.]

[*c.* 1210–15.] Grant from William de Venuz to Gilbert atte Dene of one virgate of land in Achangre to the use of Richard, son of the said Gilbert, and of Lucy, the grantor's daughter, namely, that virgate which he held of his lord John, by the grace of God King of England, to be given by the said Gilbert to the said Richard and Lucy in marriage-dowry, as soon as they come to marriageable years, to hold to them and their heirs of body, paying to the King 10*s.* annually; with reversion, failing issue, to the grantor. And the bounds of the said virgate begin at the stone bridge of Achangre to the west, through the lands of Gilbert Oyn and of Walter Burdeaus, and through the wood of Sir Robert de Mauduyt, and near (*juxta*) Bines Wythe and near (*prope*) Kyngesly, and through the lands of Ralph de Harpedene, by the old bank which goes down from the mill by Sydenemede, and from thence the same bank divides the virgate from the land of Gilbert Oyn up to the said stone bridge. Witn.: Roger de Newburgh (*Novo Bourgo*), Philip de Stane, Richard de Nortune, Richard de Bourhunte, John de Westcote, John de Andevere the forester, John son of Richard the clerk, Hugh the chaplain of Aulton, Alan son of Peter de Heȝes.—[169.]

Seal lost, but silken strings remain.

1228–29. Release from Richard [Poore], Bishop of Durham, to Peter [de Roches], Bishop of Winchester, for the sum of 70 marks, of all his right in one virgate of land in Tistede, about which they had had a contention in the Court of King Henry. Sir M. de Pateshulle, Dean of St. Paul's, London,[1] and Sir Stephen de Segrave attach their seals, at the request of the said Richard, together with his own. Witn.: Josceline Bp. of Bath, Ralph Bp. of Chichester, Walter Bp. of Carlisle, Robert de Lexintune, W. de London, H. de Breibroc, John de Baioc' [*i.e.* Bayeux], Will. de Raleghe, W. de York ["Eboraco."]—[243.]

Three seals tied up in wool; the first, representing the Annunciation, broken.

[*c.* 1230.] Grant from William de Arundel, son of Hugh de Arundel, to master Andrew of Winchester, of all the land which William Ordric held in Ledessete with the messuage, and all the briary (*brueram*) next before the gate of the messuage which is included between the way going from Ledessete to Burdunesdene on the right hand and the way which extends to la Rudeherne; paying an annual quit-rent of 6*d.* Witn.: Adam de St. Manevedo, Will. de Brembelchete, Barthol. de Ellestede, Tomas de Warbeltone, Peter de Warbeltone, Ralph de Wulfbeding, Thomas Makerel, Geoffrey de Arundel, Hugh de Arundel, Walter de Arundel, Huges de Warbelton, Will. de Widehale, Peter le Tallur.—[286.]

Round green seal, attached by dark strings; shield of arms rudely cut, apparently three lions ramp.: "Sigill' Will'i de Arundel."

[1] Appointed Dean of St. Paul's in 1228; died 14 Nov., 1229.

[*c.* 1230.] Release from Henry de Ysenherst to master Andrew, rector of the church of Chalvedone, of all his right in the lands which the said Andrew had by the gift of William de Arundel in the manor of Lidesete; notwithstanding the gift made by the said Andrew to the said Henry. Witn.: John de Venuz, John de Windelsore, John de la Stane, Mathew de Monasterio, James de Hokangre, Roger de Bradesete, Peter de Warbeltone.—[227.]

Round red seal; an antique intaglio; a winged figure, with the motto added round it, "$\overline{\text{XPC}}$ vincit, $\overline{\text{XPC}}$ regnat, $\overline{\text{XPC}}$ imperat."

[*c.* 1230.] Grant from James de Nortone to Roger de Chorlecote, for the sum of nine marks, of Adam de la Wike and Herbert of the same vill, in their homages and services, lands and rents, etc.; rendering annually one pair of gloves, value one penny. Witn.: Sir John de Venoiz, Sir Thomas Makerelle, Laurence de Heges, James de Achangre, Gilibert Conan, Mathew de Monasterio, Geoffrey de la Rude.—[179.]

Triangular green seal; a blank triangular shield within an orle: "Sigill' James [*sic*] de Nortune."

[*c.* 1225–30.] Grant from William de Arundel to the lady Sabina his sister, for the support of his daughter Maud, of that land in the vill of Lidesethe which Richard de Dunewatere held according as the hedge extends to "cheveriam," and from "cheveria" to the hedge which Ralph de la Rude held, and according as the hedge extends to the grove, and afterwards as the boundaries are marked up to the water-course, and so, opposite (*contra*) the water-course, to the well of Dunwatere; paying annually to him a quit-rent of one pair of gloves, worth one penny; in order that she may honourably provide for his daughter in the world or in some religious house, and if she be not provided for, then the said land shall revert to her upon the death of the said Sabina, or if she have deceased, then to some one of his children (*puerorum*). He grants also to the said Sabina to have 100 two-year old sheep in the common pasture, and twenty pigs in his woods free of pannage, excepting his new land (*salvo frico meo*), and twelve cows and twenty beasts in the common pasture. Witn.: Hugh de Cumbe, Will. de Brambelsete, Alan de St. Man[evedo], Will. Frest' [the Forester?], Hugh de Arundel, John Frest' [Forester?], Mathew rector of the church of Brembelsete, Henry de Bromels', Will. de Widehale, Peter Taillur.—[287.]

Round red seal; shield of arms rudely cut, apparently three lions ramp.: "Sigill' Will'i de Arundel."

[*c.* 1230–35.] Grant from Henry le Sauvage to Peter, Bishop of Winchester, for the sum of twelve marks, of all his land which he had in

Tystede by the gift of Ralph de Winesham, rendering annually one pound of cummin to the chief lord of the fee. Witn.: Roger Alis, Geoffrey de Rupibus, Thomas de Gimiges, Walter de Thigheburne, Robert Lohade, John de Venuez, Thomas de Venuez, William son of Unfrid, Roger de Molend[inis], Alard his brother, Elyas son of Roger, Nich. de Sirlege, Godfrey the Serjeant (*serviente*) of Cheritone.—[355.]

Oval green seal; the temptation of Adam and Eve: "Sigill': Henrici Savvage."

[*c.* 1230–35.] Grant from William de Arundel, son of Hugh de Arundel, to master Andrew of Winchester, of the same lands and pasturage for cattle, etc., as are granted in the deed 280, *infra* under date *c.* 1237, to the Prior and Canons of Seleburne, described in the same terms, and paying the same annual quit-rent of 12*d.* Witn.: Sir John de Venuz, Sir Adam de St. Manevedo, Sir William de Bremlessete, Thomas de Warbeltone, Peter de Warbeltone, Henry de Ysenherst, Walter de Arundel, Will. de Widenhale, Thomas de la Stiepe, Peter le Taillur, Mathew son of Nicholas, Otte Wy (*sic*).—[282.]

Round green seal; a lion courant: "Sigill' Will'i de Arundel."

Another original copy of the same grant, written by a somewhat earlier hand. Same witnesses ("Steipe," "Teillur," the last name written as one word, "Ottewy") and seal.—[283.]

A third original copy by a third hand, in which, however, there is a stipulation forbidding the grant of the property to any religious house; therefore a little earlier than either of the preceding, in both which this stipulation is omitted. Same witnesses ("Brambelsete"). Round green seal, partly broken, attached with silk strings; shield of arms rudely cut, apparently three lions ramp.: "Sigill' W . . . . . [Ar]undel."—[285.]

[*c.* 1230–40.] Grant from Adam de Rutherefeld to Roger de Cherlekote, for the sum of 100 shillings, of all his meadow of Ochangre, both that which he holds of the King, and that which he holds of the lord of Ochangre, and all the tenement which he holds there; paying an annual quit-rent to the grantor of a pair of white gloves worth one penny, and to the lord of Ochangre of 8*d*, and saving to the King the service due for such a holding. Witn.: Sir John de Venuz, Sir John de la Stone, James de Nortune, Thomas Makerel, Will. de Brambelsate, Will. de Arundel, Laur. de Hegez, Nich. of the Mills ("de Molendinis"), Rich. de Wescote, Mathew de Monasterio, Henry de Ysenhurst, Rich. de Aweltune.—[149.]

Round green seal; an eagle volant: "Sigillum Ad. . de Rederafeld."

[*c.* 1230–40.] Grant from Henry de Borrunthe to Gilebert his brother, for the sum of 30 shillings "in gersoma præ manibus" of all the land which the hedge beginning at Wyemerslade and extending to the way before the field which Richard Koterel ploughed up ("assartavit"), and the ditch made on the side of the wood of the same Henry de Borruntho, include; and two acres of land before his (Gilebert's) gate, near the great way leading from Brontelstapelo to Soynthone, and all the land which Robert the Carpenter held in the same field; paying an annual quit-rent of 12*d.*, and to the King as much as is due for the fourth part of a furlong. Witn.: Oliver the chaplain of Seleborne, Sir James de Nortone, Will. de Hockangre, Thomas Makerel, Mathew son of the Dean, Gilebert de Golleia, Roger de Bradesite, Godefrey son of the Dean, who wrote the deed.—[16.]

Round brown seal, attached by green strings, inscription broken; a fleur-de-lis: "Sigil' Henrici . . . . ."

[*c.* 1230–40.] Grant from Sabina the daughter of Hugh de Arundel to Sir William de Arundel, her brother, of all her land of la Dumwatere in Lideschete, which land he had before given to her for her life. Witn.: Sir Adam de St. Manevedo, Sir William de Brembescete, Thomas de Warbeltone, Henry de Isenherst, Walter de Arundel, William de Widehale, Thomas de Stipe, Peter le Taillur, Matthew de Bocham.—[13.]

Seal lost.

1233. Grant from James de Ochangre to Peter, Bishop of Winchester, in free alms, for the sum of 16 marks, of all his croft called La Liega, to make there a religious house of the order of St. Augustine in honour of God and of the glorious V. Mary; viz. that which going down from the water of Seleburne goes southward by ("per") the meadow which Robert de Hundesham once held, and by the brook going down from Cratewelle to the land of John de Ochangre, the grantor's uncle, and westward from the brook to the land called Thornwich. Witn.: Richard parson of Gretham, Oliver parson of Stoke, Guy chaplain of Seleburne, John de Windlesore, Will. de Ho, James de Northune, Nicholas of the Mills ("de Molendinis"), Roger le But, Gilebert Conan, Gilebert de Burhunte, clerk, John de Ochangre.—[53.]

Round green seal; a man on horseback: "S' James (*sic*) de Hocaungre."

1233. Another grant from "James" (*sic*) de Ochangre to the Bishop of Winchester of the same croft called La Lyge, for the same purpose, and for the same sum. Witnesses the same (Oliver parson of *Stokes*, John de Windelesore.)—[54.]

1233. Grant from James de Ochangre to Peter, Bishop of Winchester, for the sum of 40 marks, of the croft called la Lyghe, which goes down by the brook descending from Cratewelle to the land which John de Achangre, the grantor's uncle, held on the west of the brook, and extends from the brook westward to the land called Thornwik; also a croft called Brodecrofte which the said John his uncle held, opposite Edithesgrove up to the croft called La Bechecrofte; also a croft which Gilebert de Wik formerly held, near Brodecrofte and near the grantor's wood. Also a croft which Ralph le Niweeman held. Also a croft called Cavelescroft extending from a corner of the croft called la Lyghe to a corner between the grantor's wood and the wood which Rob. de la Rode held, alongside of the wood of de la Rode to the land of Thomas Coterel. Also a croft which Adam le But formerly held, with two increments of land on S. and E.:—in order to enlarge and make therein a religious house of the order of St. Augustine. Witn.: Richard parson of Gretham, Oliver parson of Stokes, Guy chaplain of Seleburne, John de Wyndleshore, Will. de Ho, James de Nortune, Nicholas of the Mills, Roger But, Gilbert Cunan, Gilbert de Burhunte, clerk, John de Achangre.—[55.]

Round green seal; the sun: "S' Jacobi de Hacangre."

[1233.] Grant from James de Nortune to Peter, Bishop of Winchester, for the sum of 35 marks "ad me acquietandum versus Judeos," of his water-course going down from his mill of Durtone to the wood of Will. Mauduit, with one croft called Edrichescrofte extending from the wood of the said W. Mauduit to the old ditch of Steppe, and 9 perches from the head of the said ditch, towards the E., and all the land called Stepe as it was enclosed by the old ditch up to the croft which formerly belonged to Philip of the Mills, and the said croft, and a moiety of the croft of Peter de Durtone, and a moiety of the meadow of the said Philip, with all the meadow, wood, and pasture between the said crofts and the water, to found a house of religion of the order of St. Augustine, with liberty to enclose the land, and make ponds and mills, and to have a way for cars and carts up to the highway. Witn.: Master Elyas de Derham, master Will. de St. Mary Church, master Robert Basset, master Humphrey de Milleirs, Robert de Clinchampe, Oliver the clerk, Roger Wacelin then Sheriff of Suh.,[1] John de Venuz, Will. de Ho, John Windeshore, Will. de Bira, Gilebert the Canon, Peter the Forester, Gilebert de Popham, Laurence de Heiges, Hugh de Popham, Gilibert de Burhunte, clerk.—[294.]

Shield-shaped green seal; a blank shield within a tressure or orle of (apparently) sixteen bezants: "Sigill' James (*sic*) de Nortune."

[1] He was Sheriff of Southampton from October, 1232, to October, 1234.

CHARTER FROM HENRY III FOR THE FOUNDATION OF THE PRIORY.

1233, 4 May. Henricus Dei gratia Rex Angliæ, Dominus Hyberniæ, Dux Normanniæ, Aquitaniæ, et Comes Andegaviæ, archiepiscopis, episcopis, abbatibus, prioribus, comitibus, baronibus, justiciariis, vicecomitibus, præpositis, ministris, et omnibus ballivis et fidelibus suis, salutem. Sciatis nos intuitu Dei et pro salute animæ nostræ et animarum antecessorum et heredum nostronem concessisse et hac carta nostra confirmasse pro nobis et heredibus nostris venerabili patri Petro Wintoniensi Episcopo, totam terram cum pertinentiis in manerio de Seleburne, quam Magister Stephanus de Lucy aliquando tenuit de concessione nostra, ad quandam domum religionis de ordine Sancti Augustini in eadem terra construendam, in honore Dei et gloriosæ Virginis Mariæ et omnium sanctorum. Quare volumus et firmiter præcipimus pro nobis et heredibus nostris quod Prior et Canonici in domo prædicta per eundem Episcopum fundata Deo servientes, et successores eorum imperpetuum, habeant et teneant totam prædictam terram cum pertinentiis suis et cum omnibus libertatibus et liberis consuetudinibus, in Bosco et Plano, in viis et semitis, Pasturis et Pascuis, in Molendinis, Aquis et Piscariis, infra Burgum et extra Burgum, cum Soka et sacca, Thol et Them, Infangenethef et Utfangenethef, et Hamsokne, et Blodwyte, et pecunia quæ dari solet pro Murdro et Forstal, et Flemenefrithe, et cum quietantia de omni Scotto et Geldo, et de omnibus auxiliis Regum, vicecomitum, et omnium ministrantium suorum, et Hidagio, et Exercitibus, et Scutagiis, et Tallagiis, et Syris, et Hundredis, et Placitis, et Querelis, et Warda, et Wardpeny, et de Operibus Castellorum et Pontium, et Clausuris Parcorum, et omni Careio et Sumagio, et domorum regalium edificatione et omnimoda reparatione, et cum omnibus aliis libertatibus et liberis consuetudinibus ad prædictam terram pertinentibus, sicut prædictum est. Hiis testibus, venerabilibus patribus J[oscelino] Bathoniensi, et R[icardo Poore] Dunholmensi, episcopis, Stephano de Segrave, Justiciario nostro, Thoma de Mulltone, Roberto de Lexyntone, Radulfo filio Nicholai, Godefrido de Craucumbe, Thoma de Hemmegrave, Galfrido de Cauz, Johanne de Plesseto, et aliis. Data per manum venerabilis patris R[adulfi Nevill], Cycestrensis episcopi et Cancellarii nostri apud Westmonasterium, quarto die Maii, anno regni nostri decimo septimo.—[92.]

Fragments of the great seal, attached by silk strings.

1233, 21 July, "die Jovis prox. post fest. S. Margarete Virg," 17 Hen. fil. Joh. At Aultone. Grant from John de Venuz to the church of B. Mary of Seleburne, to Peter Bp. of Winchester, and to the Prior and Canons in that church, in free alms, of the whole moor where the Beme rises, up to the head of the fishpond, that they may make in it a fishpond as great, as wide, and as deep as they wish, and pools and mills at their will; and also his meadow called Sidenemed lying on either side of the water which comes down from Bcmo and all the course of the water so descending to the mill which Paulinus held of the grantor to farm, and the mill itself, and the meadow which is called Hundeshammed and which lies on either side of the water called Lachemere, which Gilbert Oyn formerly gave to William de Venuz; also the reversion of one virgate of land in Achangre on the north of the water-course, which William de Venuz, the grantor's father, gave to Richard atte Dene in marriage-dowry with Lucy his wife, and which on the decease of the said Richard should, for want of issue, revert to the now grantor, and of which the boundaries begin at the stone bridge of Achangre towards the west, through the lands of James de Achangre up to the meadow of Sir William de Mauduyt, stretching towards the east through the lands and wood of the said Sir William towards Byneswerthe and up to Kyngesly and Oxeneye, and thence by the old bank which goes down to the aforesaid mill of Sydenemed and from thence the bank itself divides the said virgate from the land of James de Achangre up to the aforesaid stone bridge; also a quit-rent of a pair of gloves worth one penny from the aforesaid Richard for the said virgate, paying annually after the life of the said Richard for the said virgate ten shillings to the King through his bailiffs of Aultone. Witn.: Roger Wasseline, Sheriff of Suhamptone, John de Wyndesores, James de Nortone, William de Hoo, Thomas the Welshman ["Wallensis,"] James de Achangre, Laurence de Hegzes, Roger de Bradeschate, clerk, Mathew de Monasterio, Peter the Forester.—[160.]

Large round green seal; a man on horseback, with a rod in his hand: "Sigill' Joh'is de Ven' marescall' Regis."

FOUNDATION-CHARTER BY PETER DE ROCHES, BISHOP OF WINCHESTER.

1233[-4], 20 Jan. Omnibus Christi fidelibus ad quos præsens scriptum pervenerit, P[etrus], divina miseracione Wintoniensis ecclesiæ minister humilis, salutem in Domino. Ex officio pastorali tenemur viros religiosos, qui pauperes spiritu esse pro Christo, neglectis lucris temporalibus, elegerunt, speciali affectu diligere, fovere pariter et recreare, eorumque quieti sollicite providere; ut tanto uberiores fructus de continua in lege Dei meditatione percipiant, quanto a conturbationibus malignorum amplius fuerint, ex patroni provisione et ecclesiastica defensione, securi. Hinc est quod universitati vestræ notificamus, nos divine caritatis instinctu, de assensu conventus ecclesiæ nostræ Wintoniensis, fundasse domum religiosam, ordinis magni patris Augustini, in honore Dei et gloriosæ semper virginis ejusdem Dei genetricis Mariæ, apud Seleburne, ibidemque canonicos regulares instituisse: ad quorum sustentationem et hospitum et pauperum susceptionem, dedimus, concessimus, et præsenti carta nostra confirmavimus, eisdem canonicis, totam terram quam habuimus de dono Jacobi de Acangre: et totam terram, cursum aquæ, boscum et pratum, quæ habuimus de dono Jacobi de Nortone; et totam terram, boscum, et redditum, quæ habuimus de dono domini H[enrici] regis Angliæ; cum omnibus prædictarum possessionum pertinentiis. Dedimus etiam et concessimus in proprios usus eisdem canonicis ecclesiam prædictæ villæ de Seleburne, et ecclesias de Basinge et de Basingestok, cum omnibus earundem ecclesiarum capellis, libertatibus, et aliis pertinentiis; salva honesta et sufficienti sustentatione vicariorum in prædictis ecclesiis ministrantium; quorum præsentatio ad Priorem prædictæ domus religiosæ de Seleburne et canonicos ejusdem loci inperpetuum pertinebit. Præterea possessiones et redditus, ecclesias sive decimas, quas in episcopatu nostro adempti sunt, vel in posterum, Deo dante, justis modis poterunt adipisci, sub nostra et Wintoniensis ecclesiæ protectione suscepimus, et episcopalis auctoritate officii confirmavimus; eadem auctoritate firmiter inhibentes, ne quis locum in quo divino sunt officio mancipati seu alias eorum possessiones invadere, vi vel fraude vel ingenio malo occupare audeat vel etiam retinere, aut fratres conversos, servientes, vel homines eorum, aliqua violentia perturbare, sive fugientis ad eos causa salutis suæ conservandæ a septis domus suæ violenter præsumat extra[h]ere. Præcipimus autem ut in eadem domo religiosa de Seleburne ordo canonicus et regularis conversatio, secundum regulam magni patris Augustini, quam primi inhabitatores professi sunt, inperpetuum observetur; et ipsa domus religiosa a cujuslibet alterius domus religiosæ subjectione libera permaneat, et in omnibus absoluta; salva in omnibus episcopali auctoritate et Wintoniensis ecclesiæ dignitate. Quod ut in posterum ratum permaneat et inconcussum, præsenti scripto et sigilli nostri patrocinio duximus confirmandum. His testibus; domino Waltero, Abbate de Hyda; domino Waltero, Priore de Sancto Swiðuno; domino Stephano, Priore de Motesfonte; magistro Alano de Stoke; magistro Willelmo de Sanctæ Mariæ Ecclesia, tunc officiali nostro; Luca, archidiacono de Surreia; magistro Humfrido de Millers; Henrico et Hugone capellanis; Roberto de Clinchampe et Petro Rossinol, clericis; et multis aliis. Datum apud Wlvese per manum P. de Cancellis, in die sanctorum martirum Fabiani et Sebastiani, anno Domini millesimo ducentesimo tricesimo tercio.—[6.]

Oval green seal: obverse; the Bishop, in pontificals, in the attitude of blessing; inscription broken, ". . . . . . . oniensis Episcopi;" counterseal; the Bishop kneeling beneath two saints, bearing swords; "Sv̄t m' [*i.e.* mihi] sītque boni Petr' Paul'que patroni."

Appropriation to Selborne Priory of the Churches of Selborne, Basing, and Basingstoke.

1233[-4], 22 Jan. P[etrus], divina miseracione Wyntoniensis Episcopus religiosis viris Priori et Conventui ecclesiæ beatæ Mariæ de Seleborne nostræ dyoceseos salutem in omnium Salvatore. Cum ex officio pastorali sacram religionem plantare et plantatam modis omnibus fovere debeamus, et viros religiosos qui, temporalibus lucris neglectis, pauperes pro Christo esse elegerunt diligere, creare,[1] et eorum quieti sollicite providere, teneamur, Ea propter, dilecti in Domino filii, ecclesias de Selebourne, de Basinges, et Basingestoke, in dyocesi nostra sitas, quæ de advocacione vestra propria esse comprobantur cum capellis ab eisdem dependentibus, ac aliis pertinentiis suis, ad uberiorem sustentacionem vestram, et ad susceptionem hospitum et pauperum ad domum vestram de Selebourne confluencium, vobis et domui vestræ prædictæ deputamus: Concedendo vobis per præsentes [ut eas-]dem ecclesias nunc de jure et de facto vacantes auctoritate vestra propria ingredi, et in proprios usus perpetuo tenere, valeatis, salva honesta et com[petenti susten]tacione vicariorum in prædictis ecclesiis ministrancium; quorum præsentacio ad Priorem prædictæ domus religiosæ de Seleborne et canonicos ejus[dem domus in perpetu]o pertinebit, jure et dignitate ecclesiæ nostræ Wyntoniensis semper salvis. Quod ut in posterum ratum permaneat et inconcussum, præsentes literas, sigilli [nostri munimin]e roboratas, vobis fieri fecimus patentes.

Hiis testibus, domino Waltero, Abbate de Hyda; domino Waltero, Priore Sancti Swithuni; domino Stephano, Priore [de Mo]tesfunte; magistro Alano de Stoke; magistro Willelmo de Sanctæ Mariæ Ecclesia, tunc officiali nostro; magistro Luca, archidiacono Surreye; magistro H. de Millers; Henrico et Hugone, capellanis; Roberto de Clincham; Petro Russinol; et multis aliis. Dat. apud Wlvesey, in die Sancti Vincentii, anno Domini M° CC° tricesimo tercio.—[97.]

Half of the seal, oval, green; the Bishop in pontificals: ". . . . . Dei gracia . . . . . oniensis episcopi." Counterseal, as above: "Sūt m' sītque boni [Petr'] Paul'que patroni."

Charter of Liberties from Henry III.

1234, 10 April. Henricus Dei gratia Rex Angliæ, Dominus Hiberniæ, Dux Normanniæ, Aquitaniæ, et Comes Andegaviæ, Archiepiscopis, Episcopis, Abbatibus, Prioribus, Comitibus, Baronibus, Justiciariis, Vicecomitibus, Præpositis, Forestariis, Ministris, et omnibus Ballivis et fidelibus suis, salutem. Sciatis nos, intuitu Dei et pro salute animæ nostræ et animarum antecessorum et heredum nostrorum, dedisse concessisse et hac carta nostra confirmasse pro nobis et heredibus nostris Priori Sanctæ Mariæ de Seleburne et Canonicis ibidem Deo servientibus, quod ipsi et eorum successores inperpetuum habeant per terras et tenementa sua quæ habent in Seleburne, Achangre, Nortone, Bromdene, Thetdene, Basinghes, Basinghestokes, Nateleye, cum pertinenciis, Thol et Theam et Infangenethef et Utfangenethef, et quod ipsi et successores eorum et omnes homines eorum de prædictis terris et tenementis sint quieti inperpetuum erga nos et heredes nostros, et erga Vicecomites, Constabularios, Prepositos, et omnes Ballivos nostros, per totam terram nostram, de Thelonio, Passagio, Pontagio, Lestagio, Tallagio, Stallagio, et conductu thesauri, et de operationibus castellorum, domorum,

[1] *Sic*, read, recreare.

murorum, fossatorum, pontium, calcetorum, vivariorum, vinariorum, stagnorum, et clausuris parcorum, et de omnibus aliis operationibus, et de sectis Syrarum, Hundredorum, de auxiliis Vicecomitum et Ballivorum suorum, et de murdro et francoplegio, et de visu franciplegii, et de misericordiis, et de finibus pro transgressionibus et misericordiis, et pro licentia concordandi, et de escapio latronum, et de bobus de seisina, et de placitis, querelis, et exactionibus omnibus ad nos et heredes nostros, et Vicecomites, Constabularios, vel aliquos alios ballivos nostros pertinentibus. Concessimus etiam eisdem Priori et Canonicis et eorum successoribus quod nullus Vicecomes Constabularius aut aliquis alius Ballivus noster ingressum vel posse habeat in prædictis terris et tenementis, set totum ad eosdem Priorem et Canonicos et successores suos et eorum Ballivos pertineat, præter attachiamenta de placitis coronæ, ad quæ quidem cum Coronatores venerint facienda, ea ita faciant quod in nullo lædatur libertas prædictorum Prioris et Canonicorum et successorum suorum. Omnes autem prædictas libertates concessimus ita quod omnes homines sui de eis tenentes in eisdem terris et tenementis subsint et respondeant et satisfaciant prædictis Priori et Canonicis et eorum successoribus, et nulli alii, nisi de voluntate eorundem Prioris et Canonicorum et successorum suorum, de omnibus prædictis præter attachiamenta de placitis coronæ, sicut nobis aut heredibus nostris aut vicecomitibus aut constabulariis aut aliis ballivis nostris, subessent et responderent et satisfacerent de eisdem si ad nos prædicta terræ et tenementa cum pertinentiis pertinerent. Concessimus autem eisdem Priori et Canonicis quod ipsi et eorum successores distringere possint omnes homines suos de prædictis terris et tenementis ad omnia prædicta præter attachiamenta de placitis coronæ sicut nos ad eadem eos distringere possemus, aut heredes nostri, aut vicecomites aut constabularii aut aliqui alii ballivi nostri, si prædictæ libertates aut quietanciæ concessæ non fuissent. Concessimus etiam eisdem Priori et Canonicis et eorum successoribus quod omnes homines eorum de prædictis terris et tenementis sint liberi et quieti inperpetuum de omnibus juratis et assisis et recognitionibus faciendis, præterquam in attingendis propriis dominicis nostris si opus fuerit infra comitatum ubi manentes sunt si forte contentio inter nos ipsos et alios oriatur. Ita quod occasione talis juratæ, si forte evenerit, per vicecomites vel alios ballivos nostros non occasionentur, nec libertas eorundem Prioris et Canonicorum vel successorum suorum in aliquo lædatur. Concessimus insuper eisdem Priori et Canonicis et eorum successoribus quod si aliquis hominum suorum de prædictis terris et tenementis pro delicto suo vitam aut membrum debeat amittere, vel fugerit et judicio stare noluerit, vel aliud delictum fecerit pro quo debeat, catalla sua perdere, ubicunque justitia fieri debeat sive in curia nostra sive in alia curia, omnia catalla illa sint prædictorum Prioris et Canonicorum et successorum suorum, et liceat eis sine disturbatione[1] vicecomitum et quorumcumque ballivorum nostrorum et aliorum ponere se in seisinam de prædictis catallis in prædictis casibus et aliis, quando ballivi nostri si ad nos pertinerent

[1] "distributione," No. 91, incorrectly.

catalla illa in manum nostram ea seisire possent et deberent. Concessimus præterea eisdem Priori et Canonicis quod quotienscunque aliqui malefactores capti fuerint in prædictis terris et tenementis cum pertinentiis per ballivos eorundem Prioris et Canonicorum vel successorum suorum de quibus non possit vel non debeat fieri judicium in curia eorum, vicecomites et ballivi nostri recipiant prædictos malefactores sine difficultate et dilatione super forisfacturam nostram, quandocumque ballivi prædictorum Prioris et Canonicorum vel successorum suorum dictos malefactores prædictis ballivis nostris liberare voluerint. Concessimus etiam prædictis Priori et Canonicis et successoribus suis quod habeant inperpetuum omnia amerciamenta de omnibus hominibus suis prædictarum terrarum suarum et tenementorum cum pertinentiis, quæ quidem amerciamenta ad nos vel heredes nostros vel ad vicecomites aut constabularios aut ad aliquos alios ballivos nostros possent pertinere si ipsa amerciamenta eis concessa non fuissent, et quod ipsi Prior et Canonici et eorum successores habeant potestatem ad distringendum omnes prædictos ad amerciamenta eis reddenda. Prohibemus insuper super forisfacturam nostram decem librarum ne quis de prædictis amerciamentis colligendis vel recipiendis sive districtione inde facienda nisi per voluntatem eorundem Prioris et Canonicorum et successorum suorum se intromittat. Concessimus etiam eisdem quod habeant in prædictis terris et tenementis suis cum pertinentiis omnia averia quæ vocantur *Wayf* et quod talliare possint homines suos quos habent in terris suis de Seleburne sine speciali mandato nostro quandocumque nos vel heredes nostri dominica nostra talliare fecerimus. Concessimus insuper pro nobis et heredibus nostris eisdem Priori et Canonicis et eorum successoribus quod licet aliqua libertatum per nos eis concessarum processu temporis quocumque casu contingente usi non fuerint, nichilominus tamen postea utantur libertate eadem sine contradictione aliqua, non obstante eo quod aliquo casu ea usi non fuerint. Concessimus etiam eisdem Priori et Canonicis et eorum successoribus quod prædictæ terræ suæ et tenementa in Seleburne, Achangre, Nortone, Basinges, Basingestokes, Natcleye, quæ sunt[1] infra forestam nostram, sint[2] inperpetuum quieta de vasto, regardo, et visu forestar[iorum], viridar[iorum], regardatorum, et omnium ministrorum suorum, [et quoad ipsos et successores suos deafforestata][3] et quod ipsi et omnes homines sui in prædictis terris et tenementis manentes sint inperpetuum quieti de sectis Swanimotorum et omnium aliorum placitorum forestæ, et de espeltamentis canum, et de omnibus summonitionibus, placitis, querelis, et exactionibus et occasionibus ad forestam et forestar[ios], viridar[ios], et eorum ministros pertinentibus. [Prohibemus insuper super forisfacturam nostram ne aliquis eis forisfaciat in aliquo contra hanc cartam nostram sub pœna viginti librarum, Quia eos et omnes res et possessiones suas in nostram specialem suscepimus protectionem].[4] Quare volumus et firmiter præcipimus pro nobis et heredibus nostris

[1] "quæ licet sint," No. 91. [2] "sint tamen," No. 91.

[3] These bracketed words are found in No. 91.

[4] This bracketed sentence is inserted in No. 91.

quod prædicti Prior et Canonici et eorum successores et omnes homines sui quos habent in prædictis terris suis et tenementis de Seleburne, Achangre, Nortone, Bromdene, Thetdene, Basinges, Basingestokes, Nateleye, cum pertinentiis, habeant et teneant inperpetuum prædictas libertates et quietancias et amerciamenta bene et in pace, integre et plenarie, in omnibus rebus et locis, ut prædictum est. Hiis testibus, venerabilibus patribus E[dmundo] Cantuariensi Archiepiscopo, J[ocelino] Bathoniensi, H[ugone] Elyensi, T[homa] Northwycensi, R[ogero] Londinensi, R[oberto] Sarum, et W[illelmo] Exoniensi Episcopis; R[icardo] Comite Cornubiæ et Pictaviæ; W[illelmo] de Ferar[iis] Comite Derby; J[ohanne] Comite Lincolniæ et Constabulario Cestriæ; S[tephano] de Segrave, justiciario Angliæ; W[illelmo] Comite Albemar[le]; Philippo de Albiniaco; Radulpho filio Nicholai; Hugone Dispensatore; Godefrido de Craucumbe; Galfrido Dispensatore; Galfrido de Cauz[1]; Bartholomæo Peche[2]; et aliis. Datum per manum venerabilis patris R[adulphi] Cycestrensis Episcopi Cancellarii nostri, apud Westmonasterium, decimo die Aprilis anno regni nostri decimo octavo.[3]—[22, 23, 91].

Of this Charter there are three originals, varying, as seen above in one of the copies, in some details, as well as in occasional forms of spelling, but all dated alike. The inscription on the great seals attached to Nos. 22, 23, is slightly broken, but otherwise the seals are perfect and fine; of the seal attached to 91 there is only a fragment. The first is in a cover of blue serge, lined with flowered silk, and attached by red silk strings; the second is in yellow silk, with red strings; and the third in flowered woollen damask, with red and green silk strings.

1234, 9 March, 18 Hen. [III], at Northampton, "per manum Radulfi Cycenstren. episc. cancell." Grant from the King to Peter, Bishop of Winchester, of all the land and rent in the manor of Seleburne which master Stephen de Lucy formerly held, for the enlargement of the Priory and its buildings which the Bishop has there founded by the King's grant, in the land which he bought of James de Ochangre, with all liberties [everywhere] and with sok and sak, thol and them, infangenethef and utfangenethef and hamsocne and blodwite, and the money paid for murder, and forstal and flemenestriche, and acquittance from all scot and geld, and all aids of Kings and sheriffs and all their ministers, and from hidage and armies and scutage and tallage and shires and hundreds and pleas and quarrels and ward and wardpeny, and the works of castles and bridges and enclosures of parks, and carriage and sumage, and building and repairing of royal houses, and all other liberties and free customs. Witn.: J[ohn], Earl of Chester and Huntingdon, J[ohn de Laci], Earl of Lincoln and Constable of Chester, W[illiam de Fortibus], Earl of Albemarle, S. de Segrave, Justiciary of England, Philip de Albiniaco, Hugh Dispenser,

[1] "Chauz," No. 91. [2] "Pechy," *ib.* [3] "octavo decimo," *ib.*

Godfrey de Craucumbe, John son of Philip, Geoffrey Dispenser, Geoffrey de Cauz, Barthol. Peche, John de Plesset[is].—[304.]

Good impression of great seal, green, attached by red silk strings, inscription broken.

1234, 24 Oct., "nono kal. Nov.," 18 Hen. III, at Wyndesore, "per manum ven. pat. R. Cicestr. episc. canc. nostri." Confirmation by the King of the grant No. 97, 22 Jan., 1233[-4], from the Bishop of Winchester (which is recited at length) of the churches of Basinge, Basingestoke and Seleburne to the Priory of Seleburne. Witn.: W[illiam de Fortibus], Earl of Albemarle, Stephen de Segrave, Justiciary of England, Peter de Rivall[is], Hugh Dispenser, Peter (*sic*), Ralph son of Nicholas, Barthol. Peche.—[100.]

Very fine impression of the great seal, in green wax, but much mutilated at the sides.

Noted at the foot: "Ad instanciam Imberti de Montferrant. li. xvi."

1234. Confirmation by Walter the Prior and the Convent of St. Swithun, Winchester, of the foundation by Bishop Peter of an Augustin house at Seleburn and of the assignment thereto of the churches of Basinges, Basingestokes, and Seleburne.—[370.]

Fragment of seal, dark brown, round; a figure with nimbus, seated, in right hand a key, in left a book. Counter-seal: the head of a monk, with a crescent above; "Secretum Walteri Prioris."

[*c.* 1234.] Grant from James de Achangre to Peter, Bishop of Winchester, for the sum of 40 marks, of the crofts called Cavelercrofte and Brodecrofte (as described in the grant of 1233, No. 55 *supra*, with the variation of "Edrichesgrove" for "Edithesgrove"), for the increase of the houses and buildings of the Priory which the said Bishop has founded there in honour of the Blessed Virgin Mary. Witn.: the same as to No. 55 ("John de Wyndeshores;" Gilebert the clerk for "Gilbert de Burhunte, clerk.")—[189.]

Round green seal; broken: a man on horseback "S' James . . . . ."

Another copy of this grant, by another scribe, apparently written some thirty years later. Same seal, black.—[188.]

[1234.] Release from Hunfrid de Gollega to Sir John the Prior and the Convent of Seleburne, for the sum of 30 marks, of all his right in the whole tenement and in one messuage in the vill of Seleburne. Witn.: Roger Wascelin, Sheriff of Suthamtptesire,[1] John de la Stane, John de Venuz, John de Windlesore, James de Nortune, Tomas de

[1] Sheriff in 1233-4.

Giminge, William de Ho, Thomas de Venuz, Gilebert de Popham, Laurence de Heyes, Hugh de Popham, Gilebert Cunan, Roger de Bradesete, clerk.—[82.]

Round white seal; a fleur-de-lis: "S' Hunf . . . . ."

[1234.] Release and quit-claim from Hunfrid de Gollega to the Prior and Canons of B. Mary of Seleburne, for the sum of 13 marks of all his right in one virgate of land in Seleburne, which his brother, Gilebert de Gollega, formerly held by his gift, of the King in villenage, according to the custom of the manor. Witn.: Roger Wacelin, Sheriff of Suhamsire, John de la Stone, John de Venuz, John de Wildesore, James de Northune, Thomas de Giminge, William de Ho, Thomas de Venuz, Gilebert de Popham, James de Achangre, Alan de Haueclige, Gilebert Cunan, Roger de Bradesete, clerk.—[71.]

Round green seal; a floriated ornament: "Sigill' Hunfridi Gollega."

[1234.] Release and quit-claim from Richard de Suanemere to the church of B. Mary of Seleburne, and the Prior and Canons there, for the sum of 33 marks, of all his right in one virgate of land in Seleburne, as the right of their church, which Gilebert de Gollega, his uncle, formerly held in Seleburne, by the gift of the King, in villenage, according to the custom of the manor. Witn.: Roger Waceline, Sheriff of Suhamtesire, John de la Stone, John de Venuz, John de Wildesore, James de Northune, Thomas de Giminge, William de Ho, Thomas de Venuz, Gilebert de Popham, James de Achangre, Alan de Haveclige, Gilebert Cunan, Roger de Bradesete, clerk.—[3.]

Round green seal; a fleur-de-lis: "Sigill' Ricardi de Swanem."

Another original copy of this grant, with the same witnesses ("Wildelesore") and seal.—[68.]

[1234.] Grant from James de Akhangre to John the Prior and the Canons of Seleburne, in free alms, of all the moor where the Beme rises, and the land round the same moor to make a fishpond ("vivarium") as great, as deep, as wide, and as long, as they wish, and mills and pools at their will, and sufficient land all round the fishpond for dragging and drying their nets. Witn.: Roger Wascel', then Sheriff of Suhamptes[ire], John de Windeshore, James de Nortone, William de Ho, Thomas Wallensis, Laurence de Heyes, Roger de Bradesete, clerk, Mathew de Monasterio, Peter the Forester.—[136.]

Round black seal; device effaced.

1234, 6 Dec., "die Veneris, scilicet die S. Nich'i," 19 Hen. fil. Joh.[1] Release from Ameria, wife of the late Adam Gurdon, with the consent of her sons, to the Prior and Canons of B. Mary of Selebourne of all her right in heybote and housbote and common in their wood at Selebourne, and in the common pasture of Durton, which wood and pasture they have by the King's gift, of which the pasture lies between the vills of Selebourne and Thornwyke, extending in length by the water which goes down from Selebourne to the Priory on the one side, and near the lands of the Prior and Canons, of which one is called la Wrthe, and through the lands of Thomas de Bercham, near la Middelwrthe, up to Lytecoumbe, on the other side, namely on the north, and abutting on two crofts of the Prior and Canons, one called Thornwyke and the other Farncrofte, at the east end, and on the vill of Selebourne at the west end; saving to all her men of Selebourne common with all their own animals in the said pasture as in times past; releasing also all her right in all the land which Thomas de Bercham held near the water of Durtone, which lies between the land called Thornwyk and the ditch of the Prior and Canons which goes down to the said water through the middle of the meadow which was Philip of the Mill's, and in all the land which Gibert de Gollegze formerly held in Selebourne, saving an annual rent of 4*s.* 10*d.*; and her heir, when he comes of age, shall make his own charter of release which he has sworn to do, "tactis sacrosanctis," or else, if any dispute be made, eighteen marks which have been given for this release, are to be repaid; she and her eldest son, Adam (who seals with her), binding all their lands in Selebourne and Tistede for guarantee of fulfilment. Witn.: Sir Stephen, Prior of Motesfonte, master Elyas de Durham, John de Venuz, Laur. de Hegzes, Matthew de Monasterio.—[24.]

Two red seals: (1) oval, apparently a small Roman gem, but device very obscure: "S' Amirie de Gvrdvn;" (2) round, an archer shooting an arrow (drawing the bow): "Sigillum Ade de Gvrdvn."

[1234–36], 2 March, "quinto nonas Marcii," no year added; at Faverisham. Grant from Peter [de Rupibus], Bishop of Winchester, to the Prior and Canons of Seleburne of one virgate of land which he bought of Henry le Sauvage in Westistude, with messuage, wood, pasture, etc., paying to the said Henry le Sauvage an annual quit-rent of one pound of cummin. Witn.: Sir Richard, Abbot of Tychefelde, master Alan de Stoke, master William de St. Mary Church, master Humphrey de Milers, Robert de Wautham, Roger Alis, Geoffrey de

[1] *Sic;* but St. Nicholas' day, 6 Dec., fell on Wednesday in that year.

Roches, Thomas Alis, Roger Wacelin, John de Teford, John de Suwerk. "Per manum Petri de Chaunceles."—[233.]

Fragment of seal, broken in half and wrapped up in wool.

1235, 19 Hen. fil. Joh. In the Chapter of the Priory of Seleburne. Indenture by which Roger de Cherlecote grants to J. the Prior and the Convent of Seleburne in perpetual fee-farm a messuage with a croft in Hakangre Bynorthebroke, on condition that they distribute annually among the poorer persons of the parish of Seleburne, for the soul of himself, his wife Isabella, and his ancestors, six pairs of shoes, each of the value of 5½*d.* Witn.: John de Venuz, James de Nortune, knts., Henry de la Charite, John de Borhunte, James de Achangre, Gilbert Conan.—[171.]

Fragment of round green seal.

Bull of Pope Gregory IX, Confirming the Foundation of the Priory and Conferring Privileges.

1235, 1 Sept. Gregorius episcopus, servus servorum Dei, dilectis filiis Priori ecclesiæ de Seleburn, quoque fratribus tam præsentibus quam futuris regularem vitam professis inperpetuum: Quotiens a nobis petitur quod religioni et honestati convenire dinoscitur, animo nos decet libenti concedere, ac petentium desideriis congruum suffragium impertiri. Quapropter, dilecti in Domino filii, vestris justis postulationibus clementer annuimus, et ecclesiam beatæ Mariæ de Seleburn in qua divino mancipati estis obsequio sub beati Petri et nostra protectione suscipimus, et præsentis scripti munimine communimus. In primo siquidem statuentes ut ordo canonicus qui secundum Deum et beati Augustini regulam in eadem ecclesia institutus esse dinoscitur perpetuis ibidem temporibus inviolabiliter observetur. Præterea, quascumque possessiones, quæcumque bona, eadem ecclesia impræsentiarum juste ac canonice possidet, aut in futurum concessione pontificum, largitione regum vel principum, oblatione fidelium, seu aliis justis modis, præstante Domino, poterit adipisci, firma vobis vestrisque successoribus et illibata permaneant. In quibus hæc propriis duximus exprimenda vocabulis:—locum ipsum in quo præfata ecclesia sita est, cum omnibus pertinentiis suis; de Basinges et de Seleburn parrochiales ecclesias, cum de Basingestoke ac capellis aliis et omnibus pertinentiis suis; necnon terras et possessiones alias, cum pratis, nemoribus, usuagiis et pascuis, in bosco et plano, in aquis et molendinis, in viis et semitis, et omnibus aliis libertatibus et immunitatibus suis. Sane novalium vestrorum quæ propriis manibus aut sumptibus colitis, de quibus aliquis hactenus non percepit, sive de vestrorum animalium nutrimentis, nullus a vobis decimas exigere vel extorquere præsumat. Liceat quoque vobis clericos vel laicos liberos et absolutos e sæculo fugientes ad conversionem recipere, et eos absque contradictione aliqua retinere. Prohibemus insuper ut nulli fratrum vestrorum post factam in ecclesia vestra pro-

iniquitate cognoscat, et a sacratissimo corpore ac sanguine Dei et Domini Redemptoris nostri Jesu Christi aliena fiat, atque in extremo fessionem fas sit sine prioris sui licentia, nisi artioris religionis obtentu, de ecclesia ipsa discedere; discedentem vero absque communium litterarum vestrarum cautione nullus audeat retinere. Cum autem generale interdictum terræ fuerit, liceat vobis nichilominus in vestra ecclesia, clausis januis, excommunicatis et interdictis exclusis, non pulsatis campanis, suppressa voce, divina officia celebrare, dummodo causam non dederitis interdicto. Crisma vero, oleum sanctum, consecrationes altarium seu basilicarum, ordinationes clericorum qui ad sacros fuerint ordines promovendi, a diocesano suscipietis episcopo si quidem catholicus fuerit et gratiam et communionem sacrosanctæ Romanæ sedis habuerit, et ea vobis voluerit sine pravitate aliqua exhibere. Prohibemus insuper ut infra fines parrochiæ vestræ nullus sine assensu diocesani episcopi et vestro capellam seu oratorium de novo construere audeat, salvis privilegiis pontificum Romanorum. Ad hæc, novas et indebitas [exactiones] ab archiepiscopis et episcopis, archidiaconis seu decanis, aliisque omnibus ecclesiasticis secularibusve personis, a vobis omnino fieri prohibemus. Sepulturam quoque ipsius loci liberam esse decernimus, ut eorum devotioni et extremæ voluntati qui se illic sepeliri deliberaverunt, nisi forte excommunicati vel interdicti aut etiam publice usurarii sint, nullus obsistat, salva tamen justitia ecclesiarum illarum a quibus mortuorum corpora assumuntur. Decimas præterea et possessiones ad jus ecclesiarum vestrarum spectantes quæ a laicis detinentur redimendi et legitime liberandi de manibus eorundem, et ad ecclesias ad quas pertinent revocandi, libera sit vobis de nostra auctoritate facultas. Obeunte vero te nunc ejusdem loci Priore vel tuorum quolibet successorum nullus ibi qualibet surreptionis astutia seu violentia præponatur nisi quem fratres communi consensu vel fratrum major pars consilii sanioris secundum Deum et beati Augustini regulam provideant eligendum. Paci quoque et tranquillitati vestræ paterna in posterum sollicitudine providere volentes, auctoritate apostolica prohibemus ut infra clausuras locorum seu grangiarum vestrarum nullus rapinam seu furtum facere, ignem apponere, sanguinem fundere, hominem temere capere vel interficere, seu violentiam audeat exercere. Præterea omnes libertates et immunitates a Romanis pontificibus ordini vestro concessas, necnon libertates et exemptiones secularium exactionum a Regibus et Principibus vel aliis fidelibus rationabiliter vobis indultas, auctoritate apostolica confirmamus et præsentis scripti privilegio communimus. Decernimus ergo ut nulli omnino hominum liceat præfatam ecclesiam temere perturbare aut ejus possessiones auferre vel ablatas retinere, minuere, seu quibuslibet vexationibus fatigare, sed omnia integra conserventur, eorum pro quorum gubernatione ac sustentatione concessa sunt usibus omnimodis profutura, salva sedis apostolicæ auctoritate ac diocesani episcopi canonici justitia. Siqua igitur in futurum ecclesiastica secularisve persona, hanc nostræ constitutionis paginam sciens, contra eam temere venire temptaverit, secundo tertiove commonita, nisi reatum suum congrua satisfactione correxerit, potestatis honorisque sui careat dignitate, reamque se divino judicio existere de perpetrata examine districtæ subjaceat ultioni. Cunctis autem eidem loco sua jura servantibus sit pax Domini nostri Jesu Christi, quatinus et hic fructum bonæ actionis percipiant, et apud districtum Judicem præmia eternæ pacis inveniant. Amen ac Amen.

Ego Gregorius Catholicæ Ecclesiæ Episcopus.

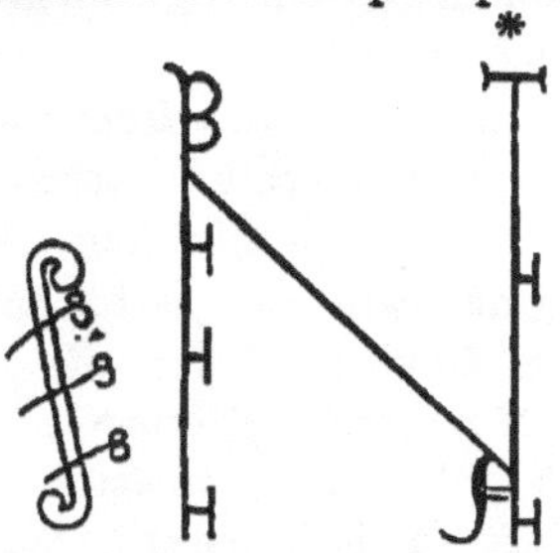

✠ Ego Thomas tit. Sanctæ Sabinæ presbiter cardinalis s[ubscripsi.]
✠ Ego Guifredus tit. Sancti Marci presbiter cardinalis s.
✠ Ego Sinibaldus tit. Sancti Laurentii in Lucin. presbiter cardinalis s.
✠ Ego Johannes Sabinensis episcopus s.
✠ Ego Jacobus Tusculanus episcopus s.
✠ Ego Rainaldus Ostiensis et Vellerrensis episcopus s.
✠ Ego Egidius Sanctorum Cosmæ et Damiani diaconus cardinalis s.
✠ Ego Petrus Sancti Georgii ad velum aureum diaconus cardinalis s.
✠ Ego Oto Sancti Nicholai in carcere Tulliano diaconus cardinalis s.

Datum Perusii per manum magistri Guillermi sanctæ Romanæ ecclesiæ vicecancellarii, kal. Septembris, indictione viij, Incarnationis Dominicæ M.CC°XXXV°, Pontificatus vero domini Gregorii papæ viiij anno nono. [Among the *Appropriations.*]

The leaden *bulla* is attached by yellow and red silk threads.

1235, 9 Oct., "die Martis, scil. die S. Dionysii," 19 Hen. fil. Joh.; in the chapel of West Werldham. Release from Ameria, who was the wife of Adam de Gurdune, with the consent of her sons, to John Prior of Seleburne and the Canons there, for the sum of 18 marks (which it is covenanted shall be repaid, under penalty of excommunication by the official of the Bishop of Winchester, if at any time any of the property shall be claimed again, or any of it lost to others, allowing for the value received, to be reckoned at five shillings per annum) of all their right [*here a line has been cut out*] in all the land which Gilbert de Golleghe formerly held in Seleburne, saving only an annual rent of 4*s.* 10*d.* from the moiety of the land, due by them to the King; granting also the land which Thomas de Bircham held near the water of

* *i.e.*, S[ubscripsi]. Bene valete.

Durtone, namely, from the land called Thornwike to the said Canons' ditch, going down to the same water through the middle of the meadow which was Philip of the Mills', together with all their right in the common of the land called Durtone, namely, from Thornwike to the said ditch, and to the head of the croft called Ferncroft, and all the land lying between Ferncroft and Otecumbe; so that their ditch shall go in a direct line from the head of the aforesaid ditch through the west end of Ferncroft to Otecumbe; paying annually one pound of cummin or 2*d*. And her heir, when he comes of age, shall make security by his own deed, as he has sworn to do "tactis sacrosanctis." Witn.: Sir Stephen, Prior of Modesfunte, Sir David, Prior of Ivychurch ("Monasterio Ederoso"), master Elyas de Derham, Sir John de Venuz, Sir John de Windlesore, Laurence de Heghes, Thomas de Bromdene, Matthew de Minster ("Monasterio"), Reginald the clerk.—[7.]

Small fragment of red seal.

[Before 1236.] Grant from Henry le Sauvage to Peter, Bishop of Winchester, for the sum of 12 marks, of all the land which he had in Tistede by the grant of Ralph de Winesham. Witn.: Roger Alis, Geoffrey de Rupibus, Thomas de Gimiges, Walter de Ticcheborn, Robert Lohod,[1] John de Venuez, Thomas de Venuez, William son of Unfrid, Roger of the Mills, Alard his brother, Elyas son of Roger, Nich. de Syrlege, Godfrey the Serjeant ("serviente") of Cheriton.—[268.]

Seal sewn up in wool. See another original copy at page 3. [355.]

1236, 2 Dec., "die Martis pr. ante f. B. Benedicti"; at Winchester. Presentation (addressed to the Bishop of Winchester) by Joan, formerly the wife of Robert Lohot, of the Prior and Canons of Selburne to the church of Westystede now vacant, which belongs to her presentation, to be appropriated to their own use for ever.—[271.]

Fragment of round green seal; a fleur-de-lis: "Sig . . . . hanne [L]ohot."

1236[-7,] 12 Jan., "secundo idus Jan." Decree of arbitration by E[lias] de Derham, Canon of Salisbury, in a suit brought by authority of the Pope before the Dean, Chancellor, and Succentor of Sarum, between J., the Prior, and the Convent of Seleburne, J. de Nortone, knt., and G. de Burhunte, clerk, about a moiety of all the tithes issuing from the demesne of the said J. de Nortone, and from the dowry of his mother Alice;—viz., that the said G. de Burhunte shall receive the said tithes during his life, offering yearly for them, on Easter Day, to the mother church of Seleburne, at the high altar, 2*s*.; that on his resignation of them, or death, they shall wholly and entirely remain for

[1] He deceased before December, 1236.

ever to the said Prior and Convent; and that on Burhunte's death or resignation the said J. de Nortune and his heirs shall present a fit clerk, who shall be admitted into the convent as a canon, and so on from time to time; and if any dispute arise as to the fitness of the presentee, it shall be determined by the official of the Bishop. Witn.: Sir John de Venoiz, knt., master John de Dertef[ord], master H., vicar of Hertele, John Terri, vicar of Hamelede, John de Caneford, chaplain, Roger de Cherlecote, Hugh de Popham, Will. de Venoiz, Sir J. de Windleshore, James de Ochangre, Mathew de Monasterio, Thomas de Chabb.', Reginald de Wiche, clerks.—[326.]

Five brown seals: (1) round, broken, a head (an antique; the seal of the arbitrator); (2) oval, the Baptism of our Lord: "Sigill' Jo . . nis Prioris de Seleburn';" (3) large, oval, the Coronation of the B. V. Mary (?): "Sigill' Conventus . . . . . . burn';" (4) shield-shaped, an inescutcheon within an orle of bezants, inscription broken; (5) oval, a head: "Sill' Gilib' Clerici de B' h' t'"; inscription engraved reversely.

1236[-7,] Feb. Lease from master Andrew, rector of the church of Chalvedone, to John, Prior of Seleburne, and to the Convent for the sum of 100s., of all the lands which he held by the gift of William de Arundel in the manor of Lydesethe to hold for the term of sixty years from the feast of the Purification of B. Mary, 1236, paying to the said Will. de Arundel, the chief lord, an annual quit-rent of 12*d.*; with power, if they have laid out costs upon improvements, to retain the land after the completion of the term until they have been repaid. Witn.: Sir Richard, Abbot of Tychefelde, Hugh, Archdeacon of Winchester, Luke, Archdeacon of Surrey, Roger Alis, Thomas his son, Reginald de Cundi, Will. de Ho, Walter de Thicheburne, Roger Wacelin, John de Kulesdune.—[289.]

Fragment of red seal, loose, wrapped up in the deed, being the other part of the seal of which a fragment is attached to No. 288, *infra*.

Another copy of the same lease by a different hand, but without the provision for improvements. Witn.: the same, adding Peter Rusinol, and spelling "Thicheburne" "Tycheburne." Fragment of the same seal, with a centaur; "S' Quec . . . . tego."—[290.]

1237, 4 June, "pridie nonas Jun."; at Farnham, "per manum P. Russinol." Confirmation by P[eter], "Minister" of the church of Winchester, of the grant by Joan, who was the wife of Robert le Hod, of the church of Westistede to the Prior and Canons of Seleburne.—[269].

Fragment of the oval red episcopal seal, sewn up in wool.
Another original copy of the same grant, but one never sealed.—[273.]

[1237.] Grant from Henry le Sauvage to Peter, Bishop of Winchester, of all his land in West Tystede, with the messuage, wood, pasture, etc., paying an annual quit-rent of one pound of cummin. Witn.: Roger Alys, Geoffrey de Rupibus, Thomas de Gimige, Walter de Tycheburne, Roger Wascelin, John de Venuz, Thomas de Venuz, William son of Humphrey, Roger of the Mill, Alard his brother, Elyas son of Roger, Nich. de Syrlege, Godfrey the Serjeant ("serviente") of Cheritone.—[260].

Seal sewn up in wool.

Another original copy of the grant, including the quit-rent, and adding that 12 marks have been received from the Bishop for the land. Witn.: the same, omitting Roger Wascelin ("Thomas de Gyminges"). Fragment of oval red seal, the temptation of Adam and Eve: ". . . Henrici le Savva . . ."—[277.]

Another original grant of the same as to the Prior and Canons of Seleburne instead of the Bishop, omitting the quit-rent of one pound of cummin. Witn. the same, (with these variations in spelling: Roger Alis, Thos. de Gimiges, Walter de Thussheberne, John de Venuez, Will. son of Unfrey, Nich. de Sirleges), oval red seal, sewn up in wool; the temptation of Adam and Eve: "S'. Henrici le Savvage."—[264.]

[*c.* 1237.] Grant from master Andrew [of Winchester], rector of the church of Chalvedone, to the Prior and Canons of Seleburne, in free alms, and for the sum of 100*s.*, of all the lands which he had by the gift of William de Arundel in the manor of Lidesethe; paying to the chief lord an annual quit-rent of 12*d.* (Written by the same hand as No. 290, *supra.*) Witn.: John de Venuz, Roger Alis, Thomas his son, Henry de Ysenherst, Roger de Bradesete, Mathew de Monasterio, John de Burhunte, Gilbert de Burhunte, Alan de Havecl[ie.]—[288.]

Fragment of round red seal; a Roman intaglio, a centaur: "S' Qv . . . . . atego."

[*c.* 1237.] Grant from William de Arundel, son of Hugh de Arundel, to the Prior and Canons of Seleburne, in perpetual alms, of all the lands which they have by the gift of master Andrew de Winton, viz., all the land of la Dunwatere which Richard de la Dunwatere held in the vill of Lydessete, and all the land of la Ruda which Walter de Arundel held in Lydessete with a messuage, and all the land before the gate of the said messuage which is included between the way going from Lydessete to Burdonesdene on the right hand and the way which goes from Burdonesdene to Rudeherne; paying the grantor an annual quit-rent of 12*d.* He grants also to the said Prior and Canons to have their pigs free of pannage in all the liberties belonging to his vill of Lydesete, except in his wood called la Frithe, and that they may have in the common pasture of Lydesete as many sorts of animals as they can. Witn.: John de Venuz, John de la Stane, James de Nortune, Alan de Haveklie, Henry de Ysenherst, Gilbert de Burhunte, Roger de

Bradesete, Mathew de Monasterio, Will. de Widenhale, Will. de Optune and Robert, clerks.—[20.]

Round brown seal; a lion courant: "Sigill' Will'i de Arundel."

1237–8, 11 March, "quinto non. Marcii"; at Faverisham, "per manum Petri de Chaunceles." Grant from Peter [de Rupibus], Bishop of Winchester, to the Prior and Canons of Seleburne, in free alms, of one virgate of land which he bought of Henry le Savage in Westtystede, with messuage, wood, etc.; paying annually to the said Henry and his heirs a quit-rent of one pound of cummin. Witn.: Sir Richard, Abbot of Tychefelde, master Alan de Stoke, master Will. de St. Mary Church, master Humphrey de Milers, Robert de Wautham, Roger Alis, Geoffrey de Roches, Thomas Alis, Roger Wascelin, John de Teforde, John de Suwerk.—[250.]

Oval red seal, large; good impression; the Bishop, full length, with pastoral staff: "Petrus Dei gratia Wintoniensis episcopus." Counter-seal: busts of two Saints, with key and sword, the Bishop kneeling below: "Sunt sītque boni Petr' Paulusque patroni."

[1238.] Grant from Joan, formerly the wife of Robert Lohod, to the Prior and Canons of Seleburne, in pure alms, of all the land between la Broch and the way which extends from Westistede towards Punesholte, namely, that which is called Trendelcrofte and Rikemanesdene in the vill of Westistede, excepting a certain "gora" towards the north, containing 3½ acres. Witn.: master Humphrey de Myllers, Hugh [de Rupibus], Archdeacon of Winchester, Luke, Archdeacon of Surrey, Walter de Tigcheburne, James de Nortune, Thomas de la Putte of Bromdene, Roger Picot.—[241.]

Round brown seal; a fleur-de-lis: "Sigill' Johanne Lohot."

1238, 4 June, "prid. non. Junii;" at Farnham, "per manum Petri Rusinol." Confirmation by P[eter], Bishop of Winchester, to the Prior and Canons of Seleburne of all the land which they have in Westistede by the gift of Joan who was the wife of Robert Lohod. Witn.: master Humphrey de Milliers, the Bishop's official, Hugh, Archdeacon of Winchester, Luke, Archdeacon of Surrey, master Elyas de Derham, Peter de Rivallis, Rob. de Clynchampe, John de Colesdone, John de Venuz, Rob. Marmiun, Will de Ho.—[257.]

Large oval green seal, good impression; same as with No. 250, *supra*.

[1238.] Grant from Joan, formerly the wife of Robert Lohod, to the Prior and Canons of Seleburne, of the church of Westistede so far as appertains to her as patroness, in free alms, for their own use. Witn.: master Hunfrid de Milliers, Hugh, Archdeacon of Winchester,

Luke, Archdeacon of Surrey, Walter de Tycheburne, James de Nortune, Will. de Dunstighele, Will. de Dreitune, Thos. de la Putte, Roger Pycot.—[263.]

Round green seal; a fleur-de-lis: "Sigill' Johanne Lohot."

[*c.* 1238.] Release and quit-claim from Henry le Sauvage to the Prior and Canons of Seleburne of all the service received by him from Peter, Bishop of Winchester, for the land given to him in West Tystede (as in preceding charters, Nos. 260 and 264). Witn.: Sir John de Venuz, John de Windeshore, James de Nortune, Adam de Lymesye, John Oysun, Robert the Serjeant ("serviente") of Suttone, Mathew de Monasterio, Will. le Bedel, William the Forester of Grutham, Reginald the clerk.—[270.]

Oval brown seal; the temptation of Adam and Eve: "S' Henrici le Savvage."

1239, 14 May, "ij idus Maii," 13 pontif. Greg. IX; at the Lateran. Bull from Pope Gregory IX (cancelled by being cut through) to the Abbot of Hyde, the Prior of Brummore, and the Dean of Winchester, forbidding the exempting the Abbot of Beaulieu Royal ("de Bello Loco Regis") from a suit brought against him, the Abbot of Tyrun (*sic*) and the Prior of Enedewell by the Prior and Convent of Seleburne respecting tithes, upon the technical grounds in the case of the first, that there was no mention of Cistercians in the Papal letters which delegated the hearing of the cause, and in the case of the others, that they were not included by a general clause of "quidam alii."—[373.]

Bulla lost.

Bull of Pope Gregory IX, respecting a Lawsuit between the Priory of Selborne and G. de Hay, respecting the Church of Tisted.

1239, 20 May. Gregorius episcopus, servus servorum Dei, dilectis filiis Decano, Precentori, et Cancellario Sarisberiensi, salutem et apostolicam benedictionem, Dilecti filii, Prior et Conventus de Seleburne, ordinis sancti Augustini, oblata nobis peticione monstrarunt quod cum magister G. de Haya, Wyntoniensis dioceseos, ipsos super ecclesia de Tychestede coram Archidiacono Surrei, auctoritate dilecti filii nostri O[thonis], sancti Nicholai in carcere Tulliano diaconi Cardinalis, apostolicæ sedis Legati, traxisset in causam, quia idem judex diebus feriatis,[1] videlicet tempore messium, ad litigandum compellebat eosdem cum non urgeret necessitas vel pietas suaderet, ipsi sentientes se indebite gravari nostram audientiam appellarunt: Ideoque discretioni vestræ per apostolica scripta mandamus, quatinus, si est ita, revocato in statum debitum quicquid post hujusmodi appellationem inveneritis temere attemptatum, in causa

[1] In vacation-time.

ipsa juxta tenorem mandati Legati prædicti ratione prævia procedatis; alioquin partes ad ejusdem archidiaconi remittatis examinationem, appellantem in expensis legitimis condempnando. Testes autem qui fuerint nominati si se gratia, odio, vel timore, subtraxerint, per censuram ecclesiasticam, appellatione cessante, cogatis veritati testimonium perhibere. Quod si non omnes hiis exequendis potueritis interesse, duo vestrum ea nichilominus exequantur. Dat. Laterani, xiij kl. Junii, pontificatus nostri anno tertiodecimo.—[252.]

With the leaden *bulla.*

[*c.* 1240.] Grant from William de Arundel, son of Hugh de Arundel, to the Prior and Canons of Seleburne of the same lands as those granted in the deed, No. 280, *c.* 1237; *adding*—all that land which Ralph de la Rude held, lying between the aforesaid lands which Richard de la Dunwatere and Walter de Arundel held, with the messuage; paying annually a quit-rent of 2*s.*; *and substituting for the pasturage, etc., the following:*—liberty to have in all the pasture belonging to the village of Lydesethe except in his arable demesne, namely, in the field called Great Burifeld, lying below his garden, and extending to the wood called la Frithe, and except in the said wood, 40 beasts, 200 sheep, 50 goats, and 40 pigs, free of herbage and pannage. Witn.: John de Venuz, John de la Stane, Adam de St. Manifedo, Hugh de Rumbe (*meant for* Kumbe), James de Nortune, Adam de St. John, Allen de Haveklie, Henry de Ysenherst, Gilbert de Burhunte, Roger de Bradesete, Mathew de Monasterio, Will. de Widenhale.—[281.]

Oval green seal; a griffin (?), "S' Will'mi de Arundel."

Another original copy of the same grant. Witn.: the same (Hugh de *Cumbe*, Alan de *Havechlye*, Henry de Ysen*hurst*), *adding the following:* John Oter, Nich. Suele, Richard the clerk, son of John the clerk. Fragment of seal in wool.—[284.]

[*c.* 1240.] Grant from Henry de Caritate to Roger de Thycheburne, knt., for the sum of 70 marks, "in arduo negocio meo," of all his tenement of la Rode. Witn.: Sir John de Bottlye, Sir Hereward de Marisco, Sir Walter Dandely, knts., Rich. de Wescote, Rich. de Nortone, Will. Gerveys, Peter de Turevile.—[362.]

Seal lost.

[*c.* 1240.] Grant from Thomas Danesy of Westworham to the Prior and Canons of Seleburne, in pure alms, of his new garden with a croft and a grove below "lalidde" of Westworham, as they extend themselves between the highway going from Westworham to Beneswortbe and the ditch of the Prior and Canons which extends from Wigesplothe to the path leading from the aforesaid highway to the chapel of Westworham, together with a curtilage between the said highway on south and the land of Will. de Borunte towards Cobbewelle. Witn.: Sir John de Wenuz, Sir William his son, Sir John de la Stane, Sir Thomas Makerel, James de Acangre, Mathew de Monasterio, Roger Wylard, Henry Wyard, Will. Baiun.—[224.]

Round green seal, broken; a fleur-de-lis: "Si . . . e Dan'si."

[*c.* 1240.] Grant from Peter de Anesy to the Prior and Canons of Selebume, in pure alms, of all his land, with a messuage, garden and meadow, below the "coftam" of West Werldham, namely, that which William the Smith formerly held. Witn.: Sir John de Venuz, Sir William his son, Sir John de la Stane, Sir Gillebert de Poppham, Sir Thomas Makerel, James de Acangre, Will. Baiun, John de Burhunte, Mathew de Monasterio.—[222.]

Oval brown seal; an eagle: "S' Petri de Anesaie."

[*c.* 1240.] Grant from Walter, son of Robert de Tottehale, to the Prior and Canons of Seleburne, for the soul of himself, his wife Eva, etc., in pure alms, of a rent of 20*d.* from the messuage which Herbert Spaule formerly held in Westwerldham. Witn.: Sir James de Nortune, Thomas Makerel, Gilebert Conan, Peter de Anesy, Mathew de Monasterio, Will. Baiun.—[223.]

Seal lost.

[*c.* 1240.] Grant from John de Ochangre to the Prior and Canons of B. Mary of Seleburne, in free alms, of a piece of land of the croft called Cavelescroft, namely, that which extends to the land of the said Canons called la Lyghe, from the corner of the land of la Lyghe to the corner between the wood which was the King's and the wood which Robert de la Rode held; and another piece of the same croft alongside of the said wood of Robert de la Rode up to the land of Thomas Coterel, as it is enclosed by the ditch of the said Canons; to make a way to the Priory; to hold of James de Ochangre and his heirs free of all service. Witn.: the same as to the following deed of James, substituting "James" de Ochangre for "John."—[37.]

Round green seal; a fleur-de-lis: "Sigill' Joh'is de Hochangre."
Another original grant of the same. Witnesses and seal the same.—[79.]

[*c.* 1240.] Grant from James de Ochangre to God and the church of St. Mary of Seleburne, and to the Prior and Canons of the order of St. Augustine there, of one piece of the croft called Cavelescroft (the same land described by the same boundaries as in the preceding deed), to make a way to the Priory; which pieces of land the said Prior and Canons had from John de Ochangre, by consent of the said James. Witn.: Sir John de Venuz, John de Windelesore, James de

Nortune, Laurence de Heyes, Gilebert Cunan, Hugh de Popham, Will. de Venuz, Geoffrey his brother, John de Ochangre, Tho. Coterel.—[19.]

Round green seal; a knight on horseback: "S' James (*sic*) de Hokaungre."

[*c.* 1240.] Release from Robert, son of Seman of Tuddene, to Warner de Isenhurste, for the sum of one mark, of all his right in the messuage and two acres of arable land in the village of Aultone, which Adam Algar formerly held of Henry de Isenhurste. Witn.: Rich. de Westcote and John de Westcote, brothers, John son of Richard, Geoffrey the Serjeant ("serviente") of the Abbot of Hyde, John Oter, Henry Wyard, William "papa" ["$\frac{a}{pp}$"], Rob. de la Wodecote.—[349.]

Seal lost.

[*c.* 1240–50?] Grant from James de Accangre to John de Venuz of a meadow called Hundeshammed, lying on either side of the water called Lachemere, extending from the meadow of Will. de Aqua to the head of the fishpond; with power to give to whom he will, except a religious house (*cf. supra*, No. 160, A.D. 1233, *et post*, Nos. 122, 209, A.D. 1254) or the Jews; paying to him annually one doe from the park of the said John at Wereldham, or if he have not a doe, 3*s*. Witn.: Sir John de Stane, Sir James de Nortone, Sir Tho. Macurel, James de Molendinis, John de Burhunte, Andrew de Heyes, Robert de Grendone, Andrew de Burhunte, Mathew de Monasterio, Thomas de Monasterio, Will. Baiun, Reginald de Coppeshurst, Peter de Heyes, Alan de Havecleye.—[214.]

Round green seal; the sun and moon: "S' Jacobi de Hacangre."
The varying dates and terms of the grants of this meadow seem puzzling.

[*c.* 1240-50.] Grant from Richard Koterel de la Rode to William de la Rode, son of Robert de la Rode and Alice his wife, for the sum of 6*s*., of a pieee of land in la Rode, in the field called Keterelesfeld, lying between the curtilage of the Lady de la Rode on north and the land of the said William on south, and containing three "daywrke"[1] and one perch; paying an annual quit-rent of one halfpenny. Witn.: John de Venuz, Will. de Achangre, Robert Marescall de la Wyke, Robert le Portir, John de Burtune.—[193.]

Seal lost.

Another grant of the same land in the same terms, but specifying 5*s*. as the price paid for the land. Witn.: Will. de Achangre, Rob. Marescall de la Wike, Walter Makerel, Rob. le Portir, John de Burtune. Seal lost.—[197.]

[c. 1240–50.] Grant from James de Acangre to the Prior and Canons of Seleburne, for the sum of 20*s*., of his born serf ("nativum meum") William de la Chappe, son of Richard de la Chappe, with all

[1] A "day-work" for ploughing was reckoned as four perches.

his following. Witn.: John de Burhunte, Andrew de Burhunte, Mathew de Monasterio, Will. Arundel, James of the Mills, Geoffrey de la Rude.—[174.]

Round green seal; the sun and moon: "S' Jacobi de Hacangre."

[*c.* 1240-50.] Grant from Gilbert de Burhunte, clerk, to God and the church of the B. Mary of Seleburne, and the Prior and Canons there, of all the land which he had by the gift of Henry de Burhunte, his brother (being the land described by the same boundaries in the deed of Henry de Burhunte, No. 16, *circa* 1230. The names are here spelled—"Wxemerslade," "Koterell," "Bramtelstapele," "Sothintune.") To hold in free alms of John de Burhunte, the grantor's nephew ("nepote"); paying to the said John an annual rent of 12*d.*, and to the King for the fourth part of one furlong. Witn.: John de Venuz, John de la Stane, John de Windeleshore, James de Nortone, Thomas Makerel, Thomas de Windeleshore, Gilbert Cunan, James de Akangre, Roger de Bradesete, Roger de Cherlekote, Matthew de Minster ("Monasterio").—[20.]

Oval reddish seal; apparently a Roman head, helmeted; inscription engraved the reverse way, beginning at the left hand corner: "Sill' Gilib' clerici de B' h."

[*c.* 1240-50.] Grant from John de Burhunte to the Prior and Canons of Seleburne, in perpetual alms, of all the land which they have by the gift of his uncle, Gilbert the Clerk, namely, that which the hedge beginning at Wiomerslande and reaching to the field which Richard Koterell ploughed up, and which the ditch made on the grantor's side, enclose; and two acres of land before his gate, near the great road which goes from Brantestapele towards Suthintun, and all the land which Robert the Carpenter held in the same field; paying an annual quit-rent of 12*d.*, and rendering to the King the service belonging to the quarter of a "ferlinge" of land. Witn.: Sir John de Venuz, John de la Stane, James de Northune, Reginald the Chaplain, Geoffrey de la Charite, Thomas de Windelsore, Roger de Bradesethe, Roger de Cherlekote, Ralph son of John de la Stane. Robert the clerk.—[296.]

Oval green seal; a fleur-de-lis: "S' Joh'is d' Burhu'te."
Another original copy of the same grant. Same seal; red.—[348.]

[*c.* 1240-50.] Grant from William the Forester, son of William the Forester, of Grutham, to the Prior and Canons of Seleburne, in free alms, of all his lands in the vill of Achangre, namely, that which is called Beme, lying between the field called Estfeld and the moor of Beme; rendering annually to James de Achangre half a pound of cummin. Witn.: John de Venuz, John de la Stane, John de Windeshore,

James de Northune, Roger de Bradesete, Mathew de Monasterio, William and Geoffrey de Venuz, Gilebert and Hugh de Popham, Thomas and William Coterel, Will. Berfray.—[131.]

Round red seal, broken: a fleur-de-lis: "Sigill' Will' For . . . . . ."

[*c.* 1240-50.] Grant from William le Forester of Grutham to Sir John, the Prior, and Canons of Seleburne, of all that cultivated land lying between his garden and the meadow which he gave to farm to Sir John de la Stane, with free ingress and egress, to hold until he shall have given them full possession of that land which he had in Achangre between the field called Estfeld and the moor of Beme which he granted to them by deed. Witn.: John de Windeshore and Thomas his son, James de Northone, Mathew de Monasterio, Laur. de Heges, Roger son of Gilibert de Bradesete, Roger de Bradesete, clerk, Thomas Coterel, Rob. de Wicke, Will. Coterel.—[146.]

Round red seal; a fleur-de-lis: "Sigill' Will' For[es]tier."

[*c.* 1240-50.] Grant from Richard de Dena, to his brother Thomas de Dena, in consideration of the receipt of 12 marks, of one virgate of land which he held of the King in Ocangre, except the meadow belonging to it, with the custom of mowing and carrying it by the villein labourers of the same holding for five Henr[ies] (pennies) to be given to the said villeins by the grantor and his heirs; rendering to the grantor annually one pair of gloves or one penny ("vel Henr'"), and to the King, 10*s.* Witn.: Sir John de la Stane, Sir Hugh de Forest, knts., Mathew de Denemede, Adam de Mora, Will. Balun, Rich. de Westcote, Rich. de Ketecumbe, Henry de Chalus, Rob. de Camera.—[153].

Round green seal; an open hand: "S' Ricardi . . . . ." (a somewhat long inscription).

[*c.* 1240-50.] Grant from Thomas de Monasterio, of Werldham, to Sir Thomas de Winton, rector of the church of Werldham, for the sum of 29 marks, of a messuage which he formerly held of Sir John de Wonoiz (*sic*), namely, that nearest to the church of Werldham towards the west, and thirteen acres of arable land in the fields of Werldham, of which three lie in Pokelescrofte, four in Wodesfoldeforlong, between the land which Matthew de Monasterio formerly held, one acre in Brodecrofte between the land of the said Matthew and that which Alice de Wonoiz formerly held, one acre in Hawenheye, one acre at the sheepfold, formerly the said Matthew's, between his land and that which Herbert le Crek formerly held, three acres in Horsemere, of which one is at the head of the seven acres of Sir John de Wonoiz, one between the land of the said Matthew, and one in Horsemerecrofte which

Gilibert de Monasterio formerly held; and seventeen and a half acres which the said Thomas de Winton formerly farmed of the grantor as they are named in a chirograph between them, and eight acres of pasture in Brodecrofte, and an annual rent of 2*s.* 6*d.*, namely, from Philip called Fitz-Count ("filio comitis"), 12*d.*, from William Wildegrim, 12*d.*, and from Reginald le Fox, 6*d.*; paying to the grantor an annual quit rent of 1*d.*, and to Sir John de Wonoiz for the messuage, 3*s.* Witn.: Sir John de Wonoiz, Sir H., then chaplain of Werldham, Hugh de Wonoiz, Robert de Grendon, clerk, Matthew de Monasterio, William the deacon, Nicholas le Stede.—[215.]

Seal lost.

[*c.* 1240-50.] Release from James de Nortune to the Prior and Convent of Seleburne for the sum of 15 marks, for himself, his heirs, and his men and tenants, by their grant and will, of all his right in the pasture of Durtune, which is enclosed with a ditch from la Worthe through Ferme Crofte up to the water towards the Priory; and also in sixty acres of land and a messuage in Seleburne, which Richard de Swanemere formerly held; and which he (the said James) had by the gift of Gilebert son of Rich. Lyps. Witn.: Master Humphrey de Millers, Sir John de Venuz, Sir John de la Stane, Robert Puntdelarche, Will. le Duc, Will. de la Bere, Rich. de la Bere, Geoffrey de Froyle, Rich. Wastehuse, Geoffrey de la Rude, Mathew de Monasteria, John Wilekin, Roger de Cherlecote.—[292.]

Shield-shaped seal, red; apparently a blank shield within a bordure of sixteen bezants; inscription illegible.

Another original copy of the same grant; seal lost.—[302.]

[*c.* 1240-50.] Release from Gilebert, son of Richard Lyps, to the Prior and Convent of Seleburne, of all his right in sixty acres of land and one messuage in the land which Richard de Swanemere formerly held in Seleburne. Witn.: Sir John de Venuz, Sir John de la Stane, Robert de Pundelarge, Will. le Duc, Will. de la Bere, Rich. de la Bere, Geoffrey de Froyle.—[84.]

Round dark seal; a fleur-de-lis: "S' Gilebeti fil' Ricardi Lelipse."

[*c.* 1240-50.] Grant from Paulinus, the Carpenter, to Robert Gaugy, with Muriel his wife, the grantor's daughter, in marriage-dowry, of all his mill of Sydenemede, and with the pasture of the meadow after haymaking, which meadow he had of the Prior and Canons of Seleburne; paying to them an annual quit-rent of 5*s.*, saving the service of the King and saving the custody of the meadow faithfully by the enclosure of the said Prior and Canons. Witn.: Sir John de Venuz, Sir Tho.

Makerel, Will. Huse, James of the Mills ("de Molendinis"), John de Burhunte and Andrew his brother, James de Ackangre, Nich. Suele, Will. de Arundel de la Wyke.—[305.]

Seal lost.

[*c.* 1240-50.] Grant from James de Nortune to the Prior and Canons of the church of B. Mary of Seleburne, in free alms, of 2*s.* of annual rent in the vill of Seleburne, from the tenement which was once Bernard le Quareur's, and which the grantor had by the gift of the Prior and Brethren of the Hospital of St. Nicholas of Portesmue. Witn.: Sir John de Venuz, Matthew his brother, Geoffrey de Rupibus, Roger Wasilin, Will. de la Bere, Oliver the Clerk, Will. de Venuz, Matthew de Monasterio.—[47.]

Reddish seal, shield-shaped; a shield (with an orle of bezants outside it) bearing apparently a double cross; "Sigillum Jacobi Nortune."

Another original copy of this grant. Witn. names have two variations, namely, the knightly title is omitted before "John de Venuz," and "Wasilin" appears in its usual form of "Wacelin." Same seal, green wax.—[49.]

[*c.* 1240-50.] Grant from Adam de Lymesie to the Prior and Canons of Seleburne, in perpetual alms, of the two messuages in the vill of Westystede which Will. Hurdman and Matilda de Seleburne formerly held of him, with all their lands, etc.; and also of all that land which lies between the quick-set hedge near the ditch of the said Prior and Canons and a certain ash tree which is on this side the highway going from Roppeley to Petersfeld, and which extends in length from the said ash tree by the said highway on south to Rompesdene; paying an annual quit-rent of one pound of cummin. Witn.: Sir Henry de Ferlye, Adam de St. Manefico, Hamon de Basynge, Rob. de Ho, John de Valletorta, Rich. de Aweltone, Will. de Dunstykel, Will. de Drayton, Thomas de Brond', Henry and Warner de Ysenhurst, brothers, Will. Bayun, Rich. de Pruuet', Mathew de Monasterio, Mathew de Hurley.—[251.]

Oval green seal; a fleur-de-lis: "Sigill' Ade de Limisi."

Another original copy of the same grant with same seal and witnesses, ["Thomas de Bromdene."] The former holder of the messuages is called "Will. Hurman."—[278.]

[*c.* 1240-50.] Grant from Henry the Clerk of Estrope to the Prior and Canons of St. Mary of Seleburne of a piece of his land, namely, that which lies at Hundesdelle, extending above the highway on the south; paying an annual quit-rent of 6*d.* Witn.: master Elyas de Derham, John de Venuz, Will. de Arundel, James de Nortune, Thomas de Bromdene, Hamo de Basinge, Rich. de London, Rich. Taun, Jervase de Ywode, Germain de Ywode, W. de Ywode.—[66.]

Oval brown seal; a fleur-de-lis: "Sigill' Henri' Destro'."

Another original grant of the same, with the same witnesses; ["Ywode" is written "Yuuode."] Same seal, oval, green: "Sigill' Henri' Destro'."—[72.]

[*c.* 1240–50.] Grant from John de Burhunte to the Prior and Canons of Seleburne, in free alms, of ten acres and a quarter of his land, with a messuage and garden which they have by the gift of Gilebert de Burhunte, clerk, uncle of the said John, in the field called Yhangre, namely, the land which lies near the highway going from Hetnesmanesburieles to Brunthestapele, and from Brunthestapele to the head of the ditch of the said Prior and Convent on south, and from thence to the highway on west going from Ymbesate to Hetenesmannesburieles. Witn.: Sir John de Venuz, Sir James de Northune, Sir Thos. Makerel, Will. Huse, James of the Mills ("de Molendinis"), Andrew de Burhunte, James de Ackangre, Will. de Arundel de la Wyke.—[123.]

Fragment of oval green seal, device effaced; wrapped in wool.

[*c.* 1240–50.] Grant from James de Achangre to John the Prior and the Canons of Seleburne of the moor where the Beme rises, (etc., *as in the deed under date* 1234, No. 136, *adding*) all the water course coming from the Beme through his lands and those of his men, at their will to lead to their mill of Oxneie. Witn. the same as to No. 130, p. 36.—[155.]

Round brown seal, wrapped in tow; a man on horseback: "S' James de Hochangr'."

1242, Sept. Indenture of an agreement between the Prior and Convent of Suwic' [Southwick] and the Prior and Convent of Seleburne, for the settlement of a suit which had been carried on before the Dean of Oxford and master Henry Bardolf, acting, by the Pope's authority, for the Prior of Christ Church of Twinham, respecting some tithes issuing from the land of la Pette and from the land of la Berghe, in the parish of Ymbesete, and respecting some others:—namely, that the Prior and Convent of Suwic' shall, by reason of the right which they have in their chapel of Ymbesete, receive all the tithes issuing from the land of la Pette, with all those issuing from all the demesne of the lord of Ymbesete, and the half of all those from the husbandmen ("colonis"), both free and villeins, and from their possessions, both moveable and immoveable, within the parish of Ymbesete, which they were wont to receive before the time of this composition: That the Prior and Convent of Seleburne, shall, in the name of their parish church of Seleburne, by reason of the partial right which they have in the tithes of the chapel of Ymbesete, receive the moiety of all the tithes of the said husbandmen and of their possessions, which they also had been accustomed to receive, with the moiety of all those issuing from the land of la Berghe, although it be in the lord's demesne. It is further agreed that this arrangement shall always stand, notwithstanding any changes in the lands to which it applies, and the following further points are added: 1. That (the vicar of Ymbesete being present and consenting), at all funerals of the parishioners of Ymbesete the chaplain of Seleburne shall celebrate the first mass, and the chaplain of Ymbesete the second, and all the oblations thereupon made shall be equally divided. 2. All legacies bequeathed by the said parishioners to the church of Seleburne, or to the chapel of Ymbesete, shall also be equally divided, but all personal legacies, left to certain persons or chaplains, shall abide by the testator's disposition. 3. The chaplain of Ymbesete shall yearly make a three-fold public denunciation of excommunication against those who maliciously withhold tithes. 4. The said chaplain has sworn, and the chaplain for the time being shall hereafter swear, to observe all that is contained in this composition, and shall make known anything done by any parishioner against the rights of either church.—[337.]

First seal (that of the ordinary, namely, master Albert de Vitriaco, official of Winchester during the vacancy of the see) lost; Second, oval, green, inscription broken, The Virgin and Child, seated: "Sigil' Sancte Marie d' . . . . ica;" counter-seal, The Virgin and Child, a figure kneeling below: "Sigill' Mathei Prioris d' S'wik."

1242, 25 Dec., "in Nativ. Dom." Lease from Cecilia de Westistede, widow of Henry le Saovage (*sic*), to the Prior and Convent of Seleburne of all the land which she had as dowry in the vill of Westistede, except her messuage; to hold for her life, paying her an annual rent of 4*s*. Witn.: Roger Picot of Bromdene, Hervic de Bromdene, John le Frankelain, Thomas le Walais of Tistede, Walter Cove, Will. de la Mare, Sir Rich. le Harepere, the mason ("cementario") of Farnham, Sir Gilbert de Burhunte.—[265.]

Round brown seal wrapped up in wool; a star: "Sigillum Cecil'." [See Nos. 267, 272, under date 1257–9.]

1245, 20 Aug., "die Domin. pr. p. Assump. B. M. V." Lease (*or* mortgage, indented) from Peter Dancsie, with the consent of his wife Cristiana, to the Prior and Convent of Seleburne, for the sum of 4 marks, which the said Peter paid to Elyas the Jew of Winchester to release his land, and 1 mark which the said Prior and Convent gave to the said Cristiana to buy a robe, of an annual rent of 10*s*., which the said Peter had in Thorneie in marriage dowry with his said wife, issuing from the tenement which Richard Quatrehomes holds of him in Thorneie; to hold for the term of fifteen years. Witn.: Sir John de Venuz, Sir John de la Stane, James de Acangre, Rich. de Warneford, Will. Baion, Roger de Bradesete, Will. de Balon', Rich. de Ketecumbe.—[297.]

Seal lost.

1246, 25 Dec, "in Nativ. Dom." Lease (indented) from William the Chaplain of Occangre to the Prior and Convent of Seleburne, for the sum of 20*s.*, for the term of ten years, of his garden of la Hunne, which is enclosed with a new ditch, and which he held to farm for the term of ten years from Peter de Cruce. Witn.: Sir John de Venuz, Sir J. de Stane, Sir Tho. Makurel, James de Occangre, Mathew de Monasterio, Roger de Cherlecote, W. Baiun.—[295.]

Seal lost.

[1247, 28 May. Grant from Thomas Danesi to Nicholas de Ewelme. Among the *Winchester* deeds in Magdalen College, No. 25.]

1249, 20 Jan., "in oct. S. Hill.," 33 Hen. fil. Joh., "in curia dom. regis apud Winton." Fine before Henry de Bath, Alan de Wasand, Will. de Wilton, Reginald de Cobeham, and Will. de Breton, the justices itinerant, by which Mathew del Moster [*Monasterio*] acknowledges that a messuage and six acres of land which he holds in Seleburne belong to the church of the Prior of Seleburne, and John, the Prior and Parson of the said church thereupon grants the same to the said Mathew to hold for his life, rendering annually 4*s.* and one pound of cummin, and doing suit of court every three weeks.—[85.]

1249, 12 March, "die S. Gregorii." [*Midhurst.*] Grant from Ralph Pichie of Midhurst to Alice, daughter of Will. le Kinge of Midhurst, in consideration of the receipt of 12*s.*, "ad arduum negocium meum," of an annual rent of 12*d.* in Midhurst, payable by Mildith, the relict of Adam the tailor [*or* clothier, "parmentarii,"] from the messuage held by her from the said Ralph, situate between the house which Thomas le Sqalle formerly held and that which Osebert le Blakesutere formerly held. Witn.: Alexendre (*sic*) le Butelyre, John le Flote, Will. de Bere, Walter Trusel, Symon the clerk, Rob. le Grant, Rich. Schererwynd, G. le Bal, Will. le Abed.—[229.]

Fragment of round white seal, effaced. *See under* 1258, No. 231.

1250, 3 Feb., "a die S. Hillarii in tres sept.," 34 Hen. fil. Joh. Fine before the Judges at Westminster (Roger de Thurkelby, John de Gatesdene, Gilbert de Prestone, John de Cobbeham, Alan de Wassand, and Will. de Wyltone), by which Roger de Cherlecote conveys to John, the Prior of Seleburne, and his Church, in free alms, one messuage, one mill, and thirty-five acres of land in Bradechete, 10*s.* of rent in la Wyke from the whole tenement which Will. de Arundol held of the said Roger in la Wyke, and one messuage, one acre of land, and three acres of meadow, in Akhangre; and the said Prior covenants that he and his Church shall provide every week for the said Roger and Isabella his wife, during their life, eighteen canonical loaves, twenty-eight servants' loaves, fifteen flagons ("lagenas") of the drink of the convent, fourteen flagons of the second beer, and 12*d.* for meat ("ferculis") and pottage: the allowance to be reduced by one-half on the death of either of them.—[177.]

[*c.* 1250.] Grant from Roger de Cherlekote, son of Walter de Cherlecote, to William, son of John de Arundel, of ten acres of land and two messuages in Wyke, namely, the land and messuage which Adam de Wyke formerly held, and the messuage which Herebert holds there; paying an annual rent of 10*s.* (*Half a line has been cut out.*) Witn.: Richard de la Bere, son of Walter de la Bere, James de Molendino, James de Ockangre, Andrew de Heyes, Will. Balun, Mathew de Monasterio, Alan de Havecleye, John Purston (*or* Thurston ?), Ralph Sturgal, Geoffrey de la Rude, Will. Baiun, Gilbert de Wyke.—[182.]

Round green seal; intaglio, a Roman head, very indistinct: "S' Rogeri de Cherlecote."

[*c.* 1250.] Grant from Peter de Cruce to the Prior and Canons of Seleburne, in free alms, of a messuage with a garden on the east side of his house, beside the highway which leads towards la Hunne. Witn.: Sir John de Venuz, Sir William his son, Sir James de Nortone, Sir John de la Stane, Sir Thomas Makerel, Roger de Cherlekote, Matthew de Monasterio, Will. Baion.—[107.]

Seal lost.

[*c.* 1250.] Grant from James de Ackangre to the Church of B. Mary of Seleburne, and the Prior and Canons there, of a croft called Brodecrofte, which John his uncle formerly held, opposite Edeithescrofte, and another croft which Gilbert de Wyke formerly held near Brodecrofte; and his whole meadow lying between his wood and the said two crofts, which Robert le Hunde formerly held of him, and a little grove in the same meadow near the ditch of the Prior and Canons; and also a croft which Ralph le Nyweman formerly held of him, extending from the garden of the said Ralph to the great ditch surrounding the Priory; and also a piece of his wood from the corner of the croft which Ralph le Nyweman held to the said meadow; and also another piece of his wood from the east corner of the said meadow to the croft of Adam le But, near the croft called Brodecrofte; in free alms. Witn.: Sir John de Venuz, Sir William his son, Sir John de Lastanc, Sir Tho. Makerel, John Brembelsete, Roger de Kelecohte, John Oter, Matthew de Monasterio, Will. Baiun, Peter de Ancsi, William Balun.—[5.]

Round green seal; the sun: "S' Jacobi . . . . Acangre."

[*c.* 1250.] Grant from James de Acangre to the Prior and Canons of Seleburne, in free alms, of 8*d.* of annual rent, which they pay him from a tenement which they had in the grantor's vill of Acangre by the gift of Roger de Cherlecote; confirming to them the said tenement and all the meadows which they have in Acangre of his fee, and all the tithes of hay issuing from his whole manor of Acangre. Witn.: Sir John de Venuz, Sir William his son, Sir John de la Stane, Sir Thomas Makerel, John de Burhunte, Andrew his brother, James de Molendinis, Andrew de Heges, Will. Baiun, Mathew de Monasterio.—[130.]

Round brown seal; the sun and moon: "S' Jacobi de Hacangre."

[*c.* 1250.] Grant from John de Windeleshore to the Prior and Canons of Seleburne, in free alms, of a piece of land of his fee, namely, through the middle of the garden of Thomas Coterel and of his land, from the highway de la Cnappe to the land of the said Canons which they had from James de Ochangre and John de Ochangre in Chavelescrofte as it is enclosed by their ditch, in order to make a road from the said road de la Cnappe to the Priory. Witn.: Master Elyas de Derham, Sir John de Venuz, James de Nortune, Laurence de Heyes, James de Ochangre, Gilebert Cunan, Hugh de Poppham, Will. de Venuz, Geoffrey his brother, John de Ochangre.—[132.]

Round brown seal; a knight on horseback, with sword drawn: "Sigill' Joh'is d' Windesore;" good impression.

Another original copy of the same grant. Witn. and seal (red) the same; good impression.—[147.]

[*c.* 1250.] Grant from Thomas Coterel to the Prior and Canons of Seleburne, of a piece of his land through the middle of his garden and of his land, [etc., *as described in the preceding deed,* 132, *relating to the same land;* "Cavelescrofte"]. Witn. the same, *omitting* Elyas de Derham, *and adding* John de Windlesore.—[133.]

Oval black seal; a fleur-de-lis, inscription engraved the reverse way: "Sigill' Thome Coterel."

[*c.* 1250.] Grant from Peter de Cruce, in free alms, to the Prior and Canons of Seleburne, of a piece of his land extending in length on the north of the grove of the said Prior and Canons up to the way leading from his house to the wood of James de Acangre, and in width from his land to that of Richard Holcvey which he had by gift of the said Peter, together with an annual rent of 2*d.* for the said land from the said Richard. Witn.: Sir John de Venuz, Sir William his son, Sir John de la Stane, Sir Thomas Makerel, James de Acangre, Roger de Cherlecote, Will. de Ysenhurst, John de Burhunte, Philip and Andrew his brothers, James de Molendinis, Will. Baiun.—[156.]

Round green seal; a cross with the sun and moon: "S' Petri de la Crus." The two last words appear both in this impression of the seal and in that which follows with the next deed [No. 157] to be engraved by mistake as "Larrvs."

[*c.* 1250.] Confirmation by James de Acangre to the Prior and Canons of Seleburne of the grant which Peter de Cruce made to them of a piece of land, and of an annual rent of 2*d.* from Rich. Holcvey. Witn.: Sir John de Venuz, Sir William his son, Sir John de la Stane, Sir Thomas Makerel, Roger de Cherlecote. Will. de Ysenhurst, John de Burhunte, Philip and Andrew his brothers, James de Molendinis, Will. Baiun.—[148.]

Small fragment of same seal as with other deeds.

[*c.* 1250.] Grant from Peter de Cruce, in free alms, to the Prior and Canons of Seleburne, of a croft of his land, extending on the east part of his grove near the highway going from his house towards la Honne, together with the said grove, and a certain increment of his garden which is between the said grove and the garden of Will. le King. Witn. the same as in the preceding grant, No. 156, *adding* Mathew de Monasterio.—[157.]

Seal, the same as above.

[*c.* 1250.] Release and quit-claim from James de Acangre to the Prior and Canons of Seleburne of all his right in a messuage and garden, situate near the highway going from the house of Peter de Cruce towards la Hunne, which Will. le Kyng formerly held of the said Peter, in free alms, as contained in the charter of the said Peter. Witn.: Sir John de Venuz, Sir William his son, Sir John de la Stane, Sir Thos. Makerel, John de Burhunte, Will. Baiun, Matthew de Monasterio.—[65.]

Round red seal; the sun; inscription broken.

[*c.* 1250.] Grant from Thomas de Monasterio to the Prior and Canons of Seleburne, in pure alms, of 12*d.* of annual rent which Nicholas le Draper of Aweltone and his heirs are bound to pay, as he has been accustomed to pay to the grantor, from seven acres of land held of him in Werlham; of which, two and a half lie in le Suthfelde, and extend above the land of Sir John de Venuz at one end and above Heggemere at the other, one acre lies in one "garstone" and two and a half in another "garstone" between the land of Tulla ("tulle") and that of Robert del Castel, half an acre lies in Svanemere, and half an acre in the field towards Netham. Witn.: Sir John de Venuz, Sir John de la Stane, Sir Thomas Makerel, Nicholas Swele, Roger Wilard, Thomas the Forester then bailiff of Aweltone, Mathew de Monasterio, John de Burhunte.—[218.]

Seal lost.

[*c.* 1250.] Confirmation by James de Accangre to the Prior and Canons of B. Mary of Seleburne of a croft which Peter de Cruce gave them, extending from the east side of the grove of the said Peter, near the highway leading from the house of the said Peter towards la Hunne, together with all the said grove, and with the increment of a garden of the said Peter, between the grove and the garden of Will. le Kyng; in free alms. Witn.: Sir John de Venuz, Sir William his son, Sir John de la Stane, Thomas Makerel, Roger de Cherlecote, Will. de Hysenhurst, John de Burhunte, Philip and Andrew his brothers, James de Molendinis, Matthew de Monasterio.—[61.]

Round dark seal; the sun: "S' Jacobi . . . . angre."

[*c.* 1250.] Release from Gervase son of Adam de la Wike to the Prior and Canons of Seleburne of all his right in the tenement and messuages which Adam de la Wike, his father, formerly held in the vill of la Wike. Witn.: Sir Robert de Popham, Nicholas Swele, Robert Gaugy, Will. de Isenhurst, Philip de Burhunte, Robert Marescall de la Wike, Ralph de la Cornere of Piperham.—[183.]

Seal lost.

[*c.* 1250.] Grant from Roger de Cherlecote, for his own soul and that of Ysabella his wife, to the Prior and Canons of Seleburne, of 10*s.* of annual rent issuing from the tenement of Will. de Arundel in la Wyke, which rent the said Roger had bought of the said Prior and Canons for 10 marks, and afterwards assigned to them, in order that they should keep after his death two days annually as the anniversaries of himself and his wife Ysabella, using the half of the said rent on each day as a bounty for their refreshment in the refectory. And for the observance of this, any subsequent ordinance of any prior or cellarer notwithstanding, the Prior and Convent have faithfully promised, and have hereto attached their Chapter seal. No witnesses.—[180].

(1) Chapter seal lost. (2) Small round brown seal; a Roman intaglio, a head; inscription illegible.

[*c.* 1250.] Grant from Robert Gaugy, with the consent of his wife Muriel, to the Prior and Canons of Seleburne, in free alms, of all his mill of la Sydenemed, which he had of the said Prior and Canons, with the pasture of the said meadow after haymaking; and the said Prior and Canons grant to him and his wife the brotherhood and benefits of their house for ever. Witn.: Sir John de Venuz, Sir Thomas Makerel, Will. Huse, James de Molendinis, John de Burhunte and Andrew his brother, Nich. Svele, Mathew de Monasterio, James de Ackangre, Will. de Arundel de la Wyke.—[353.]

Two round brown seals; (1) a circular ornament: "S' Roberti Gavgy;" (2) a female head: "Sigill' Amoris."

Another original copy of the same grant by another scribe, with the same witnesses and seals.—[354.]

[*c.* 1250.] Grant from James de Nortune to William de Arundel, son of John de Arundel, for the sum of 11*s.* 4*d.*, of all the land in the vill of Wykes in the tenement of Nortune, which Roger de Churlekote held. Witn.: Richard de la Bere, son of Walter de la Bere, John de Brambessethe, James de Molendinis, James de Ochangre, Andrew de Heyes, Will. Balun, Mathew of the Church ("de Ecclesia") Geoffrey de Larude, Gilibert de Wykes.—[76.]

Green seal, same as that attached to Nos. 47 and 49, *c.* 1260; but the shield apparently blank.

[*c.* 1250.] Grant and quit-claim from Richard de Nortune, son of James de Nortune, to Geoffrey de Creye, chaplain, in consideration of the receipt of one mark, of his serf ("nativum") William le Boþyere, son of William le Boþyere de la Wyke, with all his following. Witn.: Sir John, Prior of Seleburne, Sir John de Venuz, Sir Thos. Makerel, James de Acangre, John de Burhunte, Andrew de Burhunte, Peter the baker, Will. Arundel, Hugh the baker, Robert Marescall.—[178.]

Round brown seal; the Lamb and Flag; inscription broken and illegible.

[*c.* 1250.] Grant from Geoffrey de Craye, chaplain, to the Prior and Convent of B. Mary of Seleburne, in free alms, of William le Boþyere, son of Will. le Boþyere de la Wyke, formerly the serf ("nativum") of Richard de Nortune, whom the grantor bought of the said Richard, with all his following. Witn.: Sir John de Venuz, Sir Thomas Makerel, Will. Huse, James de Acangre, John de Burhunte, Andrew de Burhunte, and Philip his brother, William de Hysenhurst, Nich. de Ysenhurst, Will. Arundel, Robert Marescall.—[95.]

Oval brown seal; a tonsured head with a hand stretched out over it, inscription broken and indistinct: "I.H.C. O Pater eleson . . . . . . eus" (?).

[*c.* 1250.] Grant from James de Ackangre to the Prior and Canons of B. Mary of Seleburne, of all the meadows which were Richard Attenasche's, Peter le Paumer's, Will. Picot's, and Will. de la Broke's, which extend from the meadow of the said Prior and Canons called la Brodemede to the meadow of Adam de Northebroyke, as they are enclosed by the ditch of the said Prior and Canons; to hold in free alms. Witn.: Sir John de Venuz, Sir James de Nortune, Sir Thomas Makerel, Will. Huse, James de Moleudinis, John de Burhunte and Andrew his brother, Matthew de Monasterio, Will. de Arundel.—[29.]

Round brown seal; the sun and moon; inscription nearly effaced.

GRANT OF LAND TO THE PARISH CHURCH OF SELBORNE IN LIEU OF TITHES.

c. 1250-60. Omnibus Christi fidelibus ad quos præsens scriptum pervenerit Ricardus de Nortune, filius Jacobi de Nortune, salutem in Domino. Noverit universitas vestra quod ego Ricardus de Nortune concessi et confirmavi et quictumclamavi pro me et hæredibus meis Deo et ecclesiæ parochiali beatæ Mariæ de Seleburne duas acras totius prati mei in tenemento meo de Nortune. Quas acras pater meus nomine decimæ prædictæ ecclesiæ parochiali dedit in liberam et puram et perpetuam elemosinam. Quarum una acra jacet juxta viam ex parte australi, quæ via se extendit de Nortune versus Nywentune. Quam quidam acram Rector dictæ ecclesiæ debet suis sumptibus falcare, levare et cariare, sine aliquo impedimento mei vel hæredum nostrorum vel hominum nostrorum. Et altera acra jacet ex parte aquilonis, quam acram ego et hæredes mei custo nostro tenemur falcare, et salvo custodire quousque dictus Rector qui pro tempore fuerit fenum suum voluerit levare et cariare, sine aliquo impedimento ut prædictum est. Et unaquæque acra continet in se latitudinem quatuor perticarum, et longitudo acrarum extendit se per latitudinem totius prati mei. Et ego dictus Ricardus et hæredes mei tenemur warantizare, defendere, et aquietare de omnibus rebus et in omnibus locis versus omnes gentes, sicut liberam puram et perpetuam elemosinam dicti Jacobi patris mei. Et ut hæc mea concessio, confirmatio, et quicta clamancia, rata et stabilis inperpetuum perseveret, huic scripto sigillum meum apposui. Hiis testibus: domino Johanne de Venuz, domino Ada Gurdune, domino Thoma Makerel, Willelmo de Micheldefre et Galfredo filio ejus, Willelmo Huse, Johanne de Burhunte et Andrea fratre suo, Jacobo de Ackangre, Nicholao de Ishenhurste, et multis aliis.—[327.]

Seal lost.

[1250-60.][1] Grant (indented) from Ralph son of William de Wez to John Sanztere of all his land of la Syete which he had in the manor of Sultone, Roppele, la Syete, and Hedleghe, rendering to the Bishop of Winchester the accustomed services; in exchange for all the land which the said John had in the village of Overtune, and 30 marks, and four quarters of wheat and four quarters of barley, and four of oats, and four bacon-pigs ("bacones") and two robes for himself and his wife. Witn.:

[1] 1250 was the year in which the Bishop of Winchester, to whom reference is made, was elected, and he died in 1261 still unconsecrated.

master Robert de Carevile, the official of the Bishop-elect of Winchester, Sir Gerard la Grue his seneschal, Sir Oliver, seneschal of the Priory of St. Swuthun (*sic*), Sir Martin de St. Cross, Sir Walter de Briche, constable of Wulvesie, Nich. de Ychene, Will. de Dunstighele, Will. Gerveys, Will. Abintone, Nigel de Wudecote, Henry de Bromdene, Thomas de Waleys of Tystede, John de Draytun, ... de Brinckewurdþe.—[343.]

Round dark seal; a fleur-de-lis: "Sigill' Radulfi de Wez."

Another original copy. Same seal.—[333.]

[*c.* 1250–60.] Grant from John de Windlesore to William de la Rode and Alice his wife, in consideration of the receipt of 10 marks, of all the land with a messuage built thereupon, which Robert, the father of the said William, formerly held of the grantor in la Rode; paying annually one mark. Witn.: Rich. de Nortone, John de Burhunte, James de Okhangre, Roger the cook of Haveklye, Adam Oter, William de Arundell, William Sturegaf[er], Robert Marescall de la Wyke, Elyas the baker of Haveklye.—[185.]

Round green seal of arms; a bend: "S' Joh'is de Windlesor."

[*c.* 1250–60.] Grant from Adam de la Mare of Westistede to the Prior and Canons of Seleburne, in free alms, of one parcel of land in Westistede, extending in length from the highway which goes from Rompesdene to the smithy ("fabricam") of Westistede to the south, near the hedge and ditch of the said Prior and Convent to the east, and to the land which was formerly Henry the Savage's, called la Longelonde, [to the north], and by the width of two perches to the west. Witn.: Henry de Bromdene, Will. Gervais of Roppely, Geoffrey de Rumeseye, John Picot of Bromdene, John Marescal of Burhunte, Will. de Arundel de la Wike, Rob. Marescal de la Wike.—[247.]

Seal sewn up in wool.

Another original grant of the same land, with two or three slight variations, *e.g.*, instead of the clause "two perches," etc., coming at the end, it is inserted at the beginning "a parcel of ground, two perches wide." Round brown seal; a floriated ornament; "S' Ade de la Mare."—[258.]

[*c.* 1250–60.] Grant from Walter son of Thomas Makerel to Adam de Gurdon and Constance his wife, for the sum of £20, of all the land which he had by the gift of Thomas Makerel, his father, in Seleburne; rendering annually one pair of gloves of the value of one penny, and the service due to the lord of the fee as contained in the charter which he had from his said father. Witn.: Sir Will. Maudut, Sir John de Brambelsate, Ralph de la Bataille, Rich. de la Bere, Henry Wyard, Nich. Swele, James de Akangre, Andrew de Burhunte, Reginald de Kopeshurst.—[9.]

Round green seal; a fleur-de-lis: "S' Walteri Mackvrol."

[*c.* 1250-60.] Grant from brother Robert de Samford, minister of the Knighthood of the Temple in England, with the consent of their Chapter at Easter at Dincsle, to Sir John the Prior and the Convent of Seleburne, for the sum of 200 marks, to buy other lands in aid of the Holy Land, of all their tenement in lands and men, meadows, pastures and woods, which they had by the gift of Aymeric de Sasci in Seleburne. Witn.: brother Maurice and brother Edward, chaplains, brother R. de Scamelby, brother Adam de Lintone, brother William de Welleburne, brother Richard de Beugrant, brother Jordan de Berghes, brother Roger de Insula, brother Richard Carpentar, preceptor of Suthinton.—[2.]

Round green seal; the Lamb and Flag: "+ Sigillum Templi."

Another original copy of the same deed, with the same seal. (*Variations in spelling:* Roger de Scamelesby, Jordan de Bergwes, R. Carpenter, preceptor of Sudingtone.)—[26.]

[*c.* 1250-60.] Indenture of agreement between John the Prior and the Convent of Selebourne and Robert de Pontelarche, that the said Robert may have the ground for making a ditch between the wood of the Prior and Canons in the way called Merkkeweye, so that all the earth taken be thrown upon his land; if the beasts of the Prior and Canons break into the wood of the said Robert for want of sufficient enclosure, they are to be restored freely, but if the beasts of the said Robert break into the wood of the Prior and Canons for the same cause, then the said Robert shall fully satisfy for all damage according to the law of England; beyond the said ditch, the said Robert shall hereafter claim no wood nor anything else; but the Prior and Canons and all others who have had animals in his wood of Selebourne are hereafter to have free entrance and exit and chase, and free right of drinking ("potacionem") at the great mere ("maram") near the highway near the garden of the said Robert in the vill of Niwentone, but if they are hindered then they may make a free entrance for themselves to the mere called Bosmere: the ditch which Robert le Vesselyr made is to remain to him for ever; the Prior and Canons to hold all the tenements, rents and lands which they have in Ymbeschate and Bourhunte within the bounds of his demesne of Nywentone, according to the tenor of his charters made thereon, the said Robert quit-claiming anything that has heretofore been paid to him; and for this agreement he grants annually one pound of wax or sixpence to the light of the B. Mary in the monastery of Selebourne. Witn.: Sir Peter de Rivall', Sir John de Venuz, Sir James de Nortune, Sir Thomas Makerel, William le Duk, Henry de Ysenhurst, Will, Baion, Matthew de Monasterio.—[64.]

Seal lost.

[*c.* 1250-60.] Grant from John de Wyndesorre, knt., to Henry de la Charite of all his lands in la Rode; paying an annual quit-rent of 1*d.* Witn.: Sir Alan Plugenet, Sir John de Brembelschete, knts., Richard de Nortone, Will. Huse, Rich. de Westcote, John de Burhunte, James de Hockhangre.—[195.]

Seal lost.

[*c.* 1250-60.] Grant from Ralph le Nyweman to Leveva, his daughter, of the messuage with a garden which he had from James Ackangre in his manor of Ackangre, namely, that which William Andrew formerly held, lying between the land of the Prior of Seleburne and the croft which is called la Wolcroft, near the highway leading from the Priory towards the house of Peter de Cruce, alongside of the tenement which Will. Andrew held of the said James, together with seven perches of his land in length and four in breadth; paying to the lord of the fee an annual quit-rent of 14*d.*, with two suits of court, and to the grantor one pair of gloves or 1*d.* Witn.: Sir Roger de Thicheburne, knt., Will. Huse, Richard de Nortune, Gilibert Cunan, John de Burhunte, Philip de Burhunte, Andrew de Burhunte, brothers, William de Arundel de la Wike, Robert Marescall de la Wyke.—[154.]

Oval green seal; a lion counter-passant; inscription effaced.

[*c.* 1250-60.] Grant and quit-claim from John de Burhunte, in pure alms, to the Prior and Canons of Seleburne, of 12*d.* of annual rent in the vill of Burhunte, issuing from the tenement which they hold of him by the gift of Gilebert de Burhunte, clerk, his uncle. Witn.: Sir John de Venuz, Sir James de Nortune, Sir Thomas Makerel, Will. Huse, James de Molendinis, James de Ackangre, Andrew de Burhunte, Will. de Arundel, Mathew de Monasterio, Nich. Suele, Will. de Ishenhurste, Nicholas his brother.—[338.]

Oval brown seal; a female figure holding a bird (a falcon?) in the left hand, and . . . . . in the right; "S' Johannis Borhunte."

[*c.* 1250-60.] Grant from Richard de Nortune, son of James de Nortune, in pure alms, to the Prior and Canons of Seleburne, of a way from the houses of Will. de la Wyke and Will. de Boyher to the house which was the late Henry de la Cumbe's, and from the house of the said Henry, westwards, to the cross called Godecruche, and from the said cross to the highway which extends itself before the house of Will. Harolde in Nortune and so on, for cars and carts and to drive beasts. Witn.: Sir John de Venuz, Sir Adam Gurdune, Sir Thomas Makerel, Will. de Micheldefre and Geoffrey his son, Will. Huse, John de Burhunte, Andrew his brother, James de Ackangre, Nich. de Ishenhurste.—[325.]

Round brown seal; the Lamb and Flag: "S' Hamon' Lecleis d' Maling'."

[*c.* 1250-60.] Grant from Robert le Cherlecote to the Prior and Canons of Seleburne, in free alms, of all his tenement in the village of Bradesate which he had by the gift of Roger de Bradesate, with a certain addition on the east side of his house, between his old and new ditch; and all his tenement which he had in the village of Accangre by the gift of Adam de Rethersfeld; and all the land which he had in Bradesate by the gift of Laurence de Hayes, which is of the tenure of Blakemer, and 10*s.* of annual rent, with homages, wards, escheats, etc., from the whole tenement which Will. de Arundel held of him in la Wyke, in fee by the service of 10*s.*, and which the grantor had by the gift of Sir James de Nortune. Witn.: Sir John de Venuz, Sir William his son, Sir John de la Stane and John his son, Sir Thomas Makerel, James de Accangre, Will. Hysenhurste, Mathew de Monasterio, James de Molendinis, Roger Wylade, Henry Wyard, Handrew (*sic*) de Hayes, Will. Baiun.—[336.]

Round green seal; a head (very faint, an antique): "S' Rogeri de Cherlecote."

Another original copy, omitting Wylade and Wyard from the witnesses and adding John de Burhunte; seal the same.—[346.]

1250[-1], 24 Feb., "in die S. Mathie apost." Indenture of an agreement whereby Sir James de Nortune, knt., gives to the Prior and Canons of Seleburne the width of fourteen feet of his land to make a ditch between their meadow and his land, from the corner of Binlaund, and six feet of his meadow to make another ditch; and they mutually covenant that if their cattle trespass, they will, before going into their Courts about it, call each other to the churchyard of Seleburne, and there state the damage, and have it satisfied according to the view of good men. Witn.: Sir John de Venuz, Sir William his son, Sir John de la Stane, Sir Thomas Makeril, knts., James de Accangre, John de Burrunte, James de Molendinis, Will. Baud, Mathew de Monasterio.—[332.]

Seal lost.

1253, 2 Feb., "in f. Purif. B.V., anno confirmacionis nostre tercio;" at Mertone. Bond from A[ylmer] Bishop elect of Winchester to the Prior and Convent of Seleburne, for the repayment, at Mich., 1255, of 200 marks which he had borrowed in his necessity ("ad opus nostrum pro nostris necessitatibus") at the new Temple, London, under a penalty of 20 marks, to be enforced by any Bishop of the province of Canterbury.—[15.]

Oval red seal; obverse, the Bishop elect under a canopy in plain habit, holding a book, with no episcopal insignia: "Sigillū . . . . ari Dei gra. electi Wintonien;" reverse, the same figure; "Ꝯtras' [*i.e.*, contrasigillum] A. Electi Wintoniensis."

[1254.] Grant from John de Venuz, for the health of his own soul and that of his wife Amaria, and those of his ancestors and successors, to the Prior and Canons of Seleburne, of the church of Estwerldham, in free alms. Witn.: Sir Peter de Rivallis, Sir Mathew de Venuz, Sir John de la Stane, Sir James de Nortune, Sir Thomas Makerel, Hugh de Venuz, James de Molendinis, Reginald le Gupil, Thomas le Pac, Thomas Pulayn, Mathew de Monasterio.—[207.]

Fragment of green seal, same as to the following.

1254, 19 April, "die S. Elphegi archiep. et mart.;" at Seleburne. Grant from John de Venuz, for the health of his soul and that of his wife Amaria, and those of his ancestors and successors, to the Prior and Canons of Seleburne, in free alms, of all his right of patronage and claim in the advowson of the church of Est Werlham. Witn.: Sir Peter de Rivallis, Sir Mathew de Venuz, Sir James de Nortone, Sir John de la Stane, Sir Thomas Makerel, Sir John de Brambelsete, Hugh de Venuz, James de Molendinis, Will. Huse, John de Burhunte, Reginald le Gopil, Thomas le Pac, Nicholas de Hysenhurste, Will. de Burhunte, Will. de Hysenhurste, Thomas Pulayn, Mathew de Monasterio.—[206.]

Round large green seal, fine impression; a figure on horseback, holding a rod: "Sigill' Joh'is de Venz, Marescall' Regis."

1254, 19 April, "die S. Elphegi archiep. et mart." Lease from Sir John de Venuz to the Prior and Convent of Seleburne, in consideration of the receipt of 60 marks, of his meadow of Acangre which he held of James de Acangre, called Hundeshammed, lying on either side of the water called Lachemere, and extending from the meadow of Will. de Aqua to the head of the fishpond ("vivarii"); to hold for the term of 100 years, paying an annual quit-rent of 3*s*. Witn.: Sir Matthew de Venuz, Sir James de Nortune, Sir John de la Stane, Sir Thomas Makerel, Sir John de Brambelsate, James de Molendinis, Hugh de Venuz, Will. Huse, John de Burhunte, Will. de Burhunte, Reginald le Gopil, Thomas le Pac, Matthew de Monasterio, Thomas Pulayn.—[122.]

Round dark green seal; the same as the preceding.

[1254.] Grant from John de Venuz, for the health of his own soul and that of his wife Amaria, etc., to the Prior and Canons of Seleburne, in free alms, of all his land called Uggelesly, in the field of Estwerdlham called le Suthfeld, extending near the hedge of his park on the east to the ditch between his land and the land of Little Werlham, together with the advowson of the church of Werlham; also of a way for cars and carts beyond his land up to the highway near the house of Peter le Stabeler, and pasture for their oxen and beasts when ploughing the land together with his own oxen; and all his meadow of Acangre which he held of James de Acangre, called Hundeshammede, paying a rent of 3*s.* yearly to the said James. Witn. same as to the preceding deed of 19 April, 1254, No. 206.—[209.]

Seal, the same, but not so good an impression.

[*c.* 1254.] Grant and quit-claim from James de Ackangre to the Prior and Canons of Seleburne, in free alms, of 3*s.* of annual rent in the vill of Ackangre, issuing from the meadow which they hold of him by the gift of Sir John de Venuz, which is called Hundeshamemede (*as in the preceding deed*, No. 209). Witn.: Sir Matthew de Venuz, Sir James de Nortune, Sir Thomas Makerel, Sir John de Brambelsete, James de Molendinis, Will. Huse, Andrew de Burhunte and John his brother, Will. de Hysenhurste, Thos. Pulayn, Matthew de Monasterio, Will. de Arundel.—[127.]

Round dark green seal; the sun and moon: "S' Jacobi de Hacangre."

[*c.* 1254.] Grant from John de Venuz to the Prior and Canons of Seleburne, of all the particulars granted in the preceding deed (No. 209), in the same terms, except the meadow of Acangre. Witn. the same as to No. 206, of 19 April, 1254, *omitting* Nich. de Hysenhurste *and* Will. de Hysenhurste.—[210.]

Seal, the same.

ENDOWMENT OF THE VICARAGE OF SELBORNE.

1254, 29 July. Omnibus Christi fidelibus præsentes literas inspecturis A[ylmarus] Dei gracia Wintoniensis electus salutem in Domino. Noveritis nos ad præsentacionem dilectorum nobis in Christo Prioris et Conventus de Seleburne Rogerum capellenum ad vicariam parochialis ecclesiæ de Seleburne admississe, ipsumque in eadem canonice instituisse cum cura et honere residendi, salva in omnibus nostra auctoritate et ecclesiæ nostræ Wintoniensis dignitate. Taxacionem vero vicariæ ejusdem, interveniente consensu et voluntate dictorum Prioris et Conventus, fecimus in hunc modum: videlicet, quod idem vicarius et successores sui qui pro tempore fuerint recipient et habebunt omnes decimas ortorum et curtilagiorum quæ pede fodiuntur; item, omnes minutas decimas, oblaciones, legata, et obvenciones alias tam ad matricem ecclesiam quam ad capellas de Ochanger et de Blakemere pertinentes, et faciet in eisdem, prout hactenus fieri consuevit, per ministros ydoneos deserviri. Ipse quoque in matrice ecclesia personaliter residebit, et solvet annuatim in perpetuum dictis Priori et Conventui centum solidos sterlingorum ad quatuor anni terminos, videlicet, in festo Sancti Michaelis viginti quinque solidos, ad Natale Domini viginti quinque solidos, ad Pascha viginti quinque solidos, et ad festum Sancti Johannis Baptistæ viginti quinque solidos. Habebit insuper idem vicarius mansum competens ad inhabitandum prope matricem ecclesiam, et insuper terram cum gardino et curtilagio ad capellam de Ochanger pertinentem, cum omnibus suis pertinentiis. Sustinebunt autem dicti Prior et Conventus honera episcopalia et archidiaconalia et cætera ordinaria honera, et cancellum ecclesiæ cum necesse fuerit reparabunt, et omnes præsentes defectus librorum, vestimentorum, et aliorum ornamentorum ecclesiæ supplebunt, quorum librorum, videlicet, vestimentorum, et aliorum ornamentorum ecclesiæ supplecio et reparacio in posterum ad vicarium pertinebit. Honera vero extraordinaria tam Prior et Conventus prædicti quam vicarius ipse sustinebunt pro rata. In cujus rei testimonium huic scripturæ in modum cyrographi confectæ sigillum nostrum una cum sigillis prædictorum Prioris et Conventus fecimus apponi. Hiis testibus, dominis Egidio [de Bridport], decano Wellensi; Galfrido, præcentore Cicestrensi;[1] Roberto [de Karevil], thesaurario Sarrum; magistris Johanne de Cadomo, Johanne de Lyek, Petro de Sancto Mario; et aliis. Dat. apud Witteneye, die Mercurii proxima ante festum beati Petri ad Vincula, anno Domini M° CC° quinquagesimo quarto.—[42.]

Oval red seal; the Bishop-elect, under a canopy, in plain sacerdotal habit, without any episcopal insignia, holding a book in his hands: "Sigillū Ademari Dei [gracia] Electi Wīthonien." Counterseal; the same figure, smaller, without the canopy: "@tras' A. Electi Wintoniensis." See No. 15, *supra*.

1254, 23 Aug., "in vig. S. Barthol." [*Winchester deed.*] Indenture by which the Prior and Convent of Seleburne grant to Joan de Wyltone, widow of John de Wyltone, nine quarters of corn annually from their grange at Tystede, namely, five of wheat and four of barley, during her life, to be delivered at Winchester, together with 16*s.* annually; in return for her whole tenement in Sylworktenestret, and for one plot of ground behind the house which Richard de Bunteford formerly held of the said Joan in the lane between Wonegarestret and Sylworktenestret, which she, during her widowhood, gave in perpetual alms to the said Prior and Convent; with power, in case of default, to the Mayor of Winchester to compel payment by the rent which they have in Winchester. Witn.: Sir Rich. Leyres, then Mayor of Winchester, Sir Thomas Paskes, Stephen Fromund, John Edgar, William the Spicer ("speciario"), William Priur, Henry the clerk, alderman, John Cobbe, Peter Westman, Reginald Cobbe.—[248.]

Oval white seal, broken.

1255, 23 April, "die b. Georgii martiris;" at Seleburne. Grant from John de Venuz to the Prior and Canons of Seleburne of the meadow leased in No. 122, of 19 April, 1254. Witn. the same, *adding* Nich. de Hysenhurste *and* William de Hysenhurste.—[173.]

Seal lost.

[1] Not mentioned in Hardy's *Le Neve*.

1256, 20 Jan., "in oct. S. Hyllarii," 40 Hen. fil. Joh. Fine before Gilbert de Prestone, Roger de Wycestre [Whitchester], Will. de Engelfeld, Will. de Coveham [Cobham], the Justices itinerant at Winchester, by which Adam Gurdun conveys to John, Prior of Selburne, in consideration of the receipt of 5 marks, an acre and a half of land in Selburne, for which the said Prior shall pay annually one pound of cummin.—[31.]

1256, 9 Feb., "in oct. Purif. B.M.," 40 Hen. fil. Joh. Release from Alan Musard, in free alms, to the Prior and Canons of Seleburne, of two and a half messuages, three and a half acres of land, and one acre of meadow, which they have below the coft ("coftam") of Westwerldham, by the gift of Peter de Anesy and Thomas de Anesy, granting also three and a half acres of land in the same place which Walter Goghe and Amicia, his wife, formerly held; and for this the said Prior and Canons receive him to all the benefits of their church. Witn.: Sir Gilbert de Prestone, Sir Roger de Wycestre, Sir Will. de Englefeud, Will. de Cobeham, then the Justices itinerant at Winchester, John de Venoiz, Thomas de Gimminges, Walter de Andely, Hamon de Basinges, Rich. de Dimmere, Geoffrey the chamberlain, John de Brambesete, Will. de Draytone.—[216.]

Seal lost.

1256, 22 Nov., "die S. Edm. regis et mart.;" at Winton. (*See under date of* 1293, 16 April).—[220(i).]

[*c.* 1257–59?] Release and quit-claim from Cecilia, widow of the late Henry le Sauvage, to the Prior and Canons of Seleburne, for the sum of 5*s.*, "negocio meo," of all her messuage with a curtilage which she had as dowry in Westistede. Witn.: Sir John, bailiff of Suttone, William de Dunstikele, Hugh de Brinkeworde, William de Abintone, Roger Pichot, Thomas Lewaleis, John le Franckelain.—[272.]

Oval brown seal; a bird; inscription broken.

[1257–9.] Quit-claim from Cecilia le Sauvage of Westistede, formerly the wife of Henry le Sauvage, to the Prior and Convent of Seleburne, of all her land, with a messuage and its curtilage, which she had as dowry, for her life, reserving an annual rent of 4*s.* Witn.: Sir James le Sauvage, sheriff of Suhampt. [41–43 Hen. III], Sir Henry de Farnlye, Sir Geoffrey de Cundut, Sir James de Scures, Sir Hamon de Basinge, Sir John de Venuz, Sir James de Nortune, Sir Thomas Makerel, Sir John de Bradesate, Will. Huse, James de Molendinis, John de Burhunte.–[267.]

Oval brown seal; the sun and moon: "S' Cecilie Savwage."

1258, 25 Feb., "in crast. S. Mathie." [*Midhurst deed.*] Grant from Henry le Kinge of Midhurste, son of William le Kinge of Midhurste, to the Prior and Canons of Seleburne, in free alms, of 12*d.* of annual rent from a messuage which his sister Alice formerly held of Ralph Piche in the village of Midhurste, lying between the house which Thomas le Squalle formerly held and that which Osbert le Blakesutere formerly held; which 12*d.* Mildith, the widow of Adam le Parmentir, and her heirs are bound to pay to the said Prior and Canons; also of 12*d.* of annual rent from a messuage and two crofts of land in the same village, lying between the ditch called Casteldige and the house of Richard Sherewynde, which messuage and crofts Richard le Childe of Midhurste and his heirs shall hold of the said Prior and Canons for ever. Witn.: John Jokeman, William Alben (?), Gilebert the Cobbler ("Sutore"), Thomas Maunsir, John le Kinge, Thomas le Bere, John le Squalle.—[231.]

Broken oval white seal, wrapped up in tow.

1258, 3 May, "in crast. Ascens. Domini," 42 Hen. fil. Joh.; at Westminster. Indenture of a fine before the Justices Rob. de Brywes and Nich. de Handlo, by which Robert Gaugy of Benestede and Muriel his wife convey to John the Prior of Seleburne and his church the mill in Sydenemedwe, and all the pasture which they had in each year in the meadows of Sydenemedwe after the hay was carried; and the said Prior in return admits them to all the benefits and prayers of his church for ever.—[18.]

Counterpart of the indenture.—[306.]

[*c.* 1260.] Grant from Robert, the minister of the Knighthood ("milicie") of the Temple of Solomon in England, with the consent of the Chapter, to the Prior and Convent of Seleburne, of 10*s.*, to be received annually from their chamber at their house of Sudingtone, until they have provided for the said Prior and Convent ten shillings' worth of annual rent, in lands or rents within four or five leagues of the house of Seleburne, which they promise to do as soon as possible; with power of distraint in case of failure on the chattels found on the land which was Roger de Cherlecote's in Bradesethe, which is in the hands of the Templars. Witn.: brother William, brother Walter, and brother Henry, chaplains; brother Roger de Scamelesbi, brother Richard son of John, brother Warin son of Garoud, brother Hugh de Stoctune, brother John de Hotune, brother Rich. Carpenter, preceptor of Sudingtone.—[138.]

Round green seal; the Lamb and Flag: "Sigillum Templi."

[*c.* 1260.] Grant from brother Robert de Saunford, minister of the Knighthood of the Temple of Solomon in England, with the assent of the Chapter, to the Prior and Canons of Seleburne, of a sufficient way ("cheminum") for leading cars and carts, and for driving cattle, from the road which leads from Sudintone towards Blakemere beyond the land of Rich. de la Strete which he holds of the said knights in Sudintone, up to the land of the said Prior and Canons which they have in Bradesethe by the gift of Roger de Cherlecote of the tenure of Blakemere, according as the said way is bounded by the hedge ("juxta sepem") which is between the said way and the land which Will. le Stede once held of the grantors in Sudintone. Witn. and seal the same as to No. 138 preceding.—[139.]

Another original copy of same grant with same witnesses; fragment of seal.—[140.]

[c. 1260.] Grant from James de Achangre for his own soul and that of Margery his wife to the Prior and Canons of Seleburne, in free alms, of a croft of his land called Smythelcrofte, near the croft called la Hogrude on the east, the land of the Prior and Convent which is Longerude on the west, and extending to the croft of Robert de Hore on the south, with free ingress and egress through the middle of his wood called la Broke to drive all their cattle. Witn.: Sir Adam de Gurdun, knt., Sir Rob. de Popham, knt., Richard de la Bere, Henry Wyard, Robert Gaugy, John Marescall de Burhunte, Robert Marescall de la Wyke.—[88.]

Round white seal, broken.

[c. 1260.] Grant from James de Achangre, for the soul of himself and Margery his wife, etc., to the Prior and Canons of Seleburne, in free alms, of all his right in five and a half acres of his land in Achangre, that, namely, which is called la Hocrude, extending to the north to the croft which was once William Daniel's and lies near la Wrslonde, abutting on the meadow of John de la Barre called Hocmede, near the land which Philip le Wyte held; with free entrance and exit through the grantor's wood called la Brok, and also at the head of the aforesaid land which was Will. Daniel's, for cars and carts and for driving all kinds of beasts. Witn.: Sir Adam de Gurdun, Sir Rob. de Poppham, knts., Richard de la Bere, Elias Marescall, Henry Wyard, Robert Gaugy, Mathias de la Bertune, John Marescall de Burhunte, Robert Marescall de la Wyke.—[129.]

Round red seal; the sun and moon: "S' Jacobi de Hacangre."

[c. 1260.] Grant from John de Burghunte to the Prior and Canons of Seleburne, in free alms, of three and a half acres of his land, in his field of Burghunte before his gate, lying near the way from Suthingtune to

Heþennesmanneburieles to the north and extending from the way going from Burhunte to the same way to the west, and as it is bounded on the south and east. Witn.: Sir Adam Gurdun, Sir Rob. de Popham, Sir John de Brambeshate, knts., Will. Huse, Rich. de Wescote, Will. de Arundel de la Wike, Rob. le Mareschal.—[339.]

Seal lost.

[*c.* 1260.] Indenture of agreement between Gillebert son of Richard le Lypse on one part, and James de Nortone on the other, concerning sixty acres of land in demesne in Seleburne which Gillebert de Golleye held; namely, that the said Gillebert son of Richard, in return for having the legal counsel and help of the said James for acquiring the said sixty acres as his right, grants to the said James all the profit ("purchacium") which he may be able to obtain thereby by raising a plea against the Prior of Seleburne; and if it should happen that the said James should recover the said sixty acres, then he shall have the whole of the land, to hold of the King in fee without any claim or contradiction, rendering to the said Gillebert and his heirs half a pound of pepper yearly; and if the said Gillebert shall in any way withdraw from this agreement, he is bound to pay 40 marks to the said James for the costs of the plea; and for this grant the said James has paid to him 10 marks. Witn.: Sir John de Venuz, Sir John de la Stane, Sir John de Vautort, Sir William de Ho, Gillebert de Popham, Alan de Havekle, Gillebert Conan, Peter de Anese, Will. de Balun, Richard de Rutecumbe.—[40.]

Round brown seal; a fleur-de-lis: "Sigillum . . . . . Ricardi le Lipse."

[*c.* 1260–70.] Grant and quit-claim from James de Achangre to the Prior and Canons of Seleburne, in free alms, of half a pound of pepper and 2*d.* of annual rent from the garden which Will. Futhel of Seleburne formerly held of him, lying at la Hunne near the highway going from the Priory towards Blakemer; and also one pound of wax and half a pound of cummin from a messuage, with a curtilage formerly Peter de Cruce's, which the said Will. Futhel formerly held of the grantor within his manor of Achangre. Witn.: Sir Adam de Gurdun, Sir Rob. de Popham, Sir Will. Huse, Nich. Wsele (*sic*), Will. de Arundel de la Wik, Robert Mareschall de la Wik, Will. le Esquier.—[90.]

Seal lost.

[*c.* 1260–70.] Grant from Adam the Smith ("faber") of Acchangre, son of Thomas the Smith of Acchangre, to the Prior and Canons of Seleburne, in free alms, of a certain smithy ("quandam fabricam") with one messuage in Acchangre; paying an annual quit-rent to the King of 1*d.* Witn.: Rich. de la Bere, Will. Huse, Nich. Swele, James de Acchangre, Will. de Arundel de la Wik, Rob. Mareschalle de la Wike, William le Esquier.—[143.]

Round green seal; a lion counter-passant; inscription: "Sigill' G[al]fridi de la Pade" (yet the grantor says "huic scripto sigillum meum apposui.")

[*c.* 1260–70.] Grant from Thomas Paynel, knt., to Walter le Hunte of five acres of land in Seleburne in exchange for four; of which five acres, one lies between the land of the Prior of Seleburne on the east and that of Hugh Gervays on the west, one lies between the land of the Prior on the west and that of Walter son of Hugh on the east, one between the land of Stephen Umfray on the south and that of Will. Prikyel on the north, which acre is called Belsebuk, and two acres in Little Whatecumbe between the land of the Prior on either side, the west ends abutting on the bounds of the land of Fardone. Witn.: Sir James de Nortone, knt., Richard de Tystede, Henry de Estone, Peter de Heghe, Peter Doget, Roger de Bradeschate.—[89.]

Small round white seal of arms, broken; barry of three; in chief three mullets (?).

[*c.* 1260–70.] Grant from William Coterel, son of Thomas Coterel de la Rode, to William called of Adhelwoldebury, for the sum of 2*s*., of a piece of his land near la Hwitestigele, near the highway going from the King's heath ("bruera dom. regis") to Seleburne, two perches wide at the head and seven perches long, and extending to the house of the said Will. Coterel on east and to his field on west and north; paying an annual quit-rent of 6*d*. Witn.: Rich. de Nortune, James de Ochangre, Gilbert Cunan, William de Burhunte de Hertly, Will. de Arundel de la Wike, Rob. le Marescal de la Wike, Will. Lesquier, Will. de la Rode.—[202.]

Seal lost.

[*c.* 1260–70.] Grant and quit-claim from William de Arundel, son of John de Arundel, to the Prior and Canons of Seleburne, in free alms, of all his right in his whole tenement of la Wyke which he had by the gift of Roger de Cherlecote, son of Walter de Cherlecote, together with ten acres of land and the messuage which Adam de la Wyke formerly held and that which Herbert held in la Wyke; rendering annually to the chief lord 1*d*. Witn.: Sir Adam de Gurdune, Sir Robert de Poppam, Sir John de Wyldeshore, knts., Rich. de la Bere, Nicholas Suewel, Robert Gaugy, James de Achangre, Philip de Burhunte, Will. de Avecly, Robert Marescall de la Wyke.—[181.]

Seal lost.

[*c.* 1260–70.] Grant from Tomhas (*sic*) Maskerel to Adam de Gurdon and Constance his wife of all his land at Seleburne; rendering annually one pair of gloves of the value of 1*d.* Witn.: Sir John de Wynteres-hulle, Sir Will. de Wyntereshulle, Sir John de Brambelsate, Sir Peter de Sacy, Richard de Nortone, John de Burhunte, Andrew de Burhunte, John le Blunt, Richard de la Bere, Reginald de Kopeshurst, Nich. Tebbaud, Adam Oter.—[78.]

Seal, oval, green; a spread eagle: "Sigill' Tome Maskerel."

[*c.* 1260–70.] Grant and quit-claim from James de Achangre to the Prior and Canons of Seleburne, in free alms, of all his right in 3*s.* 1*d.* of annual rent issuing from a croft called la Hok and extending to the land of William the Cook westward, and from a meadow which John de Achangre formerly held of him in Achangre which extends to the meadow of the said Prior and Canons and which is called Lacheford, and from the whole land called Bim, which extends to the land of Will. de la Broke to the south; which rent the said Will. de la Broke and his heirs shall pay to the said religious for ever. Witn.: Sir Adam de Gurdun, Sir Rob. de Popham, Sir Will. de Brambesate, knts., Rich. de Westchote, Henry Wyard, Rob. Gauge, Rob. Marescall de la Wyke. —[170].

Seal lost.

Another original copy; same witnesses. Seal lost.—[121.]

[*c.* 1260–70.] Grant from Geoffrey called Achele de Lys, and Agnes his wife, called de Monasterio, of Worelham, to Sir Adam Gordon and Custance his wife of one acre of land lying between the fishpond of the said Adam and la Marlingdelle which is called Waker; in exchange for one acre in the field called Estfelde, between the land of the said Adam and Custance and that which Matthew the Wheel-wright ("rotarius") formerly held, extending towards Limenar de Stigele in la Wezforlonge. Witn.: Sir Robert de Popham, knt., Will. Linsy, Richard de Wescote, Rich. de Nortone, Henry Wyarde, Nich. Swele, Roger de Hageman, Adam Oter.—[392.]

Seal lost.

[*c.* 1260–70.] Grant from William Coterel, son of Thomas Coterel de la Rode, to Thomas son of Gilbert the Mason ("cementarii"), for the sum of 4*s.*, of all the messuage which the said Gilbert held of him, viz., that which lies between the land of John the Cobbler and the land which is called that of Dionisia Pirc; paying an annual quit-rent of 14*d.* Witn.: James de Achangre, Rich. de Nortune, Peter the baker, Hugh the baker of Seleburne, Will. de Arundel de la Wike, Robert Marescall de la Wike, Will. Lesquier, William the son of Robert de la Rode.—[367.]

Seal lost.

1261, 3 Jan., "iij nonas Jan. pontif. nostri anno vij"; at the Lateran. Bull from Pope Alexander IV addressed to the Dean and Chanter of Sumallinges, diocese of Chichester, directing them to protect the Prior and Convent of Seleburne in the possession of the church of Westistede, the revenues of which do not exceed 10 marks, and which the said Prior and Convent have acquired for appropriation, at the presentation of the patroness Joan, who was the wife of Rob. le Hout.—[274.]

The leaden *bulla* is attached.

1261, 28 Feb., "ij kal. Marcii"; in the great church of Winchester. Indenture tripartite of a decree of arbitration by Constantine de Mildehale, official of Boniface, Archbishop of Canterbury, in the diocese of Winchester during the vacancy of the see, in a controversy between Ralph de Camays, knt., and the Prior and Convent of Seleborne, respecting the right of patronage of the church of Westtisted, claimed by the said Ralph in virtue of his lordship of the manor of Westtisted, and who has thereupon presented master John de Brideport, clerk, to the said church. The decree assigns the patronage absolutely to the said Prior and Canons as having been given to them by Peter de Rupibus, Bishop of Winchester; but inasmuch as the said church is endowed with goods issuing from the said manor, and in order that the said nobleman ("nobilis") may be duly honoured by the said Prior and Canons ("condigna honoris munificentia veneretur"), ordains that he and his heirs shall always have the right of presenting one fit clerk to be admitted as a canon into the said convent, supplied by him with clothes and other necessaries at his admission, who shall there celebrate for the souls of the said nobleman and his ancestors and successors; and the said Prior and Convent shall pay to the said master John de Brideport 100*s.* annually until they promote him, or procure his promotion, to some better ecclesiastical benefice; and the said nobleman shall execute a deed of quit-claim and confirmation of the patronage to the said Prior and Convent.—[234.]

Seal lost.

1261, 1 April, "kal. Apr. pontif. an. 7"; at the Lateran. Bull from Pope Alexander IV to the Dean of Chichester, empowering him to hear a complaint of the Prior and Convent of Seleburne, against Will. Golafre, clerk, Adam de Gurdun, knt., and other clerks and laymen of the dioceses and cities of Winchester, Salisbury and Chichester, for injuries in lands and possessions.—[369.]

The leaden *bulla* is attached.

[1261.] Release from Ralph de Cameys, knt., to the Prior and Canons of Seleburne, in free alms, of all his right in the advowson and patronage of the church of Westtystede. Witn.: Sir Hugh son of Adam, the grantor's steward, Sir Henry de Brettone, Sir Henry de Chylderle, his knights, Sir Thomas de Gemynge, Sir Robert de Poppham, Sir Adam Gurdone, Will. Huse, Rich. de la Bere, John de Burhunte, Thomas Wallensis, James de Akhangre.—[249.]

Two seals:—(1) round, brown, very indistinct coat of arms; on a chief . . . (?): "Sigill' Radulfi Cameis." (2) Oval, brown, (attached "ad majorem securitatem"); four demi-figures in compartments, between them "Juste Judicate": "Sig' consistorii Wintoniensis": counter-seal: our Lord on the Cross, a figure kneeling below: "Lce (?) scripta tego Constantin' ego."

1261, 18 Aug., "die Jovis pr. p. f. Assumpt. B. M."; at Schulebrede. Release from Ralph de Cameys, knt., to the Prior and Canons of Seleburne of all his right in the land called Trendledecroft and Rykemannesdone, and in the advowson and right of patronage of the church of Westtystede, which they hold by the gift of the Lady Joan la Hood; granting them also the right of having 100 sheep in his pasture in the same village; aud confirming all the other lands and tenements which they have there of his fee. Witn.: Sir Hugh son of Adam, the grantor's steward, Sir Henry de Brettone, Sir Henry de Chylderly, his knights, Sir Thomas de Gymmingges, James de Achangre.—[256.]

Round brown seal of arms; on a chief three (?) plates: "Sigill' Radulfi de Cameis."

1262, 9 Jan., "die lune pr. p. f. Epiph. Dom.," 46 H. fil. Joh. Lease (indented) from Sir Adam Gurdon to Thomas Maskerel of £18. 6*s.* 8*d.* of annual rent from his manor of Padendene, and also of £6. 12*s.* 2¾*d.* of annual rent from his tenants of Tystede and Seleburne; viz., from Alan Plukenet, 24*s.*; from Henry Delbowe, 2*s.*; from Adam Tripot, 3*s.* 6*d.*; from Stephen le Paumer, 25*s.* 2¼*d.*; from John de Estone, 15*s.* 11½*d.*; from Gilbert Estone, 8*s.* 8¾*d.*; from the Prior of Seleburne, 4*s.* 10*d.*; from Laurence de Burcham, 8*d.*; from Richard Manser, 11*s.* 3½*d.*; from Will. le Feuere, 8*s.* 1¼*d.*; from Thomas le Stede, 4*s.*; from Gilbert Alstan, 8*s.*; from Stephen Prikel, 3*s.* 6*d.*; from John le Bac, 5*s.* 4*d.*; from Gunnilda Serle, 3*s.* 6*d.*; from Thomas Malger, 18*d.*; from Rich. de Northone, 15*d.*; from Henry le Fuwelere, 10*d.*; to hold to the said Thomas Maskerel for the term of his life. Witn.: Sir Peter de Sacy, Sir John de Wyntereshulle, Sir John de Brambelshete, Will. de Wyntereshulle, Richard de Westcote, John le Blund, Andrew de Burhunte.—[275.]

Seal lost.

1262, 22 April, "die sabb. ante f. S. Marci evang."; at Seleburne. Agreement (indented) between the Prior and Convent of Seleburne and

Adam Gurdun for the settlement of a dispute "de racionabili astuverio bosci" (*i.e.*, the right of cutting a reasonable supply of wood); whereby the said Adam quit-claims for himself and his men both of Tistede and Seleburne all the right which they have "in racionabili astuverio" for husbote and heybote in the wood of the convent in Seleburne called Norchore, saving to the said Adam and his wife Constance and their heirs and to their men of Seleburne whom they have by the gift of Thomas Makerel that their pigs shall be free from pannage in the said wood of Norchore, so many as pertain to the tenement of la Forde in Seleburne, provided that the Prior and Convent may have "parcurs tempore agistationis" (a free run in feeding-time) for all their pigs and others which are agisted in Norchore, in the wood of the said Adam and Constance in Seleburne, as formerly accustomed; and the said Prior and Convent grant in return to the said Adam and Constance and their heirs all the land and tenement which they have by the gift of Thomas Makerel in Seleburne, to hold of the said Prior and Convent. Witn.: Sir Thomas de Gimminges, Sir John de Windelsores, Sir Robert de Popham, Sir Hugh de Boclande, knts., Will. Huse, Rich. de la Bere, John de Burhunte, Gilebert Conan, Will. Arundel.—[77.]

Small round white seal of arms; three fleurs-de-lis: "Sigill' Ade Gurdun."

LICENSE TO SIR ADAM GURDUN FOR A DOMESTIC CHAPEL AT SELBORNE.

1262, 24 June. Omnibus Christi fidelibus præsentes litteras visuris vel audituris frater R., Prior de Seleburne et ejusdem loci Conventus salutem in Domino. Noverit universitas vestra nos concessisse gratiose domino Adæ Gurdun et dominæ Constanciæ uxori suæ licentiam construendi oratorium in curia sua de Seleburne quæ fuit quondam Thomæ Makerel, et in eodem quoad vixerint divina celebrandi officia, salvis in omnibus jure et indempnitate matricis ecclesiæ et dictorum religiosorum et vicarii qui pro tempore fuerit. Ita tamen quod dicti Adam et Constancia in festis sollempnibus adeant matricem ecclesiam et ibidem divina audiant, nisi debilitas corporis vel infirmitas ipsos impedient. Et salvo dictis priori et conventui quod possit sine alicujus impedimento dictum oratorium interdicere et a divina celebratione suspendere si dicti Adam et Constancia [aliquid] attemptaverint contra jura matricis ecclesiæ seu libertatem dictorum religiosorum occasione dicti oratorii, vel si per episcopum vel per aliquem ordinariorum suorum super hoc fuerint vexati vel gravati; et quod post decessum prædictorum Adæ et Constanciæ nullus heredum suorum ratione prædictæ cantariæ in dicto oratorio aliquid juris sibi vendicent. Præterea si ita contingat quod processu temporis lis vel contencio inter dictos priorem et conventum et vicarium præsentem vel futurum ratione concessionis prædicti oratorii, quod absit, oriatur, prædicti Adam Gurdun et Constancia uxor ejus tenentur prædictos priorem et conventum contra dictum vicarium defendere et in omnibus indempnes conservare. In cujus rei testimonium huic scripto in modum cyrography (*sic*) confecto sigillum nostrum conventuale una cum sigillis domini Adæ et Constanciæ uxori (*sic*) suæ, et domini Rogeri tunc vicarii de Seleburne, alternatim est appensum. Datum apud Seleburne, in Nativitate sancti Johannis Baptistæ, anno Domini millesimo ducentesimo sexagesimo secundo.—[87.]

All the three seals affixed to this counterpart are lost.

[1263-7.] Grant from James de Achangre, for the soul of himself and his wife Margery, etc., to the Prior and Canons of Seleburne, in free alms, of all his right in eleven acres of his land called la Watecrofte, near the pasture of the said Prior and Canons which extends in length from his wood of la Broke to the wood of Sir William, earl of Warewyke (*d.* 1267), and eastwards to the land which Thomas the Shepherd ("bercarius") once held of the grantor to farm, with free entrance and exit through the middle of his wood called la Broke for cars and carts and for driving cattle; and also a piece of his land which is called Bynpurtoke, which John de Hachangre, his son, formerly held of him, and which was once Richard Holewey's; with leave also to the said Prior and Canons to enclose all their pasture from the meadow which was once Peter le Paumer's up to their enclosure of la Broke. Witn.: Sir Adam de Gurdun, Sir Rob. de Poppham, knts., Richard de la Bere, Henry Wyard, Nicholas Swele, Robert Gaugy, Mathias de la Bertone, John Marescall de Burhunte, Rob. Marescall de la Wike.—[158.]

Round brown seal; the sun and moon: "S' Jacobi de Acangre."

Another original copy; same witnesses; seal lost.—[180.]

[1265] 21 Oct., "12 kl. Nov.," pontif. an. 1; at Bordeaux. Bull from Pope Clement IV to the Prior of Suthwerk, directing him to endeavour to recover for the Priory of Seleburne various possessions which the Prior and Convent and their predecessors have granted away to different persons, to some for life, to others for a long time, and to others in perpetual farm, to the injury of the monastery.—[383.]

Cancelled by being cut through and the *bulla* lost. See the similar bull of Martin IV, in 1281.

[*c.* 1265-70.] Grant from John de Burhunte to the Prior and Canons of Seleburne, in free alms, of all his land called Hywangre, as marked by boundaries. Witn.: Sir John de Bottele,[1] sheriff of Suhantesyre, Sir Rob. de Popham, Will. Huse, Richard de Nortune, Nicholas Suele

[1] Sir John de Bottele was sheriff in 1265-66 and 1268-70.

de Aweltone, James de Achangre, Andrew de Burhunte, Will. de Arundel de la Wyke, Robert Marescall.—[159.]

Oval brown seal; a figure holding a bird in the left hand and in the right [a spear-head?]: "S' Johannis de Burhunte."

1265[–6, N.S.], 3 March, "die Martis pr. p. f. S. Mathie apost."; at Seleburne. Grant from John de Burhunte to the Prior and Canons of Seleburne that they may have free ingress and egress "ad merluram (*marl-pit*) meam de Burhunte ad merlandum terram suam" which they have by his gift in the field called Hywangre. *Present:* the Sub-prior of Seleburne, brother Peter de Isenhurste, brother Mō (Matheo) de Burhunte, Rob. Marescall de la Wyke.—[340.]

Seal lost.

1265[–6], 17 March, "die Martis pr. p. Domin. qua cantatur Lætare Jerusalem" (4th S. in Lent); in the chapter house of Winchester. Confirmation by Valentine the Prior and the Convent of S. Swthin (*sic*) of Winchester of a charter (recited at length) of Peter, Bishop of Winchester, confirming the grant by Joan, who had been the wife of Rob. Lood, to the Prior and Canons of Selleburne for their own use, of the church of Westistede, together with some land, saving an honest and sufficient maintenance to the vicar.—[245.]

Large green seal, inscription broken off; a figure, with nimbus, seated, in right hand a key, in left hand a book; in back-ground, a church. Counter-seal, a small Roman intaglio; a naked figure, seated: "Valeat Valentinus."

[1266.] Grant from John *called* Saunterre to the Prior and Canons of Seleburne, in free alms, of all his tenement in Roppelyghe and Hetleghe, called la Schyte, which he had by feoffment of the late Ralph de Weis; rendering annually to the Bishop of Winchester one mark and two suits of his court of Suttone, at the two "laghedaies," namely, at the hundred of St. Martin, and at the hundred of Hockeday. Witn.: Sir Ralph de Basinges, Sir Martin de Roches, Sir Walter Daundely, Sir Roger de Ticheburne, Sir Rob. de Popham, knts., Rich. de la Bere, Nich. Martin, John de Burhunte, Nich. Swele, Henry de Bromdene, Adam de Repplinge.—[330.]

Round green seal; a star: "Sigill' Johannis Savntere."

Another original copy of the same grant. The grantor is simply "John Sawntere," the place-names are given as "Roppely" and "la Shete" (with Hetleghe); and among the witnesses "Daundely" becomes "Daundeline." Seal the same.—[342.]

1266, 1 April; at Farnham. Confirmation by John, Bishop of Winchester, of the preceding grant (which is recited at length) made by John called Saunz terre to the Prior and Canons of Seleburne of his tenement in Roppele and Hehleye called la Shete. Witn. the same: (. . . . . W. de *Aundely* . . . . . Henry de *Brundene.*)—[344.]

Oval green seal; the Bishop in pontificals, head broken off and part of inscription: ". . . . Joh . . . . Wintonien. Episcopi." Counter-seal: the heads of SS. Peter and Paul, with keys and sword; the Bishop "Joh." with clasped hands; below, "Sum vester natus provectus Pontificat'."

1266. Agreement (indented) between the Prior and Convent of New Place in Surrey and the Prior of Seleburne, that whereas the former had been called upon by the King to pay £276. 14*s.* 3*d.* of the debt of Roger de Lymesye by reason of a certain tenement which was the said Roger's in the vill of Westistede, and had by means of friends procured leave from the King to pay off the debt by annual instalments of one mark (*sic!*), and had then sued the Prior of Seleburne for aid in the payment by reason of a parcel of land held by the said Prior which was formerly the said Roger's, and it was found upon survey that the land of the Prior of New Place was worth £4 annually and that of the Prior of Seleburne 8*s.*; the said Prior of Seleburne shall pay annually to the Prior of New Place 14½*d.* as his proportionate quota until the whole debt be discharged, the first payment to be at Easter, 1266.—[266.]

Oval brown seal; the Blessed Virgin Mary, seated, holding the Child, with angels on both sides censing her; below, the martyrdom of Becket by three knights: ". . . . . Ecclesie Bēe Marie . . . . . martiris de Novo Loco Surre . . ." Counter-seal: the Cross and instruments of the Passion; inscription illegible.

1266[–7], 11 March, "die Ven. pr. ante f. S. Gregorii pape"; at Seleburne. Grant and quit-claim from Henry de la Charite to the Prior and Canons of Seleburne of all his right in one mark of annual rent from the tenement of William de la Rode, son of Robert de la Rode. Witn.: Sir Will. de Wyntereshulle, Sir Robert de Popham, John Swanecre, Richard de Nortune, Henry Wyard, James de Ackangre, Gilebert Cunan, Nicholas Suwele, Will. de Arundel de la Wyke.—[192.]

Round brown seal of arms; two bars, in chief a star: "S' Henrici de Karitate."

1266[–7], 15 March, "die lune pr. p. f. S. Greg."; in the chapter of Winchester. Confirmation by Valentine, Prior of the church of St. Swthun (*sic*), Winchester, of the charter from Bishop John, of 1 April, 1266 (No. 344), which is recited at length.—[347.]

Round brown seal; a figure with a nimbus, seated, in the right hand a key, in the left a book; inscription entirely broken off. Small counter-seal: a Roman intaglio, with one small figure: "Valeat Valentinus."

1267, 18 April, "in crast. Pasche"; at Seleburne. Grant from Henry de la Charite to the Prior and Canons of Seleburne, in free alms, of all his right in one mark of annual rent issuing from the tenement of Will. de la Rode, son of Robert de la Rode, as in the deed of 11 March, 1266[–7]; *adding* Will. de la Rode and his heirs shall be quit of frank-pledge and of view of frank-pledge. Witn.: Sir Will. de Wyntereshulle, Sir Rob. de Popham, Gilebert Cunan, Nich. Suwele, Will. de Isenhurste, Will. de Arundel de la Wyke, Robert Marescall de la Wyke.—[199.]

Round white seal of arms; two bars, in chief a star: " S' Henrici de Karitate."

1267, 9 Sept., "in crast. Nat. B. M. V.," 51 Hen. fil. Joh. Lease from Thomas de la Dene to Peter the Prior and the Convent of Seleburne, in consideration of the receipt of 60*s*., of one virgate of land which he had by the gift of Rich. de la Dene, his brother, in Ochangre, to hold for the term of three years; rendering annually one pair of white gloves or 1*d*., and to the King 10*s*. Witn.: Nicholas Svele, Ralph Paen, Will. de Arundel de la Wike, Robert Marescall, Will. le Esquier.—[119.]

Round white seal; apparently a Roman intaglio, nearly effaced; a man on horseback.

1267, 27 Sept., "die Martis pr. ante f. S. Mich.," 51 Hen. fil. Joh.; at Seleburne. Grant and quit-claim from Thomas de la Dene to the Prior and Canons of Seleburne, in free alms, of one virgate of land, which he held by the gift of his brother Richard in Ackangre; rendering annually to the grantor and his heirs one pair of white gloves or 1*d*., and to the King 10*s*. Witn.: Sir Ralph de Basinges, Sir Rob. de Popham, Adam de la More, Richard de Westcote, Henry Wyard, Will. de Isenhurste, Nich. Suwele, Ralph Payne, Will. de Arundel de la Wyke, Robert Marescall, Will. le Esquier.—[137.]

Round white and brown seal; apparently a Roman intaglio; a man on horseback, very faint; inscription broken.

[1268.] Grant from Stephen Peche to the Prior and Canons of Seleburne, in free alms, of all his tenement called Dogeferckter (*or* Dogeferckte), in the parish of Ististede; paying to the lord of the fee an annual quit-rent of 4*s*. Witn.: Sir Will. de Wyntereshulle, Sir Rob. de Popham, Sir Ralph de Basinges, John Swancere, Rich. de Wescote, Will. Huse, Henry Wyard, Nich. Suwele, Henry de Bromdene, Will. de Arundel de la Wyke, Robert Marescall.—[237.]

Round green seal; a star: " S' Stephani Peche."
Another original copy of the same; seal the same.—[246.]

1267[–8], 14 Feb., "die S. Valent. mart."; at Seleburne. Confirmation by Adam Gurdun, knt., to the Prior and Canons of Seleburne of the grant made to them by Stephen Pechi of the whole tenement of Dogefertkete, granting also all the services, reliefs, etc., due from the same, saving an annual rent of 4*s*. Witn.: Sir Will. de Wintereshulle, Sir Rob. de Popham, Sir Ralph de Basinges, Will. Huse, Rich. de Labere, John Santerre, Henry Wiard, Nich. Suele, James de Ackangre, Will. de Arundel de la Wyk, Rob. Mareschall de la Wyk, Will. le Esquier.—[254.]

Small round green seal; a shield of arms quite indistinct, and inscription illegible.

1268, "anno 52 Hen. fil. Joh."; at Seleborne. Acknowledgment by Walter Makerel, son of Sir Thomas Makerel, of the receipt from Sir Adam de Gordonc, knt., of 30 marks which he owed to him by bond for an acquittance and quit-claim for the land which the said Adam had by the gift of the said Sir Thomas. Witn.: Sir Peter de Disenhurste, Prior of Seleborne, Sir John de Bremmechate, Sir Ralph de Basinges, Rich. de Northone, Nicholasde Molendino.—[60.]

Round green seal; a cross flory: ". . . . . Walteri Makerel."

[*Beginning of* 1270.] Grant from James de Acchangre to the Prior and Canons of Seleburne, in free alms, of all his land called la Brogate, viz., that which lies between his wood called la Broke and the farm of Gilibert de Nortune, clerk, extending to the way going from la Brogate to the chapel of Acchangre; and also six and a quarter acres of his wood of la Broke, near the pasture of the said Prior and Convent on the north; also a way for cars and carts and also for driving cattle through the middle of the said wood whensoever they please from the cross de la Rode which is called Pires Cruht to the highway which goes through the middle of Acchangre and from the enclosure of the said priory up to the said way; and also 14*d*. of annual rent from the tenement of Ralph Niwemane held of the grantor within his manor of Acchangre. Witn.: Sir Martin de Rupibus, sheriff of Suhantesire,[1] Sir Adam de Gurdun, Sir Robert de Popham, knts., Rich. de Nortune, Will. Huse, Rich. de la Bere, Nich. Swele, Henry Wiard, Will. de Arundel de la Wike, Rob. Mareschalle de la Wike, William le Esquier.—[141.]

Round green seal; the sun and moon: "S' Jacobi de Hacangre."

Another original grant of the same land of "la Brocgate," etc., way, and rent; but the second portion of land is described as being "five acres of land and three quarters of an acre of his wood of la Brok." Same witnesses and seal.—[301.]

[*c.* 1270.] Grant from Henry le Mareschal of Achangre, with the consent of his wife Lucy, to the Prior and Canons of Seleburne, in free alms, of 5½*d*. of annual rent in the vill. of Achangre issuing from the tenement of Will. de Hockemore, viz., from Aschelonde, Marlacre, and

[1] He was sheriff only for the first half of *an.* 54 Hen. III; see 31st Report of Dep. Keeper of Public Records, p. 338. It is found from the *Inqq. post mortem* that he died in 1277, 5 Edw. I.

one "forhylue" in Achangre. Witn.: Sir Adam Gurdun, knt., Nich. de Thundene, Will. de Achangre, Nich. Wyard, Henry Wylekyng, Rob. Marescall de la Wyk, William Robert de la Rode.—[168.]

Oval green seal; a buckle: "S' Henrici le Mar'cal."

[*c.* 1270.] Grant from Edith Alrad, who was the wife of the late William le Messager, to the Prior and Convent of Seleburne, in free alms, of a messuage and twenty acres of land which she held of them in chief in the field of Seleburne. Witn.: Sir Henry de Sotesbroke, Nicholas de Thudde, Nicholas Wyard, Symon de Aula, Henry Willokynge, Robert Mareskall de la Wyke, Will. Roberd de la Rode.—[32.]

Oval green seal; a branch of a tree: "S' Edita Larad" (*sic*).

[*c.* 1270, *or earlier?*] Grant from William de la Rode, with the consent of his wife Alice, to the Prior and Convent of Seleburne, for the sum of 6*s.* 8*d.*, of a piece of land one perch in width, from the head of the well of Chyldewelle, through the middle of the grantor's garden, as it is marked by boundaries, which land the said Prior and Convent are bound to enclose from the beech above the well to their grove; to be held by them for the purpose of making a head in the well, "ad lavacrum suum sustinendum"; and for this the said Prior and Convent are to inscribe the names of the said William, his father and mother and wife, in their martiloge, and once in the year to celebrate for them. Witn.: Sir Adam de Gurdun, Sir Robert de Poppham, knts., Henry Wyard, Robert Gaugy, James de Achangre, John Marescall de Burhunte, Walter Drueys, Robert Marescall de la Wyke, Will. Coterel de la Rode.—[366.]

Oval white seal; the Lamb and Flag: "S' Will'i fil' Roberti."

[*c.* 1270–80.] Grant from William de Bradene and Agnes his wife to Sir Adam de Gordon, knt., and Constance his wife, for the sum of 30 marks, and for certain land which the said William and Agnes hold for their lives in Tistede and Northone of the said Adam and Constance, of all that land of la Stupe which they hold in Watceleghe, and two acres in the same, of which one is called la Stuphaker, one half-acre is called Coppehelue, and the other half is called Tyghelstichche; paying to the chief lords of the fee an annual quit-rent of 13*s.* 6*d.* Witn.: Sir John de Brembelshete, Sir Rob. de Popham, knts., John de Valletorta, Rich. de la Bere, Will. Huse, John de la Bere, Henry Wiard, Nich. Swele, John de Aultone, Peter de Benstede, Roger de Hagheman.—[255.]

Two green seals, oval: (1) a bird; "S' Will'mi Branals" (?); (2) the Lamb and Flag: "Agnus Dei miserere mei."

[*c.* 1270–80.] Grant from William Coterel de la Rode to the Prior and Canons of Seleburne, in free alms, of 8*d.* of annual rent from an acre of land in la Rode which John the Cobbler ("Sutor") formerly held of him. Witn.: Sir Adam de Gurdone, Sir Will. de Brambeshate, knts., Walter Drueys, Will. de Achangre, Henry Wyard, Robert Marescall de la Wyke, Will. Robert de la Rode.—[184.]

Oval green seal; a tree: "S' Will'i Coterel."

[*c.* 1270–80.] Grant from Henry de Watesford to the Prior and Canons of Seleburne, in free alms, of 14*d.* of annual rent from a tenement which was formerly Thomas le Mason's in la Rode. Witn.: Sir Adam de Gurdon, Sir Will. de Brambeshate, knts., Walter Drueys, Will. de Achangre, John German of Ywode, John de la Hale, Henry Wyard, Robert Marescall de la Wyke, William Coterel de la Rode. —[187.]

Oval green seal; a Roman intaglio, a small naked figure: "S' Henrici de Watsfor."

[*c.* 1270–80.] Grant from William Coterel de la Rode to the Prior and Canons of Seleburne, in free alms, of 14*d.* of annual rent which they have by the gift of Henry de Watesford issuing from a tenement which was once Thomas le Mason's in la Rode, with all that is contained in the charter of the said Henry. Witn.: Sir Adam de Gurdon, Sir John de Wyldeshore, knts., Walter Drueys, Will. de Achangre, Henry Wyard, Nich. de Thunden, Robert Marescall de la Wyke.—[161.]

Oval green seal; a tree: "S' Will'mi Coterel."

[*c.* 1270–80.] Grant from William the Tailor ("Cissor") to the Prior and Canons of Seleburne, in free alms, of a rent of 14*d.* from a tenement formerly Thomas le Mason's in la Rode (as in No. 187). Witn. the same as to No. 187, *omitting* German *and* Hale.—[190.]

Round green seal; two mailed hands, clasped; inscription indistinct ("Finali . . . . . elie"?).

[*c.* 1270–80.] Grant and quit-claim from William de Achangre to the Prior and Canons of Seleburne, in free alms, of one croft of his land in Achangre called la Grenerude, which extends eastward to la Furslonde, and westward to the land of the said Prior and Canons; and which land they have by the gift of James, father of the said William, which lies lengthways near the high road going from la Brok to the chapel of Achangre. Witn.: Sir Adam Gurdon, Sir Will. de Brambeshate, knts., Nich. de Thundene, Walter Drueys, Ralph de Heghes, Robert Marescall de la Wyk, Robert de la Rode.—[163.]

Round green seal; the sun and moon: "S' Will' Oc . . . ."

[*c.* 1270–80.] Grant from William Adam of Achangre to the Prior and Canons of Seleburne, in free alms, of 3*d.* of annual rent in the vill of Achangre for the light of the high altar of the Priory issuing from the tenements of Will. le Hunte and Agnes Martyn and Agatha her sister, viz., from "Forhilue" of the said Will., 1*d.*, and from Pukepirk of the said Agnes and Agatha, 2*d.* Witn.: Sir Adam Gurdon, knt., Nich. de Thundene, Nich. Wyard, Henry Wylekyng, Robert Marescall de la Wyk, Will. de Achangre, Will. Robert de la Rode.—[150.]

Oval white seal, effaced.

[*c.* 1270–80.] Grant and quit-claim from Lucy, widow of Henry Marescall of Achangre, to the Prior and Convent of Seleburne, in free alms, of all her right in 13*d.* of annual rent in Achangre of the fee of the said Prior and Convent, for the light of St. Katherine in their church, issuing from a meadow between la Bromcroft and the meadow of the said Prior called la Longmede, and from four acres of land in the said vill, which 13*d.* they had by the gift of her late husband. Witn.: Sir Adam Gurdun, Sir Thomas Paynel, knts., John de Venuz, John de Gatesdene, James de Nortune, John de Chiltele, Nich. Churchi, Henry Wilekynge, Peter Doget.—[151.]

Oval black seal; a Roman intaglio, very small and indistinct, a naked figure; inscription illegible.

1271, 29 March, "die domin. pr. p. Annunc. Dom.," 55 Hen. fil. Joh. Agreement (indented) by which Sir Adam de Gurdun, knt., releases to Peter the Prior of Seleburne, and the Convent there, in free alms, all his right in a place called la Pleystowe in Seleburne, to hold there their market which they have by the gift of King Henry and to build houses and shops upon it, saving reasonable way for him and his heirs to the house and croft which John le Bac holds in Seleburne near the churchyard on the south, the said Adam and his heirs claiming henceforth no right in that place nor in the land called la Buri nor in the wall of the churchyard up to the house of the said John; and the said Adam also grants, for the health of his own soul and that of his wife Constance, etc., that the said Prior and Canons shall peaceably hold the houses and curtilages which they have erected upon their lands in Seleburne in which the said Adam had right of common for himself and his men, which right he has released; and it shall be lawful for both parties hereafter to build houses and curtilages upon all their respective lands in Seleburne which touch upon the highway, without hindrance, and for the said Adam to enclose his land called la Truestede. Witn.: Sir Will. de Wintreshelle, Robert de Popham, Will. Huse, Henry Wyard, Rich. de Nortone, Nich. Swele, Will. de Arundel, Robert le Mareschal, Will. le Esquier.—[8.]

Small round white seal, nearly effaced.

1271[-2], 8 Feb., "in f. S. Edelflede virg."; at Seleburne. Agreement (indented) before the official of the Bishop of Winchester, between Sir Roger de Lechelade, vicar of Seleburne, and the Prior and Conv. of Seleburne, for settling of a controversy respecting augmentation of the vicarage, viz., that the said vicar shall have the tithes of flax of the parish, which he had formerly demised to them amongst other tithes granted to them in payment of a pension of 100*s*., and shall be released from an annual payment of 7*s*. to which he was bound by the agreement formerly made, and shall receive one quarter of corn yearly during his life; in return, the vicar covenants never again to raise any question respecting the poverty of the vicarage.—[70.]

(1) Oval white seal; the Pelican in her piety; inscription broken. (2) Seal of the official of Winchester, lost.

1274, 18 July, "die Merc. pr. ante f. S. Margarete V."; at Winchester. Judgment of Nicholas de Rokelund, official of Winchester, in a suit between the Prior and Convent of Seleburne against Sir Philip, rector of Gretham, in which the convent claim an annual pension of 2*s*. from the church of Gretham which the said Philip has withheld; and he, in return, claims the great tithes issuing from all the arable land which Peter le Foke, a parishioner of Gretham, holds of Sir Robert de Aguyband in the deanery of Aultone, of which the convent have deprived him; the convent thereupon further claim that the body of Joan called le Foke, buried at Gretham, be dug up, and her body or bones with the offerings and obventions be restored to them; and the said Philip claims that Peter le Foke, formerly the husband of the said Joan, be declared to belong with his family to the parish right ("jus parochiale") of the church of Gretham. The Judge decrees that the said annual pension be restored, with the arrears, by the said Philip; that the church of Gretham shall continue to possess Peter le Foke and his family, that the said Philip be discharged from exhuming the body of the said Joan or returning oblations, and that the convent be discharged from the suit respecting the tithes, saving to the said Philip the question of ownership should he wish to try it: both sides discharged from costs.—[120.]

Small seal, entirely broken; sewn up in linen.

1274[-5,] 13 Jan., "die S. Hillarii episc."; at Duntone. Copy by H[enry de Helingeye,] Archdeacon of Winchester, of a return made by his official to N[icholas,] the Bishop of Winchester, in pursuance of a writ from the King, certifying that upon an enquiry made by the rectors of Farendone and Gretham, the vicars of Froyle, Seleburne and Ymbesete, and the chaplains of Aultone and Benstede, it was found that the rectory of Worldham was not vacant but was held by master John de Brideport, who had been instituted by the Bishop of Winchester on St. James' day, 1262, on the presentation of the Prior and Convent of Seleburne, the true patrons.—[74.]

Small fragment of one seal: another lost.

1276, 30 Aug., "in crast. Decoll. S. Jo. Bapt."; at Seleburne. Acknowledgment by . . . . . (*torn*) de Achangre of Northebrok and William son of Adam de Achangre, that they hold all the tenements which they have in Achangre of the Prior and Convent of Seleburne by the same rent and service by which they held them on the day on which Thomas de la Deney gave the said persons to the said Prior and Convent. Witn.: Sir Robert de Poppham, knt., Rich. de Wescote, Nich. Swele, Rob. Gaugy, Will. de Arundel de la Wyke, Rob. Marescall of the same, Will. Roberd de la Rode.—[175.]

Two white seals: (1) oval, effaced; (2) round, a spread eagle, inscription effaced.

1277, 20 Aug., "die Ven. pr. p. Assumpt. B. M. V."; at Seleburne. Release from Henry de Burhunte, son of Herbert de Burhunte, to the Prior and Convent of Seleburne, for the sum of 100*s.*, of all his right in a messuage, garden, and all the land which they had by the gift of Gilibert de Burhunte in Burhunte, and in twenty acres of land which they had by the gift of John de Burhunte in Burhunte; for which he sued the said Prior and Convent in the King's Bench. Witn.: Sir Adam de Gurdun, Sir Robert de Poppham, Sir John de Wyldeshore, knts., Henry Wyard, Nich. Suwele, James de Achangre, John Marescall of Burhunte, Rob. Gaugy, Mathias de la Bertune.—[331.]

Small oval brown seal, broken; a tree with two birds: "S' Henri . . . hunte."

Another original copy, adding the following witnesses: Robert Marescall de la Wyke, Clement de Wydenale. Same seal, not broken. Written by another hand. Attached are two small strips of parchment, with memoranda of the retirement of H. de Burhunte from his suit at law with the convent before the judges R. de Settune and Ralph de Hengeham. The land is said to be at Burhunte and at Slope.—[334.]

1277, 1 Sept., "in f. S. Egidii." Agreement (indented) by which Amicia, widow of John de Burhunte, releases to Richard the Prior and the Convent of Seleburne all her right by reason of dowry in the third part of the land of Burhunte, which land they had by the gift of her said late husband; and they, in return, covenant to give to her during her life, six bushels of wheat at Michaelmas, six bushels of wheat at Easter and twelve bushels of oats at the Purification. Witn.: Sir Rob. de Poppham, knt., Rich. de la Bere, James de Achangre, Philip de Burhunte, Robert Marescall de la Wyke.—[335.]

Oval white seal; a bird, inscription nearly effaced.

1278, 3 July, "die domin. pr. f. SS. Processi et Martiniani," 6 Edw. [I] (*Monks' Sherborne*). Release from William le Waleys of his right in half a virgate of land in Syrburne Monachorum which Geoffrey Hude formerly held, about which there was a plea between the said William, claimant, and Tho. de Saunford, defendant, by the King's writ in the court of the Prior of Syrburne; confirming to Ralph de Scures and Joan his wife a grant of the said land which the said Tho. de Saunford made to them while the suit was pending. Witn.: Will. Wastehuse, Nich. Telbaud, Ralph Wastehuse, John le Waleys, Walter the Cook, Robert Franceys, Clement Hurt, Nich. Wodhorn.—[111].

Fragment of a diamond-shaped white seal.

1279, 12 March, "in f. S. Gregorii pape et conf.," 7 Edw. fil. Hen.; at Seleburne. Grant from William de Achangre to the Prior and Canons of Seleburne, in free alms, of a piece of land on the west of la Broke. Witn.: Peter de la Stane and William de Bramschate, knts.; John de Popham, Peter de Heghes, Ralph de Heghes, Robert Marescall, William Roberd de la Rode.—[134.]

Small fragment of seal, with sun and moon.

1280, 7 June, "die Ven. pr. ante f. S. Barn."; in the great church of Winchester. Judgment given by Richard, Precentor of Hyde, commissary of N[icholas,] late Bishop of Winchester, in a suit brought by Roger de Radenhale, clerk, against the Prior and Convent of Seleburne (who appeared by their proctors, Rich. de Portesye and Will. de Warneburne) respecting a claim made by him as having been presented to the church of Westistede; dismissing the said Prior and Convent from all further litigation, the said plaintiff having withdrawn from the suit, penitently acknowleding that he had no right to the church.—[244.]

Two green seals: (1) oval, three figures under canopies: "S' Precentoris b' i Petri de Hida"; (2) fragment of a small oval seal, said to be that of the Consistory of Winchester.

1280, 15 July, "in f. S. Suithuni," 8 Edw. fil. Hen. Agreement (indented) between Richard the Prior and the Convent of Seleburne, and Thomas de la Brek, Will. Adam, Robert le Hore, Will. Martin, Will. de Hockemore, Ralph de Northebroke, and Will. Doget, their tenants, by which the Prior and Convent, in consideration of the receipt of 40*s*., release to them their customary services; viz., from the tenement of the said Thomas de la Brok, 6*d*. of ripselvere, one cock and one hen, 1½*d*. for Hockemore, and 1¼*d*. for la Putacre; from the tenement of Will. Adam the same; from the tenement of Robert le Hore the same; from the tenement of Will. de Hockemore the same; from the tenement of Ralph de Northebroke, 6*d*. of ripselvere, two cocks and two hens, 1½*d.* for Hockemore, 1¼*d.* for la Putakere; from the tenement of Will. Martin, 12*d.* of ripselvere, one cock and one hen, 1½*d.* for Hockemore, 1¼*d.* for la Putakere; from the tenement of Will. Doget, 12*d.* of ripselvere and 1¼*d.* for la Putakere; saving for the lands and tenements which they hold of the Prior and Convent in Ochangre 30*s.* of annual rent, with suit of court in Ochangre above Northebroke, reliefs, heriots, wards and escheats. Witn.: Sir Adam de Gurdun, knt., Sir Robert de Popham, knt., Henry Wyard, John the clerk of Aultone, Adam Oter, Nich. de la Flode, Henry Wyleking, Will. de la More, John de Yvelie, Nich. Curci.—[86.]

Three seals lost, three small oval ones remaining: (1) a fleur-de-lis, inscription broken; (2) (3) a star (or sun): ". . . Rodulfi Binoreh . . . . ." (?)

1280, 25 July, "in f. S. Jac. Apost."; at Seleburne. Indenture of a license from the Prior Richard and Convent of Seleburne to Henry de Watesford and Nicholaa his wife, to construct an oratory in their court of Watesford, and there to celebrate divine offices at their own expense, saving the right of the mother church of Basinges and of the Convent and of the vicar for the time being, saving also to the vicar all the oblations and obventions at the said oratory; and the said Henry and Nicholaa and their heirs shall attend the mother church on solemn feast-days, if they can conveniently do so, and shall pay 12*d.* annually to the Convent.—[378.]

Seals wanting, among which was the seal of master Rich. le Beel, vicar of Basingestoke.

[*c.* 1280.] Grant from Henry Marescall of Achangre, son of Robert Marescall de la Wyke, to the Prior and Canons of Seleburne, in free alms, of 13*d.* of annual rent in Achangre for the light of S. Katherine in the said church, issuing from a meadow which lies between la Bromcroft and the meadow of the said Prior called la Longemede, and from four acres of land which Sibilia de la Lode holds in Achangre. Witn.: James de Nortune, Will. de Achangre, Symon de Aula, Rich. de Westcote, Henry de Estone, John de Thuddene, Rob. Marescall de la Wike, Henry Wilekyng, Henry de la Rude.—[162.]

Oval green seal; a buckle: "S' Henrici le Mar'cal."

Another grant of the same from the same donor, omitting the mention of the light of S. Katherine; somewhat later, as it seems, in date, as it says that Sibilia de la Lode "formerly" (aliquando) held the meadow and the four acres of the grantor. Witn. and seal the same.—[172.]

[*c.* 1280?] Release from William le Archer de la Rodo and Alice his wife to the Canons of Seleburne of all their right in a piece of land which the said Canons have by the gift of William de la Rode and the said Alice who was then his wife. Witn.: Sir Adam Gurdun, Sir Thomas Paynel, knts., John de Venuz, James de Nortone, John de Westcote, John de Candevere.—[200.]

Two green seals; (1) round, apparently a shield bearing a bar between three crosses in chief and three in base: "S' Will. . . . . . . ;" (2) oval, the Lamb and Flag; "Ecce Agnus Dei."

[*c.* 1280–90.] Grant from William le Fughel of Seleburne to Walter the Hunter ("venatori") and Agnes his wife, for the sum of 6 marks, of all the land and garden which he had by the gift of *the late* James de Achangre at la Hunne, near the highway going from the Priory of Seleburne towards Blakemere, of which one acre with a croft lies near the wood of Will. de Achangre, which [acre] is called la Brok and extends to the meadow of Will. le Wrik on the east, and to the land of the late Rich. Holewe on the west; and which garden Will. de Blakewelle, chaplain, formerly farmed of the said James, together with a meadow adjacent which the said Will. Blakewelle formerly farmed of Peter de Cruce; paying annually to the Prior of Seleburne 12*d.*, and to Will. de Achangre 1*d.*, and to the grantor during his life one overcoat ("supertunicam") worth 2*s.* Witn.: Sir Adam Gurdon, knt., James de Nortone, Simon de Aula, Will. de Achangre, Henry de Estone, Will. Gervays, Nicholas de Thuddene, John his brother, Richard de Wescote, Walter Selede, clerk, Robert Marescall de la Wyke, Henry Wylekyng, Henry de la Rude.—[58.]

Oval green seal; a floriated cross: "S' Will'i Fu'gl." [James de Achangre was alive in 1277.]

[*c.* 1280–90.] Grant and quit-claim from John de Sutheneye and Alice his wife to William de la Rode, chaplain, for the sum of 6 marks, of all their right in the tenement of the late Richard Coterel at la Rode; rendering an annual quit-rent of one pound of cummin or 1*d.* Witn.: Will. de Achangre, Henry Wylekyng, Robert Marescall, Will. Sterghaf, John the Baker.—[365.]

Seal lost.

[*c.* 1280–90?] Copy, on paper, made in the 15th century (*torn*) of a grant from Jurdan de Westþrop to the Prior and Canons of Selbourne, in free alms, of 27*s.* 5*d.* of annual rent in the village of Thuddene; viz., from the tenement of Andrew de Heyes, 7*s.* 8*d.*; from that of Henry Rufus, 9*s.* 6*d.*; from that of Geoffrey Purchaz, 7*s.* 4*d.*; and from that of Robert Clyne, 2*s.* 11*d.*; also quit-claiming to the said Prior and Canons all the land which they have in the same village by the gift of Nicholas Swele, and 10*s.* of annual rent paid by them to him; but saving a quit-rent of 20*s.* to Robert Popham. (*Witnesses omitted.*)—[379.]

1281, 10 July, "die Jovis pr. p. transl. S. Tho. mart."; at Alresford. Certificate by J. de Tybenham, official of the archdeacon of Winchester, of an inquisition made on the above day by master John de Hegghemere and John de Shypedeham, perpetual vicar of Sutthone and dean of Alresford, in pursuance of a mandate from master Adam de Hale, keeper of the spiritualities of the bishopric of Winchester, in a full chapter of the deanery, respecting the vacant church of Westistede, of which they say that the Prior and Convent of Seleburne are the true patrons, and possessors as rectors from the time of Bishop Peter, and established their right against the claim of Sir Randulf de Cameys who presented master J. de Brydeport, now rector of Great Wordlam (*see under date* 1261), and that they have held it up to the time of Geoffrey de la Flode, now lord of the village; the church is worth 10 marks annually, and the person now presented is of good life and honest conversation and in priest's orders.—[276.]

The seals of the rectors and vicars of Chyldkandevere, of Candevere Abbots, of Aventone, Bradely and Sutthone, were attached with that of the official, but only small fragments remain of any.

[1281,] 30 Nov., "ij kal. Dec. an. 1 pontif.," "apud Urbemvetenem." Bull from Pope Martin [IV] to the Prior of Southwark, directing him to endeavour to recover for the monastery of Seleburne various tithes, lands, rents, houses, etc., which the Prior and Convent and their predecessors have granted away to various persons, to some for life, to others for a long time, and to others in perpetual farm, to the injury of the monastery.—[298.]

Leaden *bulla* lost.

1282, 12 April, "prid. idus Apr."; at Reading. Confirmation by John [Peckham], Archbishop of Canterbury, to the Prior and Convent of Seleburne, made in consequence of their request made to him when at their house in the course of his metropolitical visitation during the vacancy of the see of Winchester, of the appropriation of the churches of Seleburne, Basynges and Westysted, with the chapels dependent thereon.—[21.]

Oval green seal, attached by red and yellow silk strings; inscription broken; the Archbishop in attitude of blessing, on either side a lily of the valley: "Fr̄. (Frater) Joh'es Dei . . . . . ien tocius Anglie primas." No counter-seal.

Another copy, with the same date, in which the churches are specified as Seleburne, Basynggestoke, and Westistede, the title of the Convent having been ascertained "per examinationem privilegiorum et indulgenciarum vobis concessarum per nostros commissarios diligenter factam." Half of the seal, oval, green.—[98.]

1282, 26 Nov., "die Jovis pr. p. f. S. Katerine virg."; in the church of B. Mary of Suwerk. Judgment given by the Prior of Suwerk, the delegate appointed by the Pope, in a suit brought by the Prior and Convent of Seleburne against Gilibert, vicar of Imbesshete, for a moiety of the small tithes of the villeins of Imbeshete, of which the Convent had been in possession from the time of their foundation; in which he pronounces in favour of the Prior and Convent, and condemns the said Gilibert to pay 20 marks for the tithes of which he has deprived them.—[329.]

Oval green seal; a figure kneeling before the Virgin and Child; inscription broken.

Another original copy of the decree. Seal the same: from the kneeling figure issues a scroll with the words "Ave . . . . . ." "[S] Alani prioris de Suwercka."—[345.]

1282, 17 Dec., "die Jov. pr. p. f. S. Lucie virg,"; in the chapel of the Holy Ghost at Basinggestoke. "Memorandum" that at an enquiry held by the official of the Bishop of Winchester respecting a claim made by Sir Richard, vicar of the church of Selebourne, to one quarter of wheat, one quarter of barley, one quarter of oats, and one quarter of beans, from the Prior and Convent of Selebourne, brother Richard de Portes, the proctor of the latter, produced an ordinance of W[ill. Raleigh] formerly Bishop of Winchester, and other instruments, by which it appeared that the said allowance was granted to a former vicar, Richard le Bel, only for his own personal merits and not by reason of his vicarage; and the claimant therefore acknowledged that he had no right to it.—[117.]

Small fragment of green seal.

1284, 9 Jan., "die domin. pr. p. Epiph. Dom."; 12 Edw. fil. Hen.; at Westistede. Release from Richard de Croftone, son and heir of Rob. de Croftone, to the Prior and Canons of Selborne, in free alms, of all his right in the advowson and patronage of the church of Westistede, and in the land called le Trandelcroft, which the said Prior and Canons have by the gift of the lady Joan le Hod. Witn.: Sir Simon de Wynton, sheriff of Suhant., Sir Adam de Gurdone, Sir John de Wyldeshore, Sir Hugh de Rupibus, Sir Will. de Brambeshate, knts., Will. Gervays, John Sanztere, Alan de Sutthone, Henry Wyard, Walter Huse, Rob. Marescall de la Wyk.—[262.]

Seal sewn up in wool.

[1284–5.] Release from Geoffrey de la Flode and Alice his wife, called the lady of Westistede, to the Prior and Canons of Seleburne, in free alms, of all their right in the advowson and patronage of the church of Westistede, with all the land called le Trandelcroft, which land the said Prior and Canons have by the gift of the lady Joan le Hod in the said village. Witn. : Sir Simon de Winchester, then sheriff of Suhampt.,[1] Sir Adam de Gurdon, Sir John de Wyldeshore, Sir Hugh de Rupibus, Sir Will. de Brambeshate, knts., Will Gervais, John Sanztere, Alan de Suttone, Henry Wyard, Walter Huse, Rob. Marescall de la Wyke.—[239.]

Two green seals; (1) round, a rose, ". . . . te Deum"; (2) oval, a Roman intaglio: [Jupiter (?) seated, with sun above and moon below] "S' Alicie de Croftune."

1284[-5,] 2 Feb., "in die Purif. B.M."; at Seleborne. Copy on paper (made in the 15th cent., and mutilated by rats or mice) of a grant from the Prior (Richard) and Convent of Seleburne to their beloved sister in Christ lady Ela Longespeye, Countess of Warwick, of one canon always to celebrate for her at the altar of SS. Stephen, John Bapt., and Thomas the Martyr, with the specification of the collects, etc., to be used; providing also for her daily commemoration among the founders and benefactors, and for the observance of her anniversary.—[382(i).]

[1285,] 25 Feb., "v kl. Mart.," pontif. an. 4, "Perusii." Bull from Pope Martin [IV] to the Prior of Suthwerk to the same effect as that of 30 Nov., 1281, No. 298, *supra*.—[393.]

Cancelled by being cut through, and *bulla* lost.

1285, 21 April, "die sab. pr. ante f. S. Marci evang.," 13 Edw. [I]; at Warneborne. Letters patent of Ela Longespeye, countess of Warrewyk, certifying that she is bound to the Prior and Convent of Seleburne in 100 marks for the support of one canon, a chaplain, to celebrate mass daily for her soul during her life and after her death, to be paid within the next five years; in which payment should she fail, the sheriffs of Oxon and Suhamtesire may compel payment by all her lands, tenements and goods in their bailiwick; should she die within the time, her executors to have no administration of her goods until first this payment has been made. No witnesses.—[52.]

One half of oval wax seal; the lower part of a female figure, with scroll-work pattern at the side: ". . . . . comitisse Warwik." Counter-seal: a shield of arms, six lions rampant; crest, a lion courant: "S' Ele Lungespeye . . . . ."

1285, [22 April?] "die domin. pr. ante f. S. [Marci? evange]liste"; at Seleburne. Similar copy (but more mutilated) to that in the preceding paper of 2 Feb. of a renewed and enlarged grant to Ela Longespe to the same effect; adding (*inter alia*) that mass should be celebrated monthly

[1] Sheriff of Hants, 12, 13, Edw. I.

for her at the high altar by three priests in tunic and dalmatic, that her name shall be written in every missal and in the martyrology, and her soul mentioned in all prayers when the soul of the founder is mentioned; that on the news of her death the "classicum" with all the bells shall be tolled ("pulsetur"), etc., as for a prior, every priest-canon shall celebrate 30 masses and every priest shall say 10 Psalters, and every lay-brother 150 [Pater nosters] and as many Ave Marias. "[In cujus rei] gestæ memoriam literæ hujus transcriptum in Martirologio nostro fecimus annotari."—[382(ii).]

Probably dated the day after the preceding deed of lady Ela.

1290. At Farnham, "in mancrio nostro." Copy (on vellum, made in 15th cent.) of an ordinance by John [de Pontissara, *al.* Sawbridge] Bishop of Winchester, for endowment of the vicarage of the church of Est Worldham, appropriated to the Prior and Convent of Selborne; viz., that the vicar shall have all oblations and obventions, ten acres of arable land which the rector used to hold, the tithe of wool, flax, lambs, calves, chickens, young pigs, cheese, cider, hay, and honey, and the sheaves of gardens, and of crofts which are gardens, and all places ("omnia") that are dug with the foot, and all the small tithes belonging to the altarage of the church; with one acre, for habitation thereon, near the churchyard, called Orchardscroft, which the rector used to hold; and the churchyard, and a lane lying between the Bishop's garden ("gardinum nostrum") and a croft called Wodfolde, to make his profit of; and the said Religious shall erect anew at their own expense sufficient buildings for the vicars, and shall yearly deliver at the vicar's hall three quarters of wheat, three quarters of barley, and three quarters of oats, good measure, well threshed, and if they are three months in arrear after Michaelmas they shall give double. And the said Religious shall have all the great tithes, viz., the sheaves only, and shall provide candlesticks, and books, and the bread for celebration, and shall repair and sustain the chancel, and defray all ordinary expenses. Endorsed with the following list, in English, of the crofts, etc., of which the vicar receives the tithes:—"Mem. quod vicarius prædictæ ecclesiæ percipiet decimas de istis croftis, viz., de Fowleriscroft and de Skuttslezhtone, and de Wokes, Foxys hayes, the honer crofts of Gylberd Sandale, and of the croft of Jone Balchyld of the same on ye syxte croft, ye ij acars next Boltsames yt is Hobbys, the hays of Boltsames, ye west gardyn, the calverhouse gardyn, and al Hydys hays, the carters hay, ye aslotts hays, Janottslezhtone, ye spone croft, al Gyllys crofts, al Pookks crofts, halfe the tethyng of ye Pykenots hays, ye dykers croft, ye potteris crofts, ye carpenterrs crofts, ye croft of

Huchun Sendel, ye monkenlonde, ye harpers crofts, ye freres under ye lythe, ye croft of Jonys gardyn, the croft of Saundervyle, Lurtlane croft. In the parke, ye parkefyld, ye culverhowse gardyn, ye fosters (*qu.* forester's ?) tethe, the parkers croft tethe, ye dowakes croft, ye park mede, ye ynhome, and moo other yt the vicary hadde the tethynge of or they wer take in to the parke, and therfor ye vicary shal have ye tethe in ye park of pannage of bests and of mast off swyne, and ye tethe of the dere that be yslawe, by ye grawnt and the ordennance of Kynge Edward and of hys consayl yt wer at yt tyme masterys of that place undyr the Kynge, William Wykham, Adam Hertyngdon, Thomas Harecot, and Thomas Chamburlayne."—[205*b*.]

1290, 19 May, "die Ven. in f. S. Dunstani conf.," 18 Edw. fil. Hen.; at Seleburne. Release from Roger, son of Robert Marescall de la Wyke, to the Prior and Convent of Seleburne of all his right in the tenement in Achaugre which he had by the gift of William the Cobbler ("sutoris"). Witn.: Sir Adam Gurdun, Sir Peter de la Stane, knts., Walter Drues, Will. de Achangre, Ralph de Heghes, Henry Wileking, Henry de la Rude, Will de Burhonte, Peter le Stabler.—[166.]

Round green seal; a stag: "Crede Michi."

[*c.* 1290.] Release from Galiena the widow of William Choterel de la Rode to William de la Rode of all her right in a piece of land in la Rode, lying near that land which she had by the gift of Richard Cotherel; paying her an annual quit-rent of ½*d.* Witn.: Will. de Hokangre, Rob. Marescall de la Vyche, John de Burthone, Stephen de la Rude, Rich. Cotherel.—[368.]

Oval green seal; illegible.

[*c.* 1290—1300.] Grant from Richard Coterel to John de la Rudelonde, for the sum of 10*s.*, of a part of his land in la Rode, viz., that which lies between the highway from la Rode toward the Priory of Seleburne, on the west, and the grantor's land on the east, and extends on the north from the land of Will. le Groom to the south opposite the land of William Gilerus, and contains twenty-one perches in length and two perches in breadth; paying an annual quit-rent of 4*d.* With.: James de Nortone, Will. de Achangre, Ralph de Heghes, Robert Marescall de la Wike, Henry Wylekynge, William Steregaffe, Will. de Haveele, Roger de Bradeshate, Will. Robert.—[364.]

Oval white seal; a sprig or branch: "S' Ricardi Coterel." The quit-rent of 4*d.* is struck out and altered to 1*d.*, and the following note is written on the deed: "Scribe 1*d.* pro annuo redditu; cetera ut in carta continentur." In consequence the deed has been re-written by another, although older-looking, hand, as follows:—

Another copy of the grant, fixing the quit-rent at 1*d.* Seal lost.—[359.]

See the deed of 29th Sept., 1316, No. 361, *infra*.

[*c.* 1290—1300.] Release from James de Nortone to the Prior and Convent of Seleburne of all his right in a messuage with a curtilage and half an acre of land in Akangre, which messuage and curtilage lie near the way leading from Akhangre to Kyngesleghe on the east, and the way leading from Akhangre to the house of the late Rich. de la Hacche on the south, and the half-acre lies between the curtilage of Nich le Hore on the east and the land of Will. Martyn on the west. Witn.: John de Venuz, Rich. de Tistede, John de Theddene, John de Candevere, Peter de Eldeham, John Curcy, Henry Wylekyng.—[128.]

Small round green seal of arms; a lion ramp.: "S' [Jacobi] de Nortone." The Christian name is apparently engraved as "Cojabi."

[*c.* 1290—1300.] Short vellum roll, containing copies of the legal instruments used at the election of Prior in a monastery not exempt from episcopal jurisdiction.[1]

1. "Defuncto praelato, forma petendi licenciam eligendi."
2. "Forma licencie concesse."
3. "Forma decreti post electionem conficiendi."
4. "Forma littere presentandi electum."
5. "Modus procedendi ad electionem per formam scrutinii."—[108.]

1291, 16 June, 19 Edw. [I]; at Norham. Writ from the King to the sheriff of Southampton for an inquest "ad quod dampnum" if license be given to William, son of Robert de la Rode, to give thirty acres of land in la Rode to the Prior and Convent of Seleburne.—[186(i).]

1291, 5 July, "die Jovis pr. ante fest. Transl. S. Tho. mart.," 19 Edw. [I]. Inquest "ad quod dampnum," in pursuance of the preceding writ, by Nich. Wyard, John le Waleys, Henry Willeking, Nich. Curchy, Henry atte Rude, Rich. Grim, John de Benstede, John de Marisco, John le Coc, Will. atte Vurc, Will. de Havekle, Will. Steregaffe, Henry de Estone, John Serle, Stephen de la Rude, Elyas de Molendinis, John le Bakere, Rob. Marescall and Geoffrey Martin; who return that it will not be to the prejudice of the King or others if the license be given; that the said thirty acres are held of the Prior of Seleburne by an annual rent of one mark and suit of court twice in the year, and are worth, clear, 12*s.* annually; that the said Will. de la Rode holds besides them only one messuage with a garden and a croft containing two acres of land and worth annually 3*s.*; and that the country by the gift will not be burdened except in so far as that the said William cannot hereafter be put upon assizes, juries, or recognizances.—[186(ii).]

Three small green seals; the rest broken and lost.

[1] Printed in White's *Selborne*, 4to. 1789, pp. 434–8.

1291, 9 July, "a die S. Jo. Bapt. in XV dies," 19 Edw. fil. Hen.; at Westminster. Fine before the judges John de Metingham, Rob. de Hertfort, Elyas de Bekingham, Will. de Gyselham, and master Rob. de Thorp, by which Richard de Wytheneye and Alice his wife release to Richard the Prior of Seleburne a messuage and one carucate of land which he holds in Ropele; for which they are in return admitted to all the prayers and benefits of the said church; and this fine is levied because it was found upon inquisition in the same court that the said Prior and his predecessors were seised of the said tenements by just title and without any fraud or collusion long before the publication of the statute *De Religiosis* which is called *Cum dudum*, etc.—[341.]

1292, 4 Aug.; at Waltham. License from John [de Pontissara] Bishop of Winchester to the Prior and Convent of Seleburne to appropriate the church of Great Worldham which is in their patronage whenever it may fall vacant; (for the reasons given, and in the same terms as, in the following deed of 20 April, 1293, No. 211).—[212.]

Fragment of oval green seal, showing the lower part of the figure of the Bishop.

1293, 5 April, "in crast. S. Ambrosii," 21 Edw. [I]; at Seleburne. Grant and quit-claim from John de Venuz, son and heir of Sir John de Venuz, to the Prior and Canons of Seleburne of all his right in the advowson and patronage of the church of Estworldham, and in the land called Eggesleye and in the meadow called Hundeshammede, all which they have by the gift of his said father in the vill of Estworldham. Witn.: Sir Adam Gurdun, Sir Thomas Paynel, Sir Henry de Sottesbroke, knts., Richard de Croftune lord of Westtistede, Nich. de Thuddene, Symon de Aula, Peter de Heghes, Will. de la More, Rob. Marescall de la Wyke.—[213.]

Round black seal; a rabbit: "S'. ho (?) VVisaco."

1293, 10 April, "iiij idus Apr."; at Winchester. Resignation by Richard de Torntone, clerk, to J[ohn de Pontissara], Bishop of Winchester, of the church of Great Worldham, to which he was lately presented by the Prior and Convent of Selleburne.—[225.]

Oval red seal, the seal of the official of Winchester, broken. (As attached to No. 220(ii) of 16 April following).

1293, 16 April, "xvj kal. Maii"; at Winchester. "Memorandum," or copy, by Philip, official of the archdeaconry of Winchester, of a return, dated 22 Nov. 1256, by P. archdeacon of Winton to A. the Bishop-elect, certifying that Thomas de Wynton, rector of Great Wordlam, died on the morrow of St. Martin last (12 Nov.), that he had been presented by Sir John de Venuz, but that the Prior and Convent of Seleburne are now tho patrons by the gift of the said Venuz; that the person now presented was born in wedlock, and is not in Holy Orders ("non est in sacris ordinibus constitutus" !), and that the value of the church is commonly reckoned at 16 marks.—[220(i).]

Fragment of an oval black seal.

1293, 16 April, "die Jovis pr. p. f. SS. Tiburcii et Valeriani"; at Winton. "Memorandum," or copy, of the inquisition made in 1274 by the official of the archdeacon of Winchester into the right of patronage of the church of Wordlam (*also written* Wordlham); as also found in the copy made in that year, 13 Jan. 1274[–5], No. 74, *supra* A fuller copy of the King's writ is here given, in which the inquisition is ordered on account of a claim to the patronage being made by Walter Giffard as guardian of the lands and of the heir of John de Venuz, against the Prior and Convent of Seleburne.—[220(ii).]

Oval black seal; two SS. above, two ecclesiastics below; between, the motto: "Juste judicate," ". . . . . consistorial' Wintoniensis."

1293, 20 April, "xij cal. Maii"; at Suwerk. License from John [de Pontissara,] Bishop of Winchester, to the Prior and Convent of Seleburne, to appropriate to their own use, on account of the poverty of their endowment and the number of strangers and sick and poor persons who resort to them (—"ad domum vestram prædictam hospitum pauperum et infirmorum confluit frequenter non modica multitudo, quibus vitæ necessaria et alia karitatis et humanitatis ministrare subsidia vos oportet"—), the church of Great Worldham which is in their patronage and which is now vacant; reserving to himself the assignment of a sufficient provision for the vicar.—[211.]

Small fragment of green seal.

1293, 4 May, "in crast. Inv. S. Crucis"; at Seleburne. Mandate from P[hilip Cornwaleys,] archdeacon of Winchester, to the dean of Aultone, (in pursuance of a mandate from J. Bishop of Winchester, dated at Suthwerk, 12 kal. Maii, 1293, in which the appropriation of the church of Great Werldham to the Prior and Convent of Seleb[urne] is notified), for the giving corporal possession of the said church to the said Religious.—[208.]

Oval green seal, good impression; at the top, S. Michael; in two compartments below, two Saints; at the foot, the demi-fig. of the archdeacon praying: "S' Philippi archid'i Wintonie."

1293, 8 May, "die Ven. pr. p. f. S. Joh. quod dicitur ante Port. Lat." Certificate by Stephen, vicar of Froyle and dean of Aulton, that in pursuance of the preceding mandate (No. 208) from the archdeacon of Winchester, he has inducted brother Nicholas de la Mare, canon of the church of Seleburne and proctor for the Prior and Convent, into possession of the church of Worldham.—[217.]

Small oval green seal of the deanery of Alton; a figure kneeling before St. John the Bapt. (holding the device of the Lamb and Flag): "S' decana . . . . . weltone."

1293, 8 May, "die Ven. pr. p. f. S. Joh. quod dicitur ante Port. Lat." Certificate by Stephen, vicar of Froylle and dean of Aulton, that in pursuance of a mandate (recited) from P[hilip Cornwaleys], archdeacon of Winchester, which in its turn recites a mandate received by him from J. Bishop of Winchester, he has inducted the Prior and Convent of Seleburne into corporal possession of the church of Great Worlpham, which the said Bishop has appropriated to the Convent. —[83.]

Seal lost.

1293, 6 Sept., "viij idus Sept."; in the chapter at Winchester. Confirmation by William the Prior and the Chapter of Winchester of the preceding license from the Bishop of 20 April, 1293 (No. 211), for the appropriation of Great Worldham, which is recited at length.—[212*b*.]

Very large deeply impressed green seal; a Saint, seated, in right hand a key and in his left hand a book, a church in the background; inscription broken: "Sigillum . . . . Swith . . . ." Counter-seal: a small Roman intaglio, with one figure: ". . . . . Petr. Maria."

1297, 17 June, "die lune pr. p. Transl. S. Ricardi," 25 Edw. [I]; at Seleburne, "in pleno hundredo." Publication by John le Blund of Farendone, bailiff of the hundred of Seleborne, of a writ received from the King, dated at Clarendon 27 February, that as every free man can do suit at the hundreds by attorney, the bailiffs of the hundred shall allow the Prior of Seleburne to appear by attorney whenever he wishes. Witn. to seal with the sheriff: James de Nortone, Henry de Estone, Robert Marescall de la Wyk, Stephen de la Rude, Will. Attebreche.—[4.]

Five small green seals: (1) broken, an animal with the jaws of a crocodile and the hind-legs and tail of a lion: "Pr . . . . . -lecetece" (*lege, tege ?*); (2) the Lamb and Flag: "Ecce Agnus Dei"; (3) oval, the Lamb and Flag: "S' Hugonis Ba . . ."; (4) a stag's head: "Timete Deum"; (5) a tortoise (?), inscription illegible.

1298, 14 May, 26 Edw. [I]; at Westminster. Pardon from King Edward I to the Prior and Convent of Seleborne, in consideration of the payment of a fine of 100*s.*, of their transgression in entering upon and appropriating in the time of the late King Henry, twenty-seven acres of land, one and a half acres of meadow, ten acres of pasture, and 10*s.* 5*d.*

of annual rent, and half an acre of wood, of the serjeancy of Okhangre which is held of the King in chief, without licence from the late or present King; granting them leave now to hold the said lands in free alms. Witn.: Walter de Langton, Bishop of Cov. and Lichfield, the King's treasurer.—[124.]

Fragment of Privy Seal; green. Obverse: the King on horseback (the horse trotting, not, as on the Great Seal, galloping); reverse: the shield of the royal arms, the three leopards.

1298, at Easter, 26 Edw. [I]. Memorandum of the grant of pardon as contained in the preceding writ (No. 124), adding that the King by writ of Privy Seal "mandavit eisdem quod de summa finis gratiosi existant pro paupere statu domus suæ"; and that the survey of the lands and tenements referred to remains among the inquisitions returned to the Exchequer at Easter in this year.—[167.]

Easter Day fell on 6 April in 26 Edw. I.

[*c.* 1300.] Release for James de Nortone to the Prior and Convent of Seleburne of all his right to drive cattle, cars, and carts, or to ride, on any road in le Estfelde in Seleburne. Witn.: Sir John de Tycheburne, Sir Rob. de Popham, knts., John de Dandeure, Will. de Batesford, Henry Wyard, Will. Purchaz, John ate Halle, Will. Staunford.—[102.]

Round red seal of arms; a lion rampant: "S' Jacobi de Norton."

1301, 16 May, "die Martis pr. p. f. Asscen. (*sic*) Dom.," 29 Edw. [I]; at Halkangre. Confirmation and recital by Thomas Paynel of a charter by which James de Halkangre granted for the sum of 40*s.* to Will. le Fughel of Seleborne, and Alice his wife, his garden, which the Prior of Seleborne formerly held to farm of Will. de Blakewelle, chaplain, lying "a la Hunne" near the highway leading from the Priory to Blakemere, and also his garden with a meadow adjacent, which Will. de Blakewelle, chaplain, formerly farmed of Peter de Cruce near the said way "a la Hunne"; and also a croft with an increment of three perches in width and twenty-two perches in length up to the land of Will. le Wryk on the east, and to the land of Rich. Holeway on the west, between the grantor's wood of Halkangre and the said croft which John Holeway formally farmed of him; paying annually half a pound of pepper and a pair of gloves worth one penny. Witn. to the original grant: Sir Rob. de Popham, knt., Sir Thomas Makarel, knt., John de Burhunte, Andrew his brother, Will. de Arundel, Rob. Marescall de la Wyk, Peter the baker of Seleborne, Hugh the baker of the same, Richard, chaplain of Seleborne. Witn. to the confirmation: Sir Adam Gordon, knt., Sir John de Popham, knt., James de Northone, Rich. de Systede (*sic*), John de Venuz, Rich. de Westkote, Nich. de la Floude, Peter de

Heghe, Philip de Heyforde, Will. le Balun, Stephen de la Rude, Henry Wylekyng.—[56.]

Seal lost.

1302, 4 Aug., "ii non. Aug."; at Wolvese. Grant from John, Bishop of Winchester, to the Prior and Convent of Seleburne of the appropriation of the vicarage of Great Worldham to the Priory, on the cession or death of Rich. de la Barre, the existing vicar, the endowment being too small for the vicarage, which is hereafter to be served by one of the Canons; reciting the previous grant by the same Bishop dated at Suthwerk 12 cal. Maii 1293 (No. 211, *supra*), of the appropriation of the rectory at the petition of the Convent, on account of the smallness of their means, which were insufficient for the relief of the multitude of poor and sick persons which resorted to them.—[27.]

Fragment of oval green episcopal seal, with the lower part of the Bishop's figure . ". . . . . intonien E."

1305, 2 Feb., 33 Edw. I; at Walsingham. Writ from the King to the sheriff of Southampton to enquire "ad quod dampnum," if he should grant license to the Prior and Canons of Seleburne to hold twenty acres of land in Est Worldham with the advowson of the church, which they acquired from John de Venuz, (who held, as it is said, of the King *in capite*), long before the passing of the Statute of Mortmain.—[93(i).]

Endorsed, "Cepi diligenter inquisitionem, quam quidem inquisitionem vobis mitto huic bene consutam, sub sigillo meo et sigillis eorum per quorum sacramentum facta fuit, etc."

1305, 24 Feb., "die Merc. in f. S. Mathie apost.," 33 Edw. I; at Est Worldham. Return (sewn to the preceding writ) by Thomas de Warebeltone, sheriff of Southampton, of the Inquisition made in pursuance of the said writ by John de Popham, John de Basinges, John de Theddene ("þeddene"), Rich. de Tystede, Henry de Estone, Will. de Rethercfeld ("Reþerefeld"), John Kernet, John de Corssaghe, Will. de Zabyntone, Hen. Wylekyng, James de Nortone, and Davyd de la Bere; who find that the proposed license will not be to the damage of the King or any one else; that the King receives from the present John de Venuz 100*s.* annually for the lands and tenements alienated by John his father; that the said twenty acres are worth 5*s.* a year, each acre being worth 3*d.*; that the said church is worth 8 marks yearly; and that the said Prior and Convent obtained them, in free alms, from John de Venuz, the father of the John that now is, twenty-nine years before the passing of the Statute of Mortmain.—[93(ii).]

No trace of the seals remains, but a strip appears to have been cut off from the foot of the return.

1305, 14 March, 33 Edw. [I]; at Westminster. Confirmation by the King to the Prior and Convent of Seleburne, in virtue of the preceding inquisition of 24 Feb., of their possession of the twenty acres of land in Est Worldham and of the advowson of the church.—[300.]

Good impression of great seal, in green wax; inscription slightly broken.

1305, 27 June, "die domin. pr. p. f. Nat. B. Jo. Bapt.," 33 Edw. fil. Hen.; at Seleburne. Release from Agnes, widow of Sir Adam Gurdon, to the lady Joan Achard, daughter and heir of Sir Adam Gurdon, of all her right by reason of dowry in his lands and tenements. Witn.: Sir Will. Paynel, Sir Thomas Paynel, Sir John de Poppham, knts., James de Northone, John de Venuz, Richard de Tistede, John de Westcote, Henry de Estone.—[10.]

Oval dark green seal of arms; three fleurs-de-lis, crest (?) apparently three branches of a tree, " S' Agnete (*sic*) Gvrdovn."

[*c.* 1305-10.] (*Not dated*). Grant from Joan Achard, daughter and heir of Sir Adam Gurdon, knt., to Sir Thomas Paynel, knt., of five acres of land in Seleburne, of which one lies between the land of the Prior of Seleburne and that of Hugh Gervays, one between the land of the said Prior and that of Walter son of Hugh, one between the land of Stephen Unfray and that of Will. Pikyel and that acre is called Bulsebuks, and two in Little Whatecombe, between the land of the Prior on either side, the west ends abutting on the boundaries of the land of Fardone; paying annually to the chief lords the accustomed rent, and to herself one pair of gloves worth 2*d.* Witn.: Sir James de Nortone, knt., Rich. de Tistede, Henry de Estone, Nich. Wyard, Hen. Wylekyng, John de Molyns.—[303.]

Seal lost.

1306, 16 Nov., 34 Edw. [I]; at Lanrecost. Remission by the King to Joan, daughter and heiress of Adam Gurdun, deceased, in consideration of the payment of a fine of 40 marks, of the service of half a knight's fee in Tystede and Seleburne which she ought to have done in the army of Scotland in this 34th year and did not do, and all other arrears of that said service to this day.—[253.]

No seal attached.

1306, 18 Nov., "in oct. S. Martini," 35 Edw. fil. Hen., recorded in court 1308, 29 April, "a die Pasch. in xv dies," 1 Edw. fil. Edw. Fine before the Judges at Westminster (Ralph de Hengham, Will. de Bereford, Peter Malorre, Will. Howard, Lambert de Trikingham and Hervic de Stantone, in both years the same) by which William le

Turnur and Alice his wife convey to William, Prior of Seleburn, and his church, for the sum of £20, one messuage and twenty-four acres of land in la Rode.—[203.]

The thirty-fifth, and last, year of Edw. I began on 20 Nov. 1306, and ended 7 July 1307; there consequently appears to be some mistake in the first date.

1307, 22 Jan., 35 Edw. [I]; at Lanrecost. License from the King to William le Turnur and Alice his wife (in consideration of a fine made with the King by the Prior of Seleburne in Chancery) to give to the said Prior and Convent one messuage and twenty-four acres of land in la Rode.—[126.]

Very fine impression of the great seal, perfect, in green wax, attached by red and green silk strings. Obv.: the King on a throne, of which the back and sides are of pinnacle-and-tabernacle-work, a dog on either side on its hind-legs; the King holding in his right hand the sceptre with the Dove, in his left the orb: "Edwardus Dei gratia Rex Anglie Domnus Hybernie, Dux Aqvitanie." Rev.: the King in full armour, with sword drawn, on horseback (the leopards on the *shield* passant to the left, on the *horse-cloth* to the right); inscription the same.

Endorsed with memorandum of the admission of the fine before the judges of K. B. in the same year, rot. 249.

1307, 1 May, "in f. apostt. Phil. and Jac.," 35 Edw. [I]. Indenture by which William le Turnur de la Rode and Alice his wife grant to the Prior and Convent of Selebourne a messuage with all the land which they have in la Rode, after the death of the said Alice, but so that the said Will. and Alice shall hold it during her life by fine to be levied in the King's Court and by seisin from the Prior and Convent, excepting a garden at Koldewelle which the Prior and Convent shall retain for their own use; and the said Prior and Convent grant in return to the said Will. and Alice for their life the livery of one canon, viz., one white loaf weighing 50*s*. and one gallon of beer or cider of the better drink of the Convent, with a sufficient mansion to live in from the said messuage and a garden adjacent. Witn.: Sir Thomas Paynel, Sir James de Nortune, knts., John de Venoyz, John de Westkote, Richard de Tistede, Peter de Werldham, Peter de Heges, Henry Wilkynge.—[196.]

Two green seals: (1) oval, the Lamb and Flag: "Ecce Agnus Dei"; (2) round, broken; a head: "Crede . . . . ."

1307, 7 July, "die Ven. in f. transl. S. Tho. mart. anno r. r. Edw. fil. Hen 35" (the last day of the reign of Edw. I); at la Rode. Grant from William le Turnur de la Rode and Alice his wife to the Prior and Convent of Seleburne, for 100*s*., of all the goods and chattels which they have in all their tenements in la Rode, of which tenements the said Prior and Canons are this day put in seisin by the King's precept in accordance with a fine between the parties. Witn.: Rich. de Byflet, Under-sheriff of Southampt., John Kernet, John de Chiltele, Will. de Retherfeld, Nich. Wyhard, Sampson de Gretham, John de Candevere.—[67.]

Small round green seal, broken.

1308, 29 Jan., "die lune pr. p. f. Conv. S. Pauli," 1 Edw. fil. Edw. Grant from Joan Achard to the Prior and Convent of Seleburne of all the lands and tenements which she held of them in Seleburne and which Sir Adam Gurdun, her father, had by the gift of Thomas Makerel, together with the reversion of a house and curtilage which William le Taylur holds for the term of his life in the same village, with all liberties and free customs; in consideration of the receipt of £200. Witn.: Sir Thomas Paynel, Sir James de Nortune, knts., John de Venuz, Richard de Tistede, Peter de Werldham, John Kernet, Will. de Rutherfelde, John de Candevere, Henry de Estone, John de Chiltely.—[11.]

Oval red seal, same as that attached to No. 1, under date 2 June, 1319, *q.v.*; fine impression.

Another copy of the same grant, with the same seal, green. ("Rutherfelde" is spelt "Retherfelde.")—[35.]

1308, 30 Jan., 1 Edw. fil. Edw.; at Selebourne. Grant (in French) from Joan Achard to the Prior and Convent of Selebourne of all her lands and tenements in Selebourne which were the late Makerel's, in pure alms, upon condition that within forty days after seisin is given they re-enfeoff her in the same for the term of her life; for which they are bound in a bond to Richard de Tisted for 500 marks.—[28.]

Oval red seal, the same as that attached to deed No. 1, A.D. 1319, *q.v.*; inscription broken.

1308, 31 Jan., "die Merc. pr. p. f. Conv. S. Pauli," 1 Edw. fil. Edw.; at Seleburne. Grant from Joan Achard, daughter and heiress of Sir Adam Gurdoun to the Prior and Convent of Seleburne, for the sum of £294, of all the goods and chattels in the tenements which they have by her gift in Seleburne. No witnesses.—[38.]

Oval green seal, the same as that attached to No. 1, in 1319, *q.v.*

1308, 18 Feb., "die domin. pr. ante f. Cath. S. Petri," 1 Edw. fil. Edw. Indenture by which the Prior and Convent of Seleburne grant to the lady Joan Achard, daughter and heiress of Sir Adam Gurdun, a messuage, one carucate of land, 10*s*. of rent, and ten acres of wood in Seleburne, which she had acknowledged to be theirs before the Judges of the King's Bench, and also conveyed by deed of feoffment, to hold for the term of her life without impeachment of waste, provided she do not remove or destroy any of the buildings; granting also firewood from the woods, with timber for repairs, with husbote and heybote.—[33.]

Oval green seal of Joan Achard; the same as that attached to No. 1, in June, 1319, *q.v.*

Another indenture (not the counter-part) of the same grant in another hand. Same seal.—[34.]

1308, 29 Apr., "a die Pasch. in xv dies," 1 Edw. fil. Edw. Fine (indenture tripartite) before Ralph de Hengham, Will. de Bereford, Will. Howard, Peter Malorre, Lambert de Trikingham, and Hervic de Stanton, the King's Justices, at Westminster, by which Joan, formerly the wife of Robert Achard, conveys to William, the Prior, and the Convent of the church of B. Mary of Seleburne, for the sum of 100 marks, one messuage, one carucate of land, ten acres of wood, and 10*s.* of annual rent, in Seleburne.—[43.]

[59.] One of the counter-parts.

1311, 20 Aug., 5 Edw. [II]; at London. Licence from the King to Thomas Paynel, in consideration of the payment by the Prior of Seleburne of a fine of 6*s.* 8*d.*, to give to the said Prior and Convent one acre of land in Akhangre, which he holds of the King in chief, in exchange for one acre in the same village which the said Prior and Convent also hold of the King in chief.—[125.]

Great seal, same as that attached to No. 116, of 4 Dec., 1312; perfect.

1311, 1 Sept., "die Merc. in f. S. Egidii abbatis," 5 Edw. fil. Edw. Indenture by which Sir Thomas Paynel, knt., grants to the Prior and Convent of Seleburne, two pieces of land in Okangre, of which Will. atte Barre held one of the said Sir Thomas in villenage, lying between Mauduteswode on one side and the land of the said Prior and Convent called la Watecrofte on the other, and William Toucy held the other of the said Sir Thomas, lying near the meadow of the said Prior and Convent at Oxeney on one side and the bank called Oldebroke on the other; in exchange for a croft in Okangre binorthbroke, lying between the land of the said Prior and Convent which John Oseburn held on one side, and the land of Will. atte Broke on the other. Witn.: Sir Will. Paynel, Sir John de Popham, Sir James de Nortone, knts., John de Westcote, John de Venuz, Rich. de Westcote, Peter de Worldham, Rich. Godefray, John Fruman.—[135.]

Round red seal, beautiful impression; a knight in full armour, on horseback, with armorial bearings (apparently two bars between six martlets) on shield and caparisons: "Sigill' Thome Paynel."

1312, 5 Oct., "in vig. S. Fidis virg.," 6 Edw. fil. Edw.; at la Rode in Seleburne. Grant from Richard Bakun of Holtham to John Bertin of Blakemere, for the sum of 4 marks, of all his messuage in la Rode in the parish of Seleburne between the croft which William Robert formerly held on the east and the highway to the Priory of Seleburne on the west and extending from the tenement of Rich. le Muleward on the south to the tenement of Rich. Burdun on the north. Witn.: Sir Thomas Paynel, Sir James de Nortone, knts., Peter de Heghes, John Chiltely, Will. de Haveely, Will. le Turnur, Will. de Ovinge, Rich. le Meleward.—[363.]

Small round green seal; inscription of one or two words, illegible.

1312, 4 Dec., 6 Edw. [II]; at Wyndesore. Licence from the King to Thomas Paynel, in consideration of a fine of 20*s.* paid by him, to grant to the Prior and Convent of Seleburne the fifteen acres of land and 2*s.* of annual rent in Akhangre which he holds of the King in chief, in exchange for fifteen acres which they hold of the King in the same village.—[116.]

Great seal, brown, attached by red and green silk strings; rubbed, and the inscription broken. Rev.: the King in full armour with sword drawn, on horseback, the three leopards (passant to the right) on the horse-cloth: "Edwardus Dei gracia Rex Anglic Dñs H . . . . nie, Dux Aquitanie." Obv.: the King on a throne, with back and sides of pinnacles and tabernacle-work, and the castle on each side (which distinguishes the seal of Edward II from that of his father), together with the dog.

1312, 29 Dec., "die Ven. in f. S. Tho. mart., 6 Edw. fil. Edw.; at Lydeschete. Grant from Thomas Paynel, in pursuance of the preceding license from the King of 4 Dec., to the Prior and Convent of Seleborne of fifteen acres of land in Akhangre, lying between the land of the Prior and Convent called la Broke and the way leading from the Cross of la Rode which is called Piris Crouch to Akhangre, abutting at one end on the land of the grantor and on the other on that of the Prior and Convent, of Peter the Cobbler, and Will. le Turnour; and of 15*d.* of annual rent issuing from a messuage, a garden and two crofts, which Peter the Cobbler formerly held within the grantor's manor of Akhangre; in exchange for fifteen acres in the same village. Witn.: Sir Will. Paynel, Sir James de Nortone, Sir John de Popham, Sir Nicholas Gentyl, knts., John de Venuz, John de Westkote, Rich. de Westkote, Richard de Tystede, Peter de Wordlham (*sic*), Peter de Hezes, John Courcy.—[152.]

Round brown seal, good impression, same as that attached to No. 135, of 1 Sept., 1311.

1312, 29 Dec., "die Ven. in f. S. Tho. apost." (*lege* mart.), 6 Edw. fil. Edw.; at Lydeschate. Power of attorney from Thomas Paynel, knt., to

Henry Cousin to give seisin to the Prior and Convent of Selebourne of fifteen acres of land and 15*d.* of annual rent in Achangre, in exchange for other fifteen acres of land.—[165.]

Small fragment of seal.

[*c.* 1312.] (*Date omitted*). Release from Thomas Paynel, knt., to the Prior and Convent of Seleburne in all his right in a certain way which he used to have beyond certain land in la Broke, which they have by his gift in exchange. Witn.: James de Nortone, John Popham, knts., John de Venuz, John de Westkote, Richard de Westcote, John de Candevere, Peter de Hezes, Peter de Worldham, Roger de Bradeschate, John Curcy, John Fruman.—[328.]

Seal lost.

1316, 20 Sept., "xii kal. Oct."; at "Lamht̄." (Lambeth). Certificate by Walter (Reynolds) Archbishop of Canterbury, that having cited the Prior and Convent of Selebourne before him, during the vacancy of the see of Winchester, to shew their right to the appropriation of the church of Great Worldham, they have exhibited instruments establishing that right.—[219.]

Fragment of the archiepiscopal seal, oval, green, exhibiting a knight in the act of murdering Becket before the altar.

1316, 29 Sept., "in f. S. Mich.," 10 Edw. fil. Edw.; at Aultone. Grant from John de la Rudelonde, bailiff of the Prior of Selebourne, to Robert atte Lydgate of the parish of Esbourne, for a certain sum of money, of 12*d.* of annual rent from a piece of ground which the said John demised to Galiana the wife of Will. de Ovynge; viz., that which lies in la Rode, between the highway leading from la Rode to the Priory of Selebourne on the west, and the grantor's land on the east, and extends in length from the land of Will. le Grom on the south (to) opposite the land of Will. Gylerous. Witn.: Will. Elot, John Foghelare, Will. de la Fermerye, Will. Horn, Rich. de la Lyde, Will. atte Broke, Thos. atte Broke.—[361.]

Small black seal; a cat (?) and two birds; above, "Sohovis" (?) or some strange word like this.

1317, 4 Oct., "die Martis pr. p. f. S. Mich.," 11 Edw. fil. Edw.; at la Rode. Grant from John Bertyn of Blakemere to John de Tychburne, knt., for the sum of 40*s.* of all his messuage in la Rode in the parish of Seleburne, situate between the croft which Will. Robert formerly held on the east, and the highway to the Priory of Selcburne on the west, and extends from the tenement of Rich. le Muleward on the south to that of Rich. Burdon on the north. Witn.: Sir James de Nortone and Sir Rich. de Burhonte, knts., Peter de Heghes, John de Chiltelye, Roger de Bradeshete, Robert de Tystede, Will. de Rutherefeld.—[360.]

Round red seal; a star: "S' Johannis Blakemere."

1318, 12 Nov., "die domin. in crast. S. Mart.," 12 Edw. fil. Edw.; at Selebourne. Lease from William, the Prior, and Convent of Selebourne, to William le Turnur of a messuage with a garden adjacent in la Wyk, which Alice Cappe held of them; to hold for the term of his life, rendering annually one red rose. Witn.: Sir James de Nortone, John de Candovere, John de Thetdone, John de Aultone, Adam Wylekyng, Will. de Romesy, William Marescall de la Wyke.—[75.]

Small green seal; a squirrel.

1319, 2 June, "die sab. pr. p. f. S. Petronille virg.," 12 Edw. fil. Edw.; at Seleburn. Grant from Joan Gurdun, daughter and heiress of Sir Adam Gurdun, knt., to her brother John Bastard and Gunnora Brutun his wife of a messuage with two gardens adjacent which were Angnes's, the daughter of the smith, in Seleburne, of which one garden lies above Ywhulle; and also one acre of arable land which was formerly Arnulph's, the son of Hugh, in the same vill, in the field called Pithlake, between the land of Peter the Cobbler and that of Henry Boyngeslie; paying an annual quit-rent of 1*d.* to the chief lords. Witn.: Sir James de Norton, knt., Henry de Estone, Will. de Rutherfeld, Peter de Heghe, John de la Hacche.—[1.]

Round pink seal, curious; a full length female figure, holding in her right hand a shield with three (griffins? *or* lions rampant?), and in her left a shield with a bend dancettée; on either side of her a griffin rampant: "Sigillum Joanne Achard."

1320[–1], 2 Feb., "4 non. Feb."; at Winchester. Acknowledgment by the Prior and Convent of St. Swithin, Winchester, sub-collectors in the archdeaconry of Winchester of the tenth granted by the Pope for one year to the King of England for the defence of his kingdom, of the receipt from the Prior of Selebourne of 9*s.* 9¾*d.* for the moiety of all his temporal goods; and for the moiety of the tenth of his spiritual goods, viz., the church of Selebourne with its chapel, the church of Great Worlham, the church of Tistede, and the church of Basinge and Basingestoke with the chapel, £4. 4*s.*, for the second term.—[389.]

Small fragment of red seal.

1322, 19 July, "die lune pr. ante f. S. Margarete virg." Acknowledgment by the Prior of the cathedral church of St. Swythin, Winchester, collector in the archdeaconry of Winchester for the King of 5*d.*

out of each mark of all ecclesiastical goods granted by the prelates and clergy of the province of Canterbury in the Parliament held at York, of the receipt from the Prior of Selebourne of 52*s.* 6*d.* for his spiritual goods and 6*s.* 1½*d.* for his temporal goods.—[94.]

Seal lost.

1323, 11 May, "v^{to} idus Maii"; at Winchester. Acknowledgment by the Prior and Convent of St. Swithin, Winchester, sub-collectors in the archdeaconry of Winchester of the two-years' tenth granted by Pope John XXII to King Edward for the defence of his kingdom, of the receipt from the Prior and Convent of Selebourne of £4. 4*s.*, for the ecclesiastical goods of the churches of Basingges with the chapel, Seleburne, Westtystede and Great Worldham, and of 9*s.* 9¾*d.* for their temporal goods, viz., Bromdene, Schete, Seleburne, Theddene, and rents in Winchester.—[96.]

Fragment of small red seal; obv.: two heads; rev.: a head, with sun and moon; inscription broken and indistinct.

1326, 29 Sept., "in f. S. Mich. archang."; at Selebourne. Acknowledgment by Walter de Bartone and Richard de Aultone, executors of the will of master Philip de Bartone, archdeacon of Surrey, deceased, that they have received from Walter, Prior of Seleburne, all the debts for which the said Prior and Convent were bound to the said deceased. —[358.]

Seals lost.

1327, 14 March, "prid. id. Marcii"; at Motesfunte. Acknowledgment by Richard de Aultone, one of the executors of master Philip de Barton, formerly archdeacon of Surrey, of the receipt of one mark from the Prior and Convent of Seleburne, in part payment of 36 marks for which they were bound to him and his co-executor, master Walter de Barton, by their recognizance made in the Exchequer.—[319.]

Fragment of a small green seal, with Arabic inscription: see No. 320, 2 Feb. 1339.

1328, 17 Oct., "16 kal. Nov."; at Hyde. Acknowledgment by the Abbot and Convent of Hyde, sub-collectors in the archdeaconry of Winchester of the clergy's tenth granted at Leycester to the King in aid of some weighty matters in many ways pressing on him for the defence of his kingdom, of the receipt from the Prior and Convent of Seleburne (of the same sums as those mentioned in No. 389 of 2 Feb. 1320–1, *supra*).—[391.]

Seal lost.

1329, 19 Oct., "in crast. S. Lucæ Ewang."; at Winchester. Acknowledgment by master Rich. de Barton of the receipt of half a mark from Sir Walter, Prior of Selebourne, in further payment of the debt mentioned in the preceding deed (No. 319) of 14 March, 1327.—[321.]

1336, 26 May, 10 Edw. III; at Wodestok. "Inspeximus" and confirmation by Edw. III of the charter of Hen. III of 10 April, 1234. Witn.: John, Archbishop of Canterbury, chancellor, H., Bishop of Lincoln, treasurer, R., Bishop of Durham, John, Earl of Cornwall "filio nostro carissimo," Will. de Montacute, Rob. de Ufford, steward of the household. "Ex. per Eliam de Gryme et Tho. de Capenhirste."—[110.]

Very fine impression of great seal in green wax; attached by pink and green silk strings, in yellow silk case.

1337, 3 Nov., 11 Edw. III; in the castle of Winchester. Acknowledgment by John de Scures, sheriff of Southampton, of the receipt of two marks from the Prior of Selebourne, for the use of master Walter Bartone and master Rich. de Aultone, out of a debt of 36 marks. upon a writ from the Exchequer.—[322.]

Seal lost. See above, 1327 and 1329.

1338, 6 Feb., 12 Edw. III; in the castle of Winchester. Similar acknowledgment by the same of the further receipt of 60*s*. levied on the goods and chattels of the Prior in pursuance of another writ from the Exchequer.—[317.]

Small fragment of seal.

1338, 31 Oct., "ij kal. Nov."; at Schaldeford. Return from the Dean of Guildford to Adam, Bishop of Winchester, reporting that in obedience to a writ from him (which is recited in full) dated at Merwell, ij id . . . . (*torn*), he has solemnly denounced in the churches of his deanery those who have carried off an ox from the manor of the Prior and Convent of Selebourne at Schonlonde as having incurred the greater excommunication, and that having found that Ralph (?) Poynaunt was the guilty person, he has cited him to appear before the Bishop's Commissary at Winchester, as ordered, and has also cited Rob. de Homlye, Will. Marlyn, and John de Lupere.—[14.]

Small oval green seal; an eagle: "S' Decanatus de Gildeford."

1338, 1 Nov., "in f. Omn. SS.," 12 Edw. III; at Selebourne. Acknowledgment by Walter de Bartone and Richard de Bartone, clerks, of the further receipt of 5 marks, out of 16 now remaining due. (*See preceding deeds of* 3 Nov., 1337, and 6 Feb., 1338, Nos. 322, 317.) —[318.]

Seals lost.

1339, 2 Feb., "in f. Purif. B.V.," 13 Edw. III; at Selebourne. Similar acknowledgment by the same of the further receipt of 5 marks.—[320.]

Two red seals, round: (1) a lion passant, finely engraved, inscription lost; (2) an Arabic inscription (partly broken) of three or four words, including the name of Mahomet, with an added outer inscription broken and illegible.

1338[–9], 21 Jan., 12 Edw. III; at Winchester. Indenture of an agreement between Walter the Prior and the Convent of Selebourne and Roger de Tyccheboume, son and heir of Sir John de Tyccheboume, knt., deceased, whereby the said Prior and Convent, in consideration of the grant to them by the said Roger of his whole tenement of la Rode, with its messuages, gardens, woods, etc., covenant to pay annually 6 marks to a priest-chaplain celebrating for the soul of the said Roger, his father John, and mother Amicia, ancestors and successors, in a chantry which he, with the consent of Adam, Bishop of Winchester, has established in the chapel of his manor of Tyccheboume, and which chaplain is to be admitted by the Bishop; and also covenant to admit from time to time one fit person, presented by the said Roger and wishing to live in a regular habit, as a canon into the Priory; and also to provide from amongst the canons one chaplain to celebrate daily in the conventual church, at the altar of St. Stephen, for the souls of the said Roger, John, and Amicia; under penalty of suspension, excommunication, and paying 40*s.* to the charities of the Bishop and 20*s.* to the aid of the Holy Land.—[291.]

Round red seal; apparently a flower in a flower-pot: "Ieo sui quer lel" (?)

1339, 22 April, "10 kal. Maii," 13 Edw. III; at Tycheboume. Release from Thomas de Pycheford, son and heir of John de Pycheford, to the Prior and Canons of Selebourne, in pure alms, of all his right in all services, etc., and in 1*d.* of annual rent, from the tenement of la Rode. Witn.: Sir Robert Daundely, sheriff of Southampton, Sir Thomas de Nortone, Sir Rob. de Popham, knts., Roger de Tycheboume, Will. de Overtone, senior, Will. de Overtone, junior, Roger Gervays, Richard le Beel, Thomas de Westcote, Will. Staunford, Stephen de Welewyle, John atte Hacche.—[194.]

Seal lost.

Another original copy of the same grant. ("Daundele"; Sir Rob. de Popham *omitted;* Roger "Gerveis," Stephen de "Welewyk"; "Roger de Thyddene" *added.*) Small round wax seal; the Lamb and Flag; inscription illegible.—[371.]

1339, 3 May, "die lune pr. p. f. apostt. Phil. et Jac."; 13 Edw. III; at Waltham. Grant from Roger de Tyccheboume, son and heir of Sir

John de Tycchebourne, knt., to the Prior and Convent of Selebourne, in pure alms, of all his tenement of la Rode, with all the rents and services of both freemen and serfs. Witn.: Sir John de Scures, Sir John de Roches, Sir Thomas de Coudray, Sir Rob. de Popham, Sir Thos. de Nortone, knts., Walter Wodelok, Nicholas atte Bere, William de Overtone, William de Overtone, junior, Will. Wodelok, Will. de Staunford, Valentine Bekk, John de Rutherfeld, Rich. le Beel.—[201.]

Small round red seal; a flower-pot (?); inscription illegible.

Another original copy of the same grant. (Valentine "Beck.") Fragment of seal.—[142.]

1350, 27 June, "die lune pr. p. f. S. Jo. Bapt.," 24 Edw. III; at La Rode. Grant from Joan, who was the wife of William ate Yerd of Bradeshite, to John le Hayward de la Rode, and Agnes his wife, of a messuage with a garden adjacent in la Rode near the priory of Selebourne, lying between le Park and the land of Nicholas Swel, and extending from the highway on the west to the meadow of . . . . . Pokewalle, and containing in the whole one "helvam." Witn.: John Purchas, Symon de Hezes, John de Hunte, Will. Holewey, John Smyth, Will. Tybaud, John Smoulyn, clerk.—[198.]

Round green seal; a spread eagle; inscription indistinct.

1352, 5 June, "nonas Junii"; at Winchester. Agreement (ratified by the official of Winchester) between Edmund ("Edūs") the Prior and Convent of Seleborne, as impropriators of the parish church of Seleborne with the chapels of Okhangre and Blakemere, and Sir Adam Seyncler, the perpetual vicar of the said church, for the increase of his insufficient stipend, in order to avoid a law-suit. On account of the present pestilence and the scarcity of the times, he is to receive annually for the term of his life a rent of 2*s.* 6*d.* from the tenement of the late John Bounde in Seleborne; with all the tithes of apples, pears and nuts, and all other fruit from the gardens and woods within the parish, excepting the tithe of apples from the garden of the Convent; the tithe of wool and of the mills, excepting those of the Convent; and the tithe of all hay, excepting the hay of the court ("de Cur'") of Gordon, Nortone, and Okhangre, and that of the demesne lands of the Convent originally assigned for the foundation of the conventual church. He shall have all this in augmentation of the vicarial portion for his life, and in lieu of all the small tithes from the lands and tenements of Gordon, Rode, and Tournours.—[36.]

Seal of the official of Winchester; oval, green; two saints; below, the motto "Juste judicate"; then, two bishops beneath a double-arched canopy: "Sig' Consistorii Wintonien." Another seal lost.

1352, 5 June, "nonas Junii"; at Winchester. Confirmation by Roger de Fulford, official of Winchester, of a similar agreement to the preceding (No. 36), between the Priory of Seleborne (by their proctor, Sir Ralph Tristram, rector of Gretham) and Sir Adam Seyncler, for the permanent endowment of the vicarage of Seleborne in future, as follows :—

1. The vicar shall have the house on the west side of the church, in which he at present lives, with the garden and curtilage, and a plot of ground contiguous with buildings on it, which was part of the land of the late Walter le Hunte.

2. A tenement called Prestishous, at Okhangre, with a garden, curtilage, and lands called Prestislondes, and the grass of the churchyard.

3. Four cartloads of wood annually from the nearest wood called Priouriswode.

4. One cartload of hay from the tithe-hay at Nortone.

5. One cartload of straw at the court-yard of Gordon; each of these cartloads to be such as three horses can draw.

6. Tithe of agistments of all the animals agisted in the parish and chapelries.

7. Tithe of all lands under spade-cultivation.

8. All the tithes, great and small, from the tenements and lands of the Prior and Convent which were formerly Sir Adam Gordon's, knt., Cur' de Rode, and Alice Roberd's.

9. All the tithes from all the lands and tithable things of the Prior and Convent, within the parish of Seleburne, the tithe of corn, hay, apples, wool, and those from the demesne lands of the Priory at its first foundation, alone excepted.

10. All the tithes within Okhangre and Blakemere, excepting corn and hay.

11. All the oblations at the church and chapels in legacies and requests ("requestis").

12. The moiety of all the oblations at the chapel of Waddone.

13. The moiety of all oblations hereafter or newly arising in the parish, beyond those at the church and chapels of Okhangre and Blakemere which the vicar shall have entire.

14. The portions of accustomed small tithes coming from the churches or chapels of Hertley and Imbeshete.

The vicar shall find a chaplain to celebrate in the chapels of Okhangre and Blakemere. The Prior and Convent to bear all burdens, ordinary and extraordinary. Witn.: John de Ware, rector of Cranlegh, master Robert de Lemyntone, advocate of the Consistory (? "advocato const.") of Winchester, masters Roger Bryan and Will. de Peveseye, notaries public. Attested by Roger Bryan.—[372.]

Seal of the official, as with the preceding deed; blank fragment of another seal.

1357, 24 April, "apud Hockeday," 31 Edw. III; in the Court held at Seleborne. Lease from Edmund the Prior, and the Convent of Seleborne, to John Gurdon of two crofts containing thirteen acres in Westtystede, called Merefeld, lying separately between the lands of the said John on the north and west, and the land of John Goudman on the east, and the land of Thomas Abraham on the south, together with a way at the south end of the land of John Goudman; to hold for the lives of himself, his wife Joan, and his daughters Eufemia and Agnes successively, paying an annual rent of 8*s*. Witn.: Rich. le Muleward, Thos. Artour, John le Smyth, John le Rycher, Thos. de Westcote, Stephen Welewyk, Peter Fyges, Rich. de Tychebourne, Thomas Abraham.—[259]

Small fragment, white, of the Priory seal.

1357, 25 Sept., "die lune pr. ante f. S. Mich.," 31 Edw. III; at Seleborne. Assignment by Edmund the Prior and Convent of Seleborne to William Tribon for the term of his life of an annual rent of 8*s*. payable to the said Prior and Convent by John Gurdon, Joan his wife, and Femmota (*sic*) and Agnes his daughters, for the term of their lives, for the lands held by them in Westtistede. Witn.: Rich. de Tycheborne, John atte Mede, Thomas Abraham, Rich. Germayn, Rich. le Muleward, John le Smyth, Will. le Bakere.—[240.]

Seals lost.

1358, 2 Nov.; at London. Acknowledgment by Hugh Pelegrin, Treasurer of Lichfield, nuncio of the Apost. see in England, of the receipt from the Prior of Seleburn of 28*s*. due for his procurations for the sixth, seventh, eighth, and ninth years of his stay as nuncio in England; for which he absolves him from all the sentences passed upon his proctor, master John Brown, on account of the delay.—[390.]

Fragment of red seal.

1375, 4 May. Similar acknowledgment by John de Cariloco, Prior of Lewes, commissary of John de Cabrespino, canon of Narbonne, the Papal collector. Small fragment of red seal.—[395(i)].

1362, 3 May, "die Martis in f. Invent. S. Crucis," 36 Edw. III; at Selebourne. Grant from John Grygge of Chiltecumbe to Sir Adam Seyncler of a cottage with a garden in le Rode called Goldhoppe, near the priory in the hundred of Selebourne; rendering annually one wax candle of one pound in weight, or 12*d*., at the feast of SS. Peter and Paul, to burn in the priory of Selebourne before the image of the said

Apostles. Witn.: Sir Ralph de Nortone, knt., Adam atte Burghe, John Smyht, Richard Muleward, Henry Mahu, Will. Bakere, Thos. Richer.—[191.]

Small round brown seal; very indistinct; a star, etc.

1362, 6 . . . .; at Farnham. Release granted by the Bishop of Winchester to the Prior and Convent of Selborne from a payment of £10 to which they were bound *ratione subsidii.*—[313.]

Fragment of seal, green.
(Partly illegible through damp, and the date torn.)

1364, 25 July, "die Jovis in f. S. Jacobi," 38 Edw. III; at West-tistede. Grant (indented) from Alice, widow of Richard de Tycheborne, lady of Westtystede, to Nicholas the Prior and Convent of Seleborne of a way beyond her "seperale" called le Brok in Westtystede, containing in length from the highway leading to Prenet to the field called Trandledefeld, and in width . . . . perches, to drive cattle, etc., but not to pasture there; paying to her and to her son Richard annually during their lives 12*d.*, and to their heirs after their death one clove. Witn.: Roger Gervays, Thomas Canteshangre, Walter Fyrce, John de Zabynton, Will. le Clerk, John Gurdun.—[242.]

Round dark seal; apparently a lion seizing an eagle; inscription very indistinct.

1366, 12 March, "in f. S. Greg. pape.," 40 Edw. III. Lease from Nicholas the Prior and the Convent of Seleburne, to John Denemerch, his wife Rose, and their daughter Joan, for the term of their lives, of the three crofts of land with their meadow below the "coft" of West Wordlam which they have by the gift of Peter Dansy and Alan Musard, and also three and a half acres below the same in the field called Stabler, which Walter Goghe formerly held; together with heybote and hosebote in the wood of the said Prior and Convent lying between "le lyck" (?) of the lady Agnes Markaunte and that of John Pouleyn, to build upon the said land; paying to the said Prior and Convent 7*s.* annually, with a heriot and relief and suit of court at the two "laydays" of the court of Seleburne. Witn.: Sir Ralph Norton, knt., Sir Adam, vicar of Seleburne, Robert Dogettes, Thomas Messeger, John Poleyn of West-wordlam, Walter Sexten.—[221.]

Round white seal, very indistinct.

1366, 5 Aug., "die Merc. pr. ante f. S. Laur. mart.," 45 Edw. III; at Seleburne. Acknowledgment by John Smoghelyn (*sic*), of the city of Chichester, of the receipt from the Prior Nicholas and the Convent of Seleburne of 60*s.* in full payment of a bond for £20.—[62.]

Small round black seal; a merchant's mark with I.S. "Sigillum Joh'is Smolee" (*sic*).

1379, "die sabbati in f. S. Albani mart.," 2 Rich. II; in the Chapter House. Lease from Thomas the Prior and the Convent of Selbourne to William Kambere, Agnes his wife, and John their son, of the tenement with a garden, croft, and eight acres of arable land, in Selbourne, which were formerly Luke le Glasiero's; to hold for their lives at an annual rent of 10s., with a heriot from the last survivor.—[46.]

Round pink seal, broken; a fleur-de-lis, "S' R'br'ti . . . . ." (yet said to be sealed with the common seal of the Priory).

INJUNCTIONS ISSUED BY WILLIAM OF WYKEHAM, BISHOP OF WINCHESTER, AFTER A PERSONAL VISITATION OF THE PRIORY:—

1387, 27 Sept. Willelmus permissione divina Wynton. Episcopus dilectis filiis Priori et Conventui prioratus de Selbourne, ordinis Sancti Augustini, nostræ dioceseos, salutem gratiam et benedictionem. Suscepti regiminis cura pastoralis officii nos inducit invigilare solicite nostrorum remediis subjectorum, et eorum obviare periculis, ac scandala removere, ut sic de vinea Domini per cultoris providi sarculum vitia extirpentur, inserantur virtutes, excessus debite corrigantur, et subditorum mores in nimium prolapsorum per appositionem moderaminis congrui reformentur. Hanc nempe solicitudinem nostris humeris incumbentem assidua meditatione pensantes, ne sanguis vestri de manibus nostris requiratur, ad vos et vestrum Prioratum supradictum, prout nostro incumbebat officio pastorali, nuper ex causa descendimus visitandi, et dum inter vos nostræ visitationis officium iteratis vicibus actualiter exercuimus, nonnulla reperimus quæ non solum obviant regularibus institutis, verum etiam quæ religioni vestræ non congruunt nec conveniunt honestati; ad quæ per nostrum antidotum debite reformanda, opem et operam, prout expedit et oportet, apponimus quas credimus efficaces. Infrascripta siquidem præcepta nostra, pariter et decreta sanctorum patrum, constitutionibus editis et debite promulgatis canonicisque ac regularibus institutis fulcita, vobis nostri sigilli roborata munimine transmittimus, inter vos futuris temporibus efficaciter observanda, quatinus ad Dei laudem, divini cultus ac vestræ religionis augmentum, ipsis mediantibus, per viam salutis feliciter incedatis, mores et actus vestri abstrahantur a noxiis et ad salutaria dirigantur.

The night and day Hours and the customary Masses to be attended and sung by all.

[I]. In primis, ut Domino Deo nostro, a quo cuncta bona procedunt et omnis religio immaculata sumpsit exordium, in Prioratu vestro prædicto serviatur laudabiliter in divinis, vobis in virtute sanctæ obedientiæ ac sub majoris excommunicationis sententiæ pœna firmiter injungendo mandamus, quatinus horæ canonicæ tam de nocte quam de die in choro a conventu cantentur; missæ quoque de beata Maria et de die, necnon missæ aliæ consuetæ, horis et devotione debitis et cum moderatis pausationibus celebrentur; nec liceat alicui de conventu ab horis et missis hujusmodi se absentare, aut postquam inceptæ fuerint ante completionem eorum ab ipsis recedere quovismodo, nisi ex causa necessaria vel legitima per priorem vel suppriorem vel alium præsidentem loci, ut convenit, approbanda, in quo casu ipsorum omnium conscientias apud Altissimum arctius oneramus; contrarium vero facientes in proximo tunc capitulo celebrando absque acceptione qualibet personarum regularum subeant disciplinam, acrius insuper puniendi si contumacia vel pertinacia delinquentium hoc exposcat. Si quis vero post trinam correptionem debite se non correxerit in præmissis, pro singulis vicibus quibus contrarium fecerit, ipsum singulis sextis feriis in pane et aqua dumtaxat præcipimus jejunare.

Contumacious absentees to fast on Fridays on bread and water.

The rules of silence to be observed.

[II.] Item, quia in visitatione nostra prædicta comperimus evidenter quod silentium, quasi in exilio positum, ad quod juxta regulam Sancti Augustini efficaciter estis astricti, locis et temporibus debitis inter vos minime observatur, contra observantias regulares, vobis omnibus et singulis firmiter injungendo mandamus quatinus silentium, prout vos docet regula supradicta, de cætero locis et temporibus hujusmodi observetis, a vanis et frivolis colloquiis, sicut decet, vos penitus abstinendo: illos vero qui silentium hujusmodi in locis prædictis non observaverint animadversione condigna præcipimus castigari. Et si quis tertio super hoc legitime convictus fuerit, præter regularem disciplinam die quo debite silentium non tenuerit, pane et servisia dumtaxat et legumine sit contentus.

Masses for founders and benefactors to be duly celebrated.

[III.] Item, quia nonnulli concanonici et confratres prioratus vestri prædicti validi atque sani et in sacerdotio constituti celebrationem missarum absque causa legitima indebite ac nimis voluntarie multotiens, ut dicitur, negligunt et omittunt, fundatorum aliorumque benefactorum suorum animas pro quibus sacrificia offero tenentur suffragiis nequiter defraudando, vobis ut supra firmiter injungendo mandamus quatinus vos omnes et singuli prioratus prædicti concanonici et confratres in sacerdotio constituti frequenter confiteamini confessoribus per Priorem deputandis, quos quidem confessores discretos et idoneos prout numerus personarum prædicti conventus exigit per vos dominum Priorem prædictum præcepimus deputari, missasque, impedimento cessante legitimo, tam pro vivis quam pro defunctis pro quibus orare tenemini de cætero quanto frequentius poteritis celebretis devotius, sicut decet; impedimentum vero prædictum cum contigerit, Priori vel Suppriori prioratus prædicti per illud patientes infra triduum declarari volumus et exponi, ac per eorum alterum prout justum fuerit approbari vel etiam reprobari, in quo casu ipsorum omnium tam exponentium quam approbantium apud Altissimum conscientias districtius oneramus; contrarium vero facientes primo super hoc convicti proxima quarta feria sequenti in pane, servisia et legumine, secundo vero convicti feria quarta et sexta sequentibus modo consimili, tertio vero convicti dictis feriis extunc sequentibus in pane et aqua jejunent quousque judicio Prioris se correxerint in præmissis. Statuentes præterea quod Prior et Supprior prioratus prædicti contra hujusmodi delinquentes semel singulis mensibus diligenter inquirant, et quos culpabiles invenerint in præmissis modo prædicto studeant castigare.

[IV.] Item, quia transitus communis sæcularium personarum utriusque sexus per claustrum Prioratus vestri incongruis temporibus nimium exercetur, et potissime horis illis quibus fratres de conventu in contemplatione sancta, studiis quoque ac lectionibus variis, inibi occupantur, unde dissolutiones plurimæ provenerunt, et poterunt in futuro verisimiliter provenire, ac ipsorum fratrum quieti et religionis honestati plurimum derogatur, vobis ut supra arctius injungendo mandamus quatiuus, cum secundum regulam Sancti Augustini conversatio vestra debeat esse a sæcularibus hujusmodi separata, ad animarum ac etiam rerum pericula quæ possent et solent ex concursu hujusmodi provenire cautius evitanda, transitum communem prædictum per præfatum claustrum de cetero fieri nullatenus permittatis, per quem vestra devotio et religionis honestas vulnerari vel etiam impediri valeant quovis modo, sub pœna excommunicationis majoris, quam in contravenientes intendimus canonice fulminare. Ille[1] vero ad quem ostiorum claustri custodia pertinet, si propter illius negligentiam sive culpam transitus hujusmodi sustineatur indebite ut præfertur, pro singulis vicibus quibus hoc factum fuerit, singulis quartis feriis in pane, servisia et legumine dumtaxat jejunet, et si nec sic se correxerit debite in hac parte ab officio deponatur, ac alius magis providus loco suo celeriter subrogetur.

The cloister to be no thoroughfare for lay persons of either sex, on pain of the greater excommunication.

[V.] Item, quia ostia ecclesiæ atque claustri prioratus vestri prædicti non servantur nec serantur temporibus debitis nec modo debito ut deceret, sed custodia eorundem agitur et omittitur multotiens negligenter, adeo quod suspectæ personæ et aliæ inhonestæ per ecclesiam et claustrum hujusmodi incedunt frequenter in tenebris atque umbris, temporibus etiam suspectis et illicitis, indecenter, unde damna et scandala varia pluries provenerunt, et imposterum verisimiliter poterunt provenire, vobis ut supra mandamus firmiter injungentes quatinus dicta ostia de cætero claudi faciatis, et clausa per ministros idoneos custodiri, temporibus debitis prout decet, vobis inhibentes expresse ne ostia ecclesiæ vestræ prædictæ, illa videlicet quæ inter navem ipsius ecclesiæ et chorum ejusdem existunt, nec ostia claustri quæ ducunt ad extra et per quæ introitus sæcularium in ipsum claustrum patere poterit, de mane antequam prima incipiatur in choro, aut commestionis tempore, nec etiam de sero postquam conventus collationem inceperit, nisi in causa utili vel necessaria per Priorem vel Suppriorem ut convenit approbanda, aperiantur de cætero quovis modo; ad quæ fideliter exequenda sacristam qui pro tempore fuerit, ad cujus officium præmissa pertinent, sub pœna amotionis ab officio suo arctius oneramus, acrius per nos puniendum prout nobis videlitur expedire.

The doors of the Church and cloister to be closed at due times, to prevent the grave scandals which have arisen.

[VI.] Item, quia nonnulli concanonici et confratres Prioratus vestri minus sapiunt in lectura, non intelligentes quid legant, sed literas quasi prorsus ignorantes dum psallunt vel legunt accentum brevem pro longa ponunt pluries, et e contra et per nim[i]a [?][2] gradientes, sanum Scripturarum intellectum adulterantur multotiens et pervertunt, fitque ut dum

The ignorant brethren, who cannot read Holy Scripture aright, are to be better instructed.

[1] "Illum," MS. [2] "innia," MS., as it seems.

Scripturas sacras non sapiant ad perpetrandum illicita proniores reddantur, vobis domino Priori in virtute obedientiæ firmiter injungendo mandamus quatinus, cum legere et non intelligere sit negligere, novitiis et aliis minus sufficienter literatis idoneus de cætero deputetur magister qui ipsos in cantu et aliis primitivis scientiis instruat diligenter juxta regularia instituta, quatinus in eisdem perfectius eruditi, cæcitatis squamis et ignorantiæ nebulis depositis, quæ legant intelligant et agnoscant, et [ad] contemplandum mysteria Scripturarum efficiantur, ut convenit, promptiores.

The papal constitutions concerning the Augustinian orders are to be written out, and read twice yearly in the Chapter, and the novices are to learn the rule of the order by heart, as enjoined by Card. Ottobonus.

[VII.] Item, quia Constitutiones sive Decretales Romanorum Pontificum vestrum ordinem concernentes, illæ videlicet de quibus in Constitutionibus recolendæ memoriæ domini Ottoboni, quondam sedis apostolicæ in Anglia legati, fit mentio specialis, inter vos nullatenus recitantur, prout per Constitutiones ejusdem legati recitari mandantur,[1] unde dum Decretales ipsas et contenta in eis penitus ignoratis committitis multotiens quæ prohibentur expressius per easdem, in vestrarum periculum animarum, vobis firmiter injungendo mandamus quatinus, ne ignorantiam aliquam prætendere poteritis in hac parte, Decretales prædictas, prout in præfatis Constitutionibus domini Ottoboni plenius recitantur, in quodam quaterno seu volumine absque moræ dispendio faciatis conscribi, ipsas bis singulis annis in vestro capitulo juxta formam Constitutionum prædictarum recitari clarius facientes, ad informationem rudium et perfectionem etiam provectorum, adjicientes præterea ut magistri novitiorum præsentium et etiam futurorum ipsos in regula Sancti Augustini diligenter instruant et informent, ipsam regulam eis vulgariter exponendo, quodque iidem novitii per frequentem recitationem ejusdem illam sciant quasi cordetenus, sicut in dictis Constitutionibus plenius continetur, per quam incedere poterunt via recta et errorum tenebras cautius evitare. Super executione vero præmissorum debite facienda dominum Priorem Prioratus vestri prædicti arctius oneramus, quatinus ea quæ præmisimus in hoc casu, sub pœna suspensionis ab ipsius officio per mensem, diligentius exequatur.

Clothes and shoes to be supplied when necessary, and no annual allowance in money to be made for them: old clothes to be given to the poor.

[VIII.] Item, quia canonici et confratres Prioratus vestri prædicti, ipsorum propriam voluntatem potius quam utilitatem communem sectantes, non vestes necessarias cum opus fuerit sed certam et limitatam ac determinatam quantitatem pecuniæ velut annuum redditum pro vestibus hujusmodi percipiunt annuatim, contra regulam Sancti Augustini ac domini Ottoboni et aliorum sanctorum patrum canonica instituta, fitque ut, dum effrenis illa religiosorum cupiditas aliena specie colorata vetita concupiscat, sancta religio, solutis constantiæ frenis, in luxum labentem ad latitudinis tramites quæ ducunt ad mortem miserabiliter noscitur declinare, cui quidem morbo pestifero, ne putrescat et vermes generet corruptivas, mederi citius cupientes, nihil novi statuendo sed sanctorum patrum vestigiis inhærendo, volumus ac etiam ordinamus quod canonicis et confratribus memoratis præsentibus et futuris, de bonis et facultatibus

[1] cap. xxxix: A.D. 1268. Wilkins, *Concilia*, II, 16.

communibus Prioratus vestri prædicti vestris usibus deputatis, vestes et calciamenta cum indiguerint necessaria juxta facultates prædictas, et nullo modo pecuniam pro eisdem, per eos qui super his ministrandi gerent officium de cætero ministrentur; vestes vero inveteratas et ineptas hujusmodi canonicorum camerario communi tradi volumus pauperibus erogandas, juxta regulam Sancti Augustini et alias canonicas sanctiones; contrarium vero facientes, si camerarius fuerit pœnam suspensionis ab officio ipsum incurrere volumus ipso facto, si vero alius canonicus de conventu existat præter alias pœnitentias regulares tam pecunia quam etiam indumentis novis careat illo anno.

[IX.] Item, quia nonnulli canonici et confratres Prioratus vestri prædicti, opportunitate captata, extra septa Prioratus absque societate honesta, evagandi causa, nulla super hoc obtenta licentia, se transferunt pluries indecenter, alii præterea provectiores certis officiis deputati ad maneria et loca alia officiis hujusmodi assignata equitant quando placet, ibidem manentes pro eorum libito voluntatis, nullo canonico ipsis in socium assignato, contra ordinis decentiam et religionis etiam honestatem constitutionesque sanctorum patrum editas in hac parte: Cum igitur religiosos extra eorum Prioratum sic vagari aut in eorum maneriis vel ecclesiis eis appropriatis soli (*sic*) manere expresse prohibeant canonica instituta, nos, præmissa fieri de cætero prohibentes, vobis firmiter injungendo mandamus quatinus cum aliquis Prioratns vestri canonicus vel confrater super vel pro negotiis propriis vel etiam communibus exire contigerit, prius ad hoc a Priore vel Suppriore si præsentes in Prioratu fuerint, alioquin, ipsis absentibus, ab ipso qui pro tunc Conventui præesse contigerit, licentiam habeat specialem, cui assignari volumus unum canonicum in socium, ne suspicio sinistra vel scandalum oriatur, qui, associata eisdem juxta qualitatem negotii comitiva honesta, in eundo et etiam redeundo gravitate servata modestius semper incedant, et expletis negotiis ad Prioratum citius revertantur, quæ regularibus conveniunt institutis devotius impleturi; contrarium vero facientes, absque remissione seu acceptione qualibet personarum, regularem subeant disciplinam, super quo præsidentium conventus conscientias arctius oneramus, ipsosque nihilominus pro singulis vicibus quibus excesserint in præmissis singulis sextis feriis in pane et aqua jejunent; et si officiarius fuerit, ipso facto, si aliquod canonicum non obsistat, ab ipsius officio sit suspensus.

The Canons and brethren are not to go outside the Priory without special leave, nor without a Canon as a companion.

[X.] Item, quia comperimus evidenter quod nonnulli canonici domus vestræ, secundum carnem potius quam secundum spiritum dissolute viventes, nulla causa rationabili subsistente, nudi jacent in lectis absque femoralibus et camisiis, contra eorum observantias regulares, vobis igitur firmiter injungendo mandamus quatinus vos omnes et singuli canonici Sancti Augustini regulam et in ea parte ordinis vestri canonica instituta de cætero efficaciter observetis; contrarium vero facientes singulis quartis feriis in pane servisia et legumine tantummodo sint contenti: si quis vero post trinam correctionem reus inventus fuerit in hac parte, pro singulis vicibus singulis extunc feriis sextis in pane et

The Canons strictly forbidden to lie naked in bed.

aqua hunc præcipimus jejunare; Priorem vero ac Suppriorem domus prædictæ sub pœna suspensionis ab officiis eorundem arctius onerantes quatinus super præmissis sæpius et diligenter inquirant, et quos culpabiles invenerint eos pœnis prædictis percellere non postponant.

Hunting strictly forbidden, and the keeping of hunting dogs, saving any right or custom of the Priory.

[XI.] Item, quia nonnullos canonicos et confratres Prioratus vestri prædicti publicos reperimus venatores, ac venationibus hujusmodi, spreto jugo regularis observantiæ, publice intendentes ac canes tenentes venaticos contra regularia instituta, unde dissolutiones quamplures, animarum pericula, corporumque ac rerum dispendia multotiens oriuntur, nos, volentes hoc frequens vitium a Prioratu prædicto radicitus extirpare, vobis omnibus et singulis tenore præsentium inhibemus, vobis nihilominus firmiter injungentes ne quisquam canonicorum Prioratus vestri prædicti publicis venationibus vel clamosis ex proposito intendere de cætero vel etiam interesse, canesve venaticos per se vel alios tenere, præsumat, publice vel occulte, intra Prioratum vel extra, contra formam capituli *Ne in agro Dominico*[1] et alias canonicas sanctiones. Per hoc autem Prioratus vestri prædicti nec juri vel consuetudini quod vel quam habere dinoscitur in ea parte non intendimus in aliquo derogare. Contrarium vero facientes præter disciplinas et pœnas alias canonicas pro singulis vicibus singulis quartis et sextis feriis in pane et servisia jejunando præcipimus castigari.

The officers of the Priory not to neglect attendance at the divine offices, under penalty of excommunication.

[XII]. Item, quia canonici Prioratus vestri prædicti quibus officia forinseca et intrinseca committuntur fingunt se, cum possent et deberent in choro divinis officiis interesse, in officiis hujusmodi sibi commissis multotiens occupari, quæ possent ante vel post horas hujusmodi commode fieri et etiam exerceri, propter quod cultus divinus minuitur et alii claustrales nimium onerantur, vobis in virtute sanctæ obedientiæ et sub pœna excommunicationis majoris firmiter injungendo mandamus, quatinus officiarii quicunque ecclesiæ vestræ prædictæ in choro ejusdem divinis officiis amodo personaliter intersint, nisi ex causa legitima officiorum suorum per præsidentem conventus qui pro tempore fuerit approbanda eos contigerit absentare, in quo casu de et super absentia sua legitimitateque causarum prætensarum in hac parte ipsorum præsidentium et officiariorum conscientias apud Altissimum districtius oneramus.

Two Canons to visit the manors twice every year.

[XIII.] Item, quia juxta Sapientis [?] doctrinam *Ubi majus imminet periculum ibi cautius est agendum*, volumus et etiam ordinamus quod duo canonici discreti et idonei de conventu Prioratus vestri prædicti per ipsum conventum vel majorem partem ejusdem annis singulis de cætero eligantur, qui bis in anno ad maneria tam Priori quam etiam pro sustentatione conventus hujus cæterisque officiariis assignata personaliter se transferant et accedant, statum maneriorum ipsorum tam in edificiis quam etiam in stauro vivo vel mortuo plenarie supervisuri, quique super his quæ invenerunt in iisdem conventui prædicto relationem fidelem in scriptis, ut convenit, facere teneantur, ut, si mors alicujus

[1] Constitt. Clementis V, lib. III, tit. x, cap. i; at the Council of Vienne in 1311.

officiarii vel casus alius fortuitus evenerit, de statu officii hujusmodi cujuscunque conventum non lateat memoratum. Præmissa vero vobis præcipimus efficaciter observanda sub pœna nostro arbitrio limitanda, vobis, si in his negligentes fueritis vel remissi, acrius infligenda.

The full number of Canons to be kept up, or at least so many as can be competently supported.

[XIV.] Item, quia solitus et antiquus numerus canonicorum in Prioratu vestro prædicto, quod dolenter referimus, adeo jam decrevit ac etiam minuitur in præsenti, quod ubi xiiij canonici vel circiter in habitu et observantiis regularibus in dicto Prioratu solebant Altissimo devotius famulari, quibus de bonis et possessionibus ipsius Prioratus vestri communibus quæ possidetis in victu et vestitu juxta decentiam ordinis regularis honorifice ac debite fuerat ministratum, modo vero undecim canonici dumtaxat existunt et serviunt in eodem, quo fit ut dum Regis regum cultum attenuet cohabitantium paucitas, contra multiformis nequitiæ hostem minuatur exercitus bellatorum; cum igitur juxta præfati domini Ottoboni Constitutiones[1] aliorumque sanctorum patrum canonica instituta canonicorum antiquus numerus sit servandus, ac, juxta Sapientis doctrinam *In multitude populi sit dignitas regis, et in paucitate plebis ignominia principis accendatur,*[2] vobis in virtute sanctæ obedientiæ, ac sub pœna majoris excommunicationis firmiter injungendo mandamus, quatinus cum omni diligentia et celeritate debitis de viris idoneis religioni dispositis et honestis vobis absque moræ dispendio providere curetis, ipsos in vestrum ordinem regularem in suppletionem majoris numeri requisiti, seu saltim illius numeri canonicorum ad quorum sustentationem congruam, aliis oneribus vobis incumbentibus debite supportatis, vestræ jam habitæ suppetunt facultates, super quibus vestrum et cujuslibet vestrum conscientiam arctius oneramus, celerius admittentes, ad augmentum cultus divini et perfectionem majorem ordinis regularis, pro fundatoribus et benefactoribus vestris devotius ut convenit intercessuros.

The Prior strictly charged no longer to neglect enquiry into private ownership of property on the part of the Canons twice in the year.

[XV.] Item, quia comperimus evidenter quod vos, domine Prior, cui ex debito vestri officii hoc incumbit, de proprietariis canonicis Prioratus vestri prædicti, juxta Constitutiones domini legati editas in hac parte,[3] inquisitionem debitam hactenus non fecistis, ministerium vobis creditum in ea parte negligentius omittendo, quo fit ut ille pestifer hostis antiquus pastoris considerans continuam desidiam oves miseras et errantes, ipsius hostis nequissimi fraude deceptas, in sitim avaritiæ prolabentes laqueo proprietatis seducit, contra patrum canonica instituta, in suarum grave periculum animarum, vos igitur requirimus et monemus, vobisque in virtute obedentiæ firmiter injungendo mandamus, quatinus dicti legati Constitutionibus, ut convenit, imitantes, super proprietariis hujusmodi saltim bis in anno inquisitionem faciatis de cætero diligentem, ipsos si quos inveneritis animadversione condigna juxta regularia instituta canonice punientes. Si vero id adimplere neglexeritis, administratione vestra ipso facto noveritis vos privatum, donec præmissa fueritis diligenter executi, prout in Constitutionibus domini Ottoboni legati prædicti plenius continetur.

[1] cap. xlix. [2] Prov. xiv, 28: "accendatur" is not in the Vulgate. [3] cap. xl.

Annual accounts to be rendered by the Prior and officers.

[XVI.] Item, cum secundum Constitutiones dicti legati[1] et aliorum sanctorum patrum canonica instituta abbates, et priores proprios abbates non habentes, necnon officiarii quicunque, teneantur bis saltim in singulis annis, præsente toto conventu vel aliquibus ex senioribus ad hoc a capitulo deputatis, de statu Prioratus et de administratione sua plenariam reddere rationem, quod tamen in Prioratu vestro prædicto invenimus hactenus non servatum, unde plura sequuntur incommoda et vestræ utilitati communi plurimum derogatur, vobis in virtute obedientiæ firmiter injungendo mandamus, quatinus præfati domini legati, domini videlicet Ottoboni,[2] necnon bonæ memoriæ domini Stephani [Langton] quondam archiepiscopi Cantuariensis,[3] Constitutiones editas in hac parte, faciatis inter vos de cætero firmiter observari, sub pœna suspensionis officiariorum ipsorum ab eorum hujusmodi officiis dictique Prioris ab administratione sua, quam si præmissa neglexerint observare ipso facto donec id perfecerint se noverint incurrisse, prout in dictis Coustitutionibus dicti Ottoboni plenius continetur.

Dilapidated buildings of the Priory and manors to be forthwith repaired.

[XVII.] Item, quia in Prioratu vestro prædicto et ecclesia ejusdem ac in nonnullis domibus, edificiis, muris et clausuris ecclesiæ vestræ prælibatæ, necnon maneriorum ipsius Prioratus certis diversis officiis deputatorum, quas et quæ præcessorum et prædecessorum vestrorum industria sumptuose construxerat, quamplures enormes et notabiles sunt defectus reparatione necessaria indigentes, unde statum ipsius Prioratus ac maneriorum prædictorum deformitas occupat et multa incommoda insequuntur, vobis igitur in virtute obedientiæ firmiter injungendo mandamus, quatinus defectus hujusmodi pro vestra utilitate communi absque dilationis incommodo quam citius poteritis juxta vires reparari debite faciatis; alioquin Priorem cæterosque officiarios qui in præmissis negligentes fuerint vel remissi, nisi infra sex menses post notificationem præsentium sibi factam ad debitam reparationem defectuum hujusmodi se præparaverint cum effectu, ipso facto ab officiis suis hujusmodi sint suspensi.

No liveries, corrodies, or pensions to be hereafter sold or granted without the Bishop's consent.

[XVIII]. Item, quia per venditiones et concessiones liberationum et corrodiorum hactenus per vos factas reperimus dictum Prioratum multipliciter fore gravatum, adeo quod ea quæ ad divini cultus augmentum, sustentationem pauperum et infirmorum, pia devotio fidelium erogavit, mercenariorum cœca cupiditas jam absorbet, fitque ut dum bona ejusdem Prioratus in alios usus quam debitos, ne dixerimus in prophanos, nepharie convertantur, Altissimo famulantium in eadem numerus minuitur, pauperes et infirmi suis portionibus, ac ipsa ecclesia divinis obsequiis, nequiter defraudantur, contra intentionem piissimam fundatorum, in vestrarum periculum animarum, indempnitati igitur ipsius ecclesiæ vestræ in hac parte debite providere, dictum quoque tam frequens incommodum ab eadem radicitus extirpare, volentes, bonæ memoriæ domini Ottoboni legati prædicti[4] aliorumque sanctorum patrum

[1] cap. xxxix. [2] cap. l.
[3] Conc. Oxon., cap. xxxi: A.D. 1222. Wilkins, *Concilia*, I, 590. [4] cap. xlviii.

vestigiis inhærentes, vobis tenore præsentium districtius inhibemus, etiam sub pœna excommunicationis majoris, ne corrodia, liberationes, aut pensiones personis aliquibus imperpetuum vel ad tempus vendatis de cætero vel aliqualiter concedatis absque nostro consensu et licentia speciali, præsertim cum venditiones hujusmodi, quæ species alienationis existunt, Prioratus vestri prædicti detrimentum procurent et enormem etiam generent læsionem. Si quis vero contra hanc nostram inhibitionem aliquid attemptare præsumpserit, nisi id quod sic præsumpserit revocaverit, ab officio sit suspensus, prout in Constitutionibus domini Ottoboni clarius continetur.

[XIX.] Item, quia quædam certæ perpetuæ cantariæ pro fundatoribus et aliis benefactoribus vestris tam in genere quam in specie antiquitus constitutæ per diversos presbyteros in Prioratu vestro prædicto debite celebrandæ, pro quibus plura donaria recepistis, a multis retroactis temporibus ac etiam de præsenti, ut asseritur, sunt subtractæ contra piam intentionem ac ordinationem etiam fundatorum, in vestrarum grave periculum animarum, vobis igitur in virtute sanctæ obedientiæ ac sub majoris excommunicationis sententiæ pœna firmiter injungendo mandamus, quatinus cantarias prædictas juxta formam institutionum et ordinationum earum faciatis de cætero debite celebrari ac eisdem congrue deserviri, si redditus et proventus ad hujusmodi cantarias antiquitus assignati ad hoc sufficiant his diebus; alioquin, prout redditus et proventus earum, aliis oneribus eisdem incumbentibus debite supportatis, sufficiunt de præsenti, dolo et fraude cessantibus quibuscunque, super quo vestram conscientiam arctius oneramus, amodo deserviri debite faciatis.

Chantries of founders and benefactors to be duly served, and their endowments no longer to be perverted.

[XX.] Item, vobis omnibus et singulis in virtute sanctæ obedientiæ ac sub majoris excommunicationis sententiæ pœna firmiter injungendo mandamus, quatinus elemosinas in Prioratu vestro prædicto antiquitus fieri consuetas et eas ad quas tenemini ex ordinatione antiqua pro animabus fundatorum et aliorum benefactorum vestrorum juxta facultates vestras, super quibus vestras conscientias arctius oneramus, prout divinam effugere volueritis ultionem, distribui de cætero faciatis: præcipientes præterea quod fragmenta seu reliquiæ tam de aula Prioris quam etiam de refectorio provenientia absque diminutione qualibet per elemosinarium vel ipsius locumtenentem integre colligantur pauperibus fideliter eroganda; alioquin, si elemosinarius hujusmodi remissus vel negligens fuerit in præmissis pœnam suspensionis ab officio se noverit incursurum.

Alms to be duly distributed to the poor, according to the will of founders and benefactors, and the fragments left from meals.

[XXI.] Item, quia debilibus et infirmis humanitatis præberi subsidium jubet caritas et pietas interpellat,[1] vobis domino Priori, cæteris[que] obedientiariis Prioratus vestri prædicti quorum interest in hac parte, in virtute sanctæ obedientiæ firmiter injungendo mandamus, quatinus confratribus vestris debilibus et infirmis, ipsorum infirmitate durante, in esculentis et poculentis eorum infirmitatibus congruentibus, necnon in

Sick and infirm brethren to be properly ministered to.

[1] "intelpellat," MS.

medicinis et aliis, juxta infirmitatis hujusmodi qualitatem et Prioratus facultates de bonis vestris communibus et sicut antiquitus fieri consueverat de cætero faciatis debite procurari, sub pœna suspensionis ab officiis vestris si circa præmissa negligentes fueritis vel remissi ipso facto, quousque id quod negligenter omissum fuerit perfeceritis, incurrenda, prout in Constitutionibus domini Ottoboni plenius continetur:[1] statuentes præterea quod cameræ in infirmaria vestra cum opus fuerit infirmis canonicis sint communes, ne, quod absit, aliquis sibi retineat in eisdem vel vendicet proprietatem, contra Sancti Augustini regulam et constitutiones sanctorum patrum editas in hac parte.

Offenders to be duly corrected without respect of persons; negligence herein to be visited by suspension of officers and special penance for the Prior.

[XXII.] Item, cum negligentia sive remissio in personis præsidentium sit plurimum detestanda, facilitas quoque veniæ incentivum præbeat delinquendi, vobis, domino Priori, Suppriori, aliisque conventus prædicti præsidentibus quibuscunque præsentibus et futuris, in virtute sanctæ obedientiæ firmiter injungendo mandamus, quatinus, cum correctiones in personis ipsius conventus immineant faciendæ, ipsas, prout ad vos pertinet, absque acceptione qualibet personarum juxta quantitatem delictorum et personarum qualitatem vestrasque observantias regulares, cum maturitate debita et discretione prævia, facere studeatis; alioquin, vos, Suppriorem cæterosque præsidentes prædictos, si negligentes vel remissi aut culpabiles fueritis in præmissis, canonica nostra monitione præmissa, pœnam suspensionis ab officiis vestris extunc incurrere volumus ipso facto, donec hujusmodi negligentiam, remissionem, culpam vel desidiam, a vobis excusseritis in hac parte, pœnitentia præfato domino Priori in hoc casu ut convenit infligenda nobis specialiter reservata.

Pittances and other allowances on anniversary days to be duly distributed, under penalty of double payment.

[XXIII.] Item, cum consuetudines laudabiles Prioratus cujuscumque ordinationesque ac statuta quæ usus longævi temporis approbavit merito sint servandæ, vobis, domino Priori ac singulis officiariis Prioratus vestri prædicti præsentibus et futuris, in virtute sanctæ obedientiæ et sub pœnis infrascriptis firmiter injungendo mandamus, quatinus pitancias et alias distributiones quascunque, in quibuscunque rebus consistant et quocunque nomine censeantur, in obitibus, anniversariis, festivitatibus aut aliis diebus, conventui, aut ab uno officio alii officio, ex ordinatione antiqua debitas et consuetas, si canonicum aliquod non obsistat, amodo faciatas persolvi, sub pœna portionis duplæ, cujus partem unam conventui prædicto, alteram vero partem certis piis usibus nostro arbitrio limitandis debite persolvendam specialiter reservamus.

No important business, as wood sales, and letting to farm of manors and churches, to be transacted without consent of the majority.

[XXIV.] Item, cum venditiones boscorum, firmæ maneriorum vel etiam ecclesiarum, aut alia domus vestræ ardua negotia, immineant faciendæ, illa (*sic*) sine tractatu ac deliberatione provida cum conventu prædicto ac eorum consensu expresso vel majoris et sanioris partis ejusdem, de cætero fieri prohibemus; aliter autem hujusmodi negotia ardua facta nullius existant firmitatis; et nihilominus, Priorem aliosque officiarios quoscumque qui contra præsentem prohibitionem nostram quicquam attemptaverint in præmissis pœnam suspensionis ab officiis

[1] cap. xlvi.

eorundem ipso facto se noverint incursuros, cum ex hujusmodi factis privatis ecclesiis dispendia multotiens provenerunt, illa quoque quæ omnes tangunt ab omnibus merito debeant approbari.

The common seal to be kept under five keys.

[XXV.] Item, volumus ac etiam ordinamus quod sigillum vestrum commune sub quinque clavibus ad minus de cætero custodiatur, quarum unam penes Priorem, secundam penes Suppriorem, tertiam penes Præcentorem, et reliquas duas claves penes confratres alios per conventum ad hoc nominandos, decrevimus remanere, per eos fideliter custodiendas; inhibentes prætcrea sub pœna excommunicationis ne quicquam cum dicto sigillo communi amodo sigilletur nisi litera hujusmodi sigillanda primitus legatur, inspiciatur, ac etiam intelligatur, a majore et saniore parte totius conventus, et ad ipsam sigillandum communis vester præbeatur consensus, cum ex facto hujusmodi plura possent dispendia verisimiliter provenire. Ad hæc, vobis omnibus et singulis tenore præsentium inhibemus ne compatres alicujus pueri de cætero fieri præsumatis nostra super hoc licentia non obtenta, cum ex hujusmodi cognationibus religiosis domibus dispendia sæpius provenire [1] noscuntur; contrarium vero facientes præter disciplinas alias regulares singulis sextis feriis per mensem proxime tunc sequentem in pane et aqua jejunando præcipimus castigari.

No one to be a godfather without the Bishop's leave.

The statutable boots to be worn, and not coloured shoes or leggings; offenders to be punished, if need be, by imprisonment.

[XXVI.] Item, quia nonnulli canonici domus vestræ prædictæ, fræno objecto observantiæ regularis, caligis de burneto et sotularibus bassis in ocrearum loco ad modum sotularium uti publice non verentur, contra consuetudinem antiquam laudabilem ordinis supradicti, in perniciosum exemplum et scandalum plurimorum, Nos igitur, honestatem dicti ordinis observare volentes, vobis, domino Priori, in virtute sanctæ obedientiæ firmiter injungendo mandamus, quatinos quoscumque vestros canonicos et confratres ad utendum de cætero ocreis seu botis secundum antiquas vestri ordinis observantias regulares per quascumque censuras ecclesiasticas, et, si opus fuerit, per incarcerationis pœnam, canonice compellatis, sub pœna suspensionis ab officio vestro prædicto.

Rules for dinner in the refectory, for meals with guests, and entertainment by the Prior.

[XXVII.] Item, quia tres vel duæ partes conventus domus vestræ non comedunt cotidie in refectorio, prout constitutiones sanctorum patrum sanxerunt provide in hac parte, vobis dicti Prioratus conventui firmiter injungendo mandamus, quatinus tres vel saltem duæ partes vestrum cotidie in refectorio hora prandii de cætero comedant et remaneant debite, sicut decet vobis, arctius injungentes quod nullus vestrum in mansiunculis aut locis aliis privatis etiam cum hospitibus suis regularibus vel secularibus vel confratribus suis comedat, hostilaria cum hospitibus, refectorio in communi misericordia, causa recreationis, et aula Prioris dumtaxat exceptis. Hanc tamen Prior apponat providentem diligentiam ut sine personarum acceptione nunc hos nunc illos ad refectionem convocet quos magis noverit indigere. Super executione vero debita præmissorum Priorem et alios conventui præsidentes sub pœna suspensionis ab eorum officiis arctius oneramus.

[1] "invenire," MS.

The Prior to change his chaplain yearly, for due teaching of the younger Canons, and his own security in case of slander.

[XXVIII.] Item, cum secundum sanctorum patrum constitutiones juniores canonici a suis prælatis vivendi normam habeant[1] assumere, ac iidem prælati super sua conversatione testium copiam debeant obtinere, vobis, domino Priori, in virtute obedientiæ districte præcipiendo mandamus, quatinus capellanum vestrum canonicum singulis de cætero mutetis annis, juxta constitutiones sanctorum patrum editas in hac parte, ut sic qui vobiscum fuerint in officio prædicto per doctrinæ laudabilis exercitium plus valeant in religione proficere, ac eos innocentiæ testes si vobis, quod absit, crimen aliquod seu scandalum per aliquorum invidiam imponatur prompte poteritis invocare.

All luxury in dress forbidden.

[XXIX.] Item, cum communis exquisitus ornatus præsertim in religiosis personis a jure sit penitus interdictus, vobis tenore præsentium inhibemus ne quivis vestrum de cætero in suis vestibus furruris preciosis aut manicis nodulatis, zonisve sericis auri vel argenti ornatum habentibus, utatur de cætero quovismodo, cum abusus hujusmodi ad pompam et ostentationem ac scandalum ordinis manifeste tendere dinoscatur.

Officers to be duly elected for each office singly.

[XXX.] Item, quia singula officia sunt singulis committenda personis, vobis in virtute obedientiæ et sub excommunicationis sententiæ pœna firmiter injungendo mandamus ut officia singula vestri Prioratus quæ per canonicos officiarios gubernari solebant, per officiarios hujusmodi, per vos communiter vel divisim juxta Prioratus prædicti morem solitum eligendos, quibus ipsa officia ut olim committi volumus exercenda, singulariter de cætero gubernentur.

No one without cure of souls to administer sacraments without leave.

[XXXI.] Item, cum plus timeri soleat id quod specialiter injungitur quam quod generaliter imperat, vobis omnibus et singulis inhibemus ne aliquis vestrum ad curam animarum non admissus clericis aut laicis sacramentum unctionis extremæ vel euchauristiæ (*sic*) ministrare matrimoniave solemnizare, non habita super his parochialis presbyteri licentia, quomodolibet præsumatis, sub pœna excommunicationis majoris sententiæ in hac parte a canone fulminata.

Sacred vestments and vessels to be kept clean.

[XXXII.] Item, quia comperimus in nostris visitationibus supradictis vasa et pallas altaris, necnon et vestimenta sacra ecclesiæ vestræ atque corporalia, tam immunda relinqui quod interdum aliquibus sunt horrori, ut igitur honor debitus divinis impendatur, vobis firmiter injungendo mandamus, quatinus vasa, corporalia, pallas, et vestimenta prædicta ac cætera ecclesiæ ornamenta munda nitida et honesta de cætero conserventur, hoc quoque insuper injungentes ut in ecclesia vestra celebrantibus vinum bonum purum et incorruptum ad sacramentum altaris conficiendum per eum qui super hoc gerit officium, et non corruptum et acetosum, prout fieri consuevit, imposterum ministretur; nimis enim videt absurdum in sacris sordes negligere quæ dedecerent in prophanis.

Sacramental wine to be pure and good, not sour.

Relics and sacred vessels, etc., not to be pawned.

[XXXIII.] Item, licet sanctorum reliquias, vasa aut vestimenta sacra, seu libros ecclesiæ, in vadum dari aut pignori obligari canonica prohibeant instituta, a vobis tamen in dictis visitationibus comperimus

[1] *Sic; qu.* debeant?

contrarium esse factum; vobis igitur, domino Priori, tenore præsentium firmiter injungendo mandamus, quatinus, ab hujusmodi impignorationibus extra casus a jure permissos vos de cætero penitus abstinentes, hujusmodi pignori obligata curetis recolligere, et ea ecclesiæ vestræ restituere absque moræ dispendio, sicut decet; statuentes præterea ut omnes cartæ ac munimenta quæcumque statum, bona, et possessiones domus vestræ qualitercunque contingentes sub tribus sęruris et clavibus remaneant futuris temporibus fideliter conservandæ.

Charters to be safely kept.

Diligent private reading of Holy Scripture to be kept up.

[XXXIV.] Item, cum Religiosi de bono in melius continuo debeant proficisci, ac ex Sacræ Scripturæ lectione, et inspectione qualiter id faciant, plenius instrui valeant, vobis firmiter injungendo mandamus, ut, completis his quæ ad vestri ordinis et regularis disciplinæ observantiam pertinent atque spectant, in claustro sedentes Scripturæ Sacræ lectioni sanctæque contemplationi devotius insistatis, sicque secundum regulæ vestræ exigentiam taliter codices inspiciendos requiratis ut in eis quid fugiendum, quid subsequendum, ac cujusmodi præmium inde consequendum fuerit, agnoscere valeatis.

Relatives visiting monks to be liberally entertained.

[XXXV.] Item, vobis, domino Priori, injungimus, quod cum parentes vel consanguinei alicujus confratris vestri ad eum accesserint causa visitandi eundem, liberaliter secundum statum sui exigentiam per vos vel illum qui super hoc ministrandi gerit officium infra Prioratum honeste et debite procurentur, sed videant fratres ne nimis sint in talibus Prioratui onerosi.

These Injunctions to be written out, and read before the whole Convent twice in the year.

[XXXVI.] Item, quia parum est jura condere nisi executioni debitæ demandentur, ea quoque solent labili memoriæ eo tenacius commendari quo veraciter audientium auribus fuerint sæpius inculcata, et ne vestrum quispiam ignorantiam prætendere valeat præmissorum, vobis firmiter injungendo mandamus, quatinus has nostras injunctiones et decreta pariter supradicta in aliquo volumine competenti absque moræ dispendio conscribi plenius faciatis, eaque omnia et singula bis annis singulis de cætero coram toto conventu plenius recitari. Vos nihilominus omnes et singulos monemus, primo secundo et tertio peremptorie, vobis insuper in virtute obedientiæ arctius injungentes, quatinus ipsas injunctiones nostras et decreta prædicta omnia et singula, prout ad vos et vestrum quemlibet pertinent et singulariter vos concernunt, teneatis de cætero ac etiam observetis, sub pœnis et censuris ecclesiasticis supradictis et aliis pœnis canonicis in contravenientes quoscunque, prout contumacia delinquentium exegerit, per nos imposterum canonice infligendis. Potestatem autem præmissa corrigendi, mutandi in toto vel in parte, interpretandi, declarandi, et eisdem addendi et etiam detrahendi, ac pœnas adjiciendi, suspendendi, necnon super compertis aliis in visitatione nostra prædicta procedendi, criminaque et defectus ac excessus in ipsa comperta et delata corrigendi ac canonice puniendi, et super ipsis novas injunctiones insuper faciendi, sicut et prout opus fuerit et nobis videbitur expedire, nobis etiam specialiter reservamus.

In quorum omnium testimonium sigillum nostrum fecimus his apponi.

Datum apud Wyntoniam vicesimoseptimo die mensis Septembris, anno Domini millesimo CCC? octogesimoseptimo, et nostræ consecrationis anno vicesimo.—[*Appropriations*, 15.]

On one very large sheet of vellum, 27 inches long by 20½ wide, with an additional strip, 7½ inches long by 20¾ wide, attached by a vellum label.

Oval green seal attached by a vellum label to both sheets: SS. Peter and Paul, under canopies: above, God the Father holding up the Son upon the Cross; inscription and rim slightly broken: "Willelmum Trine cum [san]ctis suscipe fine."

1413, 26 Aug., "die Sabb. pr. p. f. S. Barthol.," 1 Hen. V; at Selbourne. Release from William Self, son and heir of Walter Self of Selbourne, to John Wynchestre, Prior of the church of Blessed Mary of Selbourne, and to the Convent there, of all his right in a messuage with a curtilage and thirteen acres of land in the vill and fields of Selbourne which the said Walter held of the said Prior and Convent by the annual service of 6*s.* 6*d.* and suit of court. Witn.: John Nortone, Will. Kembere, Will. Thomas, Thomas Glasyere, Henry Dollyng.—[12.]

Small seal with initial "T."

1415, 29 Sept., "in f. S. Mich. archang.," 3 Hen. V; in the chapter house at Selbourne. Lease from John the Prior and the Convent of Selbourne to William Thomas, Alice his wife, and John their eldest son, of a messuage with a garden and two crofts, one meadow and two and a half acres in the common field of Selbourne called Kyngesfelde, of which the two acres lie between the land of John Cobham on either side and the half-acre near the land of the Prior and Convent on the west, one end abutting on the land of John Weld on the south and the other on the wood of the Prior and Convent on the north, all which were formerly Walter atte Broke's; to hold for the term of their lives at an annual rent of 8*s.*, and paying a heriot of 6*s.* 8*d.* on the death of the last, building a new grange within nine years with timber supplied by the Priory, and maintaining the "bakhous" which is at present standing. No witnesses.—[25.]

Three small red seals.

1417, 29 Sept., "in f. S. Mich.," 5 Hen. V; at Selborne. Lease from John the Prior and the Convent of Selborne to Thomas Rolf of Westtystede, Agnes his wife, and Isabella their daughter, of a messuage and three fields, called Hyfeld, Stonyfeld, and Bromfeld, in Westtystede, which Thomas Gardyner and John Payntour formerly held, together with a part of the underwood in their wood of Bromdone, viz., from

Rodegate between the way called Rodewey up to the way called Marketwey, between the way which leads back from Marketwey near Jonetwode to the upper end of Rodewey below Rodegate; to hold for their lives, with power to cut wood reasonably, excepting the oaks and great beeches, and reserving a parcel of land from the messuage opposite the grange of the rectory, three perches in width from the grange to the south, paying an annual rent for the messuage and fields of 53*s*. 4*d*. and for the underwood 6*s*. 8*d*.—[235.]

Three round red seals: the first representing two figures sitting, within a cross pattée (the Blessed Virgin and . . . . . ?); inscription illegible; the others, initial, etc.

1420, 14 July, 8 Hen. 5; at Overtone. Bond from John Forster of Overtone, yeoman ("zeman"), to John Perot of Overtone, gentleman, in £100.—[45.]

Round red seal: the creation of Eve; inscription illegible.

1425, 3 Sept., 4 Hen. VI; at Aultone. Warrant from Humphrey, Duke of Gloucester, Earl of Hainault, Holand, Zelland, and Pembroke, chief keeper of the King's forests on this side Trent, to Thomas Chaucers, esq., keeper of the forest of Wolmere and Alciesholte, reciting an order from the King that all the lands of the Prior and Canons of Selbourne in Selbourne, Achangre, Nortone, Basynges, Basyngstoke, and Natele, within the said forest, are to be free from all molestation contrary to the charters which they have of exemption from the jurisdiction of all forest-officers, and from all suits and services, as being disafforested.—[112.]

Round brown seal; the royal arms within a border of antlers rising from a deer's head: "S' H. duc' Glouc . . . . Angl ac just. et capit' cust' foreste."

1426, 16 Jan., 4 Hen. VI. Release from the Abbot Thomas, and Convent of Dureford, to the Prior, John, and Convent of Selbourne, of all actions against them.—[377.]

Round red seal, as with the following deed; good impression, but inscription broken: " . . . . cōvētus . . . . de Duref . . . . . . cestrēsis dioc."

1426, 19 Jan., 4 Hen. VI. Bond from Thomas, the Abbot, and the Convent of Dureford, for the payment of £40 to John, the Prior, and Convent of Selbourne, at Michaelmas next.—[39.]

Round red seal, fine impression, but broken; a triple canopy: in the centre the Virgin and Child; on one side a Bishop, on the other a Saint; below, a shield with a griffin, or dragon, and pastoral staff; on either side of the shield a stag couchant: "Sigillum . . . . . . de Dureford . . . . . . dioc."

1426, 20 Jan., 4 Hen. VI. Copy on paper of the condition of the preceding bond, viz., that the said Abbot and Convent shall pay annually 14 marks of ancient rent from the lands, tenements, mills, etc., which they hold of the said Prior and Convent by the said rent in Shete near Peterfeld.—[386.]

1426, 21 Jan., 4 Hen. VI. Bond from Thomas, Abbot of Dureford, to John, Prior of Selbourne, for the payment of 7 marks on St. Gregory's day next.—[324.]

Fragment of the abbey seal, as above.

1429, 6 May, 7 Hen. VI. Lease from Reginald, lord La Warre, knt., to John Stepe the Prior and the Convent of Selbourne, of the site of his manor of Okehangre, with the gardens, lands, meadows, pastures, etc., within the following boundaries; viz. between the water of Tonford up to the chapel of Okehangre, thence to le Courthacche, thence by the close of the tenants of Okehangre to le Blakelond, thence to the close of Peter le Burgheerne, thence to the lane called Honnelane and by the said lane to the west end of Wrikesgrove and the water of Tonford, thence between the close of Will. Cook and le Broke to la Redhacche, thence by the close of the said Prior to the water-course of Tonford; with all his common in the forest of Wolmere belonging to the said manor, the fishery in the pool of Okehangre, the hares ("cuniculis"), rents, services, etc.; to hold for the term of twenty years at an annual rent of 100*s.* No witnesses.—[118.]

Small red seal; a fleur-de-lis.

Draught, on paper, of this lease.—[176.]

[1429], 10 Nov. 8 [Hen. VI]. (*Deed mutilated.*) Release from Thomas Russell, citizen and fishmonger of London, Will. Hung . . . . Richard Everdone, brother of the said John, to the Convent of Selbourne, of all actions and demands.—[74.]

Small red seal; initial R.

1430, 12 Dec., 9 Hen. VI. Confirmation by Richard Tystede, lord of Westistede, to John the Prior of Selborne, of the grant of a way to the Priory, made by his grandmother Alice, widow of Richard de Tychebourne, under date of 25 July, 1364 (No. 242, which is recited at length); paying annually to him a quit-rent of one clove. Witn.: Will. Tystede, John Rutherfelde, John Sylver, John Goolde, Stephen Dyer of Aultone, Will. Astille.—[261.]

Small red seal of arms, indistinct.

1437, 15 March, 15 Hen. VI. Release from William Chamberleyne to John Stepe, Prior of Selburne, of all actions against him.—[323.]
Seal broken off.

Inventory of Vestments and Church Goods delivered to Peter at Berne, Sacrist, by Prior John Stepe.

1442, 5. Oct. Memorandum quod Johannes prior, anno regni regis H[enrici] VI xxj, die Veneris proximo ante festum S. Fidis virginis, suo fratri Petro at Bern, sacrista nunc facto ecclesiæ beatæ Mariæ Prioratus de Selbourne [deliberavit] omnia subscripta; viz., xvj capas, unde iij veteres; item xvij casulas, unde j de Halybourne; item iij casulas albas pro Quadragesima de Combe; item xiij dalmaticas, unde j debilis et ij novæ de Combe; item xxiiij amitas, unde j de Halybourne et j de Combe; item xxiiij manipulos, unde j de Combe et j de Halybourne; item xxiiij stolys, unde j de Halybourne et j de Combe; item xxvij aubys, unde j de Combe; item v aubys sine paruris pro Quadragesima; item ij pallia de serico; item j tuallum pro Quadragesima pendentem (*sic*) ad terram; item vij tuall[a] cum frontibus; item xv tuall[a] benedict[a] sine frontell[is]; item iiij tuall[a] pro lavatorio; item j velum pro Quadragesima; item tapetum de viridi pro summo altare; item vij offer[toria], unde v debilia; item vj ridell[a] pro summo altare; item j coupe; item ij osculatoria; item j osculatorium cum aure Sancti Johannis; item j crux argentea; item j cista de argento; item j ymago de argento; item j sensere de argento; item ij basonys de argento; item ij cruettes de argento de Combe; item j anulum cum saphyro; item j anulum de Sancto Edmundo; item j annulum de Sancto Ypolito; item j ouche; item j parva crux cum v reliquiis; item j pecten Sancti Ricardi; item j teca pro reliquiis imponendis; item j calefac[toriu]m Sancti Ricardi; item iiij candulstykkes, unde ij de ferro, et ij de tyn; item v calices, unde iiij deaurati; item ij vyolys of crystalle; item viij cruettes; item iiij vexilla; item ij superaltaria; item iiij pulys; item ij frontella pro summo altare; item ij tel' pro lectore; item iij quyshonya, unde j de serico; item v corprays; item ij paria de bakynghyres; item j bason de coper; item ij osculatoria de coper; item ij vasa de plumbo ad conservandum oleum; item j patellam eneam, de ferro (*sic*); item j tripid (*sic*); item j costrell continentem ij lagenas et j potel; item j terribulum eneum ("de coper" *crossed out*); item xx cerei ponderis xiijlb. et dim.; item ij torces ponderis xxlb.: item xvjlb. et dim. de cere; item j lagenam olei; item j planam eneam; item lxiiij zonæ; item lb. de frankencense; item vjlb. candel de cera; item j securim; item j schashouke; item j ledknyf; item ixlb. ponderis de plumbo; item j cista sine serura; item j vas de coper pro frankencense adimponendo; item j pixidem de yvery pro corpore Christi conservando; item j vter (*sic*) de corio continens j quarta; item j uter de corio continens j pynte; item iij anulos in pixide Sanctæ Mariæ de Waddone; item (*blank*) instrumenta pro sowdyng.—[50(ii).]

Very coarsely and ignorantly written; upon paper.

ANOTHER INVENTORY OF VESTMENTS AND CHURCH GOODS DELIVERED TO THE SAME BY PRIOR JOHN STEPE.

[*c.* 1445 ?] Hæc indentura facta die lunæ proxime post festum Natalis Domini, anno regni regis Henrici Sexti post conquestum Angliæ v. . . . . (*torn off*) inter fratrem Johannem Stepe, priorem ecclesiæ beatæ Mariæ Selborne, et Petrum Bernes sacristam ibidem; videlicet, quod prædictus prior deliberavit præfato Petro omnia subscripta: In primis, xxij amitas, xxxj aubes, unde v sine parura pro Quadragesima, xxij manipulos; item xxij stolæ; item viij casulæ, unde iij albæ pro Quadragesima; item xj dalmaticas, unde j debilis; item xvj capæ, unde iiij veteres; item unam amittam, j albam cum paruris, unum manipilum (*sic*), j stolam, j casulam, et duas dalmaticas, de dono Johannis Combe, capellani de Cicestria, pro diebus principalibus; item j amittam, j aubam cum paruris, j manipulum, j stolam, j casulam, de dono fratris Thome Halybourne, canonici; item j amittam, j aubam cum paruris, j manipulum, j stolam, j casulam, pertinentes ad altare sancte Katherinæ virginis, pro priore; item j amittam, ij aubas cum paruris, ij manipulos, ij stolas, et ij casulas, pertinentes ad altare sancti Petri, de dono patris Ricardi Holte; item de dono ejusdem ij tuella, unde j cum fruntello, et j canvas pro eodem altare; item j tuellum pendentem ad terram pro Quadragesima; item vj tuella cum frontibus, xv tuella sine frontellis; item iiij tuella pro lavatorio; item v corporas; item ij frontella pro summo altare sine tuellis; item ij coopertoria pro le deske; item ij pallias de serico debili; item j velum pro Quadragesima; item j tapetum viridi[s] coloris pro summo altare, ij ridelli cum iiij ridillis parvis, pertinentia ad dictum altare; item vij offretoria, unde v debilia; item iiij vexilla; item iiij pelves, iij quessones, unde j de serico; item ij superaltaria; item quinque calices, unde iiij de auro; item ij cruettes de argento, de dono domini Johannis Combe, capellani de Cicestre; item viij cruettes de peuter; item j coupam argenteam et deauratam; item ij osculatoria argentea; item j osculatorium cum osse digiti auricularis S. Johannis Baptistæ; item j crux argenteam et deauratam, non radicatam; item j turribulum argenteum et deauratum; item j anulum cum saphiro; item j aliud anulum Ipolitum aureum; item j anulum argenteum et deauratum Sancti Edmundi; item j ouche cum pereo infixo; item j cistam argenteam et deauratam; item j imaginem beatæ Mariæ argenteam et deauratam; item j parvam crucem cum v reliquiis; item j junctorium Sancti Ricardi; item j tecam pro reliquiis imponendis; item j calefactorium Sancti Ricardi; item iiij candelebra, unde ij de stagno et ij de ferro; item j pecten Sancti Ricardi; item ij viellas de cristallo in parte fracta; item j pelvim de coper ad lavatorium; item ij osculatoria de coper; item j parvum terribulum de latyn; item j vas de coper pro frank et sence (*sic*) conservando; item j pixidem de iuery pro corpore Christi; item ij vasa de plumbo pro oleo conservando; item j patellam eneam ferro ligatam; item j tripodem ferreum; item j costrellum continens ij lagenas et j potellum; item ij bakyngyres; item ij botelles de corio, unde j de quarte et j de pynte; item iij anulos argenteos et j pixidem Sanctæ Mariæ de Waddon; item (*blank*) instrumenta pro seudyng; item j ledknyff; item j shaffhoke; item j securim; item ij scabella de ferro pro cancello; item j plane; item j cistam sine cerura; item xiiij sonas; item xix taperes, ponderis xiij lb. et dimid; item ij torches, ponderis xx lb.; item xij lb. ceræ et dimidiam; item de candelis de cera ponderis vj lb.; item j lb. de frank et sence; item j lagenam olei; item ix pondera de plumbo. Vide de stauro in tergo. *On the back is only this short list*:—"ij vaccæ, j sus, iiij hoggettes, et iiij porcelli."—[50(i)[1].]

1447, 25 July, "in f. S. Jac. apost.," 25 Hen. VI; in the chapter house of Selborne. Grant from John Stepe the Prior and the Convent of Blessed Mary of Selbourne to Philip Squery, for the term of his life, of 20*s.* annually out of 14 marks paid by Walter the Abbot and the Convent of the monastery of Blessed Mary and St. Jo. Bapt. of Dureford in Sussex, for the lands and tenements held by the latter in farm at Shete in the parish of Petresfeld in the manor of Mapuldurham in the county of Southampton.—[69.]

Seal lost.

1448, 16 June, "in f. Transl. S. Ric. episc."; in the chapter house of Selborne. (*Midhurst.*) Lease from Sir John Stepe, Prior, and the Convent, to John Whyte, of Mydhurst, mercer, of a garden in the north street of Mydhurst, 133 feet long and 40 feet wide, between the burgage of John Brynkhurst on the north and the croft of Joan Mathew on the south, to hold for ninety-nine years, at an annual rent of 12*d.*—[226.]

Round red seal; a shield with three padlocks (?): "ancille P . . . . nam." (?)

The counterpart. Oval red seal of the Priory; two figures seated, the one with right hand uplifted over the other, and with a book in the left hand; (the Coronation of the Virgin ?); inscription broken: ". . . . . ventus . . . . . . Marie de Sele . . . . . ."—[228.]

(Northants)

[2]1452, 29 Aug., 30 Hen. VI; at Fodringey. Warrant from Richard, Duke of York, etc., Justice itinerant of the King's forests on this side Trent, to the keeper of the forest of Wolmer and Alisholt, exempting the Prior and Convent of Selborne from all jurisdiction of the foresters over their lands in Selborne, Achangre, Norton, Basinges, Basingestokes, and Nateleye, in accordance with the charters granted by Hen. III, which they exhibited before Rich. Foster, the deputy of the said Duke, Rich. Foster

[1] Printed (with many mistakes) in White's *Selborne*, 4to, 1789, pp. 463–5; and in *Notes from the Muniments of Magdalen College*, published by the editor of this volume in 1882, pp. 9—11, where it is conjectured that the date may be "undecimo anno Hen. VI," 1432.

[2] Under date of 27 May, 1451, 29 Hen. VI, there is amongst these Selborne charters (No. 81) a short inventory of the goods and possessions of the priory of Eastbourne, Sussex, with the receipts. This is printed in *Notes*, etc., as above, p. 86.

at Aultone on the Monday next after the feast of St. Bartholomew last past.—[115.]

Seal the same as that attached to the similar warrant of Humphrey, Duke of Gloucester, in 1425; No. 112: "S' Ricardi duc' Ebor' com. Marchie et Ultonie ac justic . . . . . . forestar'."

1453, 6 June, 31 Hen. VI. Unexecuted lease (without witnesses or seals) from Richard, lord La Warr, knt., to John Stepe the Prior and the Convent of Selbourne of the whole site of his manor of Okehangre, described by the same boundaries as in No. 118 of 6 May, 1429, to hold for nine years at an annual rent of 113*s.* 4*d.*—[164.]

ESTIMATE OF THE REVENUES AND DEBTS OF THE PRIORY IN 1462.

SELEBORNE PRIORATUS.

1462. Summa totalis valoris maneriorum terrarum tenementorum et pensionum ejusdem Prioratus in festo S[ti] Michaelis Archangeli, anno secundo Regis Edvardi 4[ti] ut patet Rotulis de valoribus liberatis.

iiij[xx.] vi[li.] x[s.] vi[d.]

Ultra c[s.] assignatos pro Johanne Mason, iiij[li.] pro capella de Tycheborne, c[s.] pro decima de Westysted solutos capellanis, xx[d.] pro Lussher, xx[s.] pro Thoma Taylour, and xij[d.] pro redditu prioratus de Novo Loco.

Inde in redditibus resolutis domino Papc, domino Archiepiscopo, et in diversis feodis certis personis concessis, ac aliis annualibus reprisis in eisdem Rotulis de valoribus annotatis, per annum, xiiij[li.] xix[s.] v[d.]

Et remanet de claro valore lxxi[li.] x[s.] viij[d.]

Unde assignantur pro—

Quatuor canonicis et quatuor famulis Deo et ecclesie ibidem servientibus pro eorum vadiis vesturis et dietis, ut patet per billam inde factam, per annum xxx[li.]

Diversis creditoribus pro eorum debitis persolvendis, ut patet per parcella inde facta xv[li.] xv[s.] iiij[d.]

Reparationibus ecclesiarum, domorum, murorum et clausurarum ejusdem Prioratus, per annum xv[li.] xv[s.] iiij[d.]

Annua pencione domini Prioris ei assignata per annum quousque v[ixerit] x[li.]

Modo sequitur de reformatione præmissorum.

Redditus omnes firmis et pencionibus—

Summa totalis valorum ibidem, misis et desperatis inde deductis, prout patet per declarationem domini Petri Prioris de Selborne, ad manus domini nostri Wynton. apud palatium suum de Wolsley præsentatam per ipsum ultimo die Febr. anno Domini MCCCCLXII, et penes ipsum remanentem . lxxj$^{li.}$ x$^{s.}$ viij$^{d.}$, unde per ipsum dominum nostrum Wynton. assignantur in forma sequente, videlicet—

Assignantur ut supra—

Pro quatuor canonicis et quatuor famulis Deo et ecclesiæ ibidem servientibus, pro eorum dietis, vadiis et vesturis, ut patet per billam inde factum. xxx$^{li.}$

Pro annua pencione Priori quosque vixerit x$^{li.}$

Pro diversis creditoribus pro eorum debitis persolvendis, ut patet per billam inde factam
xv$^{li.}$ xv$^{s.}$ iiij$^{d.}$ per ij annos, ad xxxi$^{li.}$ x$^{s.}$ viij$^{d.}$;
ultra lv$^{li.}$ xiiij$^{d.}$ de venditione stauri.

Pro diversis reparationibus ecclesiarum, domorum murorum et clausurarum, ut patet per billam xv$^{li.}$ xv$^{s.}$ iiij$^{d.}$ per ij annos,
ad xxxj$^{li.}$ x$^{s.}$ viij$^{d.}$

Summa totalis valoris pro debitis et reparationibus assignati, cum lv$^{li.}$ xiiij$^{d.}$ de venditione stauri, ut supra, cxviij$^{li.}$ ij$^{s.}$ vj$^{d.}$

Debita que debentur ibidem per diversos tenentes et firmarios ad festum S. Michaelis anno secundo Regis Edvardi 4, videlicet—

Abbas de Derford de feodo firmæ suæ ad ix$^{li.}$ vj$^{s.}$ viij$^{d.}$ per annum a retro xx$^{li.}$ vij$^{s.}$ xj$^{d.}$

Thomas Perkyns, armiger, firmarius rectoriæ de Estworlam, pro uno anno finiente ad festum S. Mich., anno ij Regis Edvardi 4. lx$^{s.}$

Johannes Shalmere ballivus de Seleborne debet lxxv$^{s.}$

Ricardus Tawry debet de eodem anno vj$^{s.}$

Ricardus Somere debet *xiij$^{s.}$ iiij$^{d.}$* *(crossed out)*

Summa xxvij$^{li.}$ viij$^{s.}$ xj$^{d.}$

Thomas Perkyns, armiger, debet de firma sua prædicta ad festum S. Mich. anno vij$^{o.}$ et ultra feodum suum ad xx$^{s.}$ per annum vj$^{li.}$ vj$^{s.}$ viij$^{d.}$

Thomas Lussher debet pro firma sua ad xl^{s} per annum, cum feodo suo ad xx$^{s.}$ per annum c$^{s.}$

Hugo Pakenham debet de redditu suo ad xx$^{s.}$ per annum c$^{s.}$

Abbas de Derford debet de feodo firmæ suæ pro annis iij, iiij, et v Regis Edvardi, ultra xx$^{li.}$ vij$^{s.}$ xj$^{d.}$ ut supra xxviij$^{li.}$

Walterus Berlond, firmarius de Shete, debet ix$^{li.}$ v$^{s.}$ ij$^{d.}$

Henricus Shafter, firmarius rectoriæ de Basyngstoke xij$^{li.}$ iiij$^{d.}$

Henricus atte Lede, nuper firmarius manerii de Rede (?), debet xx$^{li.}$

Summa lxvj$^{li.}$ xij$^{s.}$ vj$^{d.}$ [*lege*, lxxxvj$^{li.}$ xij$^{s.}$ ij$^{d.}$]

Totalis, iiij$^{xx.}$ xiij$^{li.}$ xij$^{d.}$ [cxiiij$^{li.}$ j$^{s.}$ j$^{d.}$]—[381.]

This paper (one folio leaf) is very roughly written, with many corrections, and with some notes struck out, and is evidently a draft copy of the statement of the condition of the Priory revenues made for Bishop Waynflete in 1462, on his issuing a sequestration in that year to provide for the repair of the ruinous buildings of the Priory. It is printed (on the whole, correctly) in White's *Selborne*, 1789, pp. 466–8.

1463–4. Seven folio leaves of paper, much injured by damp, in part torn and in part illegible, forming a portion of a book of accounts of the Priory, of expenditure and receipts, extending from 1 Jan., 2 Edw. IV [1463], to 1 Jan., 3 Edw. IV, and containing also part of the 4th year [1464]. It exhibits all the rents and miscellaneous receipts, with the names of the tenants. Of expenditure the principal entries are:—

1. Repairs of the Priory (*inter alia*, 4,000 tiles at 4*s*. per thousand, for the roof of the "frayter," the stables, and the "deyhouse," with the chancel of East Worldam), candles, bread and wine for the Priory church, glazing the windows of the chancel of the parish church.

2. Repairs of the chapel of B. V. Mary at Waddene (which had been burnt, an entry among the receipts recording that nothing had been received there for candles "eo quod post cremacionem ejusdem capelle nullum staurum cere"), and expenses for the "domus peregrinorum ibidem." The following are some of the entries:—

"Pro tectura unius domus peregrinorum cum stramine, iiij^d.

Pro cariagio ymaginis beatæ Mariæ de Waddene, videlicet de Wynton usque ad capellam prædictam de Waddene ex eo . . . . . . (?), xix^d.

Et in vadiis Johannis Gyles operantis circa fenestram majorem capellæ prædictæ . . . ." (*torn and illegible*).

Sol. Ricardo Dene operanti circa facturam domus peregrinorum ibidem per viij dies, cap[ienti] per diem iiij^d. ij^s. viij^d."

For glazing the windows of the chapel.

3. Manor of Beche.

4. Mill of Selborne.

5. Repairs of the chapel of the Holy Trinity at Basynge (nails, wood, carriage, etc.). Two mutilated entries appear to refer to some extra payments for wages "propter magnam altitudinem domus capellæ." There are payments for repairing the walls, roof, and windows of the chancel.

6. Miscellaneous expenses.

7. Payments to the Prior Peter (£10 *per an.*), to *dom.* Thomas Assheford, canon and sub-prior, and to *dom.* William Wynsore, canon and seneschal of the hospice of the Priory, as for four canons and four servants.

8. Customary annual payments: to the Bishop of Winchester for Schete, xiij^s. iiij^d.; to the Pope, vij^s.; to the archdeacon of Winchester for procurations and synodals, xxij^s. vj^d.; to the Bishop's apparitor iij^s. iiij^d.; to the sub-apparitor, viij^d.; to the sub-apparitor of the archdeacon, xvj^d., to John Tycheborne and his heirs for a chantry there,

iiij$^{li.}$; to the Prior of New Place, xvj$^{d.}$; to the lord of the manor of Ludschette, ij$^{s.}$; to the lord of Burgeham for the manor of Sholand, vj$^{d.}$; to the lord of Alton "pro secta curiæ relaxanda pro ten. in Okangre," x$^{s.}$, and for the same for the manor of Beche, ij$^{s.}$; to the bailiffs of the city of Winchester "pro curia relaxanda de Bowremete," ij$^{s.}$

9. Casual external payments, such as these: "In denariis datis domino Willelmo Wynsore canonico pro quadam sequestratione in curia Cantuar. versus dominum priorem ad sectam Johannis Hardman de London, grosere, pro debitis dicti prioris prosecuta, xx$^{d.}$ In denariis eidem datis pro contentatione debiti prædicti Johanuis Hardman solutis, xij$^{d.}$ In dono domino Willelmo Wynsore facto pro expensis abbatis de Costantynnobylle apud prioratum prædictum existentis xxvij^{o} die Julii dicto anno quarto, xj$^{s.}$ (?). (To the same) pro expensis capellani domini cancellarii Angliæ apud prioratum existentis quarto die Augusti dicto anno quarto, x$^{d.}$ In dono pro pauperibus die Cœnæ, xij$^{d.}$" (For amercements of the Prior in the preceding year in the court of the sheriff of Southampton, in a suit of John Andrewe against him for debt, xlij$^{s.}$ Further fines in this year in the sheriff's court and "coram Rege," in the same suit, with expenses thereupon.) "Sol. cuidam capellano ministranti in capella de Netley hoc anno virtute cujusdam sequestrationis domini nostri Wynton . . . . . nil, quia in anno futuro"; etc.

10. Repairing the chancel of Blakemcre church and the windows of the chancels of Okeanger, Estworlam, and Basynge.

11. Payments of debts: the total only xxxviij$^{s.}$ xj$^{d.}$

12. Repairs at the manor of Roode.

Amongst the receipts is a rent of 20*s.* *per an.* for the "tyle ovyn" at the Priory, leased to John Prat for three years, and 51*s.* 8*d.* from the sale of corn and hay of the rectory of Selborne.—[394.]

1469, 24 March, 9 Edw. IV; at Herteley. Lease from Richard Lussher to John Morton the Prior and the Convent of Selbourne of five fields of arable land separately enclosed called Candeverefeldes, lying together within the demesne of Herteley Maudite in the county of Southampton, between the land of the lord of Herteley and that of the lord of Westwordelam; and one croft of arable land called Siz acres in the aforesaid demesne, near the way leading from the village of Herteley to the wood of Herteley, between the said way and the land of the tenants of Herteley on one side and the land called Brianes on another; and also one croft of arable land called Pilcroft, on the right side of the way leading from the village of Herteley to the Priory of Selbourne, between the said way and the land of the tenants of Herteley on one side and the land of the tenants of Nortone on the other; and one meadow called Wetemede near Herteleywode; all which the said lessor had by feoffment of Joan, daughter and heir of Stephen Dier, late of Aultone; to hold for the term of ninety-nine years, paying an annual quit-rent of one penny. Witn.: William, Bishop of Winchester, Humfrey Bourgchier, knt., Thomas Selenger, esq., Rob. Wyntreshulle, esq., Thos. Basset, esq., Will. Utteworth, Henry Stoughtone.—[113.]

Small dark seal; the Prince of Wales' feathers.

1470, 16 Jan., 9 Edw. IV; at Herteley. Release from Richard Lussher to John Morton the Prior and the Convent of Selborne of all his right in the land conveyed in the preceding deed No. 113, of 24 March, 1469. Witnesses and seal the same.—[114.]

1474, 3 Jan., 13 Edw. IV; in the chapter house at Selborne. Copy, on paper (nearly contemporary), of a grant from Peter the Prior and the Convent of B. Mary of Selborne to John Wheteham of an annual rent of 20*s.* from their manor of Beche in the parish of Altone.—[17.]

1477, 4 Aug., 17 Edw. IV; at Altone. Warrant from Henry Bourgchier, Earl of Essex, Justice itinerant of the King's forests on this side the Trent, to the keeper of the forest of Wolmere and Alisholt, to the same purport as the warrants of the Duke of Gloucester in 1425 and Duke of York in 1452, Nos. 112 and 115 supra, for the exemption of the Priory of Selborne.—[205*a.*]

Bad impression of seal, black, very indistinct.

1477, 14 Nov., 17 Edw. IV. Release from Henry Percy, late of the city of Winchester, to Peter Bernes, Prior of Selburne, of all actions against him.—[396.]

Small seal.

1478, 20 March, at Brommore: 22 March, at Tortyntone. Citation from the Priors of Brommore and Tortyngtone, of the dioceses of Winchester and Chichester, appointed Visitors of the houses of the order of St. Augustine in Winchester, Chichester, and Sarum, by a general Chapter held at Leycester, to the Prior of Selborne to attend, with all the brethren and canons, their visitation to be held at Selborne on 21 April.—[41.]

Two red seals: (1) large, oval, fine impression; St. Michael treading on the dragon: "S' comune ecc̃e conventualis S . . . . chaelis de Brommore." (2) small, round; two figures (one a female, the other with a sword), under canopies; inscription (two words) illegible.

1478, 1 April. Acknowledgment by Reginald, Prior of Monemuth, the Pope's sub-collector in England, of the receipt of 7*s.* from the Prior of Selburne for procurations.—[395(ii)]

Small red seal; inscription broken; the cross-keys: "Sigillũ . . . . " (?)

1479, 12 Jan., 18 Edw. IV. Affidavit, in English, by John Scherpe, Prior of Selborne, and late Subprior of the worshipful monastery of Brewtone, Somerset, that whereas one John Danys (Davys ?) of Bristowe has taken an action of trespass against one Thomas Wykam for wrongfully taking out of his house at Bristowe a deed by which the Prior and Convent of Brewtone (the said John Scherpe being then Supprior) granted to the said John Danys certain lands, tenements, woods, etc., in demise and in reversion, in Brewtone, no such deed was ever made, granted or sealed by the said Convent of Brewtone or any of them. —[387.]

1484, 2 Sept.; at Farnham Castle. Commission by Bishop Waynflete to Richard, Prior of New Place, master Richard Hayward, LL.D., ("in legibus professori"), and Walter Hodgies, LL.B., to annex the Priory of Selebourne, in the Bishop's patronage, to Magdalen College. —[103.]

Good impression of the episcopal seal, but broken; oval, red; tabernacle-work, with three saints under canopies; at foot, the bust of the Bishop with clasped hands and his coat of arms, fusilly, ermine and sable, on a chief three lilies; on dexter side, a coat of arms, quarterly, 1st and 4th three fleurs-de-lis, 2nd and 3rd three lions passant; on sinister side, a shield with mitre and cross-keys: "Sigillum Willelmi Dei . . . . Wintoniensis . . . ."

PROCESS FOR ANNEXATION OF THE PRIORY TO MAGDALEN COLLEGE.

[A folio book, of ten leaves of parchment, in a parchment cover, numbered *Appropr.* 10.][1]

1484, Sept. 6—10.

Universis sanctæ matris Ecclesiæ filiis ad quos præsentes litteræ sive præsens publicum instrumentum pervenerint sive pervenerit, et quos infrascripta tangunt seu tangere poterunt quomodolibet in futurum, Ricardus Dei gratia Prior ecclesiæ conventualis de Novo Loco, Winton dioc., reverendi in Christo patris et domini domini Willelmi eadem gratia Wintoniensis Episcopi ad infrascripta una cum aliis cum illa clausula *conjunctim et divisim* Commissarius sufficienter et legittime deputatus, salutem in Domino et fidem indubiam præsentibus adhibere.

[1] In the following year the Process was formally repeated, in consequence (as it seems) of the Priory being then actually vacant by the cession of the Prior, and the record of this Process exists in a similar book numbered *Appropr.* 3, to which the same seals are attached. This enquiry was held before the Prior of New Place in the parish church of St. George at Esher; it commenced on 3 August, 1485, and the sentence was pronounced in the same place on 8 August. The documents are in substance the same, *mutatis mutandis.* Some verbal differences, with occasional greater variations, are given in the notes. There is also (No. 25) a copy of the first Process in a third book, which is not quite perfect at the end. An abstract of the second Process is given in White's *Selborne.*

Ad universitatis vestra notitiam deducimus et deduci volumus per præsentes quod coram nobis Commissario prædicto in ecclesia parochiali Sancti Andreæ apostoli de Farnham dictæ dioceseos, sexto die mensis Septembris anno Domini millesimo quadringentesimo octuagesimo quarto, indictione secunda, pontificatus sanctissimi in Christo patris et domini nostri domini Innocentii divina providentia Papæ octavi anno primo, judicialiter sedente, comparuit venerabilis vir magister Jacobus Preston, in sacra theologia professor, infrascriptus, et exhibuit litteras commissionis dicti reverendi in Christo patris et domini domini Willelmi gratia supradicta Wintoniensis episcopi, ejusdem loci diocesani, quas quidem litteras prædictas per magistrum Thomam Somercotes notarium publicum infra nominatum publice legi fecimus, tenorem subsequentem in se continentes :—

Commission from Bishop Waynflete.

"Willelmus permissione divina Wintoniensis episcopus dilecto nobis in Christo Ricardo, Priori ecclesiæ conventualis de Novo Loco, ordinis Sancti Augustini, nostræ dioceseos, et magistro Ricardo Hayward, in legibus professori, ac Waltero Hodgies, in utroque jure bacallario, salutem, gratiam et benedictionem. Ex parte venerabilium virorum Præsidentis et Scholarium collegii beatæ Mariæ Magdalenæ in universitate Oxon. fundati nobis humiliter extitit supplicatum, quod fructus redditus et proventus prædicto Collegio pertinentes, ad sustentationem Præsidentis et Scholarium ejusdem modernorum et futurorum, ipsiusque Collegii conservationem, et supportationem onerum incumbentium, eidem non sufficiunt, quatinus prioratum de Selebourne, nostrorum patronatus et dioceseos, cum suis possessionibus, juribus, et pertinentiis universis, eis et eorum Collegio prædicto canonice unire, annectere et appropriare dignaremur. Et quia nos aliis arduis negotiis sumus impediti quominus prædictæ unionis, annexionis, seu appropriationis, expeditionem et examinationem superintendere valeamus, ad cognoscendum igitur de et super præmissis et aliis in hac parte necessariis et requisitis, ac procedendum, in quocunque loco honesto dictæ nostræ dioceseos non exempto, in negotio unionis, annexionis, sive appropriationis, prædicti prioratus de Selebourne, cum suis possessionibus, juribus, et pertinentiis universis, ex causis præmissis, præfatis Præsidenti et Scolaribus suisque successoribus ac eorum Collegio prædicto uniendi, annectendi, appropriandi et incorporandi, ac in ipsorum proprios usus imperpetuum possideri concedendi, ita quod, Priore dicti prioratus de Selebourne moderno cedente, decedente, aut eodem prioratu qualitercunque vacante, liceat ex tunc Præsidenti et Scolaribus prædictis et eorum successoribus per se aut per procuratorem eorundem dictum prioratum de Selebourne, cum suis possessionibus, juribus et pertinentiis universis, propria sua auctoritate ingredi, ac corporalem et realem possessionem eorundem per se aut suos apprehendere ac in usus suos proprios imperpetuum possidere et tenere, dictaeque unionis, annexionis, appropriationis et incorporationis negotium, cum suis emergentibus, incidentibus et connexis quibuscunque, fine debito et canonico decidendum et terminandum, çæteraque omnia et singula in hac parte requisita seu necessaria, vocatis prius per vos in hac parte de jure vocandis, faciendum, exercendum et expediendum, vobis et vestrum cuilibet per se et in solidum, in quorum fidelitate et industria confidimus, conjunctim et divisim committimus vices nostras, ac specialem et plenam in Domino potestatem, cum cujuslibet cohercionis canonicæ exequendique quæ in hac parte decreveritis potestate. Et quid in præmissis feceritis, nos, hujusmodi negotio expedito, debite certificetis per litteras vestras patentes, totum et integrum processum unionis, annexionis, appropriationis et incorporationis hujusmodi in se continentes, seu sic certificet ille vestrum qui præsentem nostram commissionem fuerit executus per litteras suas patentes autentice sigillatas. In cujus rei testimonium præsentibus sigillum nostrum apponi fecimus. Datum in castro nostro de Farnham, dictæ nostræ dioceseos, secundo die mensis Septembris, anno Domini millesimo CCCC^{mo} LXXX^{mo} quarto, et nostræ consecrationis anno XXXVIII°."

Post quarum quidem dictæ commissionis litterarum lecturam publice factam, dictus magister Jacobus Prestone quasdam procuratorii litteras venerabilium virorum magistri Ricardi Mayewe, Præsidentis, ut asseruit, Collegii beatæ Mariæ Magdalenæ in universitate Oxon. situati, et ejusdem Collegii Scolarium sigillo rotundo communi, videlicet eorundem Præsidentis et Scolarium, in cera rubea impresso sigillatas, realiter exhibuit, cujus quidem procuratorii tenor inferius scribitur, et pro eisdem dominis suis præsidente et scolaribus fecit se partem, ac nobis cum instantia debita humiliter supplicavit quatinus onus commissionis hujusmodi in nos assumere, et juxta traditam nobis in eisdem formam procedere, dignaremur.

Ad cujus quidem magistri Jacobi Prestone procuratoris memorati petitionem et instantiam, proclamatione interim publice coram nobis facta si quis contra nos aut dictam commissionem hujusmodi objicere voluerit, nullo ibidem contradicere seu objectere (*sic*) hujusmodi comparente, onus commissionis hujusmodi ob reverentiam supradicti reverendi patris committentis in nos assumentes, vocatis de jure vocandis, pro jurisdictione ejusdem reverendi patris et nostra in hac parte pronunciavimus et declaravimus, et ad commissionis hujusmodi executionem in negotio antedicto ad instantem petitionem ipsius magistri Jacobi Preston procuratoris antedicti procedendum fore decrevimus. Necnon præfatum magistrum Thomam Somercotes, notarium publicum antenominatum, in præsenti publico nostri processus instrumento se subscribentem, in actorum nostrorum scribam nominavimus et deputavimus tunc ibidem.

No one appeared to object to the commission.

Thomas Somercotes appointed to report the process.

Consequenter tunc ibidem comparuit magister Michael Cleve,[1] sacrorum canonum professor, procurator venerabilium virorum Prioris et Conventus ecclesiæ Cathedralis Wintoniensis, et exhibuit procuratorium suum pro dictos Priore et Conventu sive capitulo dicta ecclesiæ cathedralis Wintoniensis sigillo eorum communi sigillatum, et fecit se partem pro eisdem. Deinde comparuit etiam coram nobis memorato commissario in prædicta ecclesia parochiali de Farnham dicto sexto die

Michael Cleve, proxy for the church of Winchester.

1 "Clyff" in second Process.

William Cowper, proxy for the Bishop of Winchester.

mensis prædictæ Septembris adhuc judicialiter sedente circumspectus vir [1] Willelmus Cowper, dicti reverendi in Christo patris Willelmi Wintoniensis episcopi, supradicti Prioratus de Selebourne, ordinis Sancti Augustini, ut asseruit patroni, procurator, ac procuratorium suum sub sigillo ejusdem reverendi patris sigillatum etiam realiter exhibuit, et pro eodem reverendo in Christo patre Willelmo Wintoniensi episcopo dicti prioratus de Selebourne patrono fecit se partem. In quorum magistri Michaelis Cleve, dictorum Prioris et Conventus sive capituli ecclesiæ cathedralis Wintoniensis, et Willelmi Cowper,[2] dicti reverendi patris domini Willelmi Wintoniensis episcopi patroni supradicti, procuratorum, nominibus quibus supra coram nobis comparentium, præsentia, idem magister Jacobus Prestone, procurator dictorum Præsidentis et Scholarium Collegii beatæ Mariæ Magdalenæ in universitate Oxon. prædicta, quemdam libellum sive articulum in causa sive negotio unionis, annexionis, appropriationis et incorporationis prædicti Prioratus de Selebourne, nomine prædictorum Præsidentis et Scholarium Collegii antedicti exhibuit, et admitti petiit eundem cum effectu, cujus quidem libelli sive articuli sequitur tenor :—

Libel exhibited by James Preston, proxy for the College.

"In Dei nomine, Amen. Coram vobis venerabili in Christo patre Ricardo, Priore ecclesiæ conventualis de Novo Loco, Wintoniensis diocescos, ad infrascripta commissario una cum aliis, cum clausula *conjunctim et divisim*, sufficienter et legittime deputato, Pars venerabilium virorum magistri Ricardi Mayewe, Præsidentis Collegii beatæ Mariæ Magdalenæ in universitate Oxon., et ejusdem Collegii Scholarium, dicit, allegat, et in his scriptis in jure proponit articulatim prout sequitur.

In primis, quod collegium beatæ Mariæ Magdalenæ in universitate Oxon. prædicta situatum de uno præsidente et octoginta quatuor scholaribus, præter sexdecim choristas et tresdecim servientes dicti collegii, inibi Altissimo jugiter famulantibus et in scientiis plerisque liberalibus, præsertim in sacrosancta theologia, studentibus, nedum ad ipsorum præsidentis et scholarium in dicto Collegio pro præsenti et imposterum, annuente Domino, incorporandorum in eodem relevamen, verum etiam ad omnium et singulorum tam sæcularium quam religiosorum cujuscumque ordinis undequaque illuc confluere pro salubri doctrina volentium utilitatem multiplicem et incrementa virtutum fideique catholicæ stabilimentum, ita videlicet quod omnes et singuli absque personarum seu nationum delectu illuc accedere volentes lecturas publicas et doctrinas tam in grammatíca, in loco ad Collegium contiguo, ac in philosophiis morali et naturali, quam in sacra theologia, in eodem Collegio perpetuis futuribus temporibus opportunis continuandis libere et gratis audire valeant et possint, ad laudem gloriam et honorem Domini nostri Jesu Christi et ecclesiæ suæ sanctæ exaltationem necnon ad honorem intemeratæ Virginis Mariæ matris Ejusdem, Sanctæ Mariæ Magdalenæ, Sancti Johannis Baptistæ, et aliorum sanctorum, nuper pie et salubriter extitit fundatum et stabilitum.

[1] "honestus vir ;" second Process.

[2] In the second Process Cowper's place is taken after the first day by Ralph Langley.

Item, quod in diocesi Wintoniensi fuit et est inter alia loca quidam Prioratus de Selebourne, ordinis Sancti Augustini, in quo reverendus in Christo pater et dominus dominus Willelmus Dei gratia Wintoniensis episcopus plenum jus obtinet patronatus, et sic fuit et est verum publice dictus, tentus, habitus, et reputatus palam, publice, et notorie.

Item, quod idem Prioratus de Selebourne ad tantæ ruinæ detrimentum devenit quod in eodem solitus numerus canonicorum regularium minime observatur, immo in tantum diminuitur quod Prior duntaxat ejusdem loci absque aliquo canonico obedientiario ibidem incorporato modernis temporibus residere in eodem dinoscitur. Et sic sacra religio et regulares observantiæ ibidem in ea parte non observantur, unde scandalum non modicum generatur. Fructus quoque, redditus et proventus ejusdem laicorum usibus non modicum multipliciter applicantur.

Item, quod dictus reverendus pater Willelmus Wintoniensis episcopus, dicto Prioratui et personis ejusdem pie compatiens, solicitudines pastorales, labores, et diligentias quamplurimas, tam per se quam per suos, pro reformatione præmissorum impendebat; et aliquando illius loci prioribus propter malam et inutilem administrationem et dispensationem bonorum prædicti Prioratus, suis demeritis exigentibus, amotis, alios priores in quorum circumspectione et diligentia confidebat præfecit, quos tamen male se habuisse et inutiliter administrare et administrasse usque ad præsentia tempora post debitam investigationem et examinationem factam invenit. Ita quod dictus reverendus pater statum ejusdem Prioratus reparare vel restaurare cum dictis suis solicitudinibus et laboribus gravissimis per aliquem religiosum nequivit, et considerata temporis malitia, et ex præteritis timendo et conjecturando futura, de aliqua bona et sancta religione ejusdem ordinis vel alterius, et religionis sanctis observantiis juxta piam intentionem primævi fundatoris ibidem habendis desperatur.

Item, quod fructus, redditus et proventus dicto Collegio assignati adeo tenues sunt et exiles quod ad exhibitionem dicti Præsidentis et Scholarium, Choristarum, ac eorum serventium, et aliorum onerum eidem Collegio incumbentium, minime sufficiunt his diebus.

Item, quod præmissa omnia et singula fuerunt et sunt vera, publica, notoria, manifesta et famosa, et super eisdem a diu laborarunt et laborant publica vox et fama.

Unde, facta fide in ea parte requisita, petit pars eorundem Præsidentis et Scholarium dictum Prioratum de Selebourne cum ecclesiis parochialibus de Selebourne et Basynge, una cum aliis ecclesiis et locis eidem Prioratui de Selebourne ab antiquo spectantibus et pertinentibus, cum suis possessionibus, rebus, juribus, et pertinentiis universis, Præsidenti et Scholaribus dicti Collegii et eorum successoribus ac eidem Collegio uniendum et appropriandum fore decerni et cum effectu uniri; ita quod Priore ejusdem Prioratus moderno cedente, decedente, aut dicto Prioratu qualitercunque vacante, liceat ex tunc Præsidenti et Scholaribus supradicti Collegii et eorum successoribus ipsum Prioratum de Selebourne cum dictis ecclesiis omnibus et singulis, locis, rebus, possessionibus, juribus, et pertinentiis universis, propria sua auctoritate ingredi, ac corporalem et realem possessionem eorundem per se et suos apprehendere ac in usus eorum perpetuo possidere et tenere, ulteriusque fieri, statui et decerni in præmissis et ea concernentibus quibuscunque quod juris fuerit et sacris in hac parte convenit institutis. Præmissa proponit et fieri petit pars dictorum Præsidentis et Scholarium conjunctim et divisim, non arctans se ad omnia et singula præmissa probandum, nec ad onus superfluæ probationis de quo protestatur, juris beneficio in omnibus semper salvo."

Quem quidem libellum sive articulum de expresso consensu omnium et singulorum procuratorum partium supradictarum Nos Commissarius antedictus admisimus, et ad omnia et singula in eodem libello sive articulo contenta probandum eidem magistro Jacobo Prestone, procuratori Præsidentis et Scholarium supradictorum, assignavimus terminum, videlicet decimum diem dictæ mensis Septembris. Et tunc statim et incontinenti in partem illius termini sic assignati magister Jacobus Prestone, procurator prædictus, produxit in testes magistrum Willelmum Gyfford, in sacra theologia professorem, Ricardum Bernys, in artibus magistrum, Johannem Chapman et Willelmum Rabbys, litteratos, quos nos Commissarius antedictus de consensu omnium procuratorum prædictorum admisimus, et tactis per eosdem et eorum quemlibet sacrosanctis Dei evangeliis ad ea jurari fecimus, et mandavimus de dicendo omnem et omnimodam veritatem quam noverint in ea parte superinterroganda ab eisdem. Qui quidem testes de mandato nostro sic jurarunt et eorum quilibet sic juravit, quos quidem testes nos Commissarius prædictus eodem die, tunc assistente nobis scriba supradicto, secrete et singillatim examinavimus. Quorum quidem procuratoriorum omnium et singulorum procuratorum prædictorum tenores sequuntur, et sunt tales.

Production of witnesses.

Letters of proxy of the President and Scholars of Magdalen College.

"Pateat universis per præsentes quod nos Ricardus Mayewe, Præsidens Collegii beata Mariæ Magdalenæ in universitatæ Oxon. et Scholares ejusdem Collegii magistros Jacobum Prestone et Johannem Langport, in sacra theologia professores, ac Simonem Ayleward, in artibus magistrum, conjunctim et divisim, ac eorum quemlibet per se divisim et in solidum, ita quod non sit melior conditio occupantis sed quod unus eorum inceperit quilibet eorundem id libere prosequi valeat, mediare pariter et finire, nostros veros legittimos et indubitatos procuratores, actores, factores, negotiorumque nostrorum gestores et nuncios speciales facimus, constituimus et ordinamus per præsentes, damusque et concedimus eisdem procuratoribus nostris prædictis conjunctim et eorum cuilibet, ut præmittitur, per se divisim et in solidum potestatem generalem et mandatum speciale pro nobis, et nomine nostro, ac Collegii nostri prædicti nomine, coram reverendo in Christo patre et domino domino Willelmo Dei gratia Wintoniensi episcopo, aut ipsius commissario sive commissariis uno vel pluribus in hac parte legittime deputato sive deputando, deputatis sive deputandis, comparendi, ac prioratum de Selebourne, Winton. dioc., cum suis juribus et pertinentiis universis nobis Præsidenti et Scholaribus dicti Collegii beatæ Mariæ

Magdalenæ, nostrisque successoribus ac eidem Collegio nostro, uniri, annecti, appropriari et incorporari, ac in nostros perpetuos usus possidendum petendi et obtinendi, causamque et causas hujusmodi unionis, annexionis, appropriationis et incorporationis sic ut præfertur nobis Præsidenti et Scholaribus nostroque Collegio prædicto fiendæ allegandi, proponendi, declarandi pariter et probandi, ac de veritate earundem in animas nostras jurandi et fidem faciendi; necnon hujusmodi unione, annexione, appropriatione et incorporatione sic facta, Priore conventuali Prioratus de Selebourne antedicti cedente vel decedente, vel eodem prioratu qualitercunque vacante, dictum prioratum cum suis possessionibus, juribus, et pertinentiis universis, intrandi, nanciscendi, adipiscendi et obtinendi; ac hujusmodi possessionem sic nactam et adeptam nomine nostro et Collegii nostri nomine prædicti retinendi ac continuandi; et pro præmissis, si oporteat, agendi, defendendi, excipiendi, replicandi, libellum et libellos ac quascunque petitiones summarias dandi, ministrandi et recipiendi, litemque contestandi et contestari videndi, ponendi et articulandi, ponique et articulari petendi et videndi, positionibusque et articulis ac interrogatoriis respondendi, juramentum tam de calumpnia quam de veritate dicenda et aliud quodcunque sacramentum licitum in animas nostras præstandi et faciendi, crimina et defectus objiciendi et objectis respondendi, testes, litteras et instrumenta ac alia quæcunque probationum genera producendi et exhibendi, productaque et exhibita ex adverso reprobandi et impugnandi, statusque nostri reformationem in integrum, restitutionem, dampnorum æstimationem, expensas et interesse quodlibet, necnon beneficium absolutionis seu relaxationis a quibuscunque suspensionis, excommunicationis et interdicti sententiis simpliciter et ad cautelam quotiens visum fuerit opportunum petendi, recipiendi et obtinendi, provocandi et appellandi, provocationes et appellationes notificandi et intimandi, ac eas et eorum causas prosequendi, apostolosque petendi et recipiendi, et generaliter omnia et singula faciendi, exercendi et expediendi quæ ad unionem annexionem appropriationem et incorporationem dicti prioratus de Selebourne, cum suis possessionibus, juribus, et pertinentiis universis, faciendam et ipsius negotii expeditionem necessaria fuerint seu quomodolibet opportuna, etiam si mandatum de se magis exigant speciale: Promittimusque nos ratum gratum et firmum perpetuo habituri totum et quicquid procuratores nostri seu eorum aliquis nomine nostro et Collegii nostri prædicti nomine fecerint seu fecerit in præmissis vel aliquo præmissorum, sub ypotheca et obligatione omnium bonorum nostrorum, et cautionem exponimus per præsentes. In cujus rei testimonium sigillum nostrum commune præsentibus est appensum. Datum in Collegio nostro prædicto tricesimo die mensis Augusti, anno Domini millesimo quadringentesimo octuagesimo quarto."

Letters of proxy of the Prior and Convent of the church of Winchester.

"Universis Christi fidelibus ad quos præsentes litteræ pervenerint, Nos Thomas Prior ecclesiæ cathedralis Wintoniensis et ejusdem loci Conventus, salutem in Domino sempiternam. Cum magister Ricardus Mayewe Præsidens Collegii beatæ Mariæ Magdalenæ in universitate

Oxon. et ejusdem Collegii Scholares ex certis causis rationabilibus ipsos in hac parte moventibus Prioratum beatæ Mariæ de Selebourne, Winton. dioc., cum suis juribus et pertinentiis universis, quatenus in ipsis est, eis et eorum Collegio prædicto appropriari, uniri, annecti et incorporari voluerint, Nos igitur Prior et Conventus prædicti in domo nostra capitulari capitulariter congregati dilectos nobis in Christo magistros David Husband et Michaelem Cleve, sacrorum canonum professores, nostros veros et legittimos ac indubitatos conjunctim et divisim ac eorum utrumque per se et in solidum ordinamus facimus et constitiumus procuratores, actores, factores, negotiorumque nostrorum gestores et nuncios speciales. Damusque et concedimus eisdem procuratoribus nostris et ipsorum utrique potestatem generalem et mandatum speciale pro nobis et nomine nostro coram reverendo in Christo patre et domino domino Willelmo Dei gratia Wintoniensi episcopo, aut ejus commissario sive commissariis, in negotio unionis, annexionis, appropriationis et incorporationis dicti prioratus beatæ Mariæ de Selebourne cum suis juribus et pertinentiis universis dictis Præsidenti et Scholaribus, ac eorum Collegio antedicto fiendæ comparendi et interessendi, ac cum dicto reverendo patre aut ejus in hac parte commissario sive commissariis hujusmodi communicandi et tractandi, dictæque unioni, annexioni, appropriationi et incorporationi, ac cæteris in hac parte requisitis et necessariis, nomine nostro et pro nobis consentiendi et consensum nostrum dandi et præbendi, et generaliter omnia et singula faciendi, exercendi et expediendi quæ in præmissis et circa ea necessaria fuerint seu quomodolibet opportuna, etiam si mandatum de se magis exigant speciale. Cui quidem unioni, annexioni, appropriationi et incorporationi hujusmodi sic faciendæ et fiendæ, præhabito inter nos diligenti tractatu et deliberatione sufficienti, etiam nostrum præbemus assensum pariter et consensum. Promittimusque nos ratum gratum et firmum perpetuo habituri totum et quicquid dicti procuratores nostri seu eorum alter fecerint seu fecerit in præmissis seu aliquo præmissorum sub ypotheca et obligatione omnium bonorum nostrorum, et cautionem in ea parte exponimus per præsentes. In cujus rei testimonium sigillum nostrum commune præsentibus est appensum. Datum in domo nostra capitulari quarto die mensis Septembris, anno Domini millesimo quadringentesimo octuagesimo quarto."

Letters of proxy of the Bishop of Winchester.

"Pateat universis per præsentes quod nos Willelmus permissione divina Wintoniensis episcopus, domus sive prioratus de Selebourne juxta Altone nostræ dioc. situati verus patronus, jure nostri patronatus nobis competentis dilectum nobis in Christo magistrum Willelmum Gyfford, in sacra theologia professorem, Radulphum Langley et Willelmum Cowper, litteratos, conjunctim et eorum quemlibet per se divisim et in solidum, ita quod non sit melior conditio occupantis sed quod unus eorum inceperit quilibet eorum id libere prosequi valeat, mediare pariter et finire, nostros veros et legittimos ordinamus facimus et constituimus procuratores, actores, factores, negotiorumque nostrorum gestores et nuncios speciales per præsentes. Damusque et concedimus eisdem procuratoribus nostris et eorum cuilibet, ut præmittitur, potestatem generalem et mandatum speciale pro nobis et nomine nostro coram venerabili viro Ricardo, Priore ecclesiæ conventualis de Novo Loco, nostræ dioc., in hac parte commissario sufficienti et legittime deputato, in quodam negotio unionis, annexionis et appropriationis de dicto domo sive prioratu de Selebourne cum suis juribus et pertinentiis universis Præsidenti et Scholaribus Collegii beatæ Mariæ Magdalenæ in universitate Oxon. situati, et successoribus suis ac eorum Collegio prædicto, certis de causis veris et legittimis pie et salubriter fiendæ, ubicunque hujusmodi unionem, annexionem, sive appropriationem in nostro diocesi Wintoniensi fieri et celebrari contigerit, diebus et locis ad hoc assignatis sive assignandis comparendi et interessendi, ac in hujusmodi unionis, annexionis et appropriationis negotio et super causis idem negotium concernentibus cum omnibus et singulis quorum interest tractandi et communicandi, suaque consilia et auxilia eidem unionis annexionis et appropriationis negotio impendendi, ac eidem unioni annexioni et appropriationi fiendæ nomine nostro expresse consentiendi, cæteraque omnia et singula faciendi, exercendi et expediendi quæ in præmissis et circa ea necessaria fuerint seu quomodolibet opportuna, etiam si mandatum de se magis exigant speciale. Promittimusque nos ratum gratum et firmum perpetuo habituri totum et quicquid dicti procuratores nostri seu eorum aliquis nomine nostro fecerint seu fecerit in præmissis vel aliquo præmissorum, sub ypotheca et obligatione omnium bonorum nostrorum, et in ea parte cautionem exponimus per præsentes. In cujus rei testimonium sigillum nostrum præsentibus est appensum. Datum in castro nostro de Farnham, dictæ nostræ dioc., tertio die mensis Septembris, anno Domini millesimo quadringentesimo octuagesimo quarto, et nostræ consecrationis anno tricesimo octavo."

Quo quidem decimo die dictæ mensis Septembris adveniente, sæpedictus magister Jacobus Prestone, nominibus quibus supra, coram nobis commissario præmemorato anno Domini, indictione, pontificatu et loco prædictis judicialiter sedente, comparuit, et in præsentia dictorum procuratorum quibus supra nominibus ut præfertur ad probandum contenta in memorato libello sive articulo exhibuit quasdam litteras testimoniales dicti reverendi patris Wintoniensis episcopi infrascriptas sigillo suo sigillatas[1]; necnon produxit unum testem, videlicet dominum Thomam Assheford, Priorem Prioratus de Selebourne supradicti, quem quidem testem ad petitionem dicti magistri Jacobi Prestone, ex consensu cæterorum procuratorum, admisimus, et tactis etiam per eundem sacrosanctis Dei evangeliis ad ea jurari fecimus et mandavimus de dicendo omnem et omnimodam veritatem quam sciverit in ea parte super interrogandis ab eodem. Qui quidem testis de mandato nostro sic juravit. Quem vero testem nos commissarius prædictus tunc et ibidem in præsentia prædicti magistri Thomæ Somercotes, auctoritate apostolica notarii publici, secrete et singillatim examinavimus. Et consequenter ad

[1] "Et petiit ipsas admitti, quas nos commissarius supradictus ex consensu omnium procuratoriorum (*sic*) præscriptorum partium prædictarum admisimus." Added in the second Process, which then goes on to say that Preston produced *two* witnesses, viz., Prior Assheford and William Rabbys, and the following paragraph consequently differs throughout.

instantem petionem magistri Jacobi Prestone procuratoris prædicti et de expresso consensu omnium aliorum procuratorum prædictorum depositiones et attestationes testium supradictorum in forma supradicta per nos in ea parte examinatorum publicavimus. Quarum attestationum tenores sequunter in hæc verba :—

Evidence of William Gifford, D.D.

Magister Willelmus Gyfford, sacræ theologiæ professor, ætatis lvj annorum et ultra, liberæ conditionis, testis productus, admissus, juratus et diligenter examinatus de et super libello sive articulo per supradictum magistrum Jacobum Prestone procuratorem prædictum, ut præfertur, proposito; et primo super notitia personarum et locorum in dicto libello sive articulo expressorum, ad quæ dicit et respondet iste juratus quod bene novit dictum Collegium beatæ Mariæ Magdalenæ in universitate Oxon. situatum, fundatum et stabilitum, de uno Præsidente et certo numero personarum de quo supra in libello fit mentio, inibi Altissimo jugiter famulantium et in scientiis plerisque liberalibus, præsertim in sacra theologia, non solum ad ipsorum Præsidentis et Scholarium in eodem Collegio pro præsenti et imposterum annuente Domino incorporandorum in eodem incrementum, verum etiam ad omnium et singulorum tam secularium quam religiosorum cujuscunque ordinis undequaque illuc accedere pro salubri doctrina volentium utilitatem multiplicem et incrementa virtutum fideique Catholicæ stabilimentum. Ita videlicet quod omnes et singuli absque personarum seu nationum delectu illuc accedere volentes lecturas publicas et doctrinas tam in grammatica in loco ad idem Collegium contiguo ac philosophiis morali et naturali quam in sacra theologia in eodem Collegio perpetuis futuris temporibus opportunis continuandas libere et gratis audire valeant et possint, ad laudem gloriam et honorem domini nostri Jesu Christi,[1] necnon ad honorem intemeratæ Virginis Mariæ, Baptistæ, et aliorum sanctorum, prout in dicto libello est expressum. Et ulterius interrogatus, dicit et respondet quod in diocesi Wintoniensi est quidam prioratus de Selebourne, ordinis Sancti Augustini, in quo reverendus in Christo pater Willelmus Wintoniensis episcopus plenum jus obtinet patronatus. Ac insuper interrogatus, dicit et respondet quod idem prioratus de Selebourne ad tantæ ruinæ detrimentum devenit quod in eodem solitus numerus canonicorum regularium minime observatur, immo in tantum diminuitur quod prior duntaxat ejusdem loci absque aliquo canonico obedientiario ibidem incorporato modernis temporibus residere in eodem dinoscitur, et sic sacra religio et regulares observantiæ ibidem in ea parte non observantur, unde scandalum non modicum in ea parte generatur, et quod fructus, redditus et proventus ejusdem prioratus non modicum laicorum usibus diversimode applicantur. Et dicit etiam idem interrogatus quod licet dictus reverendus pater Willelmus episcopus Wintoniensis antedictus[2] solicitudines pastorales et summas diligentias tam per se quam per suos commissarios pro reformatione præmissorum impenderit, et aliquando illius loci prioribus propter malam et inutilem

[1] "et ecclesiæ suæ sanctæ exaltationem," added in the second Process.

[2] 'dicto prioratui et personis ejusdem pie compatiens," added in the second Process.

administrationem et dispensationem bonorum dicti prioratus amotis alios priores in quorum circumspectione et diligentia pro tempore confidebat præfecit, quos tamen demum se male et inutiliter habuisse et administrasse usque ad præsens tempus post debitam investigationem factam invenit, ita quod idem reverendus pater statum ejusdem prioratus reparare vel restaurare cum dictis suis solicitudinibus et diligentia nequivit, ac quod, considerata temporis malitia et ex præteritis timendo et conjecturando futura, de aliqua debita et sancta religione ejusdem ordinis vel alterius et religionis sanctis observantiis juxta piam intentionem primævi fundatoris ibidem habendis desperatur. Insuper dictus interrogatus dicit et respondet quod fructus redditus et proventus dicto Collegio sanctæ Mariæ Magdalenæ pertinentes adeo tenues sunt et exiles quod ad exhibitionem dicti Præsidentis et personarum prædictorum et aliorum onerum eidem incumbentium minime sufficiunt his diebus.

Evidence of William Rabbys.

Willelmus Rabbys, ætatis xl annorum et ultra, liberæ conditionis ut asseruit, testis productus, admissus, juratus, et diligenter examinatus de et super omnibus et singulis super quibus dictus magister Willelmus Gyfford superius extitit examinatus; et primo super notitia personarum et locorum in dicto libello sive articulo specificatorum; ad quæ dicit iste juratus et respondet quod dictum Collegium beatæ Mariæ Magdalenæ bene novit; et in cæteris concordat iste juratus et interrogatus cum prædicto magistro Willelmo Gyfford superius examinato; et super addidit etiam quod omnia et singula in dicto libello sive articulo specificata et intenta fuerunt et sunt vera, publica, notoria, manifesta et famosa.

Evidence of Richard Bernys, M.A.

Magister Ricardus Bernys,[1] in artibus magister, liberæ conditionis, ætatis lx annorum et ultra, testis productus, admissus, juratus, et diligenter examinatus de et super omnibus et singulis super quibus prædictus magister Willelmus Gyfford superius examinatus extitit; et primo super notitia personarum et locorum in dicto libello sive articulo specificatorum; ad quæ dicit et respondet iste juratus quod dictum Collegium beatæ Mariæ Magdalenæ bene novit, ac quod in cæteris concernentibus conditionem et statum ipsius Collegii super quibus dictus magister Willelmus Gyfford deposuit, et quod fructus, redditus et proventus dicto Collegio pertinentes ad supportationem onerum eidem incumbentium non sufficiunt, concordat cum eodem magistro Willelmo; in aliis vero concernentibus statum et conditionem dicti Prioratus de Selebourne, dicit quod audivit a quampluribus personis fidedignis quibus fidem adhibuit quod idem Prioratus de Selebourne ad tantæ ruinæ detrimentum devenit quod [—etc., *almost verbally as above, in Gyfford's evidence, ending with the words* "laicorum usibus non modicum multipliciter applicantur"].

Evidence of John Chapman.

Johannes Chapman,[2] ætatis xxiiij annorum, et liberæ conditionis ut asseruit, testis productus [*etc., as above in Bernys' evidence*] Collegium beatæ Mariæ Magdalenæ bene novit, et quod in cæteris statum et conditionem ipsius Collegii concernentibus super quibus

[1] This examination is omitted in the second Process.

[2] "capellanus," added in the other Process.

dictus magister Willelmus Gyfford fuit examinatus concordat cum eodem magistro Willelmo, excepto quod nescit deponere an fructus redditus et proventus dicto Collegio pertinentes sufficiunt ad exhibitionem onerum eidem Collegio pro tempore incumbentium. Et ulterius interrogatus dicit et respondet quod novit dictum prioratum de Sclebourne fuisse et esse de patronatu reverendi in Christo patris Willelmi Wintoniensis episcopi antedicti, et quod idem prioratus ad tantæ ruinæ detrimentum devenit quod [etc., *as above*].

Evidence of Prior Ashford.

Thomas Asshford, Prior[1] dicti Prioratus de Selebourne, ætatis lxxii annorum, liberæ conditionis, testis productus, admissus, juratus, et diligenter examinatus de et super libello sive articulo per dictum magistrum Jacobum Prestone, procuratorem prædictum, ut præfertur, proposito; et primo super notitia personarum et locorum in dicto libello sive articulo descriptorum; ad quæ dicit et respondet iste juratus quod bene scit et novit dictum Prioratum de Selebourne fuisse et esse de patronatu dicti reverendi in Christo patris et domini domini Willelmi Wintoniensis episcopi; in cæteris vero omnibus et singulis in dicto libello sive articulo specificatis concernentibus statum et conditionem ejusdem prioratus de Selebourne concordat iste juratus cum Willelmo Rabbys antedicto.[2]

Tenor vero dictarum litterarum præfati reverendi patris Wintoniensis episcopi coram nobis in subsidium probationum ut præfertur exhibitarum sequitur in his verbis :—

Certificate by the Bishop of Winchester of the hopeless condition of the Priory.

"Willelmus permissione divina Wintoniensis episcopus universis et singulis litteras nostras visuris et inspecturis, salutem, gratiam et benedictionem. Noverit universitas vestra quod licet nos prioratui de Selebourne ordinis Sancti Augustini nostrorum patronatus et dioc. pie compatiens, solicitudines pastorales labores et diligentias quamplurimas per nos et commissarios nostros pro reformatione status dicti prioratus impenderimus, justitia id poscente, nihilominus tamen idem prioratus de Selebourne ad tantæ ruinæ detrimentum [etc., *in substance as in the fourth article of Preston's libel, ending* —] Quamobrem,

[1] "Dominus Thomas Asshford, nuper Prior," in the second Process.

[2] In the subsequent Process the evidence of Prior Ashford is thus recorded: "Dicit et respondet iste juratus et dicit secundum tertium et quartum articulos in eodem libello concernentes statum dicti prioratus de Selebourne fuisse et esse veros. Super aliis vero articulis in dicto libello contentis idem interrogatus dicit quod deponere nescit." In this Process Bernys' examination is not repeated, but two other witnesses are produced. "Magister Johannes Nele, artium magister, ætatis LVII annorum ut asseruit liberæque conditionis, testis [*etc.*] . . . . . primum articulum in dicto libello contentum secundum informationem fidedignorum dicit esse verum. Ac etiam idem interrogatus dicit secundum tertium et quartum articulo usque ad istam clausulam in dicto quarto articulo impositam *Ita quod dictus reverendus pater* etc. continere veritatem. Ad quam clausulam idem interrogatus dicit quod dictus reverendus pater statum ejusdem prioratus reparare vel restaurare cum dictis suis sollicitudinibus et laboribus gravissimis per aliquem religiosum dictorum præfati prioratus priorum nequivit. Et ulterius dicit quod considerata temporis malitia [*etc.*] Item dictus juratus ad quintum articulum respondet et dicit ipsum esse verum secundum quod a fidedignis dici audivit. Ad sextum articulum dicit quod præmissa modo illo prout per eum superius deposita fuerunt et sunt vera publica et famosa.

"Robertus Baron, LVI annorum liberæque conditionis ut asseruit, testis [*etc.*] . . . . super notitia personarum et locorum in dicto libello contentorum concordat cum dicto magistro Willelmo Gyfford de sua certa scientia, excepto tertio articulo in dicto libello specificato, quem quidem articulum dicit esse verum prout audivit ab aliis dici fidedignis. Et superaddidit quod præmissa ut per eum dicta et deposita vera, publica, notoria, manifesta sunt, et famosa, et super eisdem a diu laborarunt et laborant publica vox et fama."

præmissis ac moderni et futuri temporis malitia consideratis, de reparatione, reformatione et restauratione dicti prioratus in futurum de aliqua bona et sancta religione ac observantia ejusdem ordinis vel alterius ibidem effectualiter perimplenda penitus desperatur. In cujus rei testimonium præsentibus sigillum nostrum est appensum. Datum in castro nostro de Farnham dictæ nostræ dioc., primo die mensis Septembris, anno Domini millesimo quadringentesimo octogesimo quarto, et nostræ consecrationis anno tricesimo octavo."

The aforesaid evidence duly considered.

Consequenter eodem decimo die dictæ mensis Septembris sæpe memoratus magister Jacobus Prestone coram nobis Commissario in dicta ecclesia parochiali adhuc judicialiter sedente, in præsentia dictorum procuratorum quibus supra nominibus, libellum sive articulum supradictum per eum alias propositum in hac parte, singulis procuratoribus prædictis, ut præfertur, tunc et ibidem comparentibus, repetiit in vim positionum et articulorum, et petiit eos compelli respondere eisdem. Ad cujus petitionem Nos Commissarius prædictus cum eisdem procuratoribus, et præsertim cum dicto magistro Michaelo Cleve, procuratore dictorum Prioris et Conventus sive capituli ecclesiæ cathedralis Winton. dioc. de et super omnibus et singulis jam dicto libello sive articulo contentis et specificatis tractatum habuimus diligentem, et cum eisdem de unione, annexione, appropriatione et incorporatione dicti prioratus de Selebourne supradicto Collegio communicavimus, ac eosdem procuratores super omnibus et singulis in eodem libello sive articulo comprehensis interrogavimus. Qui quidem procuratores sic de, in, et super præmissis interrogati fatebantur et recognoverunt ea omnia et singula fuisse et esse vera. Deinde vero sæpedictus magister Michael Cleve, dictorum venerabilium virorum Prioris et Conventus ecclesiæ cathedralis Winton. procurator et procuratorio nomine eorundem, voluit et consentiit quod iste tractatus sic cum eo in ea parte habitus omnino habeatur et cedat in loco cujuscunque tractatus fiendi vel habendi in hac parte cum dictis Priore et Conventu. Et subsequenter Nos Commissarius prædictus prænominatis procuratoribus de eorum expressis consensu et assensu diem Sabbati tunc proxime subsequentem ad audiendum sententiam diffinitivam in ea parte et finale decretum nostrum in et super præmissis in eadem ecclesia parochiali de Farnham prædicta ferri assignavimus. Dicto vero die Sabbati, undecimo die videlicet dictæ mensis Septembris, adveniente, nos Ricardus, Prior supradictus ecclesiæ conventualis de Novo Loco, Commissarius antedictus, in eadem ecclesia parochiali judicialiter sedentes, in præsentia dictorum procuratorum partium superius descriptarum et ad eorum petitionem, sententiam diffinitivam sive finale decretum nostrum in hac parte tulimus, legimus, et promulgavimus in scriptis, ut sequitur :—

Decree of annexation of the Priory to the College, pronounced 11 Sept.

"In Dei nomine, Amen. Auditis, intellectis, et plenarie discussis, per nos Ricardum Dei gratia Priorem ecclesiæ conventualis de Novo Loco, Winton. dioc., reverendi in Christo patris et domini domini Willelmi eadem gratia Winton. episcopi, Commissarius ad infrascripta, cum clausula *conjunctim et divisim,* una cum aliis sufficienter et legittime deputatis, meritis et circumstantiis causæ sive negotii unionis, annexionis et appropriationis domus sive prioratus de Selebourne, ordinis Sancti Augustini, dictæ Winton. dioc., dicto Collegio beatæ Mariæ Magdalenæ in universitate Oxon. situato fiendæ coram nobis, ad instantem petitionem partis venerabilium virorum magistri Ricardi Mayewe, Præsidentis, et Scholarium Collegii beatæ Mariæ Magdalenæ supradicti, reverendi in Christo patris et domini domini Willelmi Dei gratia Winton. episcopi, dicti domus sive prioratus de Selebourne patroni, necnon Prioris et Conventus ecclesiæ cathedralis Winton., [procuratoribus] coram nobis Commissario prædicto legittime comparentibus, et eorum procuratoria, penes acta nostra alias realiter exhibita et in eisdem remanentia verbis, exhibentibus, quibus etiam procuratoribus de et super libello sive articulo per procuratorem dictorum Præsidentis et Scholarium memorati Collegii in causa sive negotio memorato proposito, et contentis in eodem, per nos Commissarium prædictum interrogatis et diligenter examinatis, et hujusmodi contenta in eodem libello sive articulo vera esse recognoscentibus, de et super unione, annexione et appropriatione prædicta habitis cum eisdem procuratoribus per nos Commissarium memoratum tractatu et communicatione diligentibus, ipsasque causas hujusmodi in eodem libello specificatas justas veras et rationabiles fore recognoscentibus, procuratore vero dictorum Præsidentis et Scholarium memorati Collegii beatæ Mariæ Magdalenæ supradicti sententiam sive finale decretum ferri et promulgari petente, procuratoribus vero aliarum partium superius descriptarum hujusmodi unioni, annexioni et appropriationi prædictæ nominibus quibus supra divisim consentientibus et sententiam etiam ferri petentibus:—Quia per acta inactitata, allegata, proposita, confessata *(sic)*, recognita et probata in causa sive negotio memorato invenimus et comperimus evidenter partem dictorum Præsidentis et Scholarium memorati Collegii beatæ Mariæ Magdalenæ antedicti eorum intentionem in eodem libello sive articulo per partem eorundem Præsidentis et Scholarium in hujusmodi causa sive negotio proposito, cujus libelli sive articuli tenor sequitur et est talis, "In Dei nomine, Amen [etc., *reciting at length the libel as above*], fundasse et probasse, Idcirco nos Commissarius antedictus, præhabita in hac parte regia licentia, de qua quidem licentia satis constat nobis, et quam pro inserta hic habemus et haberi decernimus, Christi nomine invocato et ipsum solum Deum præ oculis nostris præponentes, de consilio jurisperitorum cum quibus communicavimus in hac parte, de consensu voluntate et assensu expressis partium superius descriptarum, supradictum Prioratum de Selebourne, dictæ Winton. dioc., una cum dictis ecclesiis et locis eidem prioratui ab antiquo spectantibus et pertinentibus, ac rebus, possessionibus, juribus et pertinentiis suis universis, prædictis Præsidenti et Scholaribus Collegii antedicti beatæ Mariæ Magdalenæ et eorum successoribus eidemque Collegio unimus, annectimus, et appropriamus; et eundem prioratum cum dictis ecclesiis, locis, rebus, possessionibus, juribus et pertinentiis suis universis eisdem Præsidenti et Scholaribus et eorum successoribus et eidem Collegio in puram et perpetuam elemosinam perpetuo possidendum, quantum ad nos attinet, auctoritate qua fungimur in hac parte, damus et concedimus per præsentes. Ita, videlicet, quod Priore dicti Prioratus de Selebourne cedente, decedente, sive dicto Prioratu

The Royal licence pre-obtained.

qualitercunque vacante, liceat ex tunc Præsidenti et Scholaribus memorati Collegii et eorum successoribus ipsum Prioratum cum ecclesiis, locis, rebus, possessionibus, juribus et pertinentiis suis universis supradictis per se et suos libere et licite apprehendere, ac in usus suos proprios perpetuo possidere et tenere."

Lecta, lata et promulgata fuit dicta sententia sive finale nostrum decretum per nos Ricardum, Priorem dictæ ecclesiæ conventualis de Novo Loco, Commissarium antedictum, in ecclesia parochiali de Farnham prædicta sub anno Domini, indictione pontificatus, mense et die prædictis, præsentibus tunc ibidem venerabilibus et fidedignis viris magistro Ricardo Newbryche, in artibus magistro, dominis Ricardo Colyns et Johanne Singyltone, presbiteris dictæ Winton dioc., et aliis testibus ad præmissa vocatis specialiter et rogatis.[1] In quorum omnium et singulorum fidem et testimonium, Nos Commissarius antedictus hunc processum nostrum in hac parte factum per dictum magistrum Thomam Somercotes notarium publicum in hac parte actorum scribam fieri, ejusque signo et subscriptione muniri, mandavimus et fecimus, sigillumque nostrum præsentibus apposuimus. Et ad majorem fidem in omnibus et singulis præmissis adhibendum, sigillum venerabilis viri magistri Ricardi Hayward, legum doctoris, officialis consistorii Winton., præsentibus apponi procuravimus. Et nos officialis antedictus ad specialem rogatum et procurationem Commissarii supradicti sigillum officii nostri hujusmodi in fidem et testimonium omnium et singulorum præmissorum præsentibus apposuimus.

Et ego Thomas Somercotes, clericus Ebor. dioc., publicus auctoritate apostolica notarius, præmissis omnibus et singulis, dum sic, ut præmittitur, per dictum venerabilem virum Ricardum Priorem ecclesiæ conventualis de Novo Loco, ordinis Sancti Augustini, Winton dioc., reverendi in Christo patris et domini domini Willelmi Dei gratia Winton. episcopi Commissarium prædictum et coram eo, sub anno Domini, indictione pontificatus, mense, diebus et loco prædictis agebantur et fiebant, una cum nominatis testibus in prolatione sententiæ in causa sive negotio hujusmodi latæ superius descriptis præsentibus, præsens personaliter interfui, eaque omnia et singula modo et forma superius recitatis et declaratis sic fieri vidi et audivi, publicavi, et in hanc publicam for-

[1] At the promulgation of the sentence in the second Process at Esher on 8 August, 1485, the witnesses present were master David Husband, "sacrorum canonum professor," *dom.* John Smalbend, chaplain, and John Brereton, literate, of the dioceses of St. David's, York, and Coventry and Lichfield, respectively.

mam redegi. Ac præsentem processum superinde confectum in his præsentibus decem pergameni foliis fideliter scriptum, ac sigillis superius proxime descriptis sigillatum, demandato dicti Commissarii scripsi, signoque et nomine meis solitis et consuetis signavi meque hic subscripsi rogatus et requisitus, in fidem et testimonium omnium et singulorum præmissorum.

Attached by coloured silken cords, in oval tin boxes, are these seals: (1) a seated figure, before him a monk standing in supplicatory attitude with hands clasped: "S' Prioris et ꝯventus de Novo Loco Surreie ad cās" [causas]; (2) four compartments; in the two upper, half-lengths of SS. Peter and Paul, in the two lower, two figures, one of them a bishop with right hand upraised, possibly as addressing the other; between the upper and lower the words "Juste Judica": "Sig. Consistorii Wintoniensis." The same seals are attached to the second Process.

1484, 24 Sept., 3 Rich. III. Power of attorney from Rich. Mayew, the President, and Scholars of Magdalen College to Rich. Newbrige, clerk, and Simon Ayleward to take possession of the Priory of Selborne.—[375.]

Poor impression of College seal; broken.

PETITION FROM MAGDALEN COLLEGE TO POPE INNOCENT VIII FOR CONFIRMATION OF THE APPROPRIATION OF THE PRIORY.

[1485.] Supplicant Sanctitati vestræ vestri humiles et devoti oratores Ricardus Mayowe, Præsidens Collegii beatæ Mariæ Magdalenæ in universitate Oxon. fundati, et ejusdem Collegii Scolares, quatenus cum venerabilis vir Ricardus, Prior ecclesiæ conventualis de Novo Loco, Wintoniensis dioceseos, reverendi in Christo patris Willelmi Wintoniensis episcopi commissarius ad id specialiter deputatus, prioratum de Selebourne, dictæ dioc., ordinis Sancti Augustini, cujus bona in non modica quantitate in laicorum usus indebite consumuntur, et in quo solus Prior, absque alio canonico regulari obedientiario et incorporato ibidem, regularibus observantiis prætermissis, tempore unionis morari dinoscitur, licet ex illius fundatione quamplures canonici regulares cum Priore ibidem residere ac in divinis obsequiis solempniter ibidem celebrandis et regularibus observantiis communicare deberent, cum suis rebus, possessionibus, juribus et pertinentiis suis universis eisdem Præsidenti et Scolaribus, ac eorum successoribus ipsorumque Collegio supradicto, de dicti venerabilis patris domini Willelmi Winton. episcopi, ipsius prioratus patroni, necnon Prioris et Conventus seu Capituli ecclesiæ cathedralis Winton., ac Prioris prædicti prioratus de Selebourne, et aliorum in hac parte interesse habentium, voluntate et consensu, univerit, annexaverit, et appropriaverit, ita quod, dicto prioratu qualitercunque vacante, liceat extunc præfatis Præsidenti et Scolaribus ac eorum successoribus corporalem et realem possessionem ejusdem prioratus ac rerum, possessionum, et pertinentium suorum universorum, libere auctoritate propria ingredi, apprehendere, et pro perpetuo retinere, ac ipsorum prioratus et pertinentium suorum fructus redditus et proventus in suos usus convertere; cujus quidem prioratus certo modo vacantis possessionem dicti vestri Oratores adepti sunt, et in præsenti habent et retinent: Dignetur eadem Sanctitas vestra unionem, annexationem et appropriationem prædictas et illas concernentia omnia et singula, necnon inde secuta, auctoritate apostolica vestro motu proprio et ex certa scientia gratiose confirmare, ratificare et approbare, ac plenum firmitatis robur obtinuisse et obtinere decernere; Necnon tam Collegii quam prioratus prædictorum valores annuos, ac unionis dicti prioratus acta et instrumenta, et alia exinde secuta, præsentibus pro expressis habere, supplereque omnes et singulos defectus tam juris quam facti, si qui forsan intervenerint in eisdem; Ac ordinem ipsum in dicto prioratu de Selebourne et ejus dependentiam penitus supprimere et extinguere: Necnon irritum et inane decernere si cœtus super his a quoquam quavis auctoritate scienter vel ignoranter contigerit attemptari: Non obstantibus dicti ordinis statutis et consuetudinibus, juramento, confirmatione apostolica, vel quavis firmitate alia roboratis [quodque dictus prioratus per religiosos suæ vel alterius religionis forsan reformari possit],[1] ac voluntate ultima fundatorum seu testatorum et benefactorum quorumcunque dicti prioratus de Selebourne prædicta, constitutionibus apostolicis, necnon Othonis et Octoboni quondam in regno Angliæ apostolicæ sedis legatorum, cæterisque contrariis quibuscunque.—[51.]

Draft on paper.

[1485] 27 Jan. Draft of the bull first supplicated for, confirming the annexation of Selborne, Brackley, Aynho, Wanborough and Romney, as submitted for approval (as it seems) to Pope Innocent VIII, in which reference is made to the previous proceedings in England; with various corrections. A clause giving the reason for the issue of the bull in these words, "Cum autem de viribus unionum, annexionum, et incorporationum prædictarum a nonnullis hesitetur," is struck out, and noted "dematur hec clausula quia non placet." The paper is subscribed at foot (in what may be the Pope's own hand), "Fiat ut petitur de novo," and again, with regard to the proposed insertion of some additional clauses including one "ex certa scientia," "Fiat ut supra." "Datum Rome apud S̄tmpetrum sexto kal. Febr. anno primo." Endorsed "L° v° fol. c[l]xxxi°," being the reference to the official Register. See the description of this document in the following instructions to the agent of the College in this year.—[*Appropriations*, 21.]

[1] Added in the margin by another hand.

DRAFT OF INSTRUCTIONS TO THE ADVOCATE, JAC. DE MONTELATO, OF PISA, EMPLOYED AT ROME TO PROCURE THE BULL OF ANNEXATION, WITH ESTIMATE OF EXPENSES.

[On paper roll; *Appropr.* 19. A first draft is on a roll numbered 20; that is endorsed, "Conceptus M. T. Hope super supplicationibus sollicitatori missis pro bullis earundem in curia Romana expediendis."]

Domine Jacobe, Mente revolvite, exhortor, quod in prioribus annis et diebus negotia etiam majora quæ in Romana curia expedienda mihi occurrebant vobis commendabam. Ac etiam apud majores regni qui commissiones ad curiam direxerunt vos commendatum habui, uti experientia probastis. In quibus probata ac provida vestra diligentia et solicitudo me excitant ut in futurum in consultis et occurrentibus apud vos solicitandis fiduciam ponam.

Notate igitur, et diligenter ac iterum perlegite, quæ subscribuntur.

Superioribus annis reverendus in Christo pater et dominus dominus Willelmus episcopus Wintoniensis in universitate Oxon. Collegium quoddam in honore beatæ Mariæ Magdalenæ, etc., de lxxx Scholaribus, sedecim pueris et xiij servientibus fundavit, ut in informatione ac supplicationibus conceptis et cum præsentibus ad vos directis concipere poteritis. Studet igitur et curam gerit idem reverendus pater, ut prædicti scholares et alia supposita (*sic*) ipsius Collegii in futurum quietius studere, necnon Deo devotius servire et in divinum insistere, valeant, providere de fructibus et proventibus, etc., ex quibus vivere possint, sicuti et in certis provisione[m] fecit et in subjectis amplius et uberius facere conatur.

Et quia idem reverendus pater cognoscens me antiquum curialem arbitratus est in subscriptis me consulere posse ut in curia[1] sufficienter ipsa sua negotia provide ad suam voluntatem et utilitatem Collegii solicitentur et expediantur; propterea me vocavit, et ea ad solicitandum in curia mihi commisit. Recurro igitur ad vos in præsenti ex fiducia magna, et exhortor ut diligentiam in commissis subscriptis adhibere velitis.

Ecce mitto ad vos in præsentibus tenores quatuor supplicationum in quibus narrantur quinque locorum uniones seu appropriationes factæ de consensu eorum quorum intererat per diversos ordinarios in partibus, quas supplicationes, si vobis videtur quod secundum stilum curiæ conceptæ sint, bene est; sin autem, reformate. Ita tamen quod nil substantiæ omittatur.

Et licet nonnulla sint descripta in dictis supplicationibus quæ non sunt de stilo curiæ, et aliqua omissa quæ sunt de stilo curiæ, in his omnibus omissis et superfluis ac in consuetis opus erit ut provide per alias clausulas succurratur.

Habeo regulam Cancellariæ in memoria quæ canit (*sic*) quod in unionibus fiendis ac confirmandis fructus beneficiorum seu locorum

[1] curiam, MS.

uniendorum et quibus uniuntur exprimi debeant, quibus expressis compositio cameræ notior et facilior erit. Sed quia dominus meus reverendus pater episcopus petit, habeantur pro expressis ex eo capite quod nondum est plene provisum prædicto Collegio et tot personis de redditibus quod commode vivere possint, ac etiam loca unita prædicta adeo collapsa sunt et egent reparationibus, ac a locis prædictis alienati sunt fructus ac diversis acclamationibus turbati, quod grave est sibi sana conscientia verum valorem fructus eorundem æstimare. Sed describam, et dominationem suam in his specialiter exhortatus sum.

Insuper et mihi conscius sum quod frequentur uniones et acta eorum in partibus per ordinarios factæ et per Papam confirmatæ in literis apostolicis et bullis confirmationum inseri solebant; et quia dominus meus reverendus asserit acta illarum prolixa, petit tenores haberi pro expressis.

Reliquum est quod vobis intimare necesse visum est. Nam quidam Laurentius, Almanus et Romipeta, qui pluries in anno solitus est curiam visitare, cujus et notitiam arbitror vos habere, curam et solicitudinem unionum et negotiorum præmissorum superioribus diebus in Romana curia suscepit, et in his quid perfecit scietis infra, qui accessit ad dominum Antonium de Mucciarellis scriptorem bullarum, et eum fecit solicitatorem negotiorum prædictorum, et ei ostendit et tradidit informationem in partibus traditam.

Antonius visa informatione formavit supplicationem seu formari fecit, et omnes supradictas uniones quinque locorum comprehendit in una supplicatione, et illam obtinuit cum certis clausulis signari, datari, et registrari, ut patet in libro quinto Registri, fol. clxxxi. Cujus copiam vobis cum præsentibus mitto. Signatura vero fuit per hæc verba, "Fiat ut petitur de novo." Fuit et concepta minuta secundum tenorem signaturæ cujus copiam Laurentius apportavit, et in illa cavetur quomodo dominus noster summus Pontifex non confirmavit sed unit de novo loca prædicta Collegio. Habet sed sanctissimus dominus noster Papa tenores unionum et valorem fructus beneficiorum, etc., pro expressis. Sed dominus Antonius dixit Laurentio quod opus foret solvere et componere cum camera apostolica de fructibus beneficiorum unitorum tempore bullæ expeditæ semel, et in futurum imperpetuum de quindecim annis in quindecim tantum sicut in prima solutione, et quod collector domini nostri et Papæ in Anglia deberet se informare de fructibus beneficiorum hujusmodi, et certificare cameram apostolicam; qui census talis in similibus fuit et est inauditus apud nos in Anglia.

Propterea dominus meus reverendus ad evitandum hujusmodi onus et censum, qui esset periculosus et onerosus dicto Collegio in futurum si fructus diminuerentur ipsorum locorum, præterea Præsidens et Scholares, petunt confirmationes "Ex certa scientia," ut in supplicatione; etsi sanctissimus dominus noster Papa post confirmationes ad petitionem partium factas velit apponere et addicere hanc clausulam, "Et nos ex superhabundanti gratia nostra pro firmiori subsistentia prædictorum unimus etc. dicto Collegio, etc. non ad petitionem alicujus"; et hoc si obtinere poteritis dominus meus et nos optamus.

Et ita reperimus pontifices summos in similibus bullis concessisse prædicto Collegio hanc clausulam. Si obtinere poteritis probate, etiam cum aliquali pecunia et mediocri summa.

Domine Jacobe, pro laboribus vestris habebitis in Banco, solutis bullis et compositionibus, viginti ducatos. Et si clausulas obtinere poteritis quas nos addicere *(sic)* petimus, habebitis bonam propinam a domino, etc. Et si aliquas propinas ad habendum favores in aliquo officio feceritis, reverendus dominus noster antedictus ipsas refundet cum usuris. Ideo fiat diligentia ut negotia expediantur.

Valores prioratus de Selborne etc. de claro, deductis omnibus, c ducati, et de Brakley c ducati, et de Aynehoo xl ducati, et de Warnburghe viij^{xx} x ducati, et de Romenay xxii ducati; in toto in ducatis ccclij ducati, [in moneta Angliæ lxxix*li.*[1]], "ut opinatum erat temporibus unionum prædictorum locorum."[2]

Compositio per æstimationem de dictis quinque locis unitis ascendit secundum medietatem totalis valoris eorundem ad summam clxxvi ducatorum [in pecunia Anglicana xxxix*li.* xij*s.*].

Expensæ per æstimationem cujuslibet bullæ in quatuor officiis cum taxis extendunt ad summam xxiiij ducatorum [in pecunia Anglicana, cviij*s.*] In toto in ducatis iiij^{xx} xvi [in pecunia Anglicana xxj*li.* xij*s.*].

Compositio cum aliis expensis bullarum prædictis et taxis, ut supra, in toto in ducatis, feodis Jacobi exceptis, cclxxij, [in pecunia Anglicana lxj*li.* vj*s.*[3]].

Item, deponantur in Banco c ducati ultra expensas bullarum et compositionum, in casu quod non sufficerent summæ depositæ. Fiat commissio per mercatorem de Banco illo ad socios suos in curia de c ducatis solvendis dicto Jacobo de Montelato de Pissia, si necesse fuerit pro expeditione negotii prædicti. Et facta acquietancia per dominum Jacobum prædictum de illa pecunia recepta in ea parte episcopus prædictus faciet mercatorem de dictis c ducatis refundendis securum.

Fiat obligatio inter episcopum, etc., et mercatorem et socios suos de Banco de totali summa deposita in Banco quod fideliter liberabit et solvet Jacobo prædicto eandem summam, feodo Banci excepto, in Romana curia sollicitori.

Memorandum de xij*li.* dimissis in Banco de Bardis solvendis Antonio de Mucciarellis quod dictæ xij libræ sint pars summæ prædictæ deliberandæ modo dicto Jacobo.

[Totalis summa ponenda in Banco cum feodo prædicto dicti Jacobi in ducatis cclxxxxij, in pecunia Anglicana lxv*li.* xiiij*s.* Unde in Banco de Bardis sunt xij*li.*, ultra quas xij*li.* ponendæ sunt de novo liij*li.* xviiij*s.*][4]

Item, pro expeditione bullæ confirmationis de et super unione fienda prioratus de Selborne Collegio beatæ Mariæ Magdalenæ in universitate

[1] The words within brackets are struck out.

[2] These words are added in another hand, resembling Waynflete's.

[3] Struck out, and nearly illegible, but apparently this sum, although to correspond with the amounts given above the shillings should be four.

[4] The whole of this sentence within brackets is struck out.

Oxon. situato, summa ponenda in Banco primo pro expeditione supplicationis et bullæ in diversis officiis, quæ taxabitur communiter ad sex vel septem ducatos. Summa in quatuor officiis, si vadit per cancellariam, se extendit ad xxviij ducatos et x gross[os] plumbator[ibus].[1] Et in Registr[ariis?] supplicationum et bullarum ad duos ducatos ad minus; et sic ad xxx ducatos. Et si opus sit expedire per secretarium solvendæ erunt quinque taxæ.

Item, pro compositione in camera Apostolica computando fructus seu intratam Prioratus ad valorem annuum ad clx ducatos, solvendæ erunt in camera lxxx ducati, et tot mittantur ad Bancum.

[Item, solicitatori domino Jacobo de Montclato pro labore suo si expedierit cum clausulis positis in supplicatione, xij ducati.][2]

Domine Jacobo, ea quæ me movebant ut vos in notitiam reverendi in Christo patris et domini domini Willelmi episcopi Winton. præ cæteris in Romana curia procuratoribus et solicitatoribus, ejus in negotiis expediendis, præferrem et jure haberem, in principio hujus scripti annota[n]tur. Et quia superioribus diebus, postquam idem reverendus pater dominus meus Willelmus episcopus Wintoniensis consulere me dignabatur in præmissis suis negotiis et unionibus fiendis, operam dedi et literis meis absque mora vos certiores de præmissis ad vos in futurum mittendis feci, uti et vestris ad me literis directis responsum dedistis, apparet, sumus ergo nunc in opere. Deus concedat felicem expeditionem! Dominus igitur et reverendus pater conclusit ut mitterem ad vos informationes v unionum, quarum unam, videlicet de Selborne, Winton. dioc., ordinis Sancti Augustini, petit solicitari et expediri secundum tenorem informationis ac supplicationis cum præsentibus transmissæ ad vos. In qua informatione ac supplicatione reverendus pater et dominus non cupit [aliqua][3] in substantia minui, sed potius utilia addi. Fiat propterea solicitatio diligens ut expediatur illa per se in una bulla. Qua expedita et soluta, quid de aliis quatuor unionibus fiendis melius fuerit, studere et cogitare poteritis. Et quia diversæ sunt informationes, singulas percurrere et videre solerter curetis. Est enim una minuta concepta quæ comprehendit quatuor hospitalium seu locorum uniones præter supradictam de Selborne, quas in una bulla [vel diversis][2] includere, et per viam confirmationis, cum clausulis "Ex certa scientia" et cum suppletione defectuum, etiam quod fructus hospitalium, cantariarum, seu locorum, unitorum, ac Collegii cui uniuntur, non obstante regula Cancellariæ, habeantur pro expressis, ut plenius in minuta continetur, solicitare et expediri facere, [prout] facilius videbitur, date operam et expedite. Si vero aliqua difficultas oritur vel foret quod ad nutum dicti reverendi patris et secundum informationes missas res non possent expediri, rescribite de singulis.

Domine Jacobe, nosco quod secundum diversitates temporum oriuntur sæpe diversitates morum et jurium: propterea si singula quæ in infor-

[1] *i.e.*, Ten *gros* to the officers who attach the leaden seal. It would appear from the tables of money in DuCange (last edit.) that at this time the French silver *gros* was worth about 2*s.* 6*d.* *Tournois.*

[2] Struck out.

[3] Interlined by another hand.

mationibus et supplicationibus descripta per nos in partibus existunt, præcise ac de verbo in verbum in bullis non ponantur modicum refert, dummodo de substantia nil omittatur.

Similiter, licet limitavi taxas bullarum ad certum ac descripsi summas compositionum in officiis curiæ, et ita forsan res transire de faciliter non posset, propter hoc non impono vobis legem; immo habebitis arbitrium liberum tam minuendo ac etiam excedendo, non tamen nimium. Et reverendus pater et dominus noster episcopus in his confidit in fidelitate vestra, dummodo negotia feliciter expediantur.

[Summa totalis ponenda in banco cum xij*li.* existentibus in banco de Bardis, iiij^{xx} xiiij*li.* xix*s.*

Memorandum quod prædictis informationibus non obstantibus, si fieri posset, fiat simul compositio pro Celborne et aliis quatuor locis, et hoc petunt instantius præsides (*sic*) et pauperes scholares dicti Collegii, considerando senectutem, ægritudines varias et debilitatem fundatoris sui, post cujus decessum onus dicta summæ esset eis importabile tum propter paupertatem eorum et paucitatem amicorum.

Memorandum quod banckarii faciant tres billas diversas de summa imposita in bancho, quod sic solitus (*sic*) est propter securitatem nunciorum.][1]

Jacobus de Montelato.
Johannes de Jerona.
Antonius de Ewgubio.

[Memorandum quod medietates fructuum de Selborne, Bracley, Aynow, Wanborow et Rommeney extendunt se ad xlvj*li.* vij*s.*, de qua summa habet in bancho xxij*li.* x*s.*][1]

[1486.] Draft on a long narrow paper-roll of the bull to be issued by Pope Innocent VIII confirming the annexation to Magdalen College of the Priory of Selebourne and the chapel of Wanborough, mentioning also the hospitals of Romney and Brackley and Aynho. Endorsed "Billa (*sic*) nove appropriacionis per papam fiend. omnium locorum infrascriptorum."—[99.]

Another copy on a paper-roll, endorsed "Copia bulle pro Selbourne ac pro omnibus aliis hospitalibus, etc., per viam confirmacionis et eciam unionis."—[105.]

Paper roll, with the Bull for Selborne alone; endorsed "Copia bulle de Selebourne tantum per viam unionis."—[106.]

Bull of Pope Innocent VIII confirming the annexation of the Priory to the College.

1486, June 6. Innocentius episcopus, servus servorum Dei, ad perpetuam rei memoriam. Injunctum nobis desuper, meritis licet insufficientibus, apostolicæ servitutis officium mentem nostram excitat et inducit, ut hiis quæ pro ecclesiasticorum et piorum locorum, ac

[1] The passages within brackets are by the second hand.

personarum præsertim in eis literarum studiis insistentium, commodo et utilitate processisse dicuntur, ut firma perpetuo et illibata persistant, cum a nobis petitur, adjiciamus apostolici muniminis firmitatem, illaque interdum de novo concedamus: prout conspicimus id in Domino salubriter expedire. Sane pro parte dilectorum filiorum Ricardi Mayewe, moderni Præsidentis, et Scholarium Collegii beatæ Mariæ Magdalenæ in universitate Oxoniensi, Lincolniensis dioceseos, fundati, nobis nuper exhibita petitio continebat, quod cum in Prioratu de Seleborne, ordinis Sancti Augustini, Wintoniensis dioceseos, in quo juxta illius fundationem plures canonici regulares residere ac divinis obsequiis vacare debebant, solus Prior, regularibus observantiis prætermissis, moraretur, et illius bona in non parva quantitate in laicorum usus indebite consumerentur, dilectus filius Ricardus Prior monasterii de Novoloco, dictæ dioceseos, habens ad hoc, ut asserebat, a venerabili fratre nostro Willelmo episcopo Wintoniensi specialem per illius literas facultatem, illius vigore, de Willelmi episcopi prædicti, ad cujus præsentationem dictus Prioratus pertinebat, ac dilectorum filiorum Prioris et Capituli ecclesiæ Wintoniensis, necnon tunc Prioris dicti Prioratus de Seleborne, ac aliorum quorum intererat, voluntate et consensu, Prioratum prædictum præfato Collegio cum omnibus locis, membris, juribus, rebus, possessionibus et pertinentiis suis ordinaria autoritate perpetuo univit, annexuit et appropriavit: dictique Præsidens et Scholares, cum unio, annexio et appropriatio hujusmodi effectum sortire essent, unionis, annexionis et appropriationis prædictarum vigore possessionem corporalem assecuti fuerunt, quam tenent et de præsenti, Prioratus, locorum, membrorum juriumque et pertinentiarum prædictorum, prout in quibusdam autenticis literis sive publicis instrumentis desuper confectis, dicitur plenius contineri. Quare pro parte Præsidentis et Scholarium prædictorum, asserentium fructus redditus et proventus dicti Prioratus de Seleborne cum suis membris centum et sexaginta florenos auri de camera, secundum communem extimationem, valorem annuum non excedere, nobis fuit humiliter supplicatum, ut unioni, annexioni et appropriationi prædictis, pro illarum subsistentia firmiori, robur apostolicæ confirmationis adjicere, ac pro potiori cautela Prioratum de Seleborne prædictum eidem Collegio de novo unire, annectere et incorporare, ac ordinem Sancti Augustini et quascunque dependentias in eo supprimere, aliasque in præmissis opportune providere, de benignitate apostolica dignaremur. Nos igitur, qui dudum inter alia voluimus quod petentes beneficia ecclesiastica aliis uniri tenerentur exprimere verum valorem secundum extimationem prædictam etiam beneficii cui aliud peteretur uniri, alioquin unio non valeret, et quod in unionibus commissio semper fieret ad partes, vocatis quorum interesset, et idem observaretur in confirmationibus unionum jam factarum, Collegii beatæ Mariæ Magdalenæ hujusmodi fructuum, reddituum et proventuum veros annuos valores, ac verum et ultimum dicti Prioratus de Seleborne vacationis modum, qualitates et dependentias, si quæ sint, præsentibus pro expressis habentes, necnon Præsidentem et Scholares prædictos eorumque singulos a quibusvis excommunicationis, suspensionis et interdicti aliisque ecclesiasticis sententiis, censuris et pœnis, a jure vel ab homine quavis occasione vel causa latis, si quibus quomodolibet innodati existunt, ad effectum præsentium duntaxat consequendum harum serie absolventes et absolutos fore censentes, necnon ordinem et dependentias hujusmodi in dicto Prioratu, etiam si ad illum consueverit quis per electionem assumi eique cura immineat animarum, supprimentes, hujusmodi supplicationibus inclinati, unionem, annexionem et appropriationem prædictas, et prout illas concernunt omnia et singula in literis seu instrumentis prædictis contenta et inde secuta quæcunque, auctoritate apostolica, tenore præsentium approbamus et confirmamus, ac præsentis scripti patrocinio communimus, supplentes omnes et singulos defectus si quæ forsan intervenerint in eisdem. Et nihilominus, pro potiori præmissorum cautela, Prioratum de Seleborne prædictum cum omnibus et singulis membris, locis, juribus, pertinentiis et aliis supradictis, eidem Collegio beatæ Mariæ Magdalenæ dicta apostolica autoritate de novo inperpetuum unimus, annectimus et incorporamus, ita quod liceat ex nunc eisdem Præsidenti et Scholaribus per se vel alium seu alios corporalem Prioratus de Seleborne, locorum, membrorum juriumque et pertinentiarum prædictorum possessionem autoritate propria continuare et de novo apprehendere, illorumque fructus, redditus et proventus in suos et dicti Collegii usus utilitatemque convertere et perpetuo retinere, diocesani loci et cujusvis alterius licentia super hoc minime requisita. Ac præterea, quod Prioratus de Seleborne prædictus, si opus sit, per dicti Sancti Augustini vel cujusvis alterius ordinis religiosos ad nutum Præsidentis et Scholarium prædictorum eligendos ac deputandos reformari possit, eadem apostolica autoritate statuimus: Non obstantibus voluntate nostra prædicta et aliis apostolicis, necnon bonæ memoriæ Octonis, Octoboni, olim in regno Angliæ sedis apostolicæ Legatorum, ac in provincialibus et sinodalibus conciliis editis, generalibus vel specialibus constitutionibus et ordinationibus, statutis quoque et consuetudinibus dicti ordinis juramento, confirmatione apostolica, vel quavis firmitate alia roboratis, cæterisque contrariis quibuscunque: Aut si aliqui super provisionibus sibi faciendis de Prioratibus hujusmodi vel aliis beneficiis ecclesiasticis in illis partibus speciales vel generales dictæ sedis vel Legatorum ejus literas impetrarint, etiam si per eas ad inhibitionem, reservationem et decretum vel alias quomodolibet sit processum, quas quidem literas et processus habitos per easdem, ac inde secuta quocunque, ad Prioratum hujusmodi volumus non extendi, sed nullum per hoc eis, quoad assecutionem Prioratuum seu beneficiorum aliorum, præjudicium generari; et quibuslibet aliis privilegiis, indulgentiis et literis apostolicis generalibus vel specialibus quorumcunque tenorum existant, per quæ, præsentibus non expressa vel totaliter non inserta, effectus earum impediri valeat quomodolibet vel differri, et de quibus quorumque totis tenoribus habenda sit in nostris literis mentio specialis. Proviso quod Prioratus de Seleborne prædictus debitis propterea non fraudetur obsequiis, et animarum cura, si qua illi immineat, nullatenus negligatur, sed illius congrue supportentur onera consueta. Nos enim ex nunc irritum decernimus et inane si secus super hiis a quoque quavis autoritate scienter vel ignoranter contigerit attemptari. Nulli ergo omnino hominum liceat hanc paginam nostræ absolutionis, suppressionis, approbationis, confirmationis, communitionis, suppletionis, unionis, annexionis, incorporationis, statuti, voluntatis et constitutionis, infringere vel ei ausu temerario contraire. Siquis autem hoc attemptare præsumpserit, indignationem omnipotentis Dei ac beatorum Petri et Pauli apostolorum ejus se noverit incursurum. Dat. Romæ apud Sanctum Petrum, anno Incarnationis Dominicæ millesimo quadringentesimo octogesimo sexto, octavo idus Junii, Pontificatus nostri anno secundo.

Copy in an Italian hand.—[No. 101.]

Letter to the President of Magdalen College from the Agent employed by the College at Rome.

1486, Aug. 16. Reverende in Christo pater et domine mi ac benefactor observan[dissime], Com[mendo me?]. xvij° Junii scripsi vobis cum insertione copiæ literarum quas vj° Maii scripseram, et significavi quod solveram domino Bartholomæo de Perusio ducatos sex pro residuo unius duplicatæ, et solveram pro legitimatione David Ap prout ordinaveratis in bancho, ubi postea inventa fuit commissio illa novem ducat[orum] quam ipsi banchari dixerunt non habere. Item quod confirmationes omnium unionum Collegio Oxoniæ factarum erant obtentæ, ac scriptæ bullæ et taxatæ, et illæ Prioratus de Seleborne totaliter expeditæ quæ sunt in camera apostolica, quia petebant integram annatam et compositionem fructuum male perceptorum, cum Ordinarius non potuisset unire beneficium regulare sæculari, etsi Collegium non fecit fructus suos et illos male percepit, et similiter petebant de capella de Wamburghe. Nihilominus bono et secreto modo studebam, ne plus exponeremus quam misissetis, et quantocius omnia expedire curarem, quæ jam in tuto sunt. Idem nunc repeto. Recepi post hæc tres alias vestras literas, unas ij, alteras x Maii, et tertias xxj Junii, quibus respondebo. Ego P[aternitatem] vestram de negligentia, si illam incurreret, excusarem semper tanquam filius et fidelis servulus vester. Novitates et mutationes istius regni pacatas esse plurimum lætor. De molestia xlvi ducatorum, super quibus cum istis de Frescobaldis contenditis, non modicum doleo: sed mercatores, qui sciunt quod pecuniæ vigore commissionum solvendæ non dantur absque quitantiis, bene possunt certificari quod nisi ostendatur et appareat quitantia mea quod receperim xlvi ducatos, ego illos nunquam habui, et tenentur restituere deponenti, cum maxime apparuerit per sæpissimas meas literas quod commissio illa jam diu expiraverat, nec poterant expediri gratiæ in quibus tales ducatus export[ar]i debebant: qua de re etiam scribam, ut cupitis, mercatoribus supradictis et Michaeli de Ceparello ac Marco Stroctio, et quod fieri poterit cum istis de Gaddis procurabo, ne vestro bono jure fraudemini. Audiveramus ante præsentationem literarum vestrarum de obitu reverendissimi domini Cantuariensis, et successive intelleximus nominationem sive præsentationem per serenissimum Regem factam ad Cantuariensem ac Eliensem ecclesias quæ (ut accepi) cum dilatione expedientur ob penuriam nummorum.

Reposui in bancho de Gaddis die v Aprilis anni 1483 ducatos auri de camera triginta duos, quos acceperam pro expedienda quadam dispensatione matrimoniali Rogeri Bramiston, quæ non potuit expediri ob nimiam compositionem: et Hieronymus Frescobaldus scripserat ad eosdem de Gaddis ut illos repeterent, et ipsum certificarunt quod dictos xxxij ducatos a me receperant, de quibus ab ipsis Gaddis quitantiam habeo. Et sic scribent et attestabuntur quod mihi nullam pecuniæ summam aliam solverunt commissione Hieronymi Frescobaldi absque quitantiis triplicatis, ita quod dicti Frescobaldi, non ostensis quitantiis meis quod receperim xlvj ducatos pro expeditione dispensationis pro magistro H. Falke, debent cogi ad illos vobis restituendum, quos nunquam habui, nec petivi. Et sic scribam Consulibus nationis Florentinæ. Et vobis scripsi per meas literas xxv Julii 1483 quod reposueram in bancho de Gaddis dictos xxxij ducatos pro dispensatione Rogeri Bramistou constitutos. Certifico vos quod die xj præsentis mensis fuit conclusa pax inter Pontificem et Italiæ potentatus confœderatos, quam Altissimus optatam perpetuo servet nosque tueatur incolumes. Bene valete, et istis reveren[dis] dominis Archiepiscopis et Episcopis vestris me commendate. Quod Papa aliquid contra executores testamenti illius vestri domini quia non reparavit, etc., quæsierit, nihil audire potui nec intelligere; et sum certus quod sunt fabulæ. Si quid explorare vel scrutari potero, vel intellexero, statim significabo, prout vestra erga me beneficia merito exigunt et requirunt. Romæ, xvj Augusti 1486.

[*Addressed*:—]Reverendo Patri et Domino Magistro Ricardo
Præsidenti Collegii Beatæ Mariæ Magdalenæ
in Universitate Oxoniæ majori suo, etc.

In the same Italian hand as the preceding Bull.—[No. 101.]

These copies of papers are endorsed, "Copiæ mittendæ ad Dominum Thomam Hope in Anglia."

1487[-8], 2 Jan. Release from Peter [Courtenay], Bishop of Winchester, to the President and Scholars of Magdalen College of all actions and complaints for anything due by reason of the appropriation of the Priory of Selborne.—[293.]

Rather faint impression of the episcopal seal, red; the Bishop's arms on sinister base; three torteaux, a label of three points: "Sigillum Petri Courtenay Episcopi Winton." No counter-seal.

1487[-8], 3 Jan. Confirmation by Thomas, Prior of the cathedral church of St. Swithun, Winchester, and the Convent, of the preceding release from the Bishop of 2 Jan., which is recited in full. —[374.]

Fine impression of chapter seal, but inscription broken; three figures under canopies, the central one a Bishop in attitude of benediction: ". . . . cathedralis ecclesie S'or' Pet' et Paul . . . . . th'i Winton." Counter-seal same size; three canopied figures, a King between an Abbot and Bishop: "Factum ann . . . . . . onages' iiij° et anno regni regis Ed . . . . ."; two kneeling figures below.

1489, 18 April, "in vig. Pasche," 4 Hen. VII. Acknowledgment by Thomas Asshforde, late Prior of Selbourne, of the receipt from Hugh Walton, receiver general of Magdalen College in Hants, of 66*s.* 8*d.*, as his annual pension due at Lady Day.—[48.]

Small seal with initial "T."

1489, 29 July. Acknowledgment (on paper) by Symon Hyltoft, dean of the deanery of Aulton, of the receipt of the following sums from Hugh Waltham:—7*s.* 5½*d.* for the procurations of the church of Sellebume and 15*d.* for synodals; 7½*d.* for the synodals of the chapel of Okeangre; 7½*d.* for the synodals of the chapel of Blakemer; 5*s.* for the procurations of the church of Estwarlham and 7½*d.* for synodals; 22*d.* of the church of Selleburne for the expenses of the proctor of the clergy of the deanery of Aulton in the last convocation; 12½*d.* of the church of Estwarlham for the same.—[299.]

1489, 24 Oct., 5 Hen. VII. Acknowledgment by Thomas Asshforde, late Prior of Selbourne, of the receipt from Hugh Walton of his annual pension due at Michaelmas (sum not mentioned).—[44.]

Small blank seal.

Inventory of goods remaining at Selborne Priory after its annexation to the College.

1490, 16 May. Hæc indentura bonorum abbatiæ de Seleborne facta xvj^mo^ die Maii, anno r. r. Henrici septimi quinto, testatur quod hæc sunt bona dictæ abbatiæ remanencia in custodia domini Simonis Hiltofte, capellani ibidem; videlicet, in ecclesiæ duæ cruces, unde j de argento et deaurata, et alia de cupro et deaurata; unum Missale, secundo folio *Jesum Christum*; unum Gradale, secundo folio, *Salvandas*; alius liber, secundo folio, *non intellexit*; unum Ordinale, *gladio* secundo folio; unum novum volumen de canone missæ, secundo folio, *Quoniam*; unum phalterium (*sic*), secundo folio, *O Deus Meus*; alius liber parvus, secundo folio, *sapienciæ*; duæ calices; una capa de velveto, cum orfers de blew velvette cum stellis; alia capa de blodio serico cum orfers de ymaginibus; alia capa de serico de colore prædicto; alia capa nigra cum bestiis aureis de serico; alia capa nigra cum rosis albis; una pars capæ coloris yelowe; alia capa blodia cum avibus aureis; alia capa blodia cum esterige feder; ij tunicæ pro diacono et subdiacono, coloris blodii; unum dalmaticum cum avibus, stellis, et le flowre de lyez, aureis; unum dalmaticum album, cum coronis in medio; aliud dalmaticum cum cruce de chequyere; ij tunicæ pro diacono et subdiacono de ray; alia tunica alba; unum dalmaticum antiquum de bawdekyne; unum par vestimentorum viridis coloris, cum le flowre de lyez albo intexto; aliud par vestimentorum viridis coloris de plano serico, cum pare vestimentorum pro subdiacono ejusdem coloris: ij paria vestimentorum pro diacono et subdiacono de plano rubio serico; una tunica cum suis pertinentiis pro subdiacono, albi coloris; alia tunica alba cum diversis coloribus in medio; alia tunica alba cum suis pertinentiis, cum avibus in medio de argento; unum par vestimentorum cum le flowre de lyes albo intexto, modo rithis (*sic*; retis?); unum par vestimentorum cum bestiis et avibus aureis, et le orfers cum ymaginibus; unum vetus par vestimentorum blodii coloris, cum rosis rubeis et albis et aliis floribus intextis; una alba sine vestimento; alia alba pro tunica supradicta albi coloris; iij mappæ pictæ pro altaribus; unum par vestimentorum alborum, cum quo dominus Simon celebrat, et aliud par cotidianum de borde Elesaunder; iiij mappæ ad imponendum super altare, et sunt in camera quadam sub custodia dicti Simonis; xx libri secundum usum canonicum; ij cistæ in eadem camera. Et in alia camera sunt isti libri; Actus Apostolorum cum aliis contentis, secundo folio, *Quid statis*; unum Decretale, secundo folio, *puer*; Communis Glosa super Evangelia, secundo folio, *in remissionem*; Communis Glosa super Job, secundo folio, *dicebat enim*; alius liber de jure, secundo folio, *Quibus*; item M[agister] Sententiarum,[1] secundo folio, *quod est dictum*; ij pixides argenteæ cum reliquiis in eisdem contentis; unum vas æneum pro aqua benedicta facienda; ij campanæ parvæ; una campana parva quæ fuit in turre; ij candelabra de lateyne; una crux de cupro; iij pax bredc; ij vexilla; ij cistæ in vestibulo; una cista in camera nuper Prioris; unum therubulum. Et hæc omnia remanent in manu dicti Simonis ad respondendum quandocunque domino placuerit. In cujus rei testimonium huic indenturæ dictus dominus Simon subscripsit manu sua propria, signo manuali.—S. Hyltoft.—[On paper, No. 385.]

1501, 1 April. Acknowledgment by Hadrian Castellensis, Bishop of Hereford, the Pope's collector in England, of the receipt of 7*s*. from the Prior (*sic*) of Seleborne "pro procurationibus cameræ apostolicæ" for that year.—[315.]

Seal lost.

1504, 25 March. Similar acknowledgment by the same.—[314.]

[1508-9, 24 Hen. VII.] Copy (on paper) of an extract from the Sheriff's accounts for the county of Southampton, in which he prays to be relieved from the sums charged upon the Priory of Selborne and its annexed churches for the clergy's tenth granted to the King (Hen. VII?) in the 11th year, that Priory belonging now to Magdalen College, Oxford, which is exempted from payment of the said tenth.—[311.]

1509-10, 24 Hen. VII. Extract (on parchment) from the Great Roll of the acquittance of the collector from the payment of the tenth charged on the Priory of Selborne, in pursuance of the preceding representation (No. 311).—[312.]

[1] The words "Item, M. Sententiarum" are substituted for "Augustinus de Trinitate," which are struck out.

1510, 9 Feb., 1 Hen. VIII; at Westminster. Copy (on paper) of a writ from the King to the Bishop of Winchester directing him to enquire whether the Priory of Selborne is held by the President and Scholars of Magdalen College; if so, how long it has been held, and the value, etc., of the churches annexed to it.—[310.]

1509[–10], 11 Feb. Draft (on paper) of a certificate from Richard [Fox], Bishop of Winchester, to the Treasurer and Barons of the Exchequer in return to the preceding writ, that the President and Scholars of Magdalen College have held the Priory of Selborne since the year 1484, to their own use, together with the parish church of Selborne and chapels annexed, the churches of Great Wardlham, of Tystede, and of Basyng and Basyngstoke with the chapels; that the value of the said churches amounts to £9. 7*s.* 7*d.*, and that they are taxed, Selborne at 44*s.*, Wardlham at 22*s.* 8*d.*, Tystede at 17*s.* 4*d.*, Basyng and Basyngestoke at £4, and the temporalities of the Prior at 19*s.* 7*d.*—[309.]

[1510.] Acknowledgment (on paper) by W. Johnson of the receipt for John Frost, archdeacon of Winchester, from master Rich. Walter, of 11*s.* 3*d.* for the procurations and synodals of the church of Estwarleham, 19*s.* 11*d.* for those of the church of Selborne and its chapels, and 16*s.* 6*d.* for those of the church of Westistede, for the years 1509–10; together with 7*s.* 8*d.* of arrears for the years 1507–8.—[57.]

1512, 26 March. Acknowledgment by Peter Gryphus, the Pope's collector in England, of the receipt from the Prior (*sic*) of Selborne of 7*s.* for the procurations due to the apostolic chamber for the year 1512.—[63.]

Oval red seal; the tiara and cross keys; inscription broken.

1513, 26 March. Similar acknowledgment by the same of the receipt of the sum from the Bursars of Magdalen College.—[316.]

Seal broken off.

1514, 18 July, 6 Hen. VIII. Bond from John Shavyngton (signed by him), rector of Hertely Mawdytte, to the President of Magdalen College in £20, for the annual payment to the College, while he holds the living, of 5*s.*, being a pension charged upon the parsonage.—[204.]

Small blank seal.

1514, 26 March. Acknowledgment by Cardinal Hadrian [de Castello, Bishop of Bath and Wells] of the receipt of 7*s.* from the Bursars of Magdalen College for the procurations due to the apostolical chamber for the Prior of Seleborne, for the year 1514.—[395(iii).]

Fragment of seal with cross keys.

1515, 26 March. Similar acknowledgment by the same, for the year 1515.—[395(iv).]

Fragment of same seal.

1516, 26 March. Similar acknowledgment by Andrew Ammonius, the Pope's collector in England, for the year 1516.—[104.]

Small red seal; the tiara and cross keys.

1517, 26 March. Similar acknowledgment by the same, as deputy of Ha[drian] the Cardinal of Bath, for the year 1517.—[395(v).]

Small fragment of seal.

[*c.* 1516–25.] Copy (on paper) of a claim made by the President (Hygdon) and Scholars of Magd. College, by their attorney John Wyntreshulle, to be exempt, in right of their being lords of the Priory of Selborne, from all forest-jurisdiction in Selborne, Okehanger, Nortone, Basynges, Basingstoke, and Nately.—[384.]

1526, 16 April, 17 Hen. VIII. Admission at the court of the manor of Selborne of Katherine Hardyng, daughter and heir of William Hardyng (on the appearance and application of her mother Isabella Hardyng) to hold a parcel of land called Greneland, alias Pagleslese at Paglessegrene, containing four acres, and [another piece], at an annual rent of 4*s.* 2*d.*; to be held by her mother until she come of full age.—[376.]

1528, 26 April, 20 Hen. VIII. [*Midhurst.*] Surrender by Robert Okyng of Mydhurst, Sussex, to the President and Scholars of Magdalen College, for the sum of £4, of a messuage and a garden in the north street of Midhurst and all the other lands and tenements in Midhurst which formerly belonged to the Prior and Convent of Selborne.—[230.]

Small black seal with initials.

1534, 5 July, 26 Hen. VIII; in the great hall of Magd. Coll. Grant from Thomas Knolles, the President, and the Scholars of Magd. College, to Nicholas Langerige, M.A., of a chaplaincy, or salary, or whatever else it may be called ("quandam capellaniam vel salarium sive alio quocunque nomine censeatur"), in the late Priory of Selborne, for the term of forty years, if he live so long, to celebrate there for the souls of all the benefactors of the said Priory and College deceased; assigning to him an annual pension of £8 with two chambers on the north side of the said Chapel, with a kitchen, and a stable for three horses and "le orcheyerd"; and 26*s.* annually to find a clerk to serve him at the altar and in other necessary matters; and ten cart-loads of wood annually, to be given to him at the Easter progress of the President and Fellows, provided he does not sell or give away any of it; and the said Nicholas must not be absent from the said Priory more than two months in the year without special leave from the College, and must provide a sufficient substitute.—[351.]

Small fragment of the College seal, endorsed with memorandum of enrolment in the Exchequer, 8 Eliz.

1537, 9 April. Memoranda (on paper) in English, of evidence given by John May, of Faryngdon, aged seventy-two, respecting the rights of pasturage exercised by old Plummer, the farmer of Shete farm, at Swelyng and Dogford; in the presence of Nich. Knytt and Thos. Clarke; and also of similar evidence given at Sutton in the court by Jerry [*or* Herry] May, aged sixty, of Pryor's Dean, Thomas Hamme, aged eighty, and Edw. Hamme his brother, Thomas May of Faryngdon, Will. May of Petersfyld, and Thos. Aftelatte of Faryngdon.—[350.]

1542, 11 April, 34 Hen. VIII; at Twyford. Power of attorney from Thomas Wells of Twyford, esq., to Rich. Massam, to give seisin to Owin Oglethorpe of the land released in the following deed (No. 232). Signed "By me Thomas Wellys."—[357.]

Small seal.

1542, 30 April, 34 Hen. VIII. Release from Thomas Welles, esq., of Twyford, Southamptonshire, to Owen Oglethorpe, of Oxford, clerk, of all his right in a piece of his land in Westisted called le Hayes, as conveyed by him in a deed dated 30 March in the same year. Signed as above.—[232.]

Small seal.

1545, 24 April, 37 Hen. VIII. Grant from Owin Oglethorpe, of Oxford, clerk, to Nicholas Ticheborne, esq., of all his piece of land, etc., in the parish of Westistede called le Hayes, near the land of the college of St. Mary Magdalen called Trendlefeld to the west and north, the land of the said Nicholas Ticheborne called Asshewode to the south, and that of the said Nich. called Brokks to the east. No witnesses. Signed, "ꝑ me Owinum Oglethorpe."—[351.]

Small red seal, "O. O." Endorsed by Oglethorpe, with a memorandum that "these dedis" were not delivered to Mr. Tichborne "because he made no assurance to me of the tenement in Selborne now in the occupation of John Sharpe," etc.

1545, 26 April, 37 Hen. VIII. Power of attorney from Owin Oglethorpe to Rich. Massam to give seisin to Nicholas Tycheborne of Ticheborne, esq., of a piece of land, etc., in Westistede called le Hayes, according to the preceding deed dated 24 April. Signed "per me Owinum Oglethorpe."—[279.]

Fragment of small seal.

1546, 20 May, 38 Hen. VIII. Release from Thomas Wellis, of Brambrige, Southampton, esq., to Nicholas Tychebourn of Tychebourn, esq., of all his right in the lands and tenements called le Hayes in the parish of Westistede. Signed "By me Thomas Wellys."—[236.]

Seal with initials.

1546, 20 May, 38 Hen. VIII. Release from Owin Oglethorpe, S.T.P., to Nicholas Tichebourne of Tichebourne of all his right in the above lands called le Hayes. Signed "per me Owinum Oglethorpe."—[238.]

Small seal: "O. O."

1550, 4 Nov., 4 Edw. VI; in the great hall of Magdalen College. Grant from Owin Oglethorpe, the President, and the Scholars of Magdalen College to Nicholas Langrige, M.A., formerly fellow of the College, of an annual pension of £10 for thirty years if he live so long, in consideration of his resigning, on account of his advanced age, an annual stipend long since granted to him, together with two rooms and a kitchen, with stable and orchard, in Selbourne, where he now dwells, on condition of his superintending the woods, copses ("sepibus"), and enclosures there belonging to the College.—[352.]

Good impression of College seal, but inscription broken.

1567, 29 Jan., 9 Eliz. Bond from John Sharp, of Selborne, husbandman, to John Arnolde, son of John Arnolde of the same, in 40 marks, to abide by the arbitration of Ralph S[c]rope and Rich. Kingesmill, esqs., as to the title to five closes called Swangers, containing sixteen acres, and a close called Dawes, in the parish of Imshot.—[380.]

1611, Mich. Term. Decree in the Court of Wards and Liveries discharging the messuage and tenements called the Priory in Selborne (of the annual value of £10, and held from Magdalen College by George Pawlett, gent., by a demise dated 20 Nov., 43 Eliz.) from seizure by the sheriff of Southampton for a debt of £49, due to the Crown from John Sharpe of Colmer, yeoman, as executor of Margery Sharpe, widow, deceased, late wife of Innocent Sharpe, deceased, and, before that, of Richard Chase, for money remaining in his hands unpaid of the profits of lands, etc., in Petersfield, Gretham, and Hauckley.—[30.]

1718–9, 19 Feb., 5 Geo. I. Copy of a decree by L. Ch. Parker (afterwards Earl of Macclesfield) in Chancery against the College with regard to Selborne Common, in favour of the copy holders.—[397.]

INDEX.

A

B

C

D

E

F

G

H

M

P

[1] Probably there are two of the same name in this series of charters; the earlier one uses a seal representing a man on horseback, while the seal of the later one bears the sun and moon.

Q

R

S

T

[1] This abbey, situated at a place now called Thiron-Gardais, in the diocese of Chartres, had several cells in England. See Dugdale's *Monast.*, and *Gallia Christiana*, vol. xiii, col. 1264.

U

V

Y

Z

www.ingramcontent.com/pod-product-compliance
Lightning Source LLC
Chambersburg PA
CBHW030558040726
47497CB00008B/2784
9783337423827